Praise for...

SOUTHERN EXPOSURES

"Ann Jeffries definitely has a skill for storytelling...I fell in love with the Alexanders. Job well done!"
—Jessica Tilles, Author of *Loving Simone*

"I felt as though I was there witnessing everything...immediately got my attention with the colorful attention to details."
—Brenda Irons LeCesne, Esq.

"The [characters'] stories seemed most authentic and entertaining."
—Karen R. Thomas, President, Creative Minds Book Group

"I always like a happy ending and being the romantic that I am the ending makes me want the continuation to be available for me to see the two characters Vivian and Benny to have the happy ending like KJ with the respective characters Chuck and Stacy."
—Sharon Jarrett-Brown, an avid reader

ANOTHER POINT OF VIEW

"Ann Jeffries has done it again! Once you start reading you won't be able to put the book down!"
—J. A. Meinecke, Author, *A Woman to Reckon With*

AN UNGUARDED MOMENT

"Ann Jeffries does an excellent job of weaving her characters' stories together and keeping the reader captivated." —Nancy Engle, Author *Murder at Mount Joy*

"Ann has a terrific voice for romance—it [is] light, readable and the characters were a lot of fun."

—Kara Cesare, the Richard Curtis Literary Agency

"I loved the story line! A little suspenseful which I like. The story flowed and it felt like I was reading a movie. I enjoyed the book."

—Gina, an avid reader

"An engrossing and sensuous love story that immediately grabs your attention and keeps you involved till the last page."

—Abraham Leib, Esq.

"It's the kind of story you never want to end."

—Janice Sims, Author *This Winter Night*

"I really admire Ann's smooth writing style and the appealing premise of this project."
—Mavis Allen, Associate Senior Editor, Silhouette Books

TOUCH ME IN THE MORNING

"I could not put my iPad down once I started reading. Loved the characters and story line which kept me guessing what was going to happen next."

—Pauline, an avid reader.

"Ms. Jeffries characters are real life and enable the reader to eagerly ride along with them on their adventure."

—Abraham Leib, Critic

"Ann Jeffries puts so much into a book...by the time you finish reading one of her stories you feel you know the characters. Ms. Jeffries handles the romance between Satarah and Doug with realism and with passion. You really believe they're falling in love. Satarah makes him a part of her big, loving family, a multicultural clan that will steal your heart."

—Janice Sims, best-selling author, *Thief of My Heart*

Another Point of View

Family Reunion—In the Wisdom of the Ancestors Series

ANN JEFFRIES

ACKNOWLEDGEMENTS

The Creator

The Ancestors

Jessica Tilles, Editor

Abe Lieb, Esq. for all things

Management and staff, Office Depot, Myrtle Beach, SC

Management and staff, Carolina Forest Library, Horry County, SC

The journey continues and the struggle for
literary perfection shall never end.

"Whether or not one perceives it, whether or not one welcomes it, there is a universal communality which united all of man's acts and ideas not only in space but primarily in time. This intuitive, always present perception of time is after all the greatest gift available to us with which to grasp the inner meaning of all that the passage of the world has left behind, like a river leaves its alluvium. One can understand everything if one returns to the source. An African carving and a Greek marble sculpture are not as far apart as one may think."

Elie Taure
L'Espirit des Formes, 1939

"That which permeates and motivates humanity is, in the last analysis, the search for the eternal, life beyond death, which is also the search for our origins, the lost paradise of the Garden of Eden."

U. Bär Verlag,
Zurich, Switzerland, 1989[1]

---

[1] ©1990 by Facts on File, Inc., 460 Park Avenue South, NY, NY 10016 (212-683-2244 or 1-800-322-8755. ISBN 0-8160-2437-5, Library of Congress, Acatos, Sylvio)

TITLES BY ANN JEFFRIES
In the *Family Reunion—Wisdom of the Ancestors Series*

Southern Exposures

Another Point of View

An Unguarded Moment

Touch Me In The Morning

Chapter 1

On the day of her wedding . . .

JeNelle Towson awoke as the early morning salt-water breeze from the Pacific Ocean gently blew through her rear bedroom French doors. She did not open her eyes immediately, but listened to the ocean crashing against the shore and the sound of seagulls squawking as they walked along the beach or flew overhead. Her home on the shore of Santa Barbara, California, was quiet and peaceful, although she knew her mother, Canty Towson, and her mother's twin sister and her aunt, Bessie Baines, had spent the night. Yet, only the sound of the sea and birds could be heard as she reached for the peach-colored, silk-covered pillow next to her, pulling it tightly against her body. Her fiancé's Paco Rabanne's 1 Million cologne still smelled fresh as she buried her face in his pillow and squeezed it. When she opened her eyes, she glimpsed her wedding gown hanging on a form on the far side of her spacious bedroom. She smiled and felt a rush of excitement flow over her entire body; a tingling sensation that covered her from head to toe. *Could this really be happening?* Lying in the pale-peach and cream-colored bedroom with French provincial furniture, she thought about all the events, starting more than a year ago that led to this day. The day she and Kenneth James Alexander, Executive Director of CompuCorrect, Inc., would be married.

JeNelle gazed at her wedding gown again and remembered the day, the hour, and the very moment that she first saw Kenneth at the San Francisco Airport. She knew immediately that he was someone very special. She rolled onto her stomach and settled on remembering the scene nearly sixteen months earlier when Kenneth's brother, Benjamin, an Air Force pilot, flew her in a private plane from her home in Santa Barbara to a small business expo in San Francisco. As Benny helped her climb out of the Cessna, Kenneth stepped forward out of the shadows and she lost her heart at the first sight of him.

The memories were a mixture of joy and pain, she recalled. JeNelle sat up in bed, tightly bringing her knees to her chest.

Meeting Kenneth was like turning on a bright light in the darkest night. There was so much bleakness in her life until that point. She had spent years trying to avoid her former husband, Michel San Angelo, and his threats and harassment. Not knowing when or where he would attack next kept her on edge. He neither accepted nor honored the terms of their divorce. He still considered her his wife, his possession, like chattel or property. Admittedly, she was afraid of him and what he was capable of doing. He told her that it would never be over between them. That one day she would be with him again. He reminded her that no wife of an Italian man in his family was ever divorced. His threats had frightened her more than she had ever told her family or friends. Thankfully, she had the support of his family to shield her from him, and her company, INSIGHTS, to occupy her time, so she didn't think about him much. He was busy, too, building his many businesses and investments into an empire.

Michel taught her a valuable lesson though—she could not trust her judgment when it came to men. She surrendered to that prophecy, vowing never to put her judgment to the test or herself in jeopardy again.

Her family and friends tried to convince her that one bad experience with a relationship should not make her adamant against having other relationships, but she was not able to do it. Having no relationship was safe and she found comfort in her career, satisfaction in the struggle to build her business, and love from her family. That had all worked well for eleven years.

At least, it had been until the Alexander tsunami arrived.

Initially, Benjamin Alexander, Kenneth's younger brother, was in hot pursuit of her for months. He did not let her reticence dissuade him. He found any excuse to spend time with her and he was a seemingly incurable romantic, often sending flowers, cards and notes. He visited with her, planned interesting and romantic outings, and introduced her to his friends and intimating that she was something more to him than just a friend. Of course, on each opportunity she set the record straight, both privately and publicly—they were strictly platonic friends. After enduring life with Michel San Angelo for two years, she vowed that she would give herself to no one.

When Kenneth Alexander entered her life he made her live again.

Benny planned to escort her to a Santa Barbara Chamber of Commerce Gala, but had been called away at the last minute. He asked Kenneth to fill in for him. It was a magical night. She was named Woman of the Year and, floating around the ballroom in Kenneth's arms, her excitement grew…until Michel showed up.

As the evening was ending, Kenneth picked up her award and they headed for the door. Her friend and mentor, California Supreme Court Judge Johnston White Worthington and his wife, Constance, followed with their entourage. Kenneth went to retrieve her fur wrap and to order the car. She was waiting for him to return when she remembered feeling a chill come over her. When two men approached her to congratulate her on the award, something about them seemed familiar. She couldn't place where she had seen them before, until…

"Bella, Una bella donna," he said behind her, his voice low and laced with vile seduction. Without turning, she knew who it was.

She tried to walk away, but the two men blocked her path. Then she remembered who the men were and where she had seen them before. They were Michel's bodyguards and every muscle in her body had tensed.

"Michel, I have nothing to say to you," she said, still not turning to look at him.

"Bella, you are more beautiful than ever."

"Please, just leave me alone!" she said through clenched teeth, trying not to show fear.

"But you are my wife. It is time for you—"

"Stop it! I'm not your wife! We're divorced! You know that!"

"You act like a petulant child. You think that it is over because of a piece of paper! That someone, anyone can keep us apart!"

"I don't love you, Michel! I don't want to be with you ever again!"

"You can say that, but you have not looked at me. Look at me!" he demanded

She turned to see those dark penetrating eyes, smooth olive complexion, and impeccably dressed Michel Alverez Diega San Angelo. His hair was graying attractively at the temples, but his handsome, distinguished exterior did not hide his black heart from her. It was his glare that she could not withstand. His eyes silenced her and struck fear in her heart; a debilitating fear. No one crossed Michel San Angelo and got away with it. His presence made the hair on her neck stand on end. She had witnessed strong, confident men—congressmen and statesmen, captains of industry, and others—break into tears under that glare without so much as a word falling from his lips. She could not look into his face. She fixed her stare on a small cross of unusual design and beauty that hung from his neck below his black tie. She remembered that he never took it off. It was a reminder of how he hurt her, humiliated her. How it swung from his neck when he was on top of her—hurting her so badly that she prayed for sweet death.

His words were venomous and syrupy. *"What will it take, Bella? Must I show you a sign of who I am? Is that what you want to force me to do? Who shall it be, Bella? Whom do you love most? Your father? Your mother? How about your little sister, Gloria; the one I held on my knee? So eager she is for my touch. Such a young, nubile body just beginning to grow into a woman. I could have taken her in my bed many times, but I held back for you. Must you force me to take her from you now before you realize that I am your husband? That you belong to me? That no other man will ever have you? I am the only man who will be in your life and in hers! That I can have you both if I so desire?"*

"What is this? What are you saying to her? You dare to threaten her!" Chief State Supreme Court Justice Johnston Worthington interrupted suddenly, standing beside her, his body shaking with anger.

Michel did not flinch. She could still feel his steely gaze on her.

"Leave her alone, San Angelo! If you continue to harass her I'll have you back in court so fast—"

"Old man," he said still staring at her, *"Is she not beautiful, my wife . . . a Madonna? My Madonna! Hair spun by the gods. The face of my Madonna—"*

"I'm not afraid of you, San Angelo! I will find a way to take you back into court! You will lose everything! Remember, the court warned you that if you harassed JeNelle even once—"

"The court?" he said with amused disdain and with a dismissive swish of his hand as if Johnston were a servant, *"what can the court do?"*

"If not the courts, then your father!"

That got Michel's attention, she knew. Michel's eyes finally left her. Now they were on Johnston. Locked on.

Their war of words was on. Threats and counter threats until she could take no more.

"Johnston, please, let's just go. I don't want to make a scene," she recalled pleading.

"Remember, Bella. I will come for you," he said. *"No matter what you do, or who you see, you are mine. You are my wife until death!"*

From that wonderful and then horror-filled night came many disasters. The first of which was Michel San Angelo. Then a real bomb. A newspaper reporter overheard and misinterpreted tidbits of conversations during the gala and wrote an article stating that she and Kenneth were engaged. Though she wished it so, nothing at the time could have been further from the truth. So many people called to congratulate her that she had to repeat her denial so many times that she finally refused to accept any more calls. Then her mother called.

"JeNelle, baby, your daddy and I are just so happy for you. That Kenneth Alexander is everything that you said that he was and a lot more, too. You said that he was handsome and well built, but, child, he is a whole lot more than that! Your daddy and I really enjoyed talking with him at the Gala. And the way that he was looking at you ... The way that you were both looking at each other... Well, your daddy and I could just see all the love in your eyes. I just can't get over it. And that article in today's paper! You didn't say a word about your engagement to me. I'll have to get busy looking for the material for your wedding gown. Oh, and that speech that you made—baby, your daddy and I both had tears in our eyes. I don't know where you got all of that talent from, but we are so proud of you. So many people have been calling—"

"Mama, it's not true," she said quietly.

"What's not true, JeNelle? What are you talking about?"

"About me and Kenneth Alexander. We are not engaged. It was all a big misunderstanding."

"Misunderstanding? Your daddy and I weren't misunderstanding how you two were acting toward each other. We saw it with our own eyes. That man is in love, JeNelle, and so are you. You just look at that picture in the paper. I know love when I see it and I saw it at the Gala."

"Mama, Michel was there."

There was a long pause.

"Call your lawyer right now, JeNelle, and have that man locked up!"

"He didn't hurt me. He scared me, but Johnston Worthington made him leave me alone."

"Don't you be foolish, child! That man ain't right! He's crazy in the head! He's not even supposed to be in the same zip code with you! You're too easy going! Anyone who could give a speech like that—and you'd let a low-down scoundrel like Michel San Angelo mess with your head again and ruin your life! No! You do something about that Michel San Angelo right now! Do you hear me talking to you, JeNelle?"

"Yes, Mama."

"Then what are you going to do?"

"I'll go to Milo San Angelo and tell him what happened. I saw him recently and he told me that if Michel ever tried to contact me again to call him."

"You mean Michel's uncle? That nice Italian man who manages your restaurant in San Diego? The one who took care of you after Michel hurt you?"

"Yes, Mama, but I don't consider Michelangelo's as my restaurant. I haven't been involved in the business since my divorce from Michel."

"Michel gave that restaurant to you as a wedding gift, JeNelle. The divorce decree says that it is yours and a lot of money, too, that you have not touched. Now I am not going to try to run your life for you, but you were foolish to let Michel get away with what he did to you. You should have had him put under the jail and thrown away the key, but you do what you think is right with

that restaurant and the divorce settlement money. Just do not let that Michel San Angelo drag you down again. I will not forgive you if you do. You make time for that nice Kenneth Alexander. Do you hear me?"

"Yes, but it's not that easy."

"Why isn't it? What's the problem?"

"Kenneth thinks that I'm involved with his brother, Benny."

"You're not, are you?"

"No, but Benny's been on this crazy mission to seduce me. Kenneth loves his brother and I don't think that Kenneth's going to risk doing anything that he thinks is going to hurt Benny."

"The way that Kenneth was looking at you, everybody's going to know how he feels about you. His brother's bright. He's going to get the picture, too. You mark my words."

"You don't understand how important Benny and Kenneth are to each other. I will not come between them. Benny will have to understand that I just want to be his friend—nothing more."

"And what about Kenneth?"

"I don't know. If he reads this newspaper article, he will probably never speak to me ever again. Even before the Gala, he was behaving strangely. He seems to be putting up a wall…I don't know. Maybe it's my imagination, but that article surely did not help. I'm too ashamed to call Kenneth. I just hope that it wasn't in the San Francisco newspapers. If it was, I've probably wrecked his company and his good name."

"You stop hiding from life, child. You handle this situation with Kenneth. I know people and he's good people. Trust him. The man obviously comes from good Southern stock. He'll understand and be in your corner. He'll stand by you, honey."

"I'll think about it, but it's such a mess. Kiss Daddy for me and tell him that I'm sorry about the newspaper article."

She and Kenneth weathered that storm, but the dawn had not broken before another cloud burst forth. Late one night her telephone rang. It was Benny, and during the conversation she learned that Kenneth, and her associate, Lisa Lambert, were involved in an intimate relationship.

Lying awake for hours after talking with Benny, she did not know what to make of what he told her. She did not understand the ache in her heart either. Not able to sleep, she got up, went to the living room, and poured a brandy for herself. The vision of her and Kenneth dancing in the beam of light at the Gala haunted her for weeks. His face was etched in her mind. His million-dollar, polar ice-cap melting smile. The contour of his finely-sculptured body: tall, broad muscular chest and arms, narrow waist, rock-hard abdomen, firm butt and legs, a masterpiece of male physique. It wasn't just his body and handsome face that she admired, although he had more sex appeal than any other man she had ever met, he also had other qualities that she admired more. He had integrity, family loyalty, charisma, character, honesty, intellect, and a sense of soundness and completeness and humor. He was a total package. Everything that any woman would have ever dreamed of wanting in a man. He lacked for nothing. If she could have just stopped the vision of him, perhaps she could have put him out of her head and heart and then put her life back on track.

However, Benny's statement about his brother and Lisa was confirmed by another associate, Paul Garrett. Despite what her parents thought they saw sparking between her and Kenneth, he and Lisa were involved in an intimate relationship. She knew Lisa well. She was cunning and relentless when they played racquetball together. Focused on her objective, and goal oriented. If Lisa set her sights on Kenneth, she knew that Paul was right and her parents were wrong. It would be game, set, and match in favor of Dr. Lisa Lambert.

She did not see Kenneth again until the first meeting of the Governor's Blue Ribbon Panel on Youth in Business and Industry in May in Sacramento. The Panel consisted of representatives from both large and small businesses in California. There were both men and women represented on the Panel and people representing most major ethnic groups. She and Kenneth both agreed to participate on the Panel representing their individual companies.

Kenneth's was the first face that she remembered looking for as she entered the crowded conference room. During the sessions, which lasted three days once a month, Lisa Lambert monopolized most of Kenneth's time. On the final day of the conference when she was leaving the meeting room, she saw Lisa very passionately kiss Kenneth. She remembered how her disappointment grew as she saw Kenneth holding Lisa. He was treating her distantly at each monthly meeting of the Panel members. Desperately she tried to put Kenneth out of her mind; to stop having dreams and amorous feelings toward him. He was clearly having a love affair with her friend and business associate, she kept reminding herself.

Months later, in September, Benny called her and left a message on her answering machine, asking her to return the call and saying that it was very important. She returned the call the next day. When Kenneth unexpectedly answered Benny's telephone, something grabbed her in the pit of her stomach and her heart raced.

Still devastated about Kenneth's coolness toward her, when Benny called her and asked her to come to his condo in San Diego the next day, she agreed. He seemed very excited. She was totally unprepared for what she found when she knocked on Benny's door. Her heart stopped beating when Kenneth opened the door holding a newborn baby in his arms. That was when she learned that the baby girl was Benny's daughter with a young lieutenant, Stacy Greene; a woman who chose a naval career over being a wife to Benny and a mother to their daughter, Whitney Ivy. Since she and Benny had been dating she should have been upset, but she was terribly relieved. It was also the first time that she met Sylvia Alexander, Benny and Kenneth's mother; a woman whose youthful figure did not reveal the fact that she had born five children.

She remembered fearing what Benny and Kenneth might have said to their mother about her, but Sylvia Alexander's demeanor put her at ease. She seemed a woman of substance, JeNelle remembered thinking. The thick hair that cascaded over her shoulders added youth and vitality to her oval face, full lips, wide nose and smiling brown eyes. A healthy, happy looking woman the shade of an evenly brown biscuit next to her one darker and one lighter brown sons who glowed in her presence.

After learning about Benny's child, she visited Benny and Whitney as often as she could. It was Whitney who she was really there to see. Desperately she wanted a baby of her own, but Michel robbed her of her chance. She had also thought of adoption, but didn't believe that she alone could raise a baby. She was giving that idea more thought watching Benny successfully raising Whitney alone. He loved his daughter so very much that it brought tears to her eyes to see them together. He was a single parent raising his daughter and enjoying it thoroughly.

It was the last meeting of the Blue Ribbon Panel in Sacramento before the holiday break when a messenger handed a note to her. She immediately recalled Michel's threat as she read the note and felt faint and disoriented. It was blazing in her head when she grabbed her purse and bolted from the room. Gloria was in the intensive care unit at Georgetown University Hospital in Washington, DC, and that she should come immediately. Kenneth dropped everything to get her to DC. There she met Dr. Charles Montgomery, a friend of both Kenneth and Gloria's and an Emergency Room physician. Kenneth and Chuck Montgomery saw her through Gloria's crisis. Kenneth stayed with her in the Georgetown townhouse that Benny owned and leased to his and Kenneth's sister, Vivian Alexander. Vivian was a law student at Georgetown Law and sublet rooms in the huge townhouse to other Georgetown law students, including Gloria. Since it was the Christmas holiday, all the students were away when Gloria was attacked. It took a long time for Gloria to be released from the hospital, but she still couldn't remember who beat her. She was admitted to a rehabilitation facility and JeNelle stayed in Washington as long as she could until Gloria seemed to steadily recuperate. Her housemates stepped in to help Gloria heal, but Kenneth's presence and support were JeNelle's mainstays.

Months later, her father, Harvey Towson, asked, *"Who was that on the telephone, JeNelle?"* teasingly.

"Can't you tell, Harvey? Just look at her face," Canty answered in on the tease.

"Oh yes, it must have been that man of hers, Kenneth Alexander."

"Who else makes our daughter look like she just won the lottery? It was Kenneth, all right."

"Mama, Daddy, you two should stop that." JeNelle giggled.

"Okay, JeNelle. Then tell me that that was not Kenneth. I dare you."

"Mama!" JeNelle said, feigning seriousness.

"JeNelle!" Canty retorted in the same manner.

"It was Kenneth, Mama."

"See, I told you, Harvey. Our daughter has been walking on air ever since she came back from looking after Gloria. I haven't ever seen you like this."

"Don't you two go jumping to any conclusions. Kenneth and I are just good friends."

"Huh! Good friends! A good friend is someone you can have a few drinks with at a bar after work or a movie or shopping. Not someone who drops everything, charters a private aircraft to fly you both to DC, takes care of you while you're going through a crisis, calls up your parents every day to give progress reports on your sister and to check on us and helps to run your business while you're away all during the Christmas holiday. I'd call Kenneth Alexander a lot of things, but not 'just a good friend,' JeNelle."

"He has been amazing, Daddy. I don't know how he does it all. He was in the middle of making some big changes in his company when Gloria was assaulted. At the same time he was under subpoena to testify in Washington before a Congressional committee, he was helping his brother, Benny, with Whitney, working on implementing the Blue Ribbon Panel programs, working on next year's Small Business Expo, and traveling around the state giving speeches at conventions and conferences, but when I was with him, he acted like there was nothing going on. My managers, Felix, Barry, and Luke, called him all the time to ask him for his advice while I was taking care of Gloria. He always helped them come to good decisions. He even had Dr. Montgomery talking to your doctors, Daddy, while you were in the hospital."

"Yes, and he called me every day while your daddy was in the hospital to make sure that I was all right, too. Your father is right. I'd call Kenneth Alexander more than 'just a good friend'."

"You were right about something else. Kenneth comes from good Southern stock. His parents, Bernard and Sylvia Alexander, have been calling us

regularly and so have all of their children. That little sister of theirs, Aretha Grace Alexander, writes some of the nicest letters to us. She's quite a young lady."

"Yes, I know. She has been writing to me, too. I think that young lady is the reincarnation of some wise, old spirits. This couldn't be her first time on this earth. She's been here before."

"You really do look happy, JeNelle. When is the wedding going to be?"

"Mama, Kenneth hasn't said anything about getting married. He hasn't really said anything about being in love."

"Oh, the man's in love all right. He's said it in a thousand ways. Any man with his busy schedule who takes the time to write a letter to you every day is a man who's in love."

"He's an early riser. He says that he likes to watch the sun come up."

"So have you watched the sun come up with him yet, JeNelle?"

"Mama! Kenneth and I haven't been intimate."

"You mean that you haven't slept with that phine specimen of a man yet? All that time that you two were alone in DC together in the same house over the Christmas and New Year's holidays and you didn't sleep together?"

"Mama, Kenneth's not the type of man who has casual affairs."

"Yes, but he's what the young girls around here call a hunk. Tall, broad shoulders, big hands, long fingers —"

"Mama, stop it! You're even making me blush!"

"Well that man is definitely carrying some heavy luggage. I know! Just look at your daddy. Same build! He's going to be a great husband to you, JeNelle."

"When was the last time you made love, JeNelle?"

"Daddy! You're as bad as Mama. What kind of question is that to ask your daughter?"

"JeNelle, wake up! You're thirty years old. You should know that parents today had better start talking to their children as soon as they start walking. I'm ready for some grandchildren now that I've retired from the city bus company."

"You're going to have your hands full managing Towson & Towson Couture."

"*Don't try to change the subject, JeNelle. You heard what I asked you.*"

"*I know, Daddy. I haven't been intimate with a man since I was married to Michel.*"

"*What! JeNelle that was a lifetime ago! I'd better loan you some of my books so that you can read up on how it's done these days. Does Kenneth know that he's dealing with a virgin?*" Canty asked.

"*Mama, I'm not a virgin. Far from it. I was married once, remember?*"

"*Yes, JeNelle, you are. You were barely seventeen when you married Michel and only barely nineteen when you divorced him. Things have changed since then. You have the right to enjoy making love. You've got to be able to tell Kenneth what pleases you and learn what pleases him. It's not just that bim-bam, thank-you-ma'am scenario anymore. He's going to know if you try to fake it with him.*"

"*Kenneth strikes me as a man who's going to be a good teacher, Canty. He'll be patient with our daughter.*"

"*I know he will, Harvey, but JeNelle needs to learn to be creative when they make love. I'm loaning you my books and you had better read them. I'm going to quiz you after every chapter.*"

"*I don't believe it. Look, you two, you've already got me wedded and bedded just because Kenneth happened to call me while you were here. Let's finish our dinner and start working on the plans for the grand opening of Towson & Towson Couture. You know that Valentine's Day is right around the corner and we still have a lot of work to do. Constance Worthington is going to be here soon and you know how excited she is about working on the plans for the new business with you two. I need to focus on this Congressional inquiry that all these small businesses, including Kenneth's, are involved in.*"

"*Don't worry about, Kenneth, JeNelle. That man didn't do anything illegal. I'd bet my pension on that.*"

"*I'd bet my life on that, Daddy, but Kenneth isn't even going to hire a lawyer to defend himself. I'm worried about all of this negative publicity. The press has been crucifying these companies that have contracts to provide services to military installations and bases throughout the country. Kenneth's name and his company, CompuCorrect, Inc., have been mentioned prominently in connection with other companies that have received a large number of very lucrative military contracts. Kenneth acts like there is nothing going on. He won't even let me help him."*

"Kenneth knows what he's doing. He is nobody's fool. I will bet that he has an angle on this that nobody is aware of. You have to trust him and let the man do his business. You spend some time reading your mama's books and thinking about those wedding plans and my grandchildren. Let Kenneth handle this foolishness with Congress. That man didn't get to where he is without knowing how to handle something like this. You mark my words, JeNelle."

After he left her in Washington, Kenneth talked with her at least once every day. She looked forward to their conversations. She also realized that she was falling in love with him from the moment she first met him. She had to do something to help him. He was too important to her to let anything happen to him or his company when she knew that she had the means to help him through this crisis.

It took every fiber of her being, but she drove to San Diego to see Milo San Angelo at the restaurant. He was surprised, but happy to see her and they went into the kitchen to talk. Milo insisted on cooking for her, and she agreed.

"Milo, I'm here to ask a favor of you and your family. Someone who means a great deal to me is in trouble and I need your help. His name is Kenneth Alexander. He owns a company, CompuCorrect, in San Francisco. Anything that you can find out that will help him prove his innocence of these potential charges would be appreciated. I pledge on my honor that I will do whatever you ask of me in return for this favor—including reconcile with Michel."

"You're in love with this man, JeNelle?"

"Yes, Milo, I am, but he does not know that."

"Michel was not the man for you. He didn't understand who you were. That you were not Christiania."

"You mentioned her before, Milo. No one ever told me about her. She died before I met Michel."

"She was beautiful—like you—when Millos and I first saw her." He cut off his thought.

"How can you protect yourself, Milo? Michel has powerful connections everywhere."

"Familia. Family is perpetual. Should anything happen to one of us, the ultimate price must be paid."

"Vendetta."

Milo did not answer. He got up from the table and stirred the pot of sauce. He seasoned it and tasted it. He picked up a particular combination of seasonings and herbs and called to his cooks. He warned them in Italian never to use those seasonings and herbs in combination. He was noticeably angry when he returned to the table with the pasta dishes.

"You have nothing to fear, JeNelle. You have a new life with a fine man," Milo said, serving her and pouring more wine. *"This man is right for you. You have many babies together. Be happy, JeNelle. La Bella JeNelle. We will eat and laugh. Then, you will go home, JeNelle. Go back to this man, Alexander, and be happy. We will not speak of this matter again. My family owes you a debt far more than what you have asked. You will not ever have to sacrifice yourself. It shall be done."*

JeNelle recalled feeling warm and relaxed sitting in the kitchen of Michelangelo's sharing a meal with Milo. Michel gave that restaurant to her as a gift when they were first married. The same restaurant where he had publicly beat and raped her, and where she finally found the courage to leave him. She and Milo did not talk of Michel again during their meal together.

When she drove back to Santa Barbara, it was very late and her Arts Manager was camped on her doorstep. Kenneth called all over town looking for her. Felix promised Kenneth that he would not rest until he found her.

The next day she called Kenneth and he seemed to breathe a sigh of relief.

"I'm fine, Kenneth. You shouldn't worry about me so much. I'm a big girl. I can take care of myself—most of the time," she remembered saying jokingly. *"You didn't have to send out the National Guard to find me."*

"I only made a few telephone calls, JeNelle. Can I help it if Santa Barbara swings into action when its Woman of the Year comes up missing for a few hours?"

"You had people camping on my doorstep when I got home. I'd say you made more than just 'a few' telephone calls. Johnston scolded me unmercifully this morning. He told his secretary to find him no matter where he was when I called. He even left the bench when I called to say that I was fine."

"You're very important and precious to a lot of people. Especially to me."

Her heart leaped into her throat, making it hard for her to speak. *"I didn't mean to worry anyone, especially not you. You've got a lot going on with the Congressional hearings starting tomorrow. I wish that you'd let me come and be with you and help you get through this. You've done so much to help me and my family."*

"No, it's pure chaos here. There are people everywhere. My sister, Vivian, and her housemates, the Legal Dream Team, have turned this place into a legal fortress. My partners, Tom and Shirley, were saying a bunch of Hail Mary's this morning. I don't want you to be caught up in all of this confusion. It's going to work out fine and it will be over very soon."

"The press reports are vicious and slanderous. There are rumors flying all over the place, linking these allegations to people high up in the National Security Agency NSA and even to the California Governor's office. This could hurt you personally and professionally. I can't help it. I'm concerned for you, especially since you won't even hire legal representation to defend yourself. Everybody else who was subpoenaed called out the biggest legal guns that they could find."

"CompuCorrect has done nothing wrong. You'll simply have to trust me on that point."

"I'd trust you with my life. It's the politicians and the Fifth Estate who I don't trust."

"I'm glad to hear you say that."

"Say what? That I don't trust the politicians or the press?"

"No, that you'd trust me with your life."

"It's true. You're the most trustworthy, honest, upstanding, responsible—"

"Are you trying to finesse your way out of the payment that you owe me for my massage services?"

"Kenneth Alexander, how can you joke with me at a time like this?"

"Temper, temper, Ms. Towson. Remember, you'll have to trust me."

"You won't let me help. You won't let me come there. I've got to find a way to repay you for all that you've done for me, for Gloria, for my family and my business. At least, if I were there, I could find a way to say more than just thank you."

"I'll help you find some new words to say."

"You said that before. What did you mean by that? Have you thought of something that I can do to help or to say thank you?"

"I'll tell you later."

"There are times that you can be the most exasperating person I know. Have you always been this stubborn?"

"I'm sometimes an acquired taste, JeNelle. You'll get used to it."

⊶

She recalled that on the day that Kenneth was scheduled to testify, she was nervous and antsy. She wondered whether Milo found out any information that would help Kenneth, but she would not call him again. She knew that if he could find a way to help her, he would do it.

She stayed home that day and turned on the television in her study. Commentators were discussing the hearings and the list of witnesses that were scheduled that day.

"What do we know about the first witness today, Kenneth Alexander, and his company, CompuCorrect?" the program moderator asked one of the panelists.

"Good reputation from all accounts. Started the company four or five years ago after leaving Sandoval Anniston as its lead industrial engineering specialist. Worked on some top secret projects for the CIA and NSA," the panelist answered.

"Could be some tie in there to some covert operations. He was certainly in a position to know what was going on in the Pentagon and in the CIA and NSA," another panelist added.

"Are you suggesting that his company is some kind of a front for the CIA or NSA?" the moderator asked.

"I'm just saying that where there's smoke, look for a fire."

"According to CompuCorrect's Annual Report, most of their clients are non-military," another panelist added. *"There are some pretty prestigious A-list organizations listed as clients."*

"I don't need to tell you that that's how the CIA and NSA operate. Just look at what Oliver North was able to do and before that G. Gordon Liddy. I still question what Reagan or Bush knew about this investigation and when did they know it. Bush was head of the intelligence community at one time, you will remember."

"We'll have to get back to this discussion after the testimony. The hearing is about to begin. We'll take you live to the Congressional chamber after a few words from our sponsors," the moderator said.

What do they know? JeNelle recalled thinking. Kenneth was not a man who would permit himself to be used. She was positive of that.

When the coverage resumed, she could see that the Congressional chamber was packed. Television cameras panned the room. All of the major networks were carrying the hearing live. She saw the Alexander family as they entered and took seats directly behind the table where Kenneth sat alone. She saw Shirley and Tom enter the hearing room looking very nervous. She recognized Colonel JC Baker, who sat with other high-ranking military officials in the hearing room, attired in his full dress uniform. She remembered meeting Colonel Baker outside of Kenneth's home and remnants of the argument that she overheard between Kenneth and Colonel Baker. She also saw that Lisa Lambert, Kenneth's former lover, was in the hearing room. She wondered whether that was the reason that Kenneth didn't want her to be there. Was he still involved with Lisa? She couldn't think of that then.

The Congressmen and Senators entered the chamber and took their seats. Chairman Marshall called the Joint Committee of the House and Senate to order with a large gavel. The throngs of people were silent. The Chairman announced the purpose of the fact-finding, investigative hearing and then turned to the first witness of the day, Kenneth James Alexander.

"Mr. Alexander, would you state your name and address for the record?" Chairman Marshall asked.

"I am Kenneth James Alexander, formerly of Goodwill, South Carolina, currently residing in San Francisco, California," Kenneth said in a clear, cool, and crisp voice.

The room was silent.

"And your occupation, Mr. Alexander?"

"I am the Executive Director and Managing Partner of CompuCorrect, Inc."

Just then, the camera caught sight of a group of people arriving who created quite a commotion as they entered. They quickly took seats with the Alexander family members behind Kenneth.

"Mr. Alexander, are you represented here today by legal counsel?"

"No, Mr. Chairman, I am not."

The spectators gasped.

"Well, Mr. Alexander, do you have an opening statement that you would like to read into the Congressional Record?"

"No, Mr. Chairman, I do not."

The audience gasped again. Her stomach was in knots.

"Mr. Alexander, this is highly irregular. You're not represented by legal counsel and you have no statement for the record. Either you're very confident of your position or you've made a fool's mistake."

"My parents did not raise any fools, Mr. Chairman."

The audience roared and she did, too. Score one for the good guys. Even the Congressmen chuckled, but Kenneth sat straight and confidently in his chair without flinching. Calmness began to flow over her as the Congressmen began to ask questions in the order that the Chairman called their names. Kenneth answered each question clearly and concisely. The cameras captured him from every angle as other reporters snapped pictures of him. He was in full control. For that reason, as she sat there watching Kenneth testify, she knew that everything would be all right. Even from three thousand miles away, he could put her mind at ease.

"Mr. Alexander, did your company bid on ten military contracts and receive all ten?" Chairman Marshall asked.

"Actually, eleven military contracts. Yes, we did, Mr. Chairman."

"Isn't it highly unlikely that a small company like yours should be so favored as to have received all of the contracts that it bid for?"

"No, Mr. Chairman. CompuCorrect is a growing company with highly-trained, competent, qualified, and energetic people."

"But, weren't these contracts inflated, Mr. Alexander?"

"Yes, they were, Mr. Chairman."

The spectators gasped. Reporters pulled out cell phones and started calling in their stories. The video media took close-up views of Kenneth. JC Baker shifted; it seemed uncomfortably, in his seat and whispered something to the other military officers. A murmur could be heard through the room. The Chairman banged his gavel and the noise ceased.

"Mr. Alexander, are you admitting wrongdoing in the acceptance of these contracts?"

"Absolutely not, Mr. Chairman."

Kenneth's words were still hanging in the air when a woman came into the chamber, handed a copy of some papers to Chairman Marshall and whispered something in his ear. The Chairman covered his microphone, looked over the papers while the woman handed a copy of the papers to each member of the Committee. There was a flurry of activity from the congressional aides as their congressional representatives conferred with them. The Chairman returned to the microphone.

"Would William Anthony Chandler, David Burnham Carter, III, Alan Keanu Lightfoot, Melissa Bernice Charles, and Vivian Lynn Alexander please rise if you are in this Chamber?" Chairman Marshall asked.

They all rose and she recognized David and saw Kenneth's sister, Vivian, and the other housemates. Vivian was very attractive, she had thought, but she wondered what the housemates had all done to be singled out by the Chairman in that manner.

"Mr. Alexander, do you know these people?"

A slight amused smile crossed Kenneth's face.

"Yes, Mr. Chairman, I do know them."

"Have you authorized them to act on your behalf, Mr. Alexander?"

"No, Mr. Chairman, but I'll take full responsibility for whatever they have done."

"Thank you, Mr. Alexander," Chairman Marshall had said, *"you are excused while we examine certain new information which has been brought to this Committee's attention."*

Suddenly, she thought of Milo San Angelo. She had a strong feeling that he may have been successful in finding some vital piece of information that would help Kenneth.

Kenneth got up and sat next to his parents.

"This Committee calls a Corporal Samuel Yeager to the witness table."

The crowd began to murmur loudly. Reporters started looking around to see the witness. She noticed that JC Baker seemed to nearly leap out of his skin. The Committee room doors opened and Corporal Yeager marched in. He was attired in his spit and polish, full-dressed military uniform. He marched to the front of the room, the clerk swore him in, and he took a seat at the witness table.

"Corporal Yeager, I'm holding an affidavit, which appears to have your signature affixed and notarized," Chairman Marshall said.

The Clerk handed a copy of the document to Corporal Yeager.

"Is that your signature?"

"Yes, Sir," Corporal Yeager had said.

"Son, would you tell us in your own words what is contained in this document?"

"Yes, Sir. I have been Colonel JC Baker's assistant and driver since he came to the Pentagon, Sir. During that time, Colonel Baker and other military officials attempted to coerce Mr. Alexander into overpricing projects while he was at the Sandoval Anniston Corporation. Mr. Alexander refused and left the company. Since then, Colonel Baker worked with Dr. Lisa Lambert to distract Mr. Alexander while he slipped some RFPs through Mr. Alexander's company. Colonel Baker was concerned that Ms. Shirley Taylor, a partner of Mr. Alexander's, might discover the overpricing and alert Mr. Alexander,

so he started an affair with her to keep her from finding out. Colonel Baker instructed Dr. Lambert to use Ms. JeNelle Towson, or anyone else, to distract Mr. Alexander. They were concerned about using Ms. Towson because of her relationship with California State Supreme Court Judge Johnson Worthington and the San Angelo family in New York; Ms. Towson and Judge Worthington were two people who they thought wouldn't permit themselves to be used. Colonel Baker and Dr. Lambert have been pushing overpriced RFPs into California and other states so that the military budget could not be cut, and so that military bases would not be closed. Colonel Baker and other military officers have had their intelligence operations going in each state similar to the one in California. In Florida and Texas…"

She recalled that the mentioning of her name sent shockwaves through her body, but even more importantly, she was overwhelmed by the soldier's testimony concerning Lisa Lambert. She recalled wondering whether Lisa was simply using Kenneth for all those months to slip the military contracts into his company. However, something about the company, Sandoval Anniston, stuck in her mind. She couldn't remember why, but she had other things to think about. She would have to Google them. When she did, she knew why the corporate name sounded familiar. It was because Michal owned it.

The audience sat in absolute silent amazement as Corporal Yeager spoke for nearly an hour of other transactions he witnessed. When Corporal Yeager finished, pandemonium broke loose.

The Chairman banged the gavel loudly several times.

"Corporal Yeager, do you have anything else to add to your testimony?"

"Well, I left out the part about Dr. Lambert and Colonel Baker having sex in your office, on your desk, Sir, and in the Heritage Foundation Board Room, but I'll put that all in my book when it's published," Yeager said proudly.

Pandemonium broke out again and the Chairman banged the gavel, *again.*

"In my office! On my desk!" the Chairman yelled. *"Son, do you have any evidence to back up these allegations?"*

"No, Sir, just my word, but I am from Holly Hill, South Carolina, Sir, and in South Carolina, a man's word is his bond."

The audience laughed.

"I'm sure that's true, Son, but we can't charge highly-decorated officers of our military with these unspeakable acts without proof."

"I have proof, Mr. Chairman," Kenneth interrupted, as he walked to the witness table.

The audience hushed.

Kenneth took his pager off his waist and placed it before the microphone. He flipped a switch and his and Baker's voices could be heard arguing over many of the facts to which Yeager testified.

Then Kenneth gave a closing statement without benefit of notes or teleprompter. She beamed with pride at his words and his demeanor. Score another one for the good guys. Tears filled her eyes. He was magnificent. She tingled all over just thinking about him. Her telephone began constantly ringing, but she refused to answer it. She sat in the glow of her admiration for him for hours. When she heard Kenneth's voice come over her answering machine, she leaped for the telephone.

"Kenneth, you were brilliant. I'm so proud of you. I could hardly believe it."

"You've been a busy lady, Ms. Towson, haven't you?"

"Me? You're the one who the television commentators are saying ought to be in public office. They're praising you on every network and on every channel!"

"Don't try to change the subject. I believe that you had something to do with Corporal Yeager's key testimony."

"Now, Kenneth, I only made a simple request of an old friend. Can I help it if this country turns out in force when its Man For All Seasons skips by a little bump in the road?"

"Touché, Ms. Towson, but from now on let's not be out of touch so that neither one of us has any reason to worry. Agreed?"

"Agreed, Mr. Alexander."

She recalled how they continued to talk on the telephone several times each day. She thought that they were beginning to find any reason to call each other. One day she did not hear from him at all. She was swamped with preparations for the grand opening of Towson & Towson, the renovations to INSIGHTS, and the student trainees running her new mail-order business. She recalled not feeling comfortable because Kenneth hadn't called. She went into her office to call him.

"Greetings, this is CompuCorrect, Northern Division. How may I direct your call please?" Sara McDougal answered.

"Sara, good morning. This is JeNelle Towson. How are you?"

"Hi, JeNelle, I'm fine. How are you?" she answered with a strange lift in her tone. *"I'm fine, Sara. Is Mr. Alexander in the office this morning?"*

"No, JeNelle. He left on an extended business trip."

"That's funny. He didn't mention anything to me about going away."

"Oh, I'm sure that he'll be in touch with you real soon," she recalled Sara saying with a giggle.

"What are you so happy about, Sara?"

"Love, JeNelle. Ain't love just grand!" she said rhetorically with wistfulness in her voice.

"I suppose so, Sara," she said, but was confused by Sara's statement. *"Will you tell Mr. Alexander that I called?"*

"Sure, JeNelle, but I'm sure that you'll probably hear from him long before I do," she said with a certain joy in her voice that made her even more confused.

"Thanks, Sara. My best to everyone."

She recalled shaking her head and going back to work. She had a full day of work ahead of her.

"Ms. Towson, would you come to the front desk. You are wanted on the telephone and you have a special delivery," Wanda said over the store's intercom.

She was a little annoyed because she asked Wanda not to interrupt her when she was meeting with her student trainees. Excusing herself, she went to the front of the store. It was quite a walk since, what used to be a stock and storage room, was now an active back-office operation. The store had now doubled in size. The finishing touches were also being made on yet another project next door to INSIGHTS for the opening of another small business venture. She and her new partners would unveil the new business at an open house celebration over an upcoming holiday weekend. She and her parents went into partnership in Towson & Towson Couture. Her mother taught a group of young people to sew and make clothing that they sold to their customers, some of whom were very wealthy, like Mrs. Johnston White Worthington, who had become a regular customer and who had brought many of her friends to the shop. Others were young people looking for the latest new outfit.

"Wanda, I thought that I asked you not to disturb me when I'm working with our new employees, unless it is very important."

"I know, Ms. Towson, but this seems to be very important," Wanda said apologetically. *"Mrs. Worthington is on line three and you have a special delivery."*

She looked at Wanda's very apologetic demeanor, smiled at her, and shook her head. She took a deep breath and answered the telephone.

"Constance, I'm sorry to keep you waiting. How can I help you this afternoon?"

"Oh, I know how busy you are, JeNelle, and I won't take up much of your time. I just need to get a few details cleared up."

"All right, Constance. If this is about Towson & Towson Couture, what do you need to know?"

"Well, I've got the announcements and invitations all worked out. I've been working with that nice young man, Paul Garrett. He really selected a beautiful beige onion-skin paper and the raised embossed printing in script is simply divine. He thought that you might like that. He's worked with you before and I think that he's captured your spirit—and Kenneth's, of course. Well, anyway, the guest list is completed. It's just going to be a small affair with just your family and Kenneth's and three hundred of your closest friends. Johnston and I are so glad that you and Kenneth agreed to let us host your engagement party. The catering is all arranged, but I need to know what color scheme you're going to have at the wedding so that I can incorporate those colors into the decorations for the engagement party. Kenneth didn't say. All he said was that you would tell me later. I know that he's just as busy as you are with his new office, but color schemes are very important, too."

As Constance Worthington spoke, her eyes had grown wider and her mouth had dropped open. She didn't believe what she was hearing, but then there was that noise from the construction going on across the street. Or had Constance finally gone 'round the bend'! She wondered whether Johnston knew that his wife had flipped her wig.

"Engagement party! Color scheme! Catering! Invitations! Constance, are we talking about the opening of Towson & Towson Couture?"

"Oh, JeNelle, I know that these are not things that you have a lot of time to deal with right now, but since the announcement is already in this afternoon's newspaper, I thought that I'd better get it all cleared up before we're swamped with calls and acceptances. So you just think about it, dear, and give me a call later when you and Kenneth have made a decision."

Constance hung up and she was in total bewilderment. Wanda quickly placed a stool behind her and helped her to sit down. She handed her a copy of the Style section of the afternoon paper and stepped back. Wanda remembered the last time that she got news from the newspaper. She was not taking any chances this time. She was completely innocent.

"It wasn't me, Ms. Towson. I swear!" Wanda said, holding her hands up in the air.

She began to read the article.

"Dr. and Mrs. Bernard Alexander of Goodwill, South Carolina, are pleased to announce the engagement of their eldest son, Kenneth James Alexander, formerly of San Francisco, to Ms. JeNelle Elise Towson, daughter of Mr. and Mrs. Harvey Towson of Santa Barbara. Ms. Towson is the owner of INSIGHTS, and Towson & Towson Couture of Santa Barbara and is a leading citizen of the Santa Barbara community. She was named Woman of the Year last year by the Santa Barbara Chamber of Commerce and currently serves on the Governor's Blue Ribbon Panel on Youth in Business and Industry and as the President of the California State League of Business and Professional Women.

Mr. Kenneth Alexander, the Executive Director of CompuCorrect, stated, in an exclusive interview, that he and his lovely bride-to-be will reside most of the year in Santa Barbara where Mr. Alexander is opening his new offices, but that they would also maintain a home in Goodwill, South Carolina.

Judge and Mrs. Johnston White Worthington will host the happy couple's engagement party at their estate on Valentine's Day. Mr. Alexander stated that the date of the engagement party was chosen carefully to coincide with the one-year anniversary of their love for each other. The wedding date has not yet been disclosed, according to Mr. Alexander, but he stated that he would prefer a short engagement since the couple is planning to have a very large family.

It was nearly one year ago that this reporter covered the selection of Ms. Towson as the recipient of the prestigious Chamber of Commerce award. The question then was, 'Who would move for love?' It appears that Mr. Alexander has answered that question loudly and clearly. We wish the happy couple well."

Just as she finished reading the article and looked up, the noise from the construction stopped and she saw a sign going up on the building across the street. The sign read, in bold letters:

FUTURE HOME OF COMPUCORRECT, INC.
SOUTHERN DIVISION
KENNETH J. ALEXANDER, EXECUTIVE DIRECTOR

She had blinked her eyes rapidly. She couldn't believe what she was seeing.

"First Constance, then the article, now this? What is going on!" she exclaimed aloud.

"You forgot about your special delivery, Ms. Towson," a very familiar voice said to her.

She turned to see Kenneth leaning against the bookshelves in that same sexy stance of his, wearing that same warm, million-dollar, polar-ice-cap-melting smile. He walked toward her, took a box from behind his back, and handed it to her. She looked at him, still dazed by the events.

"Kenneth, what …"

He kissed her on the lips. Her bewilderment grew. It was the first kiss that they shared. She dreamed of what his kiss would feel like. She totally underestimated how wonderfully powerful it actually was.

"Open the box, JeNelle," he said, looking into her eyes.

She took the box and started to open it, but kept looking at him as she fumbled with the ribbon and paper. As she unfurled the tissue paper inside the box, she saw the beautiful crystal bowl that she admired in Tiffany & Company in San Francisco. Her eyes began to water. It was more beautiful than she remembered.

"Kenneth, how—"

He kissed her on the lips again, and she started to feel those amorous feelings growing rapidly inside her.

"Open it, JeNelle."

She had looked at him as she removed the lid of the crystal bowl. The aromatic scent of rose petals wafted out of the container and into the air. A red satin box sat in the middle of the white rose petals.

"Kenneth, who—"

He kissed her lips again, and she felt pure excitement building up inside her. Her heart was racing.

"Open it, JeNelle."

She opened the box and found a beautiful star, diamond engagement ring with many beams of light. Tears were rolling down her cheeks.

"Now, if you're ready for your vocabulary lesson, Ms. Towson, repeat after me: Kenneth James Alexander, I love you as much as you have loved me. We will love each other more tomorrow than we do today. We will love each other and our children—"

She didn't let him finish. She leaped from the stool and kissed him with all of the passion that she had locked away for far too many years. She was oblivious to everyone and everything around her. She only felt the bliss of holding the man that she loved in her arms.

In the early morning the next day, Kenneth stood on the deck of her home looking at the beautiful beginning of a new day and the peaceful ocean as it rolled gently onto shore. He folded his arms across his bare chest and looked up at the last glimmer of the stars as the day began to overtake the night. He seemed to be saying a silent prayer.

She went out onto the deck from her bedroom where they had shared their first night together making love. She kissed his bare back, put her arms around him, and stroked his chest and his abdomen. She laid her cheek against his warm back and pressed her body against his.

He kissed her fingers and the ring on the third finger of her left hand.

"I missed you when I woke up and you weren't there," she said, as she held him.

"I came out here to thank my ancestors for bringing me to this point. I'm in love for the first time in my life."

She moved around to face him, put her arms around his neck, and kissed him with all of the passion within her. She looked into his eyes.

"And I'm in love for the last time in my life."

◦═◦

As Constance Worthington had promised, there was only Kenneth's family, her family, which numbered more than three hundred of their closest family members and friends. It was a beautiful afternoon engagement party on the lawn of Johnston and Constance's palatial estate in Montecito. She and Kenneth walked hand-in-hand, greeting each of their guests. People from his office in San Francisco were there, her employees, and people who she worked with on different projects, including the mayor and city council. Both their parents and siblings attended. It was a long afternoon, but she didn't feel fatigued with Kenneth by her side.

Lights illuminated the lawn and Kenneth led her to a beautifully-decorated chair that was placed on a platform in front of the bandstand. She did not know what to expect, but she trusted him unequivocally. The lawn lights dimmed and a single spotlight shinned on them as he seated her in the chair. She remembered how she tingled as he smiled at her and knelt before her on one knee. The guests at the reception all gathered around.

"JeNelle Elise Towson, I'm in love with you. I have loved you since the first moment that we met. I love the warmth in your eyes when you look at me. I love the excitement in your voice when you speak to me. I want to spend the rest of my life with you. Loving you. Sharing every day and every night with you. Raising a family with you. I promise you that I will always be there for you whenever you need me. I want you to reach for each and every dream that you have and I will be there to help you make each one come true. I promise you this before God and all of our families and friends who are gathered here today. JeNelle Elise Towson, will you marry me and make me the happiest man in the universe?"

She remembered crying as he spoke to her so tenderly, but her answer came without question or reservation.

"Yes! Yes! Yes! A million times yes!" she said, as she cupped his face in her hands. He rose and held her close to him. She kissed him with all the joy in her heart, body, and soul. The combo began to play "You Are So Beautiful," as they again danced in a single beam of light with their families and friends surrounding them, cheering and clapping wildly.

She was glad that Kenneth asked Benny to be his best man. She and Benny were good friends now. They talked about his feelings for her and resolved them. She knew that he was not in love with her, but with Navy Lieutenant Stacy Greene and she hoped that one day soon Stacy would come back to him. He and their daughter, Whitney Ivy, needed Stacy in their lives.

Her sister, Gloria; Kenneth's siblings, Vivian, Aretha, Gregory; his business partners, Tom Jenkins and Shirley Taylor; their friends, Chuck Montgomery, Janice Atterly, and Cecil Jordon; her cousin, Timothy Baines, and his cousin, James Dixon, also agreed to be in the wedding. Gloria was reluctant since she still had difficulty walking. The scars from the brutal beating healed, but it left deeper scars on her heart and soul. She pleaded with her sister to seek counseling or to join a focus group of battered women, but Gloria refused. Instead she hired the best lawyers that she could find and filed suit against Tony Jamerson, her former fiancée, the San Diego Chargers, because he had played wide receiver for them, and the Washington Hotel because of what she described as their lax security. Gloria, she thought, was on a vendetta. She hoped that her sister would begin to heal herself as she helped her plan for her wedding to Kenneth. It seemed that all the wedding festivities, the bridal showers, and the bridal party dinner only made her more bitter.

David Carter, one of the law school housemates, was constantly with Gloria, providing moral support.

Although Gloria wasn't enthusiastic about her upcoming wedding, Vivian, Kenneth's sister, was a ray of sunshine as they talked about the plans. She had good reason to be happy. She met Derrick Jackson, Vivian's boyfriend, a former professional basketball icon, who was now a noted pediatrician. They seemed to be floating on air whenever she saw them together. She was sorry that Derrick might not be there for the week-long wedding festivities. His medical practice in Washington, DC, kept him busy for months, but he told Vivian that he would make every effort to be there for the wedding. All of the housemates were there, though, including Anna Menendez-Gaza, the housekeeper and cook, and her two children, Angelique and Miguel.

Aretha Grace Alexander, Kenneth's youngest sibling, was the true cheerleader for the wedding. She would be a junior brides maid and asked to play and sing a special song for her and Kenneth during the wedding ceremony. Aretha Grace kept her FAX machine, text, and e-mail humming with wedding information, like bridesmaids' dresses, cake decorations, bridal shower etiquette and a myriad of other details that she didn't want her to forget. She was a real live wire at the bridal shower the week before the wedding, as she folded each piece of wrapping paper carefully after she opened each gift. She asked Aretha Grace why she was treating the wrapping paper so carefully and was told that she should use the paper to line the drawers of hers and Kenneth's bedroom furniture so as to always remember how happy they were. Aretha also threaded each ribbon through a hole in paper plates. She didn't know why Aretha did that until last night at the wedding rehearsal. As the members of the wedding party came down the aisle, they carried the ribbons on the paper plates as if they were real flowers. Aretha didn't miss a trick, but she would not divulge what she decided to perform. It was a secret.

Dr. Charles Montgomery was there as a member of the wedding party. He was a friend of the housemates and had personally taken care of Gloria after the assault. He took good care of her, too, with his warm and caring ways. She could hear the excitement in his voice when she and Kenneth called him using a speakerphone and asked him to be in the wedding. He let out a yell that would have made the rodeo circuit proud. He helped Benny, Gregory, and Tom plan Kenneth's bachelor party, too. Judge Johnston White Worthington, her friend and mentor, attended that bachelor party and he turned beet red whenever she asked him what went on. He consistently took the Fifth Amendment against self-incrimination and swore that he would take the secrets of that bachelor party to his grave. He still said that he would perform the wedding ceremony with a clear mind, but a guilty conscience.

Vivian and Chuck looked cute pretending to be her and Kenneth at the wedding rehearsal, but Gregory Alexander, Kenneth's youngest brother, got most of the attention. He had all of her young cousins salivating—some of the older cousins, too. The young female students in her store and her parents' couture boutique couldn't function whenever he was around during the week-long festivities. She noticed that Raymond, one of her clerks, who happened to be gay, actually did cartwheels down the aisles whenever Gregory was in the store. Gregory did have sex appeal, but all of the Alexander men did. Even her future father-in-law, Dr. Bernard Alexander, had a striking appearance with loads of charisma, but he clearly only had eyes for one person, Sylvia Benson Alexander, his wife and the mother of their five children. They still held hands after thirty-six years of marriage.

Even her parents, Harvey and Canty Towson, were thrilled after finally meeting them in person. They spent many days together sharing stories and no doubt, secrets about their children, including her and Kenneth, she was sure.

Meeting so many of the Alexander family was bewildering. So many of them and the people from Kenneth's company in San Francisco were coming to Santa Barbara for the week-long festivities that she selected multiple hotels to house them Their guest list had grown rapidly. Sylvia Alexander e-mailed a list of names and addresses of relatives and friends that took up many pages. She didn't know how the church was going to hold all of the people who were going to be invited to attend the wedding, but Kenneth insisted that he wanted their wedding day to be the most special day of their lives. He simply decided to change the wedding venue to the Atrium Ballroom. He helped with every detail of the planning, but he was always the calm in the eye of the storm. His calm, careful, and thoughtful demeanor got her through some tense periods of anxiety, like the days after the wedding invitations were mailed when mail trucks of all types and description pulled up in front of her home to deliver wedding gifts. Kenneth simply started stacking them, unopened, in a POD storage container parked next to her house and said that they would open and acknowledge each one after they returned from their three-week honeymoon, but he still wasn't saying where they were going. They were having work done to her bungalow to add two additional levels while they were away. On another occasion, when she began to panic about the wedding costs, Kenneth simply picked up the telephone and called some of his clients. Within a few hours, everything was arranged. Flowers, catering, cars, valet services, wait staff, and the musicians for both the wedding and the reception. He could do anything with such ease and poise. That's why he was the Executive Director of CompuCorrect, Inc., and the man that she loved.

Initially, her relationship with Kenneth was one disaster after another. First, it was Benny's relentless pursuit of her, and then Kenneth's determination not to fall in love with her because of Benny. Kenneth went to great lengths to mask his feelings for her. He even permitted himself to carry on a very open affair with Lisa Lambert.

Disasters kept them apart, but, ultimately, it was another disaster that brought them together: Gloria was allegedly attacked by her fiancée. Kenneth was with her at a meeting when she got the news. It was only his strength that got her though the ordeal, particularly when a newspaper reporter dug up information that she, too, was the victim of domestic violence at the hands of Michel San Angelo that had hospitalized her for six months. Kenneth comforting presence led her to reveal the whole sordid story to him. She told him how Michel raped and beat her in a fit of rage in a public parking lot while customers were held at bay by Michel's armed bodyguards. Only Milo San Angelo's intervention stopped Michel from killing her.

Chapter 2

"What's wrong, Shirley?" Tom Jenkins asked, as he sat down beside her on his bed. Shirley Taylor studied Tom's face, unsure of her ground. Except for the pretty green eyes instead of blue, she always thought that he could be the clone of the actor Simon Baker, who played Patrick Jane in the television drama *The Mentalist*. What she saw was a mixture of love and concern radiating there.

"I'm not so sure that it's a good idea for me to spend the night with you when your children are here," Shirley said, looking away from him, nervously, unnecessarily smoothing her pink silk nightgown over her knees.

He took her busy hands in his to steady them, then with a finger to her cheek, turned her face toward his and kissed her troubled brow. It was funny how often she was mistaken for the Canadian actress Tamara Taylor who played Dr. Camille Sarayan on the crime drama *Bones*.

"My children love you, Shirley, and so do I. Of course, it's all right."

She looked into his green eyes. "What will they think of me being here with you like this?"

One side of his mouth hitched up into a grin. "That you're a lustful woman hell bent on making their father very happy every night."

Shirley pursed her lips, frustrated. "Tom, don't joke about this. This is too important. Children are very impressionable, I hear. We're going to have a hard enough time with an interracial relationship. I know how hard that can be because my parents have gone through it for forty years. I don't want to complicate things by having trouble start with your children." Shirley frowned.

It was so like her to be concerned for someone else, never for herself. That was one of the many things that so endeared her to him, but he wanted, no *needed* to reassure her that she had no need for concern.

Heaven knew that they had come such a long, hard way to get to this point. He wasn't going to let anything interfere with the future that he wanted for them both.

"My children are bright and articulate. If they begin to have a problem with our relationship, they'll tell us. I'm not worried though."

"Why not?"

"We've talked about this. We learned how to talk with each other when we were all in group therapy after Deidre and I divorced. Aaron was sullen and Ericka would whine and fight with little or no provocation. They were both very unhappy little children. Deidre and I were arguing a lot before we divorced. We didn't know that the children heard us. We were fighting about who the children should live with most of the time. The children thought that it was their fault that their whole universe was ending."

"That's terrible, Tom. What did you do?"

"The therapist told us that the acrimony had to stop. That it was tearing the children apart and the children were trying to hold Deidre and me together by acting out all the time. The therapist helped Aaron and Ericka work out their anger and frustration. That helped me and Deidre, too."

"Oh, Tom, I'm glad to hear that."

"Although we couldn't live together anymore, family is very important to both of us. That's why we're able to share custody of our children and not kill each other in the process. The children now know, and more importantly, understand that they weren't the reason that we divorced and that we, as parents, weren't divorcing them. We have good, loving bonds between us now. What my children need now is to see good, stable, healthy relationships between men and women. I'm not going to hide you away in some closet. You're an important part of my life, Shirley. You're a beautiful woman—black or white, or anything in between."

Shirley hugged Tom and rested her head on his shoulder, stroking the arm he had around her. "How'd you get so smart?"

"Your friend and mine: Kenneth Alexander. He taught me a great deal about the family unit. That's where he learned about the perceptions and attitudes that affect relationships. I sure don't know it all, but I'm learning."

"Kenneth and JeNelle are going to have a wonderful marriage. They're so right for each other. I'm excited about being a part of their happiness."

"We'll be there, too, Shirley."

"Marriage? Oh, I don't know, Tom. We've only been seeing each other socially for six months."

"We've known each other for nearly nine years and we've been business partners for many years now."

Shirley shifted away from Tom. "Let's not rush into anything."

Gently, Tom took her by the shoulders and shifted her back toward him. "I keep getting this nagging feeling that something's wrong; that you're reluctant to make a commitment to this relationship. Am I wrong or what?"

"This all happened so fast," she said, her hands aflutter.

Warmly, he smiled at her. "Not for me it didn't. Why do you think my wife and I were arguing so much?"

"I thought that it was about your children," she said, puzzled.

"That came later. Deidre knew that I wasn't in love with her anymore. She accused me of having an affair with you."

Shirley's eyes widened with shocked distress. "But we weren't involved. I mean, we were friends and then business partners, but nothing more than that."

"She could detect that I had feelings for you and finally I couldn't deny it. It blew her mind that I wanted you—a Black woman—instead of her. She didn't understand that it had nothing to do with color or race. The chasm that developed between Deidre and me began because we wanted different things out of our marriage. She wanted the security of a big house in Marin County, expensive cars, membership at the country club, our children in the best private schools, expensive vacations to exotic places. She wanted someone to take care of her." He took a deep-cleansing breath and then continued.

"I wanted love. I wanted someone to love me whether I was rich or poor. When Kenneth, you and I left Sandoval Anniston to start CompuCorrect, Deidre went ballistic. She thought that she was going to lose her security blanket. It didn't matter that I wanted to own my own business. Work for myself. Build something that I could be proud of. That I needed her support. She didn't believe in me and wouldn't even give me her moral support. That killed it for me. I didn't start out looking for an affair outside of my marriage, but I needed someone who did want to be in my corner. I found her. You, Shirley Taylor. I'm committed. Are you?"

"I'm feeling a little uncomfortable, that's all. I'm not sure that I can handle all of this."

Tom huffed out a breath. "If I were Kenneth would we be having this problem?"

"That's not fair, Tom. This isn't about Kenneth."

"Then what's it about?"

"I just don't know whether I'm ready for a sexual relationship, yet."

"*What?*" he yelled.

"Tom, calm down."

"Calm down, hell! Six months of holding hands is long enough, Shirley. We aren't silly, immature kids with nothing on our brains but a quick screw!"

"I just don't know—I mean, I've never slept with—"

"A white man? Is that the problem? You think I'm made differently from any other man or something? Well, I'm not! Look for yourself!" He pulled off his robe and turned slowly with his arms outstretched. "See, no horns!"

Shirley giggled. "You're purple."

"You should see me when I really get excited," Tom said, folding his ire into a laugh. "Now you do it."

"Do what?"

"Take off your robe, stand up, and turn around."

"You're crazy."

"No, I'm not. I'm in heat. I'm in love. But I'm not insane. If the only thing standing between us is our skin color then let's take a good look and move to the next step."

Shirley reluctantly and slowly did as Tom asked. He guided her to a full-length mirror and they gazed at each other's nude body, smiles growing on their faces.

"Now," he said, getting into bed and pulling back the cover, "let me show you how I can love you and your beautiful skin."

Chapter 3

"I've had it!" Janice Atterly yelled, as she came into the condo and slammed the door behind her.

"What's wrong with her?" Charles Easton asked, as Janice breezed by the living room.

"Probably another wasted date," Cecil Jordon said dispassionately, as she uncurled her long, shapely legs from Charles' lap.

"Wasted? What do you mean wasted?"

"My condo mate is the world's greatest eternal optimist. She wants it all; the perfect man and the perfect life. She keeps putting herself out there and coming up empty. She'll never learn."

"You sure are rough on a brother, Cecil."

"As if you 'brothers' don't deserve it," she joked, as she reached for her wine glass, taking a sip.

"Some of us do, but you sistahs are rough to handle these days. You all want the perfect man. He's got to be kind, handsome, loving, supportive, and rich. He's also got to be able to fix everything under the sun—materially, emotionally, and sexually. You women live in some kind of fantasy world and it's driving us brothers to run the other way."

"Ha!" Cecil laughed without humor. "Do you have it wrong or what? First, Charles Easton, women don't want to be 'handled' any way but gently. Second, as for the 'perfect man', there ain't no such animal. Third, any and every man should be kind, loving, and supportive. It doesn't cost anything. Any man can afford that. Fourth, as long as the man doesn't need fixing, most sistahs can cope. Finally, and most importantly, you brothers want the ultimate fantasy. You want to find a replacement for your mothers. Submissive, accommodating, attentive, and supportive to the nth degree. You want the twenty-first century woman to be a bitch in the boardroom and a babe in the bedroom. You want unconditional love, but conditional relationships."

"I'm just saying that relationships ought to be built on realities about each other. Black men aren't just studs ready to be ridden like in some damn steeplechase. Jump this hurdle. Cross that barrier and getting whipped on the ass every step of the way. We aren't all prize-winning stallions. We have faults and shortcomings just like anybody else, but to the Black woman, every man has to be a superman or out you go. Yes, we want to be pampered and maybe we do look for those same qualities in women that our mothers had, and maybe we do want you women to seduce us in the bedroom, but what the hell is wrong with that? Can't today's Black woman give a little emotional sustenance anymore?"

"Hell no! We gave at the office. When is it a Black woman's turn to be pampered and given some of that same emotional sustenance that you men lust after?"

"Hey, whatever you want, whenever you want it, Cecil. I'm single, educated, have my own business... Some women think I'm not a bad catch."

"I may spend a lot of time in the ocean, but I'm not a fisherman looking for the 'catch' of the day. I'm not talking about us."

"How long are you going to keep up this man-sharing position of yours, Cecil?"

"What are you talking about now?"

"You know that I see other women and I know that you see other men."

"So?"

"So when are you going to stand still and let me 'catch' you?"

"Hey, hold on. Maybe you need to hook up with Janice. She's the one looking for a stable relationship, not me."

"Most women I know are willing to go to extremes to keep their men away from other women, including changing who they really are or getting pregnant or becoming a fatal attraction, but you? Hell, you avoid commitment just like some men do. What gives with you, Cecil?"

"I've learned to love and take care of myself. Relationships are hopeless; too many games. It's not that I can't keep up; it's that I don't want to. I've seen too many women get trapped into unsatisfying relationships just to be able to say that they've got a man, and then they can't get out of it. Too many pressures to keep up appearances, getting the material things, having children, social pressures. Fear of failing, fear of being alone. It's crazy. Some women stay in a bad relationship for the most asinine reasons. Always crying about why her man did her wrong—why he doesn't love her anymore. Then they run out making Mary Kay rich, aerobicizing every molecule, trying on this diet or that fad to get a man or keep a man. Trying to make themselves feel better. And what do they get for the makeovers, the aerobics and the diets? A bill from Visa! Hell, I can feel good or bad by myself and I don't have to carry anyone else's emotional baggage or pay for it either."

"No man in his right mind would step out on you, Cecil—I know that I wouldn't. You'd be gone before I got back!"

Cecil's impressive face, her dark golden and fiercely seductive eyes smiled, like a feline cat ready to lap up a bowl of cream. "Isn't it great that we don't even have to think about things like that? You are at liberty to see and do anyone you want, any time you want to. No strings attached."

"That's not how I want it, Cecil," he said and huffed, frustrated. "I want you more than part time. More than friends with benefits."

The mood she was desperately trying to recapture since Janice came home was broken again. All she wanted to do was to pin this hunk in her bed and get her sex on. She rolled her eyes, sat back, and drank more wine. She curled her long, lush body into him, testing; ready to pounce, to take. "It works for me."

"It doesn't work for everybody. Look at your friend, Benny. He had your version of the ultimate relationship with Stacy Greene. He had it all. Freedom to see and 'do' anyone he wanted. Now look at him. Stacy's gone and he can't get it together to be with anyone else. Can't find that same groove with any other woman that he had with her. He has alternatives—plenty of options—but he's realistically confronting the fact that he wants just one person in his life just like I do. Someday, Cecil, you will, too, and I'll be there waiting."

"Ha! Don't hold your breath, pal," she said dismissively with a flip of her hand. She stood up to get more wine. "Benny is different. He is a total and complete package, but he's in a painful dilemma. He's got a baby, Whitney Ivy. He loves that little girl and her mother. He's had to cope with the possibility of raising Whitney alone. Stacy threw him a curve. He just hasn't had the time to recover, yet. He'll get back on his feet."

"Cecil, like I said, you women don't give men an even break."

Totally out of the mood for sex now, she leaned an elbow against the bar and sipped her wine. "Isn't it time for you to go home, Charles?"

Charles stood to his impressive six-five height, approached Cecil, slight panic rising in him. He was looking for ways to move his relationship with Cecil to another level; an exclusive one. Their discussion provided the opening he needed, but if he could not get her back into a romantic mood, he feared that he would be losing a lot more than time.

"Oh, so just because I don't agree with you I don't get to spend the night?"

"I'm leaving town tomorrow, remember?"

"I know. You're just going to Santa Barbara to be in a wedding, Cecil. It's not like when you're leaving for months on one of your expeditions. I'll leave early if you want."

"Don't you have someone else you can call?"

"That's not the issue. I know where I want to be."

"I need to check on Janice. Make sure that she's all right."

"Fine, I'll take a shower, open another bottle of wine and wait for you in your bed," he said, leaning into her, effectively trapping her against the bar. The scent of her slid into him. He brushed his mouth over her exposed left shoulder, up her long neck to her ear. "We can mother each other and give each other sustenance all night."

Cecil shook her head and rolled her eyes. He kissed her quickly, grabbed another bottle of wine and strolled away whistling. She levered away from the bar and went into Janice's bedroom. Janice was stretched out on her bed. She rolled to her side when Cecil entered and sat down on the edge.

"How you doing, girlfriend?"

"Don't ask," Janice said, rolling her eyes and pursing her lips.

"Kinda rough out there, huh?"

"The pits!"

"What was wrong this time?"

"The turkey was married!"

"That's news. Who was it?"

"Norman Cobb."

"Who's he?"

"You remember. The guy I met at that party last month. Account Executive with MCI. He and Charles are frat brothers."

"Oh, yeah. The one who comes down from LA a few times a month and hangs out with Charles."

"Yes, that's the one. Claimed that he was single."

"Don't they all. How do you know that he's married?"

"He blew it. He asked me to put something in his glove compartment while we were at the beach. When I opened it, there was a picture of him, his wife and two children. He tried to tell me that they were separated and getting a divorce. I believed him until tonight."

"What happened?"

"His wife rolled up on us, complete with their children! Was that ugly or what?"

"What did she say?"

"Told Mr. Cobb that she was sick and tired of him having affairs behind her back, she was leaving him, and that he could take care of their children from now on. Then he had the nerve to say that she wasn't going anywhere because she couldn't find another 'good' man like him. The woman got back in her car and left. The jerk just stood there! I hailed the first cab I saw and left him standing there with his children.

"I'll tell you, I've about had it with men. Before, it was Burke Peters at the office and before him Malik Spooner, and before him Slater Hurston.

"Aren't there any decent guys left in this world anymore? All I want is a man who can tell the truth. He doesn't have to be a star, just someone who understands who he is."

"Fantasies," Cecil said, rolling her eyes.

"I should have known better than to talk to you about an affair of the heart. The original Ice Princess."

"Don't say I didn't warn you, Janice."

"More than once. I know the drill, Cecil. Love 'em and leave 'em, right?"

"It's a numbers game. Men think that they can just act any way that they want to because there's a pitiful shortage of men—and they're right. Between joblessness, murder, drugs, homosexuality, and jail there aren't any left worth bothering about."

"Ha! You can talk! You don't seem to have any trouble finding the good ones. Your problem is that you don't want to keep any of them. You could have married any one of ten eligible bachelors we know, including Charles."

"Marry? Who wants to get married?"

"Certainly not you, Cecil Jordon."

"Got that right!" She chuckled. "I'm not brave like you, Janice."

"Yeah, right. Get out of here and go break Charles Easton's heart some more, why don't you?" Janice fussed without heat. "I'll bet he's waiting for you to hurt him again. You got your whip?"

Cecil rolled her eyes and sucked her teeth, but her concern for her pal was there on her face.

"You okay?"

"Yeah, I'll be fine. Maybe I'll meet someone at Kenneth and JeNelle's wedding."

"Give me a break, Janice," Cecil said and huffed, frustrated. "You just said that you have had enough, didn't you?"

"Good night, Cecil."

◦━◦

"What were you and Janice talking about for so long," Charles asked, as Cecil slipped into bed and turned out the light.

"Fantasies."

"Sounds good to me. I have a few that you can help me with."

"You want to make it quick. I need to get some sleep."

"Damn, Cecil! You take all the romance out of it."

"Charles Easton, you know where the door is. You don't have to be here, ya know?"

"Come here, woman. Let me mother you a little," he said, pulling her close to him and kissing her.

⚬══╼

"What time did Charles leave this morning?" Janice asked.

"I don't know, why?"

"His office is looking for him. Something about some important business deal he was supposed to take care of. Sounded urgent. He's not in any kind of trouble, is he?"

"No, not that I know of. How much trouble could he be in? He owns the dealership. I think that he would have mentioned it to me if there was a problem."

The doorbell rang and Janice answered it. Benny Alexander came in pushing his daughter, Whitney Ivy, in her stroller.

"You two ready to go?" he asked.

"I am," Janice smiled, as she lifted Whitney into her arms, kissed her and squeezed her. The baby giggled.

"What about you, Cecil?"

"I'll be ready in a minute. I want to make a phone call."

"Okay, we'll meet you at the car."

Benny and Janice left and Cecil dialed Charles' cell number.

"Everything all right with you?" she asked when he answered.

"Why, were you worried about me?"

"Your office called."

"Oh, that, uh, well, uh. I've taken care of that, but I'm impressed."

"About what?"

"That you cared enough to call. That mothering that I did last night must be paying off. Are you sure that you don't want me to come to Santa Barbara with you? I could really show you what a mother I can be."

"No way. I don't need a mother anymore."

"Somebody might try to steal you away from me. I need to protect my woman."

"I'm not your woman, Charles."

"Not yet, maybe, but don't go falling for someone in Santa Barbara. I've got enough competition here in San Diego."

"Goodbye, Charles."

"Call me when you get back."

"Maybe," she said, hanging up.

The telephone rang again.

"Charles, I told you—"

"Hey, Cecil, it's me, Vivian Alexander. Who's Charles?"

"My mother."

"Your what?"

"Don't sweat it. What's up, lady?"

"Is everything set for the bridal shower?"

"Yes. Where are you?

"Still in DC, but we'll be leaving soon."

"You're bringing this new man with you?"

"No, not this trip. He had an emergency. His nephew is sick."

"You come on. We'll have fun anyway."

"I'll see you later. I've got another call coming in."

"Ciao."

Chapter 4

Benny Alexander landed the Cessna at the Santa Barbara Airport and taxied the aircraft to an unloading area. A man approached the airplane and Benny beamed.

"Hey, cousin!" Benny said, as he climbed down out of the aircraft. Cecil handed Whitney to Benny.

"Hey, yourself!" the man said with a broad smile as they embraced. "Good to see you finally. And look at Miss Whitney Ivy," he said, taking the grinning baby from Benny to hug and kiss her.

"Yeah, a little turbulence. Thanks for picking us up. Let me introduce you to my friends," Benny said, helping Janice and Cecil out of the aircraft. "Janice Atterly and Cecil Jordon, this is my cousin James Edward Dixon from Goodwill, Summer County, South Carolina."

"Nice to meet you both," he said, shaking Cecil's hand, but smiling broadly at Janice.

"I believe that Benny has mentioned you before. You and he are first cousins, right?" Janice asked and smiled back, as she eyed the gold chain around his neck that read "**FAMILY**."

"Yes, we are, and you're the biochemist, right?"

"Yes, I see that Benny's been talking about a lot of people."

"Family trait. We talk with each other a lot."

"So he tells me. He mentioned that you teach."

"Lecture, actually, at South Carolina University, but only part time. My father and I manage a hydroponics and livestock farm for our family consortium in Summer County."

"Uh, you two want to get a move on or go through life standing on the tarmac?" Benny joked.

"Oh, uh, sorry, cousin. You're right... We should get going," James said while still holding Whitney and looking at Janice. "The van is right over there," he said, leading Janice and Cecil toward the van without taking his eyes off Janice.

Benny and Cecil winked at each other as they pulled luggage behind them. They could see the instant interest James and Janice had in each other. Benny loaded the luggage into the back of the van. James handed Whitney to Benny then he took Janice's hand and helped her climb into the front seat of the van. He pulled the seat belt across her and latched it, smiling at her as it snapped into place. Benny and Cecil grinned at each other. James and Janice talked together all the way to the McCoy Suites Hotel. He even carried her luggage to the suite that she, Cecil, Vivian, Shirley, and Melissa would share.

"Janice, would you like to have lunch…I mean are you hungry?" James asked, a little uncertain with this lovely woman. "I know you just got here, but…"

"Yes, where should we go?"

"You mean you will?" James asked, surprised.

"I know this nice little place not far from here…" she said, taking his arm and gliding out of the room.

"Oh, well," Cecil said, and smiled at Benny.

"Looks like my cousin's taken care of."

"Just you and me, kid," Cecil winked.

"And baby makes three," Benny said, kissing Whitney's chubby cheek. "Let me unpack, get Whitney's go bag, and we'll find someplace to eat."

Benny left the suite and went across the hall to the suite that he would share with Kenneth and Gregory. He opened the door and found his younger brother locked in a compromising position with a young woman. The pair untangled themselves as Benny and Whitney came in.

"Oh, hey, Big Ben," Gregory said, quickly pulling up his swimming trunks as he rose from the sofa. "Uh, I didn't expect you this soon."

"That's obvious," Benny said, grinning.

"Uh, this is, uh, uh—"

"Kendra Johns," the young woman said, pulling up her bikini bottom and getting to her feet.

"Uh, yeah, Kendra," Gregory said, embarrassed at having forgotten her name.

"You must be Benjamin Alexander," Kendra said, flirtatiously.

"Yes, uh, how did you—"

"Oh, I picked up Gregory, Aretha, and some of your other family members from the airport this morning. Gregory was just telling me about your family. JeNelle and I are distant cousins."

"I see, so you two just met today?"

"Uh, yeah," Gregory said, chagrin. "We went swimming and just got back...and, uh, we were going to change into dry clothes and uh, …"

"Uh huh," Benny intoned, grinning.

"Oh, Whitney Ivy," Gregory said, taking his niece from Benny.

Whitney giggled and Gregory hugged her.

"Gregory, I'll see you a little later. Nice to meet you, Benjamin. I'm going to count on seeing you again real soon, too," she cooed, as she left the suite.

Benny folded his arms across his chest and glared at Gregory after Kendra left.

"What?" Gregory asked with innocence.

"You know what."

"She's a nice girl," Gregory said sheepishly, kissing Whitney under her chin.

"Girl! She's twenty-five if she's a day and you're nineteen. What have I told you about having unprotected sex?"

"Got it covered," Gregory smiled, producing an unwrapped condom from the lining of his swimming trunks.

Benny shook his head, as Gregory smiled broadly and kissed Whitney again, making the baby giggle.

"Two seconds later and I would have—"

"I get the picture, little brother. Just don't ever forget it, but you can't just go around sleeping with every girl or woman you meet."

Cecil knocked on the open door.

"Ready, Benny?" she asked, coming in.

"*Whoa!*" Gregory said, eyeing Cecil as she came in.

Gregory playfully pushed Benny aside, handed Whitney to him, and approached Cecil.

"Calm down, little brother. This is my friend, Cecil Jordon."

"*Well, hello, Cecil!*" Gregory said, demonstratively.

"This must be Gregory." Cecil laughed, noticing Gregory's suggestive stare and tone and the gold chain that read "FAMILY" that hung from his neck. "Good looks do run in the Alexander family," she said.

"Cecil, if we hurry, we can be married before lunch and on our honeymoon by—"

Cecil smiled as she stood on her tiptoes and planted a kiss on Gregory's cheek. "We'll talk about it over lunch," she said in a sexy, husky voice.

Benny buried his face in one hand and shook his head. He loved his younger brother, but a woman, like Cecil? Well, even *he* wasn't brave enough to step to her.

"Vivian here yet?" Benny asked Gregory.

"Naw, they haven't left DC yet. They'll be here later today."

Chapter 5

"*Oh, Alan!*" Melissa Charles moaned haltingly, as they made love in her bedroom.

He kissed the back of her neck and traced circles on her back with his tongue slipping in and out of her slowly, but methodically. Melissa moaned in ecstasy, grabbed the sheets and dug her nails into the bed. He got to his knees and pulled Melissa onto him, rotating her hips as she reached back for him. Their bodies slapped together as the sweat rolled down between them.

Alan Lightfoot looked at Melissa's pure white, flawless skin as he slid her back and forth. He took one pink nipple in his hand and massaged it. Melissa shrieked and intensified her movement, calling his name repeatedly as they reached climax together. Alan cupped her butt and spread her cheeks as he lay against her back breathing hard. Melissa collapsed on the bed as he stroked her smooth skin. He turned her over, bit and suckled her nipples into his mouth. He stroked her flawless face and looked into her deep blue eyes.

"Don't you think we ought to get ready to go?" Alan asked, breathless.

Melissa peeked at her clock, rolled Alan onto his back and got on top of him.

"It's not 6:00 A.M. yet. Our flight doesn't leave until ten," she panted.

"Don't you have some packing to do?"

"No, I'm ready."

"What about everybody else?"

"They'll be ready."

"Maybe we'd better check."

Melissa raised her head and looked at Alan without expression. "What is it?"

"Nothing, I want to make sure that we don't forget anything," he said, looking away from her stare.

"It's that comment that my father made, isn't it?" Alan didn't answer her. "That is it, isn't it?"

Melissa rolled off Alan, onto her back and looked blankly up at the ceiling.

"Your parents have a right to their opinion."

"That doesn't make what my father said right."

Alan rolled to his side and sat up on the edge of Melissa's bed, rubbing his face with both hands. Melissa stroked his long, damp, black hair.

"I didn't realize how racist and bigoted my parents are, Alan."

He stood up and removed the condom, slamming it into the trash. Melissa stood up behind him and embraced him.

"I'm not my parents," she said, resting her head against his strong, broad back.

"Maybe they're right. Maybe you shouldn't be with an alcoholic, shiftless, good-for-nothing redskin."

"Alan, please," Melissa begged, with tears welling up in her eyes. "They just don't know you. You're not like that."

"They think that I am. They've got me all figured out. I'm some low life from the dregs of society, trying to get into their world by banging their lily white daughter."

"Stop, please, Alan," Melissa said, tightening her hold on him. "They just don't matter."

"Of course, they matter. They're your parents, Melissa. They matter a lot because they're your family."

"Not to me. Not to what we have between us."

"They've got plans for you and those plans don't include you shacking up with a redskin mongrel."

"I won't listen to any more of this!" Melissa shrieked, pushing away from Alan to pace.

He turned to face her as she crisscrossed her steps, agitated.

"I'm a proud man. I'm not ashamed of my heritage. I fought for this country as a Marine as did my father, grandfather and beyond, but I won't make you choose between me and your family. Your history."

Melissa bit back a sob. "You're going to let my parents come between us?"

"Maybe we should cool it. Put some distance between us for a while. It wasn't that long ago that you and Chuck were involved. He'd be more acceptable to your parents because he's rich, white and a doctor. It might work if he wasn't secretly in love with Vivian. Still, your parents want you to move back to Rhode Island and marry that Arrington Kennedy Prescott, III dude. Raise little Prescotts and be the dutiful wife. That's what they've been grooming you for, isn't it?"

"That's not what I want. When we graduate from law school and pass the bar exam I want to stay here and start a career and be with you."

"I may not be here. I'm thinking about going back to New Mexico. Live and work on the Res."

"Then I'll go with you."

"No, Melissa! Let's just let it rest for a while. Get our heads on straight."

"We've known each other for nearly three years and we've been sleeping together for nearly two years now, Alan. You're going to throw that away? Just like that?" She snapped her fingers.

"Maybe it's for the best."

"Best for whom? Certainly not for me," she bit out, stalking toward him. "I'm not a child that my parents can dictate to anymore. I got out of Rhode Island because they were smothering me. Priming me to be a proper Stepford wife. I couldn't be who I wanted to be. They don't own me so they can't tell me who to love or who to marry."

"Think about it, Melissa." He slipped away from her, put on his cut-off jeans and stormed out of her bedroom door, slamming it behind him.

"What was that?" Sidney asked, as she heard a loud bang.

"Melissa and Alan. They're at it again," Bill Chandler answered and then yawned as he rolled over onto his stomach before he buried his face in his pillow.

"Do they have to be so loud?" Sophia asked, as she laid her head on Bill's back and stroked his butt. "Can't get any sleep around here."

"They've been fighting for a few weeks now," Bill said into his pillow. "It gets a little crazy sometimes. Go back to sleep, ladies. Sounds like they're through with round one."

"When are you leaving, Billy baby?" Sidney asked, as she licked his shoulder and neck.

"Later—much later," he moaned into the pillow.

"Then we've got time to—"

"Uh huh," Sophia said, as she buried herself under the cover and began biting and licking Bill's butt.

The two women rolled Bill over, tied his hands and feet to the bedposts, and began making erotic and passionate love to him.

"Not again," he moaned.

"You're going to be gone a long time," Sidney cooed.

"Only ten days," he gasped, as the women sent waves of tingling sensations over his body.

"That's ten days too long," Sidney said, burying her tongue in his open mouth and pinching his flat tits between her fingers. "You're always away modeling, doing commercials or acting somewhere like Europe, Asia, South America, Canada, not to mention California, New York, and Miami."

"Or you're studying for some big exam in law school," Sophia added.

"Got to make a living while I'm young because you two are killing me," he panted.

The two women giggled. Bill felt Sophia masturbating him under the covers. He grabbed the bedposts to steady himself as his nature rose. His iPod alarm clicked on and music filled the room, covering the sounds of his ecstasy.

⊙═◦

Vivian Alexander hung up the telephone after talking with Derrick Jackson. She smiled to herself and rolled onto her stomach. She heard

Melissa's door slam loudly. *What in the world?* She lifted her head. *It's too early in the morning for this.* She buried her head under the pillow. Then she heard Bill calling for divine intervention. *He must have company again*, she thought. Then she heard Gloria and David's voices raised in acrimony. *That did it!* No more rest. She got out of bed and went to the kitchen to start the coffee. While she was waiting for the coffee to drip, she sat on the semi-circle banquette that curved around the ceiling to floor window, looking out into the mist rising in the early morning over her backyard and Rock Creek Park beyond. She was thinking about Derrick when she noticed a shadow then another below the kitchen window. She peered into the mist and saw two figures embracing tenderly. The figures paused for a long, slow kiss and Vivian's eyes widened when she recognized her neighbor, Fenster Jones. Mr. Jones, a middle-aged bachelor, was a famous concert violinist who often played with the National Symphony Orchestra and toured the world giving solo performances. He taught music to young virtuosos in his spare time in his home. He was teaching Angelique Menendez-Gaza to play the piano and he and David Carter were teaching her little brother, Miguel, to play the violin. He certainly wasn't teaching music at that early, predawn hour, Vivian mused to herself, but she could not distinguish who the person was with him. Then Vivian heard the door open on the ground level of the house. She crept to the stairs just in time to see Anna Menendez-Gaza scurry into her apartment. Vivian smiled to herself with some surprise in her discovery. She crept back into the kitchen and poured a mug full of coffee for herself and sat at the table watching the sun rise.

"*Ola, Señorita* Vivian. You are awake?" Anna asked with her Peruvian accent, as she came into the kitchen slipping into a robe.

"Yes, Anna, I can't seem to sleep this morning. There seemed to be an unusual number of things going on around here," she said, smiling.

"*Si, Señor* Bill, he have, how you say, uh, mannaj..."

"*Ménage à trois.*"

"*Si. Très!* And *Señorita* Gloria, she *mucho* mad. Not want to go to *Señorita* JeNelle's wedding. *Señor* David, he say 'yes she go'! *Señorita*

Melissa, she, well, she the same with *Señor* Alan—they fight," Anna said, hands aflutter.

"And you, Anna, how are you this morning?" Vivian asked with a wry smile and a little lift in her voice.

Anna glimpsed Vivian's face and smiled shyly.

"This good day," she said, smiling back at Vivian.

"Must have been a heck of a night, too."

Anna didn't answer. She giggled and began making breakfast.

The front door opened and shortly, nearly seven-foot tall, Dr. Chuck Montgomery came into the kitchen.

"Ummm, that's what I like. My woman making breakfast for me," he said, grabbing Anna around the waist, lifting her in his arms, and squeezing her. Anna giggled like a school girl when he put her on her feet again.

"I think you've got competition, Chuck," Vivian said, wryly.

"Competition? It's the story of my life. You mean somebody is trying to take my Anna away from me, too? Who is the scoundrel?" Chuck joked, as he poured a mug of coffee and sat at the table across from Vivian.

"I think it's Fenster Jones."

"Fenster? You mean the fiddle player next door?"

"He's been up to something other than playing a fiddle," Vivian joked.

"This true, Anna? You've traded me in on a fiddle player?" Chuck asked.

"You big boy now, Dr. Chuck. You need young woman," Anna joked.

Chuck buried his face in his hands. "Every time I find someone, along comes some Johnny-come-lately and takes her away from me," he joked.

"You have to move faster, Chuck," Vivian joked, as she rose from the table. "You have to say what you mean and mean what you say."

Chuck was tempted to tell Vivian exactly what he wanted, that he was in love with her, but he let the moment pass as Vivian left the kitchen and headed up the steps to her bedroom.

He felt Anna's eyes on him and he glimpsed her face. She came toward him and cradled his head in her arms, rocking him. He knew that she understood.

❦

"Are you comfortable, Gloria?" David Carter asked, sitting next to her in the 747's connoisseur-class cabin. "May I get anything for you?"

"Yes, you can get lost, David Carter, III!" Gloria Towson said snidely, while leafing through *Elle*.

David didn't reply, as he put his earphones on and listened to a Wagner opera, while he began reading a legal journal. The music was enchanting and he removed his glasses, closed his eyes, and leaned his head back against the seat to listen to a particularly compelling segment of the second movement. He wanted to share its lusty rhythm with Gloria and opened his eyes. She wasn't in her seat. He looked around the aircraft cabin and spotted her sitting with a stranger, smiling broadly. He watched momentarily as she talked with the man. She caught him staring at her and rolled her eyes. David looked away, put on his glasses, and opened the journal again. Later, Gloria returned to her seat and began writing on a legal pad.

"Do you have the *Black's Law Dictionary* app on your iPad, David?"

"Yes," he said, reaching into his oversized briefcase at his feet and retrieving his electronic notebook. He handed it to her and she began going through the pages and jotting down more notes. He noticed that she was writing fast and furiously.

"It is certainly refreshing to see you so eager to study, Gloria."

"Study? I'm not studying. I'm writing the terms of my contract."

"Contract?"

"Yes, that guy over there is with *Today's Sportsman*, a cable network show. He's interested in paying me a lot of money for my story."

"You mean about your assault?"

"Of course, David." She rolled her eyes.

"You would be ill-advised to enter into any binding agreement about this tragic case."

"Shut up, David. I can't concentrate when you're nagging at me."

"I caution you, Gloria, that to take any action of the nature that you are contemplating would be scandalous at best. You have your reputation to consider. Moreover, the grand jury has not determined whether the police have enough evidence against Tony Jamerson to bring criminal charges against him. You should also consider that your civil case has not been decided either."

"He wants an exclusive now," Gloria said, as she continued to write. "This case is taking an eternity. I can't wait that long. This money will make me relatively independent. I can take a real vacation. Go to France, Italy, Germany or even Africa, if I want. Maybe go with Bill to Majorca for the season or with Derrick. Now that would be a real vacation. Spending time with Derrick on some deserted beach ..."

"Gloria, if you persist in this folly, I will withdraw my assistance as your legal advisor." David said, sternly.

"Oh, no you won't. You're kidding, right?"

"I kid you not, Ms. Towson!" David looked directly into her eyes with his usual starched demeanor.

"But, David..."

He looked away from her, placed the earphones in his ears, and returned to his reading.

Gloria knew that he meant what he said and that if he followed through on his threat she would be lost without his guidance. She retained legal counsel to represent her, but she trusted David's knowledge of the law far more than she trusted the lawyers that she hired. The law firm was impressed with David, too. They offered him a position once he graduated from law school and passed the bar. They were taking no chances. The law firm knew that he had many other offers and had asked her to use whatever influence she had with David to convince him to associate with their firm. They wanted David badly and they were proposing a handsome salary to get him and a potential partnership down the road. In the interim, she needed him to help her with her case. She balled up the sheets of the legal pad and caught the eye of the producer. He shrugged his shoulders and nodded his head with an understanding glance. He wasn't going to get his exclusive tell-all story.

Melissa and Alan sat together as the airplane droned through the sky. Alan was asleep, but Melissa sat looking out on the fluffy white clouds, which looked like different shapes of animals to her. Fluffy horses, and cute teddy bears, and a kitten, she thought. Anything to get her mind off Alan's suggestion that they stop seeing each other. That wasn't the option that she wanted. *What if he started seeing someone else?* No, that would never do. She could not let that happen. She could not risk losing him, but what could she do? How could she hold on to him? She could, of course, get pregnant. She immediately dismissed the notion. Alan was painstakingly careful about using condoms and he always made sure that she was wearing her diaphragm. *Wouldn't her parents flip out over that prospect? What would his family do or say? His family.* She didn't know his family. He didn't talk about them to her. Maybe that was the thing to do. Get his family on her side. Get them to support her being with him. Maybe that would work to her advantage. If they liked her they could be her allies. Most people she met liked her. His family would, too. She'd see to that. She would have to wait for precisely the right time to ask him to take her to meet his family. He might not just do that on his own.

Melissa formulated a plan in her head, as she continued looking out of the window. She suddenly felt Alan's hand on hers. She laced her fingers in his and wiped her tear-stained face. She turned and looked at him. His eyes were still closed when she kissed him, but he responded gently to her.

When the blanket slipped off Bill Chandler's shoulder, Vivian reached across him to cover him again. Bill repositioned himself on her shoulder, but did not awaken. Vivian continued reading *Invisible Life.*

"You and Derrick seem to be getting serious," Chuck said, sitting on the other side of her on the aircraft reading a medical journal.

"I think so."

"I know so."

"We were together yesterday and I suddenly thought about Carlton Andrews and...well...you know..."

"Yes, I remember."

"It's hard not telling Derrick the whole situation. I feel like I'm lying to him about what happened between Carlton and me."

"Don't do this to yourself. I haven't said anything to him and I won't."

"But, Chuck, he's your best friend."

"Our friendship, yours and mine, is just as important to me, Vivian."

"If Derrick and I were getting serious, how would you feel about that?"

"Me? What have I got to do with it?"

"You're his best friend—and mine, too."

Chuck looked at Vivian. "I didn't know that. I mean, that you considered me one of your best friends."

"There's no prize attached to it." She smiled. "You didn't win anything."

"Yes, I did," he said quietly.

Vivian looked at him. "We've come a long way, haven't we?"

Chuck chuckled. "Light years."

Vivian grinned. "Was it that bad?"

"Annie Oakley, you're a piece of work, but I wouldn't change one thing about you."

"Annie—you remember when you started calling me that?"

"I didn't start it—you did."

"Your memory must be failing in your golden years."

"Not mine. I'm only thirty-four, but I remember like it was yesterday. We were strangers. I offered to give you a ride home from Reagan

National Airport in a blizzard. I asked you your name and you said, 'Just call me Annie. Annie Oakley, partner'."

Vivian smiled. "You're right. We have come a long way. You've always been there when I needed a friend."

"Nothing will change. I'll still be there whenever you need me."

"I depend on that, Chuck."

"You should. I mean it."

"Now that you two have settled that, you can kiss and be quiet. I need my sleep," Bill grumbled, repositioning his head on Vivian's shoulder. "Me first."

Chuck and Vivian laughed and Vivian kissed Bill on the forehead quickly. Bill didn't open his eyes, but smiled broadly.

"I'll pass," Chuck laughed. "You're my friend, but you're not my type."

Miguel stood by Bill's leg and pulled at the cover. Bill opened his eyes, shifted and without a word lifted little Miguel onto his lap, rested Miguel's head against his chest, covered him with the blanket, and kissed him on the top of his head.

Vivian and Chuck looked on smiling as Miguel closed his eyes and burrowed into Bill's embrace. Vivian turned to Chuck, still smiling.

Vivian's lips were only inches away from him. He wanted desperately to kiss her. To take her in his arms right then and there on that jet headed to California. To tell her that he was in love with her. To tell her that he had always felt that way since the moment he first laid eyes on her. She was looking into his eyes with such warmth and openness. Her beautiful, bright, brown eyes were mesmerizing until Derrick flashed across his mind. He caressed Vivian's face and planted his kiss on her forehead. They smiled at each other knowingly and went back to reading. Angelique was watching them from the seat in front. She giggled and covered her smile. Chuck and Vivian smiled at her and Chuck playfully pinched her nose.

"*Amore,*" Angelique said, giggled.

She slid back down into her seat out of sight.

In the morning, Tom and Shirley put the breakfast dishes away while his children put their luggage in his van. Shirley was quiet most of the morning, talking with the children about school, their playmates, and their plans for the summer. Tom smiled, as he watched her interact effortlessly with his children. He hadn't pressed Shirley to talk about their first night together. They were about to leave for the airport when Shirley caught his arm and kissed him on the lips.

"You think that we can get some time alone together while we're in Santa Barbara?"

"I suppose so, why?"

"I want to see it turn red hot again." She smiled.

Chapter 6

JeNelle Towson came out of her shower, dried herself and stretched out across the bed, thinking about Kenneth and their wedding day. They participated in one wedding event or the other for the last few weeks and now, within hours, they would be married. She would finally be free of Michel, she mused. When the telephone rang, she noted the caller ID, and smiling, answered the call.

"Hello."

"Good morning, Ms. Towson. Are you ready to become Ms. JeNelle Elise Towson-Alexander?" came from Kenneth's deep voice on the line.

"No," she joked.

"'No'? You mean that you've forgotten all about me already after just a few nights of being away from each other?"

"No, I mean that I'm ready to become Mrs. Kenneth James Alexander. I really missed having you next to me at night. I've been laying here thinking about you and hugging your pillow."

"I'm glad to hear you say that because I don't intend to ever spend another night away from you. It took too long to find you. I don't want to miss one minute of our lives together."

"That's one life together, Mr. Alexander, and don't you forget it. When 3:00 P.M. comes today, we give our lives to each other. We become one person in two bodies. Are you ready for that kind of commitment?"

"JeNelle, I've been ready since the day that I met you at General Aviation, Hanger number 3 at San Francisco Airport."

"Me, too. I'm so excited, Kenneth. I can hardly believe that it's really going to happen. I've been laying here in bed thinking of all of the things that we've been through. It frightens me to think that we almost let love slip away from us."

"We didn't, JeNelle, but I do have another question to ask you."

"Yes, Kenneth?"

"Are you ready to become the mother of our children?"

"Kenneth, I've been ready since the day that I met you."

"*Touché*, Ms. Towson. I love you."

They hung up the telephone and Kenneth lay back in his bed at the McCoy Suites Hotel where his family and friends were staying during the weeks before the wedding. He put one hand behind his head, stroked his bare chest with the other, and thought about the first night that he and JeNelle spent together. They arrived at her home late in the afternoon. Her face was aglow as she led him into her bedroom. He cupped her face in his hands and kissed her gently on her lips.

"Make love to me, Kenneth. I want you. I need you," she had whispered.

She was trembling slightly and tears were in her eyes. He undressed her slowly, removing her blouse and kissing her breast. He unzipped her skirt and it slipped to the floor. Unsnapping her garter, he removed her stockings, and kissed her navel. She stood before him in her shiny, baby-blue bra and thong. Her butter, biscuit-brown skin was soft and supple as he touched her. When he pulled his sweater over his head, she kissed his bare chest and defined six-pack abs as she unbuttoned and unzipped his slacks. Moving closer to him, she ran her tongue along his neck and slipped her hands into his jockey shorts cupping his butt in her caress. He loosened her hair and let it fall to her shoulders and down her back. She looked up at him and smiled through her tears. Her body was pressing against himas she fit so perfectly in his arms. She put her arms around his neck and he lifted her in his arms and carried her to a large, wide chair with a barrel back that sat beside French doors leading to the deck overlooking the Pacific Ocean. He sat with her in his lap, kissing her and caressing her body, but she was still trembling as he unfastened her bra and removed it. He stroked her full breasts, her nipples hardening as he took each one into his mouth. She tasted better than he had imagined she would. She kissed his eyes, his nose, and his mouth. Her kiss was passionate. Her tongue found its way into his mouth and searched for its companion. His nature rose effortlessly and quickly. He believed that she, too, felt it, as she gazed into his eyes and smiled. She rose from his lap and led him to the bed. He reached for his condom in the pocket of his slacks. She removed it from his hand and tossed it on to her dresser.

"We don't need that," she had said softly. *"No one has touched me in nearly eleven years and I trust you completely."*

She lay on the bed and reached for him. He lay beside her.

"JeNelle, are you sure that you're ready for this. I want this to be as special for you as I can make it, but I want to make love to you so badly that I may not be able to control myself for long."

"Make love to me, Kenneth. I don't want you to hold back. I've waited for this moment and for you for far too long. I want to feel again. I'm in love with you and we're going to be husband and wife soon for a very long time."

He was rock hard as he began to guide himself inside her. Her body was cool and she trembled as he entered her. He had not been intimate with anyone without wearing a condom. The feel of her heighten his nature. Still, her body stiffened and she seemed to wince in pain. He started to pull back, but she caught him and pulled him into her. He worried that he was too large or too long, but she held him fast and kissed him, nearly blanking his mind. Barely, he held himself in check for some time before their union became too overwhelming for him. His nature broke forth with uncontrollable force. His heart was beating wildly. He held her in his arms and caressed her, but he was aware that no matter what he did to bring her to a heightened state, she still trembled and seemed to freeze up.

They repeated their lovemaking several times that first night together, but each time there was the same result. She trembled and never seemed to fully let her passion loose. Still, she was the woman that he loved and ached for, but he worried that he could not satisfy her. It wasn't enough to simply satisfy himself. He wanted her to feel the excitement that he was feeling. The joy of their union. The ecstasy that they should be sharing together.

He thought that perhaps he was too distracted with getting CompuCorrect's Southern Division up and running to be an attentive partner. So he had instituted some changes that would relieve him from many of the day-to-day details of the construction, purchases for office furniture, supplies, and other minutiae that took up so much of his time. He knew exactly what he had to do.

Months earlier, he put his plan into action with one of two telephone calls. The first one was to his San Francisco office.

"Good morning. This is CompuCorrect, Northern Division. How may I direct your call?"

"Sara, this is Kenneth Alexander. Turn on Skype, please."

"Oh, hi, Mr. Alexander," Sara McDougal said with excitement and joy in her voice, as she turned on the viewer. *"We sure do miss you around here."*

"That's why I'm calling, Sara. I have something to talk with you about."

"What is it, Mr. Alexander? You look serious."

"Is there anything that would keep you from moving to Santa Barbara and running the office here?"

Sara screamed so loudly that he momentarily had to turn down the volume.

"Oh, no, Mr. Alexander, I'd love to come to Santa Barbara. You wouldn't even have to give me a raise or anything. I could get everything set up for you and I could even start training the secretaries and getting the supplies in order! Oh, and did you get the exercise equipment, yet? You know that we need to do that because—"

"Slow down, Sara." He laughed, as she went through a litany of things that she wanted to do. He finally calmed her down, but she was still excited. *"Now, if you're sure that you want to come and live here, this will be a completely new position for you and, because of the additional duties and responsibilities you'll be taking on, your salary will increase substantially to match your new job title. All of your other benefits will be transferable. The company will pay for your relocation costs, including costs associated with staying in a residential hotel while you look for some place to live. Now, are you sure that you want to do this?"*

"Yes! Yes! Yes!" Sara screamed. *"I can be there tomorrow, Mr. Alexander! I'm so excited that I can't stand it."*

Kenneth laughed. *"Let's see what Tom Jenkins and Shirley Taylor say about it. You're a valuable part of that office. They're not going to be happy with me for taking you away from them."*

"Please don't let them change your mind, Mr. Alexander. I really want to come and work for you even without the new title and increased pay. There's nothing to keep me here. It's just me and my cat, Dimples, and I can come right away. I know that you've had your hands full with the construction of the new office building, the remodeling on your and JeNelle's house in Santa Barbara and the construction of the one in Goodwill, and the wedding plans and I really want to help. Please, please, please, Mr. Alexander. Can I come?"

"Sara, you've got the job. I'll work it out with Tom and Shirley, but would you mind calling me Kenneth? We are going to be working very closely together."

"Only when no clients are around. You deserve respect, Kenneth, and if I'm going to be the new Office Manager of CompuCorrect's Southern Division, everyone is going to treat you with respect!" she had said emphatically.

"Thanks, Sara, now would you get Tom and Shirley on a video conference line for me please?"

"Right away, Mr. Alexander!"

She had connected the lines.

"Kenneth, how's it going, old man? Are you calling to tell us that you're coming back?" Tom had asked jokingly. *"You've only been gone a couple of months and I'm swamped. I don't know whether I'm ready to run the Northern Division without you here every day. I don't know how you did this."*

"He's doing just fine, Kenneth," Shirley chimed in, *"We're all feeling a little lost without you around, but we're handling it."*

"I'm not calling to make your lives any easier," he said, smiling. *"I've asked Sara McDougal to come to Santa Barbara as the new Admin officer as a part of my local management team and she's accepted."*

"Oh, is that why she's out there turning cartwheels in the reception area?" Tom added with a laugh. *"You're going to start a stampede once the other employees hear about this. Some of them have been asking us about the possibility of transferring to the Southern Division. Obviously, it must be*

the climate that you Southern residents seem to have. It certainly couldn't be because of your sterling qualities, Kenneth."

"You're right, Tom. It must be the climate. How would you and Shirley feel about opening up the positions here in Santa Barbara to the San Francisco staff?"

"The Southern Division is going to be much larger than the Northern Division. You're going to need experienced people to get it up and running and to do the orientation and training for new employees. I think that we can do it. What do you think, Shirley?"

"We can do it from a budgetary standpoint, too, Kenneth. Aside from the staffing positions that I've already budgeted for, we still have ample resources for costs associated with moving and relocation expenses. That doesn't include the revenue from the new clients that Tom brought in."

"But none of them are military contracts, Kenneth. I promise! I've learned my lesson. I'm not moving on any new clients without your approval," Tom hastened to add. *"I've been running full background checks on every potential client and I just sent the dossiers to you this morning."*

He laughed.

"Tom, I trust you and your judgment. Don't let what happened in that Congressional hearing change your way of doing things. I know that you're the best public relations and sales and marketing man in the business and you're going to do equally as well running the Northern Division. With Shirley at your side as our Comptroller, how can you miss?"

"Thanks, Kenneth. I just don't want to let you down again."

"You've never let me down, Tom. Believe me when I say that. Shirley, I'm thinking of bringing in a deputy director for the Southern Division. How are we situated for executive pay and benefits?"

"Fine, Kenneth. I see no problems. Who is this person?"

"A bartender I met in Sacramento last year."

"A what!" Tom yelled. *"You're thinking of hiring a bartender as a deputy director! Has the climate down in Santa Barbara affected that brain of yours?"*

"Do you trust me, Tom?"

"Without question or reservation, Kenneth, but a bartender? What's his background?"

"I haven't got a clue, but he knows people and that's what I need in the Southern Division."

"It's your call, Kenneth. You're the boss and I'm confident that you wouldn't be considering this person if you didn't see something in him. What's his name?"

"Joe Grayson."

"You're kidding right? Joe the Bartender?"

"When I first met him he told me that Joe's his name, bartending is his game."

"You do what you have to, Kenneth. I can make it work financially," Shirley said confidently.

"Great! Contact me if anything comes up, but I want to spend as much time with JeNelle as I can to get ready for the wedding."

"Oh, yeah, when is the wedding?" Tom asked.

"June, but it could be today as far as I'm concerned."

"You sound very happy, Kenneth," Shirley said.

"So do you and Tom, Shirley."

"We are, Kenneth. Tom and I may have something to tell you and JeNelle soon," Shirley said.

"I want to tell you now, Kenneth, but Shirley won't let me and, no disrespect, Kenneth, but she's really my boss."

"It doesn't take a Dunn and Bradstreet lawyer to figure this one out," he said, *"and I didn't come down with yesterday's rain either. I'm happy for you both. JeNelle and I will wait for the formal engagement announcement."*

Tom and Shirley laughed.

"I'll talk with you two soon," he said and then hung up.

He made his second important call to Joe Grayson in Sacramento. *"Joe, do you remember me? Kenneth Alexander from CompuCorrect, Inc., in San Francisco?"*

"Sure, Mr. Alexander. I saw you on television. You were awesome! You made me proud to be an American citizen. Everybody on the hotel staff was talking about you. I told everyone that I had served you in the bar when you were here. You're the one that I told about the KIS MOM methods. Of course, I remember you. How did it all work out? Did you finally land that lady that you were in love with?"

"The wedding's in June and you're partly responsible."

"Congratulations, Mr. Alexander. I'm glad that it all worked out for you. It's good of you to call and tell me that. Most people don't remember the little things in life that make someone's day a little brighter."

"What's it going to take to get you to come to Santa Barbara and make a lot of people's lives a lot brighter?"

"You're offering me a job, Mr. Alexander?"

"Not just a job, Joe. A career change at our new Division in Santa Barbara."

There was a long pause.

"Mr. Alexander, I barely got out of high school and that was eons ago. I had a couple of years in junior college, but I didn't go on and finish at a university or anything. I don't know anything about computers, computer programs or computer networks. Hell, I can barely operate the new cash register that the hotel installed."

"It's not your computer skills that I'm looking for, Joe. It's your people skills and as far as I'm concerned, you've got a PhD in that specialty."

"Mr. Alexander, I don't know if I can do this."

"Let's use your KIS method, Joe."

"What do you mean?"

"Take your current salary and triple it. Add a potential for a five-percent raise every year based on merit and performance, full health insurance plan, and life and disability plans. A healthy retirement program. A company car and you are the second in command in the Southern Division. I can promise you long hours, hard work, and barely enough time to shit, shave and shower. Construction noise and confusion. Purchase orders and scheduling problems. Zoning ordinances. Equipment maintenance snafus. Delivery schedules. Endless meetings and professional social obligations. A month's vacation every year that you'll probably have no time to enjoy. All the joys of working with a great group of people, the majority of whom you're going to hire for us, and you won't have to polish another glass or serve another drink if you don't want to and that's the easy stuff."

There was another long pause.

"When did you say that you wanted me to be there, Mr. Alexander? I should at least give the hotel twenty-four hours' notice."

"Call Sara McDougal at my San Francisco office. She'll arrange all of the details for your travel and relocation expenses."

"It's just me and my cat, Mr. Alexander. We don't need a lot, but I'll call your secretary right away."

"Sara's my new Office Manager, Joe. She's going to be moving to Santa Barbara, too. You two will be working together very closely especially while I'm planning for my wedding and while I'm away for an extended honeymoon. I'll work with you personally on what this company is about, but by June, I'm confident that you're going to be right on top of it all."

"Mr. Alexander, has anyone ever told you that you've raised the KIS method to an art form?"

"Every day, Joe, every day. Let me know what your travel plans are. Sara knows how to reach me. Plan to spend some time at our San Francisco Division before you come to Santa Barbara. Tom Jenkins and Shirley Taylor are expecting you. They'll take good care of you while you're in San Francisco. You can stay at a house that I own up there. It's in Marin County, but close to the office and it should be comfortable."

"How did you know that I'd accept your offer, Mr. Alexander?"

"It's Kenneth, Joe, and you taught me the ropes, remember? KIS, Keep It Simple!"

Joe laughed. *"I'll be on my way tomorrow, Mr. Alexander, I mean, Kenneth. Thanks! You've given me an opportunity that I've always dreamed of, but never thought that I'd ever have, especially at my stage of life."*

"Don't thank me yet, Joe. I'll see you sometime next week."

When Joe Grayson arrived in Santa Barbara after spending two weeks in San Francisco, he was eager to go and he did well over the five months since he started with the company. He was everywhere all at once. Kenneth thought Joe and Sara hit it off immediately and their work habits complemented each other. They spent long hours and usually seven days a week dealing with everything from construction schedule to the purchase of paper clips. Sara, he thought, was amazing. She wouldn't spend one dollar more than absolutely necessary and she bartered for everything. She took the position that the sticker price for any item was the price from which she started downward. Everything was negotiable as far as she was concerned and she saved the company more than forty percent on large and small ticket items. She was enjoying her new role and handling it well. Most of the time, he found himself with little or nothing to do in the office except cultivate their client base. Joe and Sara would send him out of the office and he would walk across the street to JeNelle's shop or to her parents' boutique to get out of their way.

JeNelle's managers, Felix Olson, Barry Kennedy, and Luke Malone were taking on more of the responsibility at INSIGHTS, relieving JeNelle of a lot of work and long hours. She had also promoted one of her long-term employees, Wanda Willis, to floor manager, freeing up her time for focusing on the macro issues of a rapidly growing business.

As a result of their combined efforts, he and JeNelle were able to spend a lot more time together. They went sailing at least once a week, did some sightseeing, and even traveled to San Diego to visit with Benny and Whitney and Cecil and Janice. They had attended numerous dinner parties or other social events together. One dinner party at Johnston and Constance Worthington's estate had even included the President and First Lady among the notable dinner guests. Apparently, Johnny Worthington and the President were lifelong chums. Surprisingly, Johnston and the President were also best buds with Gustafson "Gus" Fehey, Vivian's law professor and mentor.

He and JeNelle both accepted speaking engagements, but only if it meant a short one-day trip. They slept together every night since their engagement had become inseparable.

He only packed up his personal items when he left San Francisco. He and JeNelle had spent days making room in her three-thousand-square-foot, single-level, three bedroom beachfront house for his belongings. It was clear that no matter how much they discarded or stored, they were clearly going to need more space. So, they hired an architect and construction company to build two additional levels onto JeNelle's bungalow. They liked the beachfront property's location. Neither of them wanted to move to a larger house somewhere else. They were already planning to build a home in Goodwill, South Carolina, on the land that his grandparents had given to him. Each of his brothers and sisters had received equally large parcels of land, too.

A month after he moved to Santa Barbara, he and JeNelle were lounging in the living room.

"Kenneth, when can we go to Goodwill?"

"Whenever, you want, JeNelle. Why?"

"I've been looking at the pictures of your land there and thinking about what kind of home we should build. Gregory did a video tape of the property. I have a few ideas and I want to see whether they would work." JeNelle lay on the floor in her living room with pictures of the land and house plans spread out around her.

He was reclining on the sofa, drawing some ideas for plans of his own.

"What have you come up with so far?" He put down his plans and lay on the floor beside her.

"I like this one with the southern exposure." She picked up a picture of a large house with an expansive open floor plan and showed it to him.

"This house has six bedrooms and four and a half baths. There are only two of us now."

"Yes, but there are going to be more of us soon."

He had looked at her and she had smiled at him broadly.

"How soon?" he had asked.

"Oh, I'd guess maybe November or December. The doctor isn't sure." She smiled broadly.

He rolled over on his back and pulled her on top of him.

"Ms. Towson, have you been keeping secrets from me again?"

"No, Mr. Alexander, I wasn't sure until today."

He kissed her. *"Ms. Towson, have I told you how much I love you today?"*

"Yes, Mr. Alexander, but I want to hear it every day all day and I'll tell you a secret if you tell me where we're going on our honeymoon."

"No deal, Ms. Towson."

"*Then I'll keep my secret to myself,*" she said, pouting prettily.

"*You'll know where we're going when we get there. Then you can tell me your secret.*"

"*But, Kenneth, how will I know what to pack if you don't tell me where we're going?*"

"*Your mother has already taken care of that.*"

"*You told my mother, but you won't tell me where we're going?*"

"*I promise you that it's the only secret that I'll ever keep from you after we're married.*"

"*Then you'll tell me what you did at your bachelor party last weekend?*"

"*Well, maybe, only one secret that I'll keep from you.*"

"*Why is it that nobody's telling what happened at that infamous bachelor party?*"

"*We would all be arrested, JeNelle. We're protecting ourselves from self-incrimination.*" He smiled, embarrassed.

"*I won't tell you what happened at the bridal shower then.*"

"*Oh, you mean with over a hundred women and the Chippendales erotic male dancers?*" He laughed.

"*Kenneth! Who told you?*" JeNelle had bristled.

"*I saw the video tape. I didn't know that you could move like that! And my mother! Well, I hope that my father never sees that tape. Tell me, honey, did your mother ever get that twenty-dollar bill in that guy's G-string just using her teeth? And your Aunts Ruth and Bessie, what ...*"

"*Kenneth! If you ever show that video tape to anyone, you'll probably wreck a lot of happy homes.*"

"*Not to mention sending some husbands and other partners into cardiac arrest!*"

JeNelle laughed. "*Especially, Johnston Worthington,*" she added.

"*Do you think that he's seen that purple birthmark on Constance's ...?*"

"*Kenneth James Alexander!*"

They both laughed.

"*That bridal shower did lack a certain amount of decorum,*" JeNelle blushed. "*Our sisters, bridesmaids, and mothers really know how to throw a bridal shower.*"

"Yes, and about some of those bridal shower gifts that you conveniently left in the trunk of your car. Were you planning to use some of those 'toys' on me?" he asked with a questioning smile.

"That's why I left them in the car. I need to read the instructions to figure out what to do with them first."

He had found that particularly amusing. *"JeNelle, you're all the stimulation that I'm ever going to need, especially now that we're going to have a baby,"* he had said as he kissed her, *"but if you want to model some of those negligees, I won't complain at all."*

"Oh, no, Mr. Alexander. I'm saving some of those things for our honeymoon and some for our new home in Goodwill."

"Save some for the remodeling of this home, too, JeNelle." He reached for the sketches that he had been working on and handed them to her.

She had rolled off him and sat up. Her eyes narrowed as she looked at the sketch, which included adding a second and third level to her beachfront house. There were notations on the pad. There was a huge bedroom suite with ample walk-in closet space for both of them, a bathroom suite including a whirlpool tub and walk-in shower. Next to the bedroom was a room marked 'Nursery' and a notation that read, 'Must be completed in six months.'" She had looked at him lying on the floor beside her.

"You knew!" she accused, as she put down the pad, sat on top of him, and grabbed his hands.

He laughed, coughed, and doubled over as she landed on his chest, but she was holding his hands down against the floor. He couldn't stop laughing.

"Tell me the truth, Kenneth," she said with a questioning smile. *"Did you know that I was pregnant?"*

"I guessed," he said between bouts of laughter. *"We've been together every day, JeNelle. I could see the glow on your face and that sparkle in your eyes. I've seen it before when my mother was carrying my sisters and brothers. I've been looking at that beautiful body of yours for a while now, too. Seems like there's a little more of you for me to feast my eyes on."*

"So that's why you were so calm when I told you."

"I've been walking on air for weeks, waiting for you to say the magic words and tell me that you're carrying our child. I can't even tell you how excited I am, but I can show you," he said, with a twinkle in his eyes and a suggestive grin on his face.

JeNelle released his hands and he sat up and held her close to him. Her legs straddled him. He began caressing her and kissing her. She went cold and her body began to tremble in the same way that it had each time that they made love. He looked at her face. He could see the tears forming in her eyes.

"What is it, JeNelle?" he asked softly. *"Am I doing something that you don't want me to do? Have I hurt you?"*

"No, oh no, Kenneth. I love you. You haven't hurt me."

"Then tell me what it is."

"It's nothing, Kenneth. Make love to me. I want you to."

"I can't help if I don't know what the problem is. You have to talk to me. You have to trust me. I love you and I don't want to do anything that's going to hurt you."

"Just love me, Kenneth," she whispered, as she put her arms around his neck and hugged him.

He complied, but he still worried that she was not fully enjoying their lovemaking.

As he lay in the bed on the morning on his wedding day remembering the past, he knew that something had to be done. He decided to start working on it as soon as they returned from their honeymoon.

He heard Whitney Ivy start to cry in another bedroom of the hotel suite. He got up and crossed the living room to Gregory and Benny's bedroom. Benny was awake giving Whitney her 6:00 A.M. bottle after her cereal and fruit, and talking to her as he came into the bedroom. Gregory was still asleep face down and buried in his pillows. Kenneth sat on the bed next to Benny.

"How is Miss Whitney this morning?" Kenneth asked, as he lifted his ten-month-old niece from his brother's arms.

"She's got me under control as usual," Benny said, as he yawned and stood up to stretch. He lay down on the bed and buried his head in the pillow.

"Pretty tough raising Whitney alone," Kenneth said, as he fed her.

Her big, light-crystal brown eyes were shinning, as she played and drank from her bottle. She smiled at Kenneth and a broad smile crossed his face.

"It's tough being away from her, but I wouldn't trade her for anything in this universe," Benny said, as he rolled over and propped his head up on his hand.

"Whitney is a beautiful little girl," Kenneth said.

"She looks just like Stacy," Benny said, looking at a picture of Stacy that was framed and sat on the nightstand by his bed.

"You haven't heard anything from her?"

"Nothing since she sent that note to Mom and Dad before Thanksgiving."

"Did that information that I gave you about her father help?"

"I have an address for him in Asheville, North Carolina, but there was no telephone listing. I'm going to see if I can find him when I go home for the Fourth of July family reunion."

"What about Stacy's mother?"

"No luck yet. She apparently moves around a lot. The last address was in Champaign, Illinois. You really have done a lot though. Thank you for that. I don't know how you came up with the information that you've given me."

"It's no secret. Computer networks. When you gave me a copy of Stacy's application to the Naval Academy that you got from Senator Mitchell, her parents' social security numbers weren't redacted on it. That's all I needed to find their places of employment and home addresses listed on the employment records."

"It certainly has helped. I hope that when I find Stacy's parents, one of them can tell me where she is or how I can get in touch with her."

"Benny, wherever Stacy is she must be on an important mission. Her status is classified 'top secret, highest national security'. Even my contacts at NSA couldn't access her location."

"I know. I've tried my contacts at the Pentagon, the CIA, the FBI, the Secret Service and even Homeland Security. All that I could find out was that wherever she is, she's not in the United States. Since I know that she speaks fluent Japanese, I checked with the naval base in Japan, but my contacts there tell me that she's not in Japan."

"You'll find her, Benny."

"I have to. She doesn't know that I'm in love with her, KJ. When she left, she thought that I was in love with JeNelle. I want the chance to tell her that I'm in love with her and to see whether we can't make things work out between us."

"Everyone thought that you were in love with JeNelle. Even you."

"Everyone except Mom, Dad, and Aretha."

"Are you going to be all right today?"

"What? Being the best man at your wedding?"

"I don't want you to do it if it's going to be painful."

"KJ, I'm responsible for bringing you two together in the first place. It would have been painful if you hadn't asked me to be your best man," Benny said, as he smiled at his brother.

"Can't a man get any sleep around here?" Gregory grumbled, as he opened one eye and looked at his brothers.

"He speaks!" Kenneth said jokingly.

"Barely," Gregory grumbled.

"What's up with you, G?" Kenneth asked.

"Our little brother, the new Olympic-class lover, hasn't been able to find his way back to the hotel before dawn any day this week," Benny said sarcastically without heat.

"Man! These California women are all of that!" Gregory said with much emphasis. "They've got it going on! I've got to get back to South Carolina to get some rest!"

"Three young women showed up here last night after the rehearsal dinner, to take our brother out. When he came in this morning he had sand in his—"

"You didn't have to go there, Ben!" Gregory interrupted.

Kenneth laughed. Whitney finished her bottle and reached for Kenneth's neck. He lifted her to his shoulder and patted her on her back. She burped and giggled, as she bounced on his lap. Kenneth kissed her on her stomach and she giggled more. She climbed onto the bed, crawled to Benny, and kissed him. He hugged her and she was off again. Kenneth lowered her to the floor and she crawled to Gregory's bed. She climbed to her feet and reached for Gregory. He lifted her into his bed and she snuggled close to him.

"That's what Olympic-class loving will do for you," Benny said to Gregory.

Gregory reached into the pocket of his slacks that lay in a heap on the floor by his bed and pulled out several packets of condoms.

"Not yet it won't," he said as he tossed the packets to Benny with a broad smile. "I love my niece, but I'm only nineteen and I'm not ready to be anybody's father, yet!"

Gregory kissed Whitney. Kenneth and Benny laughed. The door to the bedroom opened suddenly and a young, attractive cleaning lady, who looked like she was in her mid-twenties, came in. The three brothers were only wearing their briefs and looked up suddenly. The young woman smiled broadly as she looked at the brothers' bodies.

"Oops! Sorry! I knocked on the door to the suite, but apparently you didn't hear the knock or me call out housekeeping when I entered. I'll start in the other rooms and I'll come back to clean up in here later, Gregory," she said with a wink and a smile.

She closed the door and left. Kenneth and Benny looked at each other with shocked expressions and then they looked at Gregory.

"Yep, California women give new meaning to the term *room service*," he said matter-of-factly while leaning back and lacing his fingers behind his head.

Benny and Kenneth tossed the condoms back to him.

"You'd better hold on to these, G," Benny said. "Looks like you're going to need a new supply very soon!"

The three brothers laughed. The door opened again and Bernard Alexander entered. He heard his sons laughing and looked at their nearly nude bodies.

"What's so funny?" he asked, as he sat on the bed next to Gregory and Whitney, taking his granddaughter in his arms. "And who was that woman who just smiled at me?"

His sons laughed loudly again.

"Nothing, Dad," Gregory said.

Bernard picked up one of the condom packets and looked at it.

"Huh! After Kenneth's bachelor party, I'm not sure whether I raised you boys right."

"You did fine, Dad," Kenneth said.

"Chuck Montgomery though—I'm not so sure about him. That doctor is out there!" Benny said.

They all laughed.

"Yeah, that was some stag party," Bernard said, almost blushing.

"Did somebody say stag?" another voice came from the door.

"Come on in, Bill," Kenneth said as Bill Chandler entered with Chuck Montgomery, Alan Lightfoot, and David Carter.

"Did I hear someone say stag?" Bill asked again, as he pulled a chair up next to Bernard, sat down, and propped his feet up on Gregory's bed.

"Yeah, Bill, my father was still talking about the bachelor party."

"Oh, yeah! There were a bunch of queens at that party, too," Bill said.

"Queens?" another voice said from the doorway. "Who's a queen?" Tom Jenkins asked, as he came in and seated himself next to Bill.

"At the bachelor party, Tom," Kenneth answered. "Bill was just saying that there were a lot of queens there."

"*Shhh!*" Tom said excitedly. "Don't talk too loud. You never know who might be listening. If Shirley knew what I did at that stag party, she'd kill me!"

"Not that type of queen," Benny said, laughing at Tom. "Bill was saying that there were a lot of gay and bisexual men at the bachelor party."

"Where? I didn't see any gays! What would a gay man be doing at a bachelor party?" Tom asked, confused.

"Cruising! What else?" Joe Grayson said, as he entered the room and overheard the conversation.

"Naw," Tom said, with his green eyes wide, looking from face to face. "I can spot a gay man a mile away. You know how they act. Always switching around, trying to be a woman."

"Are you sure about that, Tom?" Alan asked.

"Sure, they're always so obvious. They don't even look like us real men."

"I'm sorry to break your illusion, Tom, but you're wrong. There were a lot of gay and bisexual men at the party. Not that it mattered," Chuck said, grinning.

"Where, Chuck? They must have been hiding in the closet," Tom said, laughing at his own joke.

"No, Tom," Kenneth said slowly. "Do you remember the singer who was wearing the cowgirl outfit? The one with the dimples and long blond hair?"

"Sure, that babe was gorgeous. If I didn't love Shirley so much, she could have sat on my lap all night!" Tom said, with a twinkle in his eye. "I got a hard on just from looking at her!"

"She did sit on your lap all night, Tom," Kenneth said, "and I was wondering what you were whispering in her ear."

"Shhh, Kenneth! I told you. Don't talk so loud! I was just asking her how she got that beautiful body of hers into that tight little outfit. All of those female entertainers were gorgeous, though. That little red-headed babe kissed me so hard over behind that big flower pot that my toes curled!"

"Females! There weren't any women at the bachelor party, Tom," Gregory said with a broad smile. "It was a stag party."

"No, Greg, I'm talking about the entertainers. You know, the women who did the great impersonations of famous people and sang so well. Like the one who looked like Dolly Parton with the big bosom and the one who did the Diana Ross impersonation! She really could sing like her, too."

"They weren't women, Tom. They were female impersonators," Gregory said, as he tried to stifle his amusement.

Tom's green eyes widened. He nearly jumped out of his seat. "*What!*" he yelled. "You mean that gorgeous creature that was sitting on my lap was a man? And that red-headed . . . *oh my God!*"

The men couldn't hold it in any longer. They all broke out in uproarious laughter at Tom. Bernard laughed so hard that he had to lean back on Gregory's bed. Kenneth stood up laughing and staggering around the room. Benny rolled over and over on his bed, doubling up and holding his stomach as he laughed. Bill tried to give Alan a high five, but they were laughing so loudly and falling over that they barely could touch each other's hands. Joe laughed so hard that he rushed to the bathroom to avoid urinating in his pants. David rolled over and over on the floor. Tom sat there in shock, looking at everyone's laughing face. The men tried to compose themselves, but when they looked at Tom's shocked and scandalized face, they all broke up in uncontrollable laughter again.

They finally got control of themselves and talked about the stag party. Each man described something funny that he observed between the guests and the entertainers. Each story was more hilarious than the last. Chuck rolled on the floor, pounding his fist on the carpet. Kenneth put both hands on the wall, trying to catch his breath. Alan jumped up and down, stomping his feet and falling to his knees. The stories got funnier and funnier as the men talked. Tom's eyes went from face to face, as he listened to each story in disbelief.

". . . And then when Judge Worthington jumped up on the dance floor between those twin sisters and started stroking them and wringing and twisting, I thought that I was going to lose it all. He had that long-stemmed red rose between his teeth and was snapping his fingers over his head like he was a Flamenco Dancer..." Joe said between bouts of laughter.

Joe was laughing so hard he couldn't finish the story.

"Yeah and that attorney friend of JeNelle's, Floyd Ewing, jumped up on the table and started doing a strip tease act with the Diana Ross impersonator, I thought that the cops were going to have to take him away, birthday suit and all!"

"Yes, if they had been real cops they might have, but when they snatched off their uniforms and started dancing, that's when I realized that they were a part of the show!"

"That was some bachelor party," Chuck said, his face beet red, "but no more stories guys, please. We've got to see all of those men again at the wedding today. I might not be able to do it with a straight face."

"Straight!" Bill said, still laughing. "That's the operative word all right, Chuck."

The men all broke up into laughter again.

Tom's face was flushed. "Well, you guys really put one over on me," Tom said, chagrinned. "I'll know better the next time," he said confidently.

Bill put his arm around Tom's chair. "Yeah, we guys have to stick together, right Tom?" Bill asked nonchalantly.

"Damn straight!" Tom said. "I mean, not straight, but you're right. You can't always tell the players without a score card anymore."

Bill leaned in close to Tom, cupped his crotch and whispered, "You've got that right, Tom. Batter up!"

Tom leapt from his chair so quickly as if lightening had struck him, face flushed red as an American Beauty rose. The men all broke out in laughter again. They were whooping and hollering at the top of their voices.

Tom's green eyes were flashing around the room at the men laughing. Then he stared at Bill. *"You're gay?"* Tom asked, amazed.

A grin crossed Bill's handsome face. "Bisexual is more politically correct, Tom, but I'm available for service whenever you want to call."

"But you're a model—a high-priced man's clothing model! I've seen you in *Gentlemen's Quarterly* and *Esquire!* And you're a law student at Georgetown, too! You live with Kenneth's and JeNelle's sisters, Vivian and Gloria, and with Alan and David, too! You can't be bisexual!"

"Which role is it that you think that gay or bisexual men can't play, Tom? The model, the attorney, the friend or the housemate?" Bill asked, laughing at Tom's expression. "Don't misunderstand. I do love women. Slept with some beautiful and exciting ones in my time, too, but I've had a taste of some beautiful male bodies since I've been here this week, thanks to that bachelor party. I may be back here after I pass the bar, so look out, Tom. I may be knocking on your door real soon."

Bill was laughing so hard that he had to steady himself in the chair. None of the men could stop laughing.

"Oh, no, I'm strictly straight! I mean heterosexual, and I live in San Francisco, not Santa Barbara," Tom said, having trouble with the nomenclature.

"San Francisco?" Bill laughed. "The Western Gay Mecca. Remember Harvey Milk? This is where the Gay Revolution began."

Tom flushed. "I don't understand how you can all take this so lightly."

"We've evolved, Tom," David said. "I have accompanied Bill on many occasions and I'm heterosexual. I'm not intimidated by his sexuality."

"But, Bill, how can you... I mean... how do you—"

"Spit it out, Tom," Alan said.

"I just don't understand how a gay... I mean, bisexual man can have sex with both a man and a woman."

"I usually don't at the same time, but it's an intriguing thought, Tom. What did you have in mind?" Bill asked, with a devilish, matinee-idol smile on his too handsome face.

"No, no, I'm just curious about how... Oh never mind..."

"Come on, Tom. Ask your question, man. I didn't mean to embarrass you," Bill said sincerely.

"Loving a woman has got to be different than, you know, fooling around with a man. I mean, a woman is soft and giving. I mean, look at Kenneth or Benny or even Gregory! They have masculine bodies, but they don't turn me on. I couldn't imagine fooling around with any one of them."

"Doesn't it take imagination to make love to a woman, Tom? Don't you have to caress a woman, fondle her, kiss her?"

"Sure, but that's different."

"No, it isn't. I like to be caressed, fondled, and kissed. Don't you?"

"Sure, but not by someone who has as much hair on his chest as I do. And I can't imagine someone poking me in my ass."

"I'm heterosexual, Tom, but I understand what Bill is saying," Alan added. "On the reservation, homosexuality is forbidden, but we have all been curious at some time in our lives. The measure of manhood starts at age thirteen on the Res. That's the time in a young boy's life when he starts comparing his body and skills to the same boys that he's played kid's games with. You do find yourself looking at another male body, usually just to see whether you measure up. Bill measures up. I can look at Bill's body and not feel a thing. He's bisexual, but he's also my friend. I'm sharing a suite with him, David and Chuck, but I don't want to sleep with him and he's never approached me for sex. I'm a full-blooded Navajo, but Bill hasn't treated me with anything but respect since I moved into the house with them. I respect him for who he is. No matter what his sexual preferences, I consider him my brother. He also brings home some beautiful women, too!" Alan said, with a sly smile, "And he always makes sure that I and David have great dates for any social occasion!"

"Bill, you're probably a nice person—everybody here seems to like you, but I'm still confused."

"About what, Tom? How I make love? Do you need some instructions to follow?"

Tom blushed. "No, give the instructions to Kenneth. He's the one who's going to need them," Tom said, laughing.

"I've tried to teach KJ everything that I know, but I'm not sure that he took enough notes," Benny joked.

"Who taught who?" Bernard asked his son with a confident grin.

"Well, you schooled me on how to protect myself, Dad, but after that—"

"After that Whitney was born," Gregory added. "Your notes must not have been too legible."

The men all laughed.

"Kenneth James knows what to do," Bernard said confidently of his other son, "and more importantly what not to do."

"Would you clarify that point for us, Dr. Alexander?" David asked.

"It's not difficult, David. There are some basic things to keep in mind when you're making love to your partner, male or female, although I've never had a male-on-male relationship either," he mused. "I call them the Ten Commandments of Love. First, don't let her feel that her gratification is less important than yours. Second, don't start if you can't finish. Third, don't make love if you're distracted. Fourth, don't let your partner think that you're not enjoying the moment. Fifth, don't expect to receive all if you're not willing to give all. Six, don't fantasize about someone or anything else while you're in the throes of passion. Seven, don't forget foreplay. Eight, don't think that it's over after you cum. Nine, don't forget to talk about what your partner needs and wants. Ten, and most importantly, don't forget to say please, I love you, and thank you."

David was taking notes. "Was number seven the one about fantasizing, Dr. Alexander?" David asked to be sure that he didn't miss anything.

"No, David, fantasizing is number six. Foreplay is number seven," Gregory added. "Dad grilled all of us, including KJ, on the Ten Commandments of Love."

"Do I remember those discussions!" Benny added, demonstratively.

"Did you remember them, Kenneth," Chuck asked, with a grin.

"Backwards and forwards," Kenneth answered.

"He just didn't take time to practice them," Tom added.

"He'll get all the practice time he can handle with a woman who looks like JeNelle!" Alan added.

"Yeah, my future sister-in-law registers ten on the Richter scale. Practice time is over, KJ. Now comes the real deal! Do you need some pointers?" Gregory asked.

Kenneth laughed at his youngest brother.

Bernard was looking at his son's face and noticed something in his eyes. "Well, it's almost lunch time. Why don't we all go down to the pool for a swim before we eat?" Bernard suggested.

Everyone agreed and the group broke up. Kenneth headed across the living room suite to his bedroom to dress. His father followed him.

"Kenneth James, what is it? What's wrong?" Bernard asked, as he entered Kenneth's bedroom and closed the bedroom door behind him.

Kenneth sat in the chair by a window and rested his arms on his knees. He stroked his face with one hand and looked at his father.

"I don't know yet, Dad," he started slowly.

"I'll understand if you don't want to talk with me about this, Kenneth James," Bernard said, sitting across from Kenneth and assuming a similar position.

"No, it's not that, Dad. I've always been able to talk with you and Mom about everything, including sex. You've always answered my questions honestly. What I'm trying to figure out is why I can't seem to satisfy JeNelle sexually."

"Does she satisfy you sexually?"

"I love her, Dad. Our lovemaking has been physically satisfying for me, but I'm not emotionally satisfied because she isn't enjoying our lovemaking."

"Is it your technique?"

"I've tried everything over the past five months. She hasn't responded to anything. She's been very submissive. When I touch her she goes cold, she trembles, and she cries. If I don't touch her, she pleads for me to make love to her and tells me how much she loves me."

"Does she initiate your lovemaking or take an assertive role?"

"No, never, but if I don't initiate it, she believes that something is wrong. That maybe she's not exciting or stimulating to me and nothing could be further from the truth."

"Have you talked with her about it?"

"Yes, I've tried too many times. Professionally, JeNelle is a dynamic, aggressive, and articulate woman. She thinks clearly and acts rationally. She's got a great sense of humor and she's extremely creative, but we haven't reached the levels of intimacy that I know we can go together. I know that she loves me as much as I love her, but she won't let herself go. She won't let herself feel."

"Has she had other sexual encounters? Maybe something or someone she can't forget?"

"You know that she was married and divorced at a very early age. While she was still a teenager, in fact. What you may not know is that she was battered and brutalized by her former husband, but that was eleven years ago. The first night that we spent together, she told me that no man had touched her since her divorce. I believe her. If my brother couldn't get her into his bed, nobody could."

"But she wasn't in love with Benjamin Staton. She was in love with you. Apparently she's been badly hurt, Kenneth James. That's the only logical conclusion that I can draw from what you've told me."

"I know, Dad. I've come to the same conclusion and I'm going to work this all out with her. We both want to have the same kind of marriage that you and Mom have. The same kind of loving marriage that her parents have. We're going to have to work this out between us. I'll never give up on that goal no matter what it takes."

Chapter 7

"JeNelle, are you awake?" Vivian whispered, as she knocked on the door and peeked in.

"Sure, Vivian, come in," JeNelle said, with a broad smile. She patted the bed and beckoned Vivian to sit down. "I've been just laying here being lazy and thinking about that wonderful brother of yours."

"He is on the right side of perfect, isn't he?" Vivian asked rhetorically.

"Yes, he is. I'm a very lucky woman to have found him. He's a rare breed of man. All of your brothers are and your father, too."

"Yes, they are special men, but Kenneth is also lucky to have found you, JeNelle. He's usually a happy man, but I've never seen him this happy. Nobody has."

"I love him so much, Vivian, that sometimes I can't catch my breath just thinking about him. I just want him to hold me in his arms. He's so attentive and loving. He makes me feel like I'm beautiful and loved and needed, and like such an important part of his existence. I never dreamed that I'd find a man like him. I didn't think that men like him existed. I owe it all to Gloria and Benny."

"Are you and Benny all right?"

"Yes. We spent a lot of time together after Whitney was born. We talked about his feelings for me and he admitted that it was Stacy that he loved all of the time that he thought that he was falling in love with me. Now we talk about Stacy. He loves her so much andhe's hurting very badly because he never told Stacy how he truly feels about her. When she left, she thought that he was in love with me. Benny told me that Stacy always gave him good advice on how to handle his relationships with women, especially with me."

"I know. Benny and I have had some very long talks about Stacy, too. I met her when he brought her home to meet us and tell us that they were expecting Whitney Ivy. They both kept insisting that they were only good friends with benefits who had an 'unguarded moment', but everyone else could see how much they were in love with each other."

"Then she does love Benny."

"I think so and so does everyone else in our family who's seen them together."

"Benny told me that when Stacy found out that she was pregnant, she wanted to have an abortion, but he wasn't going to let that happen."

"No, he wasn't. That's why he brought her to Goodwill. She told me that he said that she could try to convince all of us that an abortion was the right solution. Stacy said that after being at home with us the very first day that she and Benny arrived, she knew that she couldn't go through with an abortion. She told Benny that she would have his baby for him, but that she couldn't raise it. He would have to raise Whitney Ivy without her. She and I talked on the telephone every week during her pregnancy. Stacy really wanted to get back to her career, but she wanted to give her best friend what he wanted, his daughter."

"She must be a strong woman, Vivian. To go through the ordeal of a pregnancy and childbirth for a friend, even a good friend like Benny. That's more than a notion."

"She's a hell of a woman. Stacy is one of the most dynamic women I've ever met. She wasn't born with a silver spoon in her mouth. Growing up in the old Cabrini Green section in Chicago, she lost her twin sister to a drug overdose when they were both very young. Her mother left after her sister died because she couldn't handle the pain. Stacy's father raised her and her younger brother alone. It doesn't get much tougher than that. Now she's a career Navy Intelligence and Security Communications Officer who knows her stuff. She's tough, too. She told me that she came a long way from the slums of Cabrini Green, but she had a long way to go to reach her goals."

JeNelle and Vivian both turned when someone knocked on the door. "JeNelle?"

"Hi, Janice! Hi, Cecil! Come on in," JeNelle said joyfully.

"What are you two doing in here?" Janice Atterly asked.

"We were talking about Stacy Greene," Vivian answered.

"Oh, that's my girl!" Cecil Jordon said. "Ms. Career Woman Personified!"

"Yes, that's what we were just saying," Vivian said.

"Yeah, when I grow up I want to be just like her!" Cecil said.

"Right, Jordon! Doctor of Oceanography and you, too, Dr. Janice Atterly, Doctor of Biochemistry! Benny told me that you two finished your dissertations and received your Doctorates!"

"Oh, that," Janice said blandly. "That and seventy-five cents wouldn't get you a small cup of coffee at Starbucks."

"You're not saying that getting your Doctorate wasn't worth it, are you?" JeNelle asked.

"Hell, no, JeNelle! I'm glad that Cecil forced me to do it. It was a hell of a lot of hard work, but I'd do it again. Didn't hurt the paycheck at the Salk Institute either, I might add," Janice said.

"I was real happy that the Scripps Institute dug deep into its pockets, too," Cecil added. "But don't mind Janice. She's feeling like her biological clock just went haywire."

The women all laughed.

"I don't know what you're talking about, Janice. Stacy's done a lot with her career, but she hasn't achieved what you have," Vivian said.

"Yeah, but she's younger than I am. She will in time and she's enjoyed being in the Navy doing what she's been doing a hell of a lot more than I have enjoyed my career," Janice added. "I'm in the lab so much that I'm afraid that life is rushing past me."

"So many men to choose from and so little time!" Cecil added hauntingly. "Stacy had men falling overboard for her and she could have cared less! She had career on the brain and my condo mate has love and marriage on the brain these days."

"Yes, but she and Benny—"

"Yeah, I know what you're going to say, JeNelle. She and Benny had a good thing going," Cecil said dryly.

"Yes they did. I called it unique. Stacy was seeing this Adonis Lieutenant something…" Janice added.

"And that fine Marine from Camp Pendleton, Ted Peterson! Girl, what I wouldn't have given to make muster with him!" Cecil joked.

"You did, Cecil, remember?"

"Oh, I did, didn't I?"

"Benny and Stacy were in love with each other," JeNelle added.

"If they were they sure didn't know it or act like it. They had a real modern and enlightened love affair," Janice said. "Benny knew all about the men that Stacy was seeing and Stacy knew all about the women Benny dated. Even you, JeNelle. They used to talk about their relationships together even during the time that they were sleeping together."

"Who wouldn't want to sleep with Benny? Hell, I considered it a few times myself!" Cecil added laughing. "Half the women in the San Diego Standard Metropolitan Area would have gladly paid to get into Benny's bed. The man's hung like a damn horse and I hear that he knows how to graze in the grass, too!"

"Hey, hey! TMI! He's my brother and I love him, but I think that he did service a lot of the Washington, Maryland, and Virginia areas as well when he lived in DC," Vivian added dryly. "I still call his house Benny's Bordello."

"Yes, but when it comes to good looks and physique, Kenneth Alexander takes the prize and JeNelle's got that stallion roped and tamed!" Janice said with a broad smile.

JeNelle blushed. "If you're trying to say that my fiancé is a handsome and physically attractive man, you'll get no argument out of me, Janice Atterly, but Gregory's going to break a lot of hearts."

"He already has," Vivian added dryly, "and a few family records, too."

The women all laughed.

"Damn! Dr. Alexander had me fanning myself!" Cecil added. "What did you put in those Southern genes, Vivian?"

"Beats the hell out of me!"

"I hear that your Dr. Jackson is a heart stopper too, Vivian," JeNelle said with a smile. "Gloria tells me that he's built like a Greek God."

"Oh, yes! Derrick's got it all in the right places. Carries some healthy luggage, too, I believe," Vivian said, smiling broadly.

"What! You haven't nailed this vision yet?" Cecil asked with a raised eyebrow.

"Not yet! Almost did though just before I came out here, but Chuck Montgomery called and Derrick had an emergency."

"You know, I haven't crossed the color line yet, but that Chuck Montgomery could operate on me anytime he wanted to!" Cecil said.

"Get in line! Melissa Charles had first dibs on his bedside manner and then there are about two hundred females at Georgetown Hospital that are lining up just to change his sheets," Vivian joked.

"Melissa? I don't think so, Vivian," JeNelle said. "Melissa and your other housemate, Alan, were playing kissy face at that party that Kenneth's and my employees threw for us this week at that country club."

"Are you sure, JeNelle?" Vivian asked.

"I saw them in the garden at the country club. Melissa's got a hot-blooded Native American on her agenda, not Chuck Montgomery."

"I wonder whether Chuck knows," Vivian said aloud with some concern.

"Sure, he does. He pointed them out to me. He thought that they made a great couple." JeNelle added.

"Bill Chandler isn't chopped liver either," Janice said.

"I noticed that, too. Great dancer. Extraordinary good taste in men's fashion. Looks like he can handle himself in close situations," Cecil said.

"Vivian, how can you live in a house with three gorgeous men with great qualities and still find someone else?" Janice asked. "I've been looking for so long that I've just about given up until I met your cousin James."

"It ain't always easy, believe me, but Derrick gets my juices flowing and I can't wait to let it flood!"

The women all laughed.

"That's what Benny says about Stacy. They used to get these 'rushes'. Benny gets his from flying jets and Stacy gets hers from sailing," Janice said. "Those two should be together. They're like perfectly matched bookends. Benny hasn't been the same since she left. He's not even dating anymore."

"I know. It's just him and Whitney Ivy. He's a wonderful father to her and he loves Whitney so much," Vivian said. "I want Stacy to come back to him and my parents believe that she will one day, but I'm not so sure. Benny and Stacy were magic together though. They kept us awake at night and woke us up early in the morning with their lovemaking when we were in Goodwill."

"That's how they were in San Diego, too. Benny changed after he and Stacy started sleeping together. He wasn't out there partying that much. He was ready for a commitment, but Stacy wasn't. She used to say that Benny was the dangerous type. The type of man that women fell in love with and went crazy over. She said that insanity didn't run in her family and that she wasn't putting herself in harm's way. I don't think that she knew that he cared so deeply for her," Janice said with a sigh.

"She had to have known something, Janice. Otherwise, why hasn't she called or written to him?" Vivian asked.

"You've probably got a point, Vivian, but I think that she realized how much Benny really meant to her and decided to get out of Dodge. Remember Stacy probably thinks that Benny wanted to marry JeNelle," Janice said.

"I wish I knew where she was. I'd be there today, on my wedding day, explaining how much she means to Benny. He and Whitney deserve to be happy," JeNelle added.

"Wherever Stacy Greene is, it's an important mission. Of that, I'm sure. What she and Benny had just didn't work out. Next!" Cecil said blandly.

"That's my condo mate for you," Janice said dryly. "She and Stacy have nothing on their minds but making it through life without a full-time mate."

"Is that true, Cecil? You're not going to find someone special?" Vivian asked.

"Not on purpose. Don't misunderstand. I do enjoy having male companionship as much as the next woman, but it's not a requirement that I fall in love, get married, and have babies, in that order."

"That's so cold, Cecil," Vivian said.

"Cold! You haven't seen my iceberg condo mate in action. She's got a full social calendar, but she doesn't give two hoots in hell for any of them."

"You just haven't met your match, Cecil. You need somebody who can get past your resolve," JeNelle said confidently.

"I'm not looking for a match. Just because I prefer not to do the love and marriage thing, everyone wants to find a match for me."

"Cecil, you do have some unconventional views. I don't know anyone else who doesn't want to find a soul mate."

"A soul mate? That's why I have you three, my sistahs!"

Everyone laughed.

"Yeah, but pairing is a natural thing. You just have to kiss a lot of frogs to find your prince," Janice said, with a sigh.

"Somebody's been watching too much television. I'm nobody's princess. Besides, what is it that a man can do for me that I can't do for myself?" Cecil asked.

"Give you babies!"

"You're a biochemist, Janice. You should know that those come in test tubes now."

"Are you saying that men are unnecessary?" JeNelle asked.

"No, but they aren't critical to the process of being happy, fulfilled, successful—"

"Don't get her started," Janice sighed. "I've been her friend for a lot of years, since we met and shared a house our first year in undergrad. I already know that there is no use starting this conversation."

"I understand what you're saying, Cecil. I hadn't planned to find Kenneth, fall in love with him, or want to marry him."

"Thanks, JeNelle. I'm glad somebody understands."

"Come to think of it, after Carlton and I broke it off, there was a period of time when I wasn't interested in a love relationship either."

"Oh no, please don't give her any more ammunition! I've been trying to convince Cecil that she should leave herself open to the idea of being with someone special."

They all turned when someone knocked on the door and peeked in.

"You girls have been in here for a long time. Shirley Taylor just arrived. Now come get some of this bridal lunch. We have a wedding to go to today."

"Okay, Mrs. Towson," Cecil said.

"No, dear, I'm the other one, Bessie Baines. I'm JeNelle's aunt."

"Oh, I'm sorry. You and Mrs. Towson must be twins."

"We are. You girls come along now. Lunch is ready."

JeNelle smiled to herself and absently rubbed her abdomen. Then her mood changed. "I'm coming, Aunt Bessie. I just want to have a word with Vivian."

Vivian came back to JeNelle's bed and sat down.

"What is it, JeNelle? You look concerned about something," Vivian said.

"I am. How do you think that Gloria is handling this?"

"Not real well, JeNelle, I'm sorry to say. Your sister almost didn't come. She's been consumed with the idea of suing Tony Jamerson for allegedly beating her. Although the police have pretty much cleared him from allegations that he assaulted her, all that she talks about is taking him to the cleaners. The District Attorney is considering taking the case before a grand jury based on what little information and evidence he does have."

"That's what I was afraid of. I'm not sure what to do."

"I've tried to talk with her. Even Chuck couldn't get her to budge, but for some reason David did."

"What do you mean?"

"Well, Gloria decided that she wasn't coming to the wedding because she sometimes still needs a wheel chair. Even Chuck, who, as you know, she respects for taking care of her, couldn't change her mind, but when David heard that she wasn't coming he went into her room and we could hear them arguing. Then David came out carrying Gloria over her shoulder. She was kicking and screaming and he put her in the van. He told her, in no uncertain terms, that if she wasn't coming with us, then she was going to have to walk back to her room by herself. She didn't say a word after that. When we got to the airport, David told her that she had three choices She could walk to the plane, ride in the wheel chair or he'd carry her, but one way or the other, she was going to get on that plane."

"David did that? Mild mannered, the original Erkle, David?" JeNelle asked in total amazement.

"The brother was fierce! Scared me! David rarely speaks above a whisper and he's certainly not the most athletic figure I've ever seen, but something got into the man and he let Gloria have it with both barrels. This is a Black man who can spell rhythm, but can't find it. I think that he must be confusing himself with Wesley Snipes! I thought that he was having an out-of-body experience!"

"They do resemble each other except for the thick glasses," JeNelle said.

"Bill, Chuck, and Alan took David to get contact lens. He's beginning to look a lot better," Vivian said. "Bill's even got him dressing better. David doesn't even look like a nerd anymore."

"I did notice that he seemed different. I only met him after Gloria was assaulted. I'm certainly grateful to him and to all of you for sticking by my sister."

"She's family, JeNelle. All of us in the house are."

There was a knock on the door and Shirley peeked in.

"Hi, Shirley," Vivian and JeNelle said in unison.

"Is this one of those meetings in the ladies' room or can anyone come in?"

"Come on in here, Shirley," JeNelle said smiling.

Vivian hopped off the bed and hugged Shirley

"I'm going to feed my face," Vivian said.

"Okay, Vivian. Thanks, and I love you."

Vivian winked at JeNelle and closed the door as she left.

Shirley paced the room and looked out at the women having a bridal luncheon on the deck overlooking the vast Pacific Ocean. JeNelle noticed her discomfort.

"What's wrong, Shirley?"

"I have something to tell you, JeNelle, and I'm ashamed."

JeNelle got off the bed and went to Shirley. She embraced her. "This is about you and Kenneth, isn't it?"

Shirley's eyes widened and her mouth dropped open. "He told you?" she asked, stunned.

"No, you know Kenneth better than that. He's been your friend for seven years and your business partner for four years. He'd never betray a friendship or confidence."

"Then how did you know?"

"I guessed."

"You knew that I had this huge crush on Kenneth and you still asked me to be in your wedding?"

"Of course, but I also know that Tom's very much in love with you. He's a fine man."

"I know. Tom and I may be ready to walk down an aisle someday soon, too."

"You deserve the best."

Shirley hugged JeNelle. "You know, Kenneth and I were never intimate. He never even looked at me with anything other than platonic friendship in mind."

"It certainly wasn't because you're not an attractive woman, Shirley, but you know Kenneth when he's clicking on all cylinders, he's passionate about his work."

"You sure revved up his engine. I was so jealous when he met you, I couldn't stand it. He fought so hard not to fall in love with you because of Benny, but it was hopeless. I could see it in his eyes."

"I know how he felt. I was fighting a losing battle, too, because I didn't want a man in my life again. Not after my marriage to Michel San Angelo, but Kenneth was too special to walk away from. I love Benny, but only as a good friend and soon-to-be brother-in-law. He's not Kenneth."

"You're going to be very happy. You and Kenneth have this great chemistry between you and he loves you completely."

"There is no greater love than what I feel for him. Just wait. You and Tom are headed in the same direction."

"I know and I appreciate and admire you for being so gracious and understanding. I'm not sure that I would have been as forgiving if I were in your shoes."

"You and I are good friends now. I hope that you feel the same way about me."

"I do, JeNelle. I truly do."

They embraced. Just then, Canty Towson came in through JeNelle's French doors from the deck.

"Okay, you two. This bridal luncheon is ready and I want you two to come and eat so that you won't faint from starvation or dehydration during the wedding."

JeNelle put on her robe and she and Shirley followed her mother out to the deck. It was a bright sun shinny day. They all laughed and talked.

"Now, we come to the most important part of the female bonding wedding ritual," Cecil said.

"And what is that, Cecil?" JeNelle asked.

"The gifts to the bride, of course!" Cecil said.

"Oh no! Not another gift! Kenneth and I can't get into the other bedrooms as it is!"

"This is different. It's time for the something old, something new, something borrowed and something blue gift giving."

"Oh, okay. This I can handle," JeNelle laughed.

"Don't be so sure, JeNelle."

"This sounds ominous."

Cecil pulled a blue thong out of a bag and handed it to JeNelle.

"Okay, this takes care of the something blue part," JeNelle said.

"Oh, no, JeNelle. That's the borrowed part."

"I don't understand. You want me to wear these and then give them back?"

"Almost. You are to wear the underwear and then loan them to Lisa Lambert!"

The women all fell out laughing.

"You're wicked, Cecil," JeNelle said. "If I wear this rubber band that you call underwear, I'm not going to send them to Lisa on loan."

"You should, JeNelle, for what she tried to do to Kenneth and to you," Shirley said.

"Give the woman a break. She didn't succeed and now I hear that she lost her job as Economic Affairs advisor to the Governor. Remember, ladies, and I do underscore the word *ladies*, she's a sister down on her luck."

The bridesmaids looked at each other and booed JeNelle. She laughed. They went on with their ritual and JeNelle gave each of them the coffee table book, *I Dream A World*. The women sat there for some time, lost in the pages of the beautiful book until it was time for them to begin dressing for the wedding.

⚷

"I'm not doing this!" Gloria stormed, as she sat in JeNelle's den.

"Gloria, this is your sister's wedding day. She's in her bedroom getting dressed. She expects you to be her Maid of Honor. Are you going to disappoint her now?" Vivian asked.

"Disappoint her! What's she got to be disappointed about? She's got it all! It's me who has nothing! She's always been the prettiest! The most gracious! Everyone looks up to her! Now she's getting married to a man who loves her and can take care of her! And what about me? What do I have? I should be the one getting married. The one that everybody's making such a big fuss over! Not her! She's been married before!" Gloria yelled, collapsing into tears and burying her face in her hands.

Vivian went to her and hugged her. She rocked her in her arms. "Gloria, she's your sister and she loves you. Look at you! You're gorgeous. Men are always taken by you. You walk into a room and everyone takes notice. JeNelle has a different type of style and beauty. She's not in competition with you. She hasn't had it easy either. Her first marriage ended in disaster. You read that newspaper article. You know how JeNelle suffered. She's overcome a lot."

"It was her fault what happened to her. She deserved it!"

"Bull!" Cecil raged. "How dare you say that! No woman deserves to be beaten and raped! But I'm beginning to believe that maybe you're the exception to that rule!"

"Cecil, that's not fair," Shirley said. "Now everyone's a little edgy. Let's not have any more of this. This is supposed to be a happy occasion. JeNelle and Kenneth have worked hard to make this a very special event not just for themselves, but for everyone."

"Yeah, and Ms. Spoiled Brat here is trying to screw it all up just because of some damn sibling rivalry. Well, it ain't happening like that, Gloria Towson! Do you hear me? It ain't happening!" Cecil shouted.

"Cecil, we aren't going to get anywhere if we don't handle this thing calmly. Gloria's come through a lot, too," Janice said.

"Ha! She got her ass kicked because her fiancée, Tony Jamerson, walked in and caught her screwing two of his best friends! It wasn't enough that she was skewing anything that wasn't nailed down! Oh, no! She has to go after the big money, too! I saw you oozing all over the team owners while Tony was out there getting his butt kicked on the football field. He could have been a great football player, but the minute you stepped on the scene, his stats took a nosedive. People started talking behind his back saying that he was pussy whipped! Everyone knew what you were doing, Gloria Towson! You didn't even have the decency to cover it up! Tony still tried to defend you and your behavior, telling everyone that you were just high spirited and still giving you everything that you wanted! Jewelry, furs, cars, trips, and an unlimited bank account, but that wasn't enough for you! You had to rub his face in the dirt, and for what? What did the man ever do to you, but love the hell out of your last year's underwear!" Cecil argued.

"He beat me! That's what he did to me!" Gloria yelled.

"I'm a woman and I'd beat your ass, too!"

"Cecil! Come on everybody. This is neither the time nor the place to have this kind of conversation. Save it for the Business and Professional Women's Conference!" Vivian pleaded.

"What do you know about how I feel, Vivian?" Gloria yelled. "You've got Derrick! I don't have anybody!"

"Gloria, Derrick means a great deal to me, but he doesn't define who I am. No man can do that. I'm a whole person regardless of whether I'm with a man or not. I carry my own weight."

"And she won't have anyone if she keeps suing everyone. Suing Tony for twenty million dollars! The man's probably going to lose his contract with the Chargers!"

"That's what he gets for putting his hands on me!"

"Gloria! Listen to me! Now enough is enough! This isn't about you. It's about my brother and your sister! Someday someone special is going to happen to you just like JeNelle has happened for Kenneth and Derrick has happened for me. Would you want this type of foolishness going on, on your wedding day?" Vivian asked patiently, trying to reason with her.

"Who cares? Nobody is ever going to want me again. Not like this!"

"Holy...!" Janice said, throwing up her hands in frustration.

"Janice, please," Vivian pleaded, as she pushed some buttons on the telephone.

"Who are you calling, Vivian," Shirley asked.

"David," Vivian answered.

"*David!*" Gloria yelled.

"Yes, David! He seems to be the only one who can reason with you these days."

"No! Don't do that, Vivian," Gloria yelled. "Please! Don't call David!"

"Then are you going to cooperate?"

Gloria sulked.

"Hello, McCoy Suites Hotel," a voice came over the speaker.

"McCoy Suite number 452, please. Mr. David..."

Gloria pressed the disconnect button. Cecil and Janice shook their heads.

"Are you girls ready yet?" Canty Towson asked, as she came into the den smiling. She looked around at all of the faces and apparently sensed that something was going on. "All right, what's wrong?" she asked, her smile slipping from her face.

"Nothing, Mrs. Towson. Just a little pre-wedding jitters. We'll be—"

"Stop covering up, Cecil. I know something is wrong. I can feel it in the air." She looked at Gloria. "Gloria, I'm waiting for an explanation."

Gloria didn't look at her mother.

"Gloria!" Canty said, raising her voice.

Gloria still didn't answer.

"All right, young lady. Let me tell you one damn thing! You're my daughter and I love you, but if you screw up this wedding, I'll never forgive you! That's a promise!" she said with her eyes flashing. "Now the limousines are here. We've got one hour before the wedding starts and it's starting on time or my name isn't what it is! Six hundred people are going to be at this happy event and, Gloria Elaine Towson, every one of them had better see a happy, united family!"

She left the room.

The bridesmaids applied the last touches on their makeup, finished dressing in silence, and stood by the door looking at Gloria. Gloria looked up at their faces and slowly stood and walked through the door using a cane to steady herself. The women all sighed in relief.

The limousines pulled up to the south portico of the Atrium Manor at 2:10 P.M. The groomsmen, pages, and ushers were all standing, awaiting the arrival of the bride and her bridal party. They greeted the bridesmaids warmly and complimented them on their attire. James Dixon made a special effort to be the one assisting Janice Atterly from the car. He was all smiles, as she took his hand and stepped out of the limo. She was smiling radiantly at him, too.

"You look quiet handsome, James," Janice said, with a coy smile.

"You're breathtaking, Ms. Atterly. Simply breathtaking," he said slowly, awed.

"James, don't you think that we know each other well enough to dispense with the formalities? I mean, we have known each other for a week now and I'd like to get to know you better," she said.

James' smile grew broader. "That's the best news that I've heard this year, Janice."

Vivian whispered something to one of the young pages who then scurried away.

Harvey Towson helped his daughter, JeNelle, from the limousine and everyone turned and marveled at how absolutely gorgeous she looked. Her radiant smile lit up everyone's face, as Harvey proudly escorted her.

They all went inside and, as they began to ascend the wide staircase, David, Bill, and Alan appeared at the top of the balcony. David fixed his stare on Gloria and walked confidently down the staircase. He said nothing, but approached her confidently. He held out his hand to her. She looked up at him. A humming moment later, she finally extended her hand and he assisted her up the steps. Alan and Bill moved to help, but David waved them off.

"I'll always be here for you, Gloria," Vivian overheard David say. "Always."

Gloria did not acknowledge him, but she held on to his arm and walked into a salon with the rest of the wedding party awaiting the final moments to expire before the wedding began.

"Nice move, Vivian," Cecil said quietly. "Someone ought to give you a medal for patience in the line of fire and beyond the call of duty."

"Gloria's had a lot of disappointments, Cecil. I love her like a sister. That's what family does."

"I'm beginning to believe you, Vivian. It must be all of that Southern gentility."

Chapter 8

Mr. and Mrs. Harvey Moore Towson

Request the honor of your presence

at the wedding of their daughter

JeNelle Elise

to

Mr. Kenneth James Alexander

son of

Dr. and Mrs. Bernard Thomas Alexander

on Saturday, the first day of June

at three o'clock in the afternoon

at

The Atrium Manor

20000 Main Street

Santa Barbara, California

Chapter 9

It wasn't merely a wedding; it was *the* event, a happening that everyone had been waiting for. Guests of the couple arrived in their finest attire and smiled broadly and gaily, as they strolled among the grounds and gardens that led to the opulent Atrium Manor, the epitome of grace and glamour, in the hills overlooking the City of Santa Barbara. It was a beautiful, sunny day not uncharacteristic for the area, which conjures up images of a modern day Eden. The guests entered the anteroom, and oohed and aahed at the beautiful and physically magnificent decorations.

Some very notable, prestigious, and influential people, the rich and the famous, were in attendance along with a substantial number of family members and other friends of the couple. All of the employees of both INSIGHTS and Towson & Towson Couture, and CompuCorrect's Northern and Southern Divisions, and many of their business associates and families were there as well.

The press and news media were there, too, buzzing around each car as the valets opened the doors and the guests got out. The Mayor and City Council worked the room while businessmen and women pumped their hands vigorously along with members of the Chamber of Commerce and the Board of Trade. Guests fell into lines to receive their envelopes with seating placements, white carnations with nametags attached, and wedding procession event cards.

Hot and cold hors d'oeuvres and Champagne were being served, as people milled around talking about the happy event and couple. A group of musicians played mellow tunes, as the guests arrived. The Anteroom was tastefully and beautifully decorated in large, potted greenery with many pairs of white doves cooing in large, gilded cages. Ice sculptures of wedding bells, a couple embracing, wedding bands, and other wedding scenes were placed strategically around the room on tables gaily dressed in the wedding couple's colors with tiers of food and beverage trays beautifully staged. The official photographers snapped pictures of the guests and videographers panned the anteroom from the floor and from the mezzanine above.

Sara McDougal and Joe Grayson accepted and stored gifts that were brought in by the guests and attended to the comfort of the guests.

At exactly three o'clock, the music ended, and chimes could be heard being played by young people who worked for the couple's companies in their respective youth-at-risk programs. They were dressed in traditional Mexican wedding attire and came down the two, wide, curved, cascading staircases at opposite sides of the anteroom. The young people wore stoic expressions, marking the solemn significance of the occasion.

A hush fell over the crowd, as the children played the chimes and moved to positions in front of the large doors that led to the inner chamber ballroom. The guests were silent as one young boy rang out three chimes clearly and slowly, as the doors to the ballroom swung open. The guests silently followed the young people through the doors and were awestruck by the beauty of the hanging garden scenes that graced Grecian columns. Large, white, arched columns held hanging plants and greenery cascading over and around the columns. Each round table—covered in starched white linen clothes, crocheted netting and bunting with light burgundy silk ribbons draped across the tables separating them into slices—sat twelve guests. A single crystal vase on each table held a beautiful array of flowers of all hues of pink, purple, lavender and burgundy. Tapered, hand-dipped candles surrounded the flowers and fine bone China, Waterford crystal, and silverware gleamed in the candle light. It was a magical scene and the guests moved quietly and reverently toward their appointed seats and sat silently.

The young people moved to the front of the room where a wide, but shallow staircase stood, adorned with archways and greenery. They struck three chimes in unison and the Honorable Judge Johnston White Worthington, Chief Justice of the California State Supreme Court, entered wearing his black judicial robe and carrying a white Bible and moved to the center of the room.

The wedding party stood poised in the doorway. Three bells sounded and Gregory escorted Gloria's mother, Canty Towson, into the room. She was wearing a silver-grey, organdy, long formal gown with matching wide brim hat and gloves. She carried a bouquet of white roses in her hand. As she was seated, three bells sounded and Bernard escorted his wife, Sylvia, into the room and seated her. She was wearing a crystal blue crepe gown, which flattered her full head of hair beneath the matching pillbox hat and small veil on her head. She also carried a bouquet of white roses. Bernard was wearing a Pierre Cardin tuxedo with a single white rose in the lapel.

Once they were seated, three bells were sounded and Kenneth and Benny moved into position, facing their guests. The audience reacted to the very debonair brothers in the pearl-grey Pierre Cardin tuxedos. The brothers were both smiling broadly, as the young people moved out of position and the musicians began to play. The ring bearer, Timothy Baines, entered and walked slowly to his position beside the groom. Tom Jenkins entered, escorting Shirley Taylor. His green eyes were sparkling and Shirley was smiling. He positioned her and moved in beside Benny Alexander. Next, James Dixon entered, escorting Janice Atterly, Gregory Alexander escorting Cecil Jordon, and then Chuck Montgomery escorting Vivian Alexander. Each had walked proudly and happily down the aisle.

Gloria entered alone, solemnly with tears streaming down her face. When she was positioned, two ushers rolled the white covering down the aisle and up the shallow steps to the foot of the Judge. Aretha entered and dropped flower pedals as she walked along. When she was positioned, the lights dimmed and a single beam shined as JeNelle and her father momentarily stood at the door.

The guests rose to their feet quietly and were obviously awestruck as JeNelle entered, escorted by her father. She was radiant in her floor-length wedding gown of ivory with an elbow-length chapel train. The gown was covered by what appeared to be thousands of points of light all sparkling and shinning like glitter. Her hair was mounted gracefully atop her head with sprigs of heather and baby's breaths adorning her face.

The bride glided down the aisle and tears of joy could be seen flowing on many faces of the guests. Kenneth moved into position, facing JeNelle. Harvey escorted Canty to stand behind JeNelle. Bernard escorted Sylvia to stand behind Kenneth.

"On behalf of Kenneth James Alexander and JeNelle Elise Towson, I welcome you to the union of these two extraordinary people. They invite you to share with them the beginning of their new life together and to witness the unadulterated love that they share. A love that is patient and kind. A love that is always proud. A love that keeps a record of joy and happiness. A love that celebrates truth, honor, and integrity. A love that is unyielding and never relents or fails to sustain them." Judge Worthington spoke in a clear voice and continued his uplifting and sincere presentation. The parents of the bride and groom gave their orations of happiness then took their seats. Then each of the brides' maids and groomsmen recited their presentations to the couple. When they finished, Aretha took to the baby grand piano and began to play and sing "Someone to Love" in a pure, vibrant, and enchanting voice and finished with "Because You Loved Me." The orchestra accompanied her as she smiled at the couple. Then Kenneth and JeNelle faced each other.

"I, Kenneth James Alexander, ask you, JeNelle Elise Towson, to be my wife and to share my life. I will love you always and with this ring I pledge you my heart and endow you with all of my worldly possessions." He placed the ring on her finger and kissed it.

"I, JeNelle Elise Towson, ask you, Kenneth James Alexander, to be my husband and to share my life. I will love you forever and with body, mind and spirit I endow you with all of my worldly goods." She slipped the ring on his finger and kissed it.

They were handed lit candles by Benny and Gloria that they joined together and then proceeded to light individually the candles held by their families and their families passed the flame to their friends until the dimmed room was aglow with hundreds of lit candles. Then they joined their candles and lit a single candle together.

Vivian smiled at Chuck, with tears rolling down her face. Gloria caught David's eye. Tom winked at Shirley who blushed. Janice and James beamed at each other. Bernard and Harvey both kissed their respective wives and Benny smiled broadly at Whitney.

"All assembled by the lighting of these candles know that you obligate yourselves to the support and the integrity of this union. By the power vested in me by the State of California, I pronounce that Kenneth and JeNelle are now one. Ladies and Gentlemen, I have the profound and distinct honor and pleasure of presenting to you Mr. and Mrs. Kenneth James Alexander on the first day of their new life together. Kenneth, you may now salute your bride."

Kenneth took JeNelle in his arms and they gazed into each other's eyes.

"Forever," JeNelle whispered.

"And always," Kenneth answered.

They kissed in the glow of the candlelight, with a single pure light illuminating their union. The guests applauded them.

The seven-course meal was served by skillful wait staff who kept the wine and water glasses filled with each course.

Kenneth and JeNelle sat at a center table reserved for the wedding party, ate their first meal together as husband and wife, and then mingled with their guests. They took to the floor for their first dance, still gazing deeply into each other's eyes. Then they danced with their parents, as the rest of the wedding party and guests joined in.

"That was some ceremony," Chuck said, as he held Vivian in his arms and danced.

"They're very happy. You can see it in their faces." Vivian glimpsed Kenneth and JeNelle as they danced.

"They sure are. Is this the type of wedding you see for yourself?"

"This was just perfect for Kenneth and JeNelle, but something a lot less opulent would suit me just fine." Vivian smiled.

"Make a wish," a familiar voice came from behind Vivian.

Turning, she was surprised, but pleased to see Derrick Jackson's smiling face.

"Glad to see that you could make it, DJ," Chuck said, releasing Vivian to Derrick's arms.

Tears welled in her eyes, as Derrick took her in his arms. Derrick's heart beat faster as he kissed her.

"Thanks to you, Chuck. Ahkmed Sudah-Ryheme came on board on Monday and has been working out just fine. Thank you for recommending him."

"Ahkmed? Isn't that—" Vivian began to ask.

"The same," Chuck answered.

"You know him, Vivian?" Derrick asked.

"I've met him. Chuck gave him a ride home from the airport the same night that I met Chuck. I didn't know that you two kept in touch, Chuck."

"Sure, he's been training at Georgetown since he arrived. I've had him on my Emergency Room rotation for six months now. He's a very talented pediatrician and works very hard. Cares about his patients."

"He certainly does. He's covering the emergency calls. That's why I am able to spend some quality time with you," Derrick said, holding Vivian.

"You two look like you can handle it from here," Chuck said, as he left Vivian and Derrick standing on the dance floor.

"Thanks for taking care of my lady," Derrick called after Chuck. Then he turned to Vivian and took her in his arms. "Make a wish," Derrick repeated, brushing his mouth over hers.

She put her arms around his neck. "I have my wish," Vivian answered. "You're holding me in your arms. What more could I wish for than that?"

"If you could be anywhere in the universe, where would that special place be?"

"Anywhere in your arms," Vivian said quietly.

Derrick beamed, as he looked at Vivian beautifully attired in her wedding ensemble. He pulled a card from his suit jacket and handed it to her.

She looked at him quizzically, as she opened the card and noted that it was an invitation for a week in an undisclosed location beginning that evening. There was also a copy of a medical report, indicating that Derrick had tested negative for HIV.

"Where are we going?" Vivian asked.

Derrick laughed.

"We're going through Miami," he said, with a smile.

"Okay, to where?" she asked. "Jamaica? Barbados? The Bahamas?"

"So many questions, Counselor." He smiled, as they began to dance.

"And so few answers, Doctor."

"Are we going to make this flight?"

She looked at the invitation again. "I think that I can fit this into my schedule."

"That's the best news that I've had since you left me over a week ago. I've missed you."

"Not as much as I've missed you." She kissed him.

⚬⚬

"Mmm, that must be the good doctor over there with Vivian," Janice said.

"Uh huh," Cecil answered not really paying attention, as she spied a tall, well-built man across the room.

Peering in the same direction as her friend, "Who are you looking at, Cecil?" Janice asked,

"That vision over there with James," Cecil answered.

"Oh, that's Don, James' twin brother, Donald Dixon," Janice answered.

"All right, I'm listening. What's the story on him?"

"I don't know that much about him. He isn't married though and he's here alone. He didn't bring anyone with him."

The women continued to talk.

⚬⚬

"James, who's that gorgeous creature with Janice?" Don asked.

"Oh, that's Dr. Cecil Jordon, Janice's condo mate. She and Janice live in the same building with Benny. Real nice lady, too. Lot of fun to be around."

"Medical doctor?"

"No, she's an oceanographer for Scripps Institute in San Diego."

"I take it that she's not married then."

"No, brother, she's single. Not seeing anyone seriously that I can tell. She's been here all week—by herself. I'll introduce you to her if you like, but with your hectic career—"

"Just introduce us. I'll worry about career matters later," Don insisted.

"My pleasure. It gives me an excuse to spend some more time with Janice."

Donald halted his brother before he could move away. "Wait a minute. You've been talking about Janice Atterly all week. What's the deal?"

"I like her style—a lot! We've been spending a little time together this week. I'm going to fly back to San Diego with Cousin Benny for a visit for a few days, maybe as much as a week or two after we leave Santa Barbara. Hadn't really had a lot of time to visit with him and Whitney since we've been here. Every day something was scheduled. JeNelle and Kenneth certainly do have a lot of friends—especially Janice."

"Are you sure that it's Benny and his daughter that you're going to see?"

James laughed. "Sure, brother, but if Janice is around, all the better!"

The two men approached the women and began a lively conversation.

"So, Cecil, I understand that you're an oceanographer."

"Yes. I hope that your next question isn't going to be 'What's that?'"

Don laughed. "A person who studies the geography of the five principal salt water divisions of the Earth's surface that constitute the Atlantic, Pacific, Indian, Arctic or Antarctic Oceans that cover more than two-thirds of the Earth's surface."

Cecil smiled. "Mmm, not bad. I'm impressed."

"How impressed?"

"More than mildly, but less than extremely," Cecil said.

"Then what would I have to do or say to assure that you're extremely impressed?"

"Is that important to you?"

"Extremely."

They laughed.

"Donald and Cecil seem to be enjoying each other's company," Janice commented as she and James are now seated at a table alone.

"I'm more interested in whether you're enjoying my company, Janice," James said rather bashfully.

Janice smiled.

"Is that smile a yes, Janice?"

"It's a yes, James."

"Good!" he said rather excitedly. "Then I take it that you wouldn't mind if I called you sometime?"

"I wouldn't mind, but, James, you live in South Carolina."

"I was thinking that I don't get to the West Coast very often and I have never been to San Diego."

"Yes, and…."

"Well, Benny and I have been talking about my coming down there after the wedding and spending a week or so with him…I mean, I wouldn't want to presume that you'd have much time…I mean, if you weren't busy…I mean, I know that an attractive woman like you probably has a full social calendar…I mean, if you thought that it was too forward of me to suggest—"

"James, you know I was just sitting here thinking of an idea. I mean, do you mind if I make a suggestion?"

"No, Janice, what is it?"

"Well, you probably are a very busy man, but since you've come all the way to California it would be a shame for you not to come down to San Diego for a while. I'm sure that Benny would enjoy the company and since I don't have a lot to do for the next week or two…I mean, if you can find the time, I could show you around San Diego. We have some very interesting attractions. For example, there's the San Diego Zoo. Now with your background in Animal Husbandry, I'm sure that you could turn this little side trip into an educational, as well as pleasurable experience."

"You know, Janice, you're a very bright and astute woman with great ideas."

They both laughed.

⚏

"Yo, Big Ben, check out the cousins tryin' to rap to your phine friends," Gregory said, trying not to be too obvious with his glances.

"Not bad form if I do say so myself," Benny mused, as he glimpsed his twin cousins, Donald and James, with Cecil and Janice.

"So when you gonna hook me up with one of your fresh friends, my brother?"

"G, I don't think that you need any help finding the ladies." Benny laughed. "Just stand still for five seconds. You've been a moving target all week!"

"But, Ben, I'm still a growin' country boy. I need nuturin'. You know—from the more mature woman—say about twenty-five or twenty-six or so."

Benny laughed. "If you want to keep growing, you'll stick with those young women who have been booking you all week and wait for them to get, uh, more mature!"

"But, Ben, look at some of these phine hunnies in here! I mean, they've been tryin' to rap to you all day! They've been walkin' all over me to get to you! Can't you give a brother a break and let's, uh, enhance my education?"

Benny laughed. "Sorry, my brother. You're on your own. I've got my girl right here," he said, as he kissed his baby daughter while she giggled.

"Aww, Ben, just look around you! How can you deny these beauties the pleasure of my company?"

"Because you're not ready yet," Aretha said, as she hugged Gregory from behind and kissed him on the cheek.

"Aww, Retha, I almost had Benny sold and now here you come," Gregory fussed, with a sigh.

"And remember, Gregory Clayton, you have to go back home with me and I'll be seeing Charlotte, Ellen, Leslie, Ann, Regina, Jennifer, and even Lucille and Geneva when we get back. Do you really want me giving your home girls the 411 on Conchetta and Carlotta Domingo-Garcia and Karen Braxton?"

"I see your point, little sister."

"If I have failed to mention it, Gloria, you look particularly ravishing today," David said, as he sat down beside her. "Would you honor me with a dance?"

Gloria rolled her eyes. "You don't dance, David. Remember?" she said sarcastically.

"I am familiar with the process and if you will await a melody, a waltz perhaps, I believe that I am capable of—" he stopped talking when he noticed that Gloria was eyeing Derrick and Vivian. "Gloria, are you distracted?"

"Sure. Sure, David. Look, uh, I want you to dance me over there to Derrick and then ask Vivian to switch partners and dance with you?" she said rather excitedly.

"I do not want to dance with Vivian."

"So what? Just ask her!"

David did as Gloria asked.

"Salutations, Vivian, Derrick. Would you two care to switch partners?" David asked.

"Certainly, David," Derrick said. "I'll let you know when," he said, as he danced Vivian away from David and Gloria.

"May I have the pleasure of this dance?" Bill asked, extending his hand next to Tom and Shirley.

Tom laughed nervously. "You're kidding, right, Bill?" Tom asked.

"I'll let you lead," Bill smiled smugly.

"Uh. Uh, Bill, I mean, uh—"

"Shirley, your friend doesn't seem to be able to make up his mind. Why don't we show him what he's missing?"

Shirley laughed and took Bill's outstretched hand.

"Now, Tom, take notes," Bill said jokingly.

Tom relaxed and Shirley laughed as Bill took her in his arms.

"You're wicked, Bill," Shirley said, laughing. "You shouldn't tease Tom like that. He's a good man."

"He's got a good woman beside him, Shirley. How could he miss?"

Shirley blushed. "Tom told me that you gave him a real education in humility, propriety, and consciousness raising."

Bill laughed. "I don't believe that Tom will ever forget this week," Bill mused. "I'm glad that he found it enlightening, but don't worry, Shirley. He's not my type."

"Not long ago, I didn't think that he was my type either, but we're learning." She smiled knowingly.

"That's all that counts. Whether you're Black or white or gay or straight or rich or poor or anything in between. First and foremost, we're all human beings in need of higher and constant education."

⚬—‹›

"Alan."

"Yes, Melissa?"

"Since we're out here, couldn't we take a side trip to your home?"

Alan looked at Melissa quizzically, as they danced. "To the Reservation?"

"Yes. I'd like to meet your family. You know, see where you grew up."

"I guess so, Melissa, but why would you want to do that? I mean, there are a lot of places that you could visit up and down the Pacific

Coast. I'm not sure that a young woman from Rhode Island would enjoy visiting the Res. There aren't many fancy hotels or motels around."

"Your family wouldn't let me stay with them?

Alan was really confused. "Sure, but—"

"I want to go there, Alan, and I didn't think that you were going to invite me on your own."

"It's not the place for—"

"A white woman like me? Is that what you were going to say, Alan?"

"Well, no, but Melissa, it's not easy…I mean, I've lived there all of my life. I'm used to the customs, people, isolation, the desolation of the wilderness. I mean, to me it's beautiful, but I don't know whether you'd enjoy it."

"Then why don't we both find out. I'd like for you to take me there to meet your family and friends."

"Okay, Melissa. If you say so, but I can't promise you—"

"I don't think that you understand what I'm saying, Alan. I want to meet your family so that they'll approve of me."

"Approve of you? Melissa, if this is just some flight of fancy, some misplaced or misguided idea that it would be just 'peachy keen' to—"

"Oh, so are you saying that I'm okay to sleep with in Washington, but I'm not good enough to be around people you know? That you should hide me away somewhere like some dirty little joke? That I can't expect or hope for a life with you? I can't expect to bear your children because I'm not a Native American? That I can't measure up to—"

Alan kissed her passionately. "We can fly into Farmington, New Mexico, and then drive the rest of the way or we can rent a car here and drive there. It would take us about two days to get there if we don't drive straight through. That's a little longer, but—".

Melissa's kiss interrupted him. "Let's take the slow route, if you don't mind, Alan. I want to get a good look at my new home."

"Dr. Chuck, you not happy man," Anna commented, sitting next to him.

"Anna, it's been a great day. Kenneth and JeNelle are going to be very happy together. I'll bet that they'll have a family started before the end of their first year of marriage."

"*Si, tu necesita a tener muchos niños y. una familia grande*, but you, Dr. Chuck. What you do now? Your friend, *Señor* Jackson, he muy loco with *Señorita* Vivian."

"*Si, el es muy loco para ella, mi amigo.* I guess you'll just have to marry me, Anna, *Si?*"

"*Estas loco,* Dr. Chuck," Anna laughed.

"Then how about a dance with *estas loco*, doctor, *Señora* Anna Menendez-Gaza?"

"*Si,* Dr. Chuck," she smiled.

⚬━━◦

"You know, lass, you're a chip off the old—"

"Aww, go on with your blarney, Joe Grayson. You could charm the elves out of their gold with your—"

"No, no, Miss McDougal, I be tellin' it to ya straight as an arrow. I swear on my dearly departed father's grave. If I was a laddie, oh say ten years younger, I'd—"

"You'd what, Joe Grayson?"

"Well, I'd a come a courtin'."

"Joe Grayson, you know where I live, don't you?"

"Yes, but Lass, I be on the shady side of thirty."

"And I'm on the shady side of twenty. Time to put a little sunshine in all this shade, wouldn't you think?"

"And you said that I kissed the blarney stone, Sara McDougal."

"It's the luck of the Irish in me, Joe Grayson."

They laughed.

⚬━━◦

"So, Retha, how can a young brother be picking up some digits, you know, so as I can speak at you?" Timothy Baines, the ring bearer, asked as he danced with Aretha Alexander.

"I have not decided when I will be prepared to accept phone calls from gentlemen callers, but I am accustomed to receiving letters from pen pals. If you'd care to write to me, then I will be happy to furnish my address."

"Wow, Retha, I never heard a girl talk like you do. I mean, you've got a fresh little rap going! You say you're from South Carolina? I like the rest of the package, too!" Timothy said, eyeing Aretha's fourteen-year-old frame.

"Yes, I am. I'm sure that you meant that as a compliment or at least that is the way that I choose to accept it, but if you move your hand one inch further down my hip, I'll bust your balls! How you like me now?"

⚬⟞⟝⟞

"Well, Bernie," Sylvia Alexander said, smiling. "Kenneth and JeNelle finally made it."

"Yes, they'll be as happy as we are one day," Bernard Alexander said, as he danced with his wife and smiled at her.

"I don't know about that. No one is as happy as you make me feel every day." She smiled back at him.

He kissed her gently on the lips.

"Now, if we can just find Stacy, maybe Benjamin Staton will find what we have."

Judge Worthington and his wife, Constance, danced alongside Bernard and Sylvia. "Dr. Alexander, Mrs. Alexander, I'm sure that this is a very happy occasion for you two," he said. "I'd be honored if you'd permit me to dance with the lovely mother of the groom. You two have been dancing together like newlyweds all afternoon."

Sylvia and Bernard smiled at each other.

"We are newlyweds, Judge. We've only been married for thirty-six years," Bernard said.

⚬⟞⟝⟞

"Are you happy, JeNelle?" Kenneth asked, as they danced.

"Who?"

"Oh, I mean, are you happy, Mrs. Alexander?"

"Say it again, Kenneth. I love the sound of that."

"I love you, Mrs. Alexander."

JeNelle beamed. "I love you, Mr. Alexander."

Harvey and Canty Townsend danced toward the couple. "Well now that you two have settled the question of who you are and who loves who, may I dance with your wife, my former little daughter?" Harvey asked, jokingly.

"Only, if I can dance with my new mother-in-law," Kenneth added.

They exchanged partners.

"JeNelle, you look wonderful," Harvey beamed. "Are you happy?"

"Oh, yes, Daddy. I can't explain how I feel. There are no words to adequately describe it. I've never felt this way before so I can't compare it with anything. I didn't know that it was possible to feel like this."

"It can only get better, honey. Kenneth is a good man. He loves you. Treat him well—with respect, I mean. He'll always be there for you. He'll never let you down or disappoint you."

"You really believe that, don't you, Daddy?"

"Yes, I do. The man has substance, but you have to be there for him, too. He's got to know deep down inside that you love him, trust him, and respect him. He's your partner for life now. It's not the way it used to be in the old days. There are no roles to play anymore. It's okay now for a man to feel things, express them openly, and not fear that he'd be considered less than a man. It's also okay for a woman to take the lead sometimes and tell her man what she needs to be happy. He'll listen to you and you listen to him. Hear and feel what each of you is saying. That way nothing will ever be left unsaid."

JeNelle kissed her father's cheek and hugged him tightly.

"You'll always be my daddy though, won't you?"

"You'll have me always, JeNelle, but Kenneth is all that you'll ever need in your life."

"Kenneth, now you remember what I've told you. JeNelle is almost a virgin. You'll have to teach her a few things about how to love you the way a man needs to be loved."

"JeNelle and I will be fine. We'll make time to be together."

"And time to give me some grandbabies, too. None of this waiting-around-until-the-time is-right nonsense."

Kenneth laughed. "We'll see what we can do about filling your request."

"That's good! Now I promise that Harvey and I won't be interfering in-laws, but when the babies start coming, all bets are off! We intend to spoil them rotten. We're fixing up JeNelle's old room as a nursery so that we can take our grandbabies off your hands whenever you want. Now Sylvia and Bernard said that they're going to do the same thing. We're going to work out a schedule so that—"

Kenneth laughed and Canty blushed.

"Listen to me," she mused. "I've already got the babies born and sharing them with your parents. I don't know, Kenneth. I'm just so happy for you and my daughter. I just want everything in your lives to be perfect."

"We'll make it that way. We've got the main ingredients: love, trust and mutual respect."

"I know you do. My daughter is a very lucky woman to have found you and your family."

"We're both lucky. I imagine that if I had searched the universe I couldn't have found any more loving and giving parents than you and Harvey. I'm a very lucky man."

Canty kissed her new son-in-law on the cheek and hugged him tightly as they danced. He returned the kiss as they spun around the dance floor.

⚬—⟊⟊—⟊

JeNelle and Kenneth started up the back steps to change into their traveling clothes. JeNelle spotted the catering trucks lined up and men putting equipment in the trucks. She looked at Kenneth and he released her hand with a smile.

"Take all the time you need," he said, kissing her gently on the lips.

JeNelle went into the kitchen and saw Milo San Angelo orchestrating the packing of his equipment. The leftover food was being put into serving trays and Milo was telling the driver to take the food trays to the homeless shelter when the driver noticed her standing there and smiled broadly. Milo turned and a broad smile grew on his face.

"*Balisimo, bella, bella,*" he gushed, as he walked toward her, his hands outstretched. When he reached her, he kissed her knuckles. "You are beautiful, JeNelle, but you should not be in this kitchen. Something might stain your beautiful wedding gown." He led her out of the kitchen into an anteroom.

They sat together on velvet benches, as Milo beamed at her with tears in his eyes.

"You look like my Christiania. So beautiful."

"Christiania? Wasn't that Michel's, Antonio's, and Maria's mother?"

Milo wiped his tears. He looked away and sadness crossed his face, too.

"Yes, you look like her. She was a Madonna, so fragile...so—" He choked.

"Milo," JeNelle leaned in to comfort him. "I'm sorry. I remember. You told me about her."

"This is not for you today, *Bella*. Be happy, JeNelle. Have many babies."

JeNelle kissed Milo on the cheek and hugged him. "I'm pregnant, Milo," she whispered.

Milo's face lit up. He kissed the palms of her hands and cupped her face.

Milo walked JeNelle out to Kenneth. He placed her hand in his and smiled at them both.

"This is good," he said, smiling. "This is very good."

The last morsel of food had been eaten. The last toast of many had been made. The wedding cake had been cut, and distributed in neat little white boxes, saving the top tier for their first anniversary. The last congratulatory note had been read and Kenneth and JeNelle stood before the happy crowd, poised in their traveling clothes with the wedding bouquet and bride's garter in hand.

They said their final goodbyes and turned to toss the last mementoes over their heads to their friends. The eligible men stood waiting on one side of the room and the eligible women on the other. Up went the bouquet and arched high over Sara, Shirley, Vivian, Gloria, Janice, and other women. Hands were raised and bodies leaped.

The men readied themselves for the garter. Up it went. Grunts and groans could be heard from Alan, Bill, David, James, Chuck, Derrick, Tom, Donald, and other less limber souls.

The newlyweds made the traditional dash toward a waiting limousine amid a hail of birdseed, after kissing and hugging their parents and siblings goodbye.

Bernard and Harvey stood talking together as they waved goodbye.

"You know, Harvey, I don't think that we're going to have to wait too long to be grandparents," Bernard said.

"You know, Bernard, I was just thinking the same thing. That daughter of mine has a certain glow about her and it wasn't just her makeup either."

"Yep, Harvey, I've seen that same glow on my Silvy's face five times."

"I've only seen it on my Canty's face twice, but I remember it very well."

The two men laughed and embraced.

"Canty, we're all set. You and Harvey are going to come to the Fourth of July reunion in Goodwill," Sylvia said.

"We're looking forward to it, Sylvia. Harvey and I haven't been on a real vacation in years and neither one of us has ever been to South Carolina."

"You two plan on staying with us for at least two weeks. Between your sewing and my knitting we'll have a complete wardrobe ready for when our grandbaby is born."

"From the look of things, Sylvia, I think we'd better double that wardrobe. In addition to me and my sister, we've got a few more sets of twins in our family."

"I think you're right. We have some twins in our family, too. Bernard and his sister, Olivia, are twins and Olivia and her husband, Romello Dixon, have twin sons, Donald and James."

The two women laughed and hugged each other.

"Imagine those two children of ours thinking that they could hide the fact that JeNelle is pregnant from us," Canty mused.

"They're young. This is the first time for them. They probably just want to surprise us later."

"Me and Harvey will act real surprised when they decide to tell us."

"Bernard and I will try to be surprised, too, but Kenneth James knows us too well. He's always been an intuitive, insightful and attentive son. He may pick up on any subterfuge real easy. Plus my Aretha probably already told him the month, day, and time that our grandbabies are going to be born," Sylvia said, laughing.

"Mm mum, that Aretha is something else, Sylvia. She's an angel sent from heaven. She's got the wisdom of old spirits guiding her."

"Yes, I know. We're proud of all five of our children, but Aretha's going to be the one to watch."

⌖

"Cousin, I'm out of here," Donald Dixon said, as he and Benny embraced.

"You working?" Benny asked.

"Yeah, man. Just got enough time to see KJ jump the broom."

"When are we going to get together and just kick back?" Benny asked.

"Man, you're in retirement, I hear. It's not like the good old days when we used to party—hard! Looks like this Stacy Greene's got you on total lockdown!"

Benny smiled slightly.

"Oh, it's like that, is it?" Donald laughed.

"We'll see…if I ever find her."

"I heard the shout out. I'm working on it."

"Looks like you're working on my friend, Cecil, too."

"Hey, man, if I had known that you had a friend like Cecil Jordon in the neighborhood, I would have made time to visit you more often!"

"Don't be messin' around, starting something you won't finish, Cousin. Janice and Cecil are family. This ain't like playtime."

"All right, Benny. I hear you. James says that he's hanging out with you in San Diego for a few weeks. Maybe I can swing through for a couple of days before he leaves to go home. In the meantime, your mission is to make sure that Cecil Jordon doesn't fall for anyone else before I can get to there."

"Oh, it's like that, is it?"

Don smiled. "We'll see, Cousin."

The two men embraced again and Don started to leave the Atrium Manor, but not without saying a special goodbye to Cecil.

"So, Benny, what's the story on Donald Dixon?" Cecil asked, as they watched Don leave. "You never told me about him before."

"Yes, I did, Cecil. I'm always telling you and Janice about my family."

"You must have left the chapter on Don out."

Benny laughed. "With Don, there's more than what meets the eyes."

"He's not hard on the eyes, that's for sure. Doesn't talk about himself a lot though. He and James are twins, but they seem very different."

"Yeah, James Edward moved back home to Goodwill a long time ago. He worked for the Farm Industry in Chicago, after college, grad school and getting his doctorate, but he heard the Call of the South. Don, well, he heard the Call of the Wild," Benny mused.

"A real nature lover, huh?" Cecil asked, with tongue firmly planted in cheek.

Benny laughed. "You could put it that way. Let's just say that he taught me a lot about big game hunting."

Cecil smiled broadly. "Load and lock, huh?"

Benny nodded. "He invented the game."

Cecil grinned. "We'll see if I can perfect his game."

"Hey, you two," Chuck said as he approached Cecil and Benny, "let's finish our duties, help Joe and Sara make sure that the gifts get packed up in the storage unit out back, sent over to Kenneth's and JeNelle's place, and then find someplace to party."

"Sounds like a plan," Cecil said, happily. "I'll round up the crew."

Cecil left the two men standing together.

"I'll help get these gifts packed up, but then I'm spending my time with Ms. Whitney tonight."

"Thought you might say that, Benny. I've already talked with Aretha. She's got Whitney Ivy and she's already taken her back to the hotel. No excuses. You're partying tonight, partner!"

Benny laughed. "Okay, Chuck. You can be my date tonight. Where are Vivian and Derrick? Have they already left for their mystery flight?"

"Uh, yeah, they had a plane to catch."

"Does my little sister know that you're carrying around this big torch for—"

"Let's just get going, man," Chuck interrupted. "I feel a party coming on."

"All right, Chuck, I'm with you," Benny said, as they left the Atrium Manor.

⚷

The limo pulled into a restricted area of the airport and into a General Aviation hanger. A Cessna sat waiting, as the chauffeur opened the door.

"Kenneth, is this what I think it is?"

"Well, Mrs. Alexander, if you think that it's an airplane, you're right. It's all loaded and ready for our departure."

"Where's the pilot and where are we going?"

"I'm the pilot and you'll see where we're going when we get there. All aboard, Mrs. Alexander," Kenneth said, with a smug smile.

JeNelle climbed aboard and Kenneth strapped her in. She looked at him quizzically, as he started the engines and the ground crew pulled the jet out of the hanger. She was awed by his mastery of the aircraft, as he contacted the Santa Barbara tower and prepared to line up for takeoff. He checked each procedure in detail and lifted the plane off the runway into the setting sun out over the deep blue Pacific Ocean below.

Chapter 10

A jazz band was warming up on the terrace of the El Encanto when the wedding group arrived, and was immediately seated. The terrace seating overlooked the City of Santa Barbara whose lights twinkled like so many diamonds strewn across a dark velvet background. The combo began to play as the waiter took drink orders. Bill Chandler, James Dixon, and Joe Grayson were the first to spring to their feet with Cecil Jordon, Janice Atterly, and Sara McDougal. Bernard and Sylvia Alexander and Harvey and Canty Towson followed close behind.

Alan Lightfoot and Melissa Charles helped to sort out the drink order when it arrived, aided by Benny Alexander and Chuck Montgomery. Gregory Alexander toured the crowded terrace, scoping out the bevy of beauties assembled for an evening's entertainment. Gloria Towson finally asked Alan Lightfoot to dance while Tom Jenkins danced with Melissa Charles. David Carter and Anna Menendez-Gaza sat watching their friends on the dance floor and enjoying the warm, summer night air.

"You dance very well," Bill said to Cecil, as they swayed slowly to the music.

"So do you, Bill. It seems that you do a lot of things well."

"Oh, for example?"

"High-fashion model, movie actor, business man, and attorney for starters. I'd say that you're multi-talented."

Bill smiled. "Careful, Cecil, you're going to make my head swell. Compliments like those from a beautiful woman—"

"Are very sincerely meant," Cecil said, with a knowing smile.

"Cecil, are you making a pass at me, I hope?"

"I hadn't thought about it, but would you be receptive if I were?"

"Very receptive, but I'm not sure if you know that I'm not heterosexual."

"I'm glad to hear you say that."

Bill craned his head and grinned at Cecil looking for more of an explanation for her comment. Cecil noticed and smiled at him.

"That's a compliment, Bill. I appreciate a man who can be honest and forthcoming with someone he barely knows about an issue as personal as his sexuality. Those qualities are so very rare in so many men that I meet. Too many men on the down low."

"I see. It's refreshing to meet anyone who can appreciate my need to have a sexual option. I think that we are going to be good friends—at a minimum." Bill smiled.

"And at a maximum?"

"Something incredibly special." He grinned.

⚬

"Janice, I've worked out an arrangement with Benny to stay at his place, but unfortunately he's going to be working almost every day," James Dixon said.

"That's wonderful."

"It is?"

"Yes, but do you mind if I monopolize your time while Benny is away?"

"No, certainly not. I'm looking forward to it, but are you sure that it's not going to be inconvenient?"

"I'm sure, but even if it were, I'd work it out."

James smiled. "Careful, Janice, I could get to like this western hospitality a great deal."

"I hope so, James. I truly hope so, but..."

"But what?"

"I need to ask you a question."

"Anything. What's the question?"

"Are you married?"

James looked at her questioningly. "No, Janice, I'm not married."

"Are you sure?"

"I think that I would have noticed if I were."

"Do you have children?"

James stopped dancing and looked at Janice, perplexed. "I just said that I'm not married and I don't make babies with just anyone, Janice. I'm single and I have no children. I'm unattached to anyone, emotionally except my family. I'm heterosexual, HIV negative, gainfully employed and over thirty years old. I did my undergrad degree in Animal Husbandry at the University of Chicago, my graduate degree at the University of Texas and my doctorate at the Institute of Genetics and Animal Breeding at the Polish Academy of Science. I lecture at the University of South Carolina, part time, and I own a 140-acre hydroponics family farm in Goodwill, Summer County, South Carolina, that's been in my family for decades. I raise horses, cows, pigs, chickens and assorted other farm animals, cotton, peas, beans, tomatoes, cucumber, lettuce, corn, greens of all varieties, and fruit, including apples, pears, peaches, grapes, cherries, oranges, and strawberries. I have my own home, which is paid for, two vehicles, one of which is a truck, and I have a modest bank account. I don't owe any money or other debts to anyone. I enjoy doing a lot of things, including all outdoor sports. I'm not a bad poker player, I can hold my own at backgammon, but I'm better at chess and checkers. I don't smoke, chew tobacco, do drugs or heavy alcohol, or chase women. Maybe I should say that I haven't made a practice of chasing women— until I met you. Now, whatever else you need to know you can ask me."

"As I was saying, western hospitality includes breakfast, lunch, dinner, and late night suppers, James." Janice smiled as they resumed their dancing.

⚓

"So when are you and Alan leaving, Melissa?"

"Early in the morning, Tom. Alan says that it's about a sixteen-hour drive from here to where his family lives on the Navajo Reservation in New Mexico. We'll stop somewhere overnight and then get to the reservation late the following day."

"Sounds like you two have it all worked out."

"The trip part, yes. I just hope that his family likes me."

"What's not to like?"

"I hope that his family agrees with you. That's very important to me."

⚯

"So, you say you're from South Carolina?"

"Yes, a little town called Goodwill in Summer County."

"Do you get to California often?"

"No, I'm out here for my brother's wedding."

"You're Kenneth Alexander's brother?"

"Yes, Gregory Clayton Alexander. How did you know that?"

"It's been in all the newspapers. The wedding was today, wasn't it?"

"Yes, you're very well informed."

"I tend to pay attention when one of the most eligible bachelors in California gets married. Lucky woman, your new sister-in-law."

"They both are, but, uh I rather talk about you."

"What do you want to know?"

"Everything."

"You're pretty smooth, you know?"

"And you're very pretty, you know?"

"Is this some of that South Carolina charm?"

"I don't know. Is it working?"

"What are you doing later?"

"Sleeping alone, I suppose."

"Not if you keep working that South Carolina charm on me you're not."

⚯

"Our son, Gregory, is at it again, Sylvia."

"You mean *still*, don't you, Bernard? It's that Alexander charm. Drives women wild."

"I guess maybe I need to have a little talk with him."

"Not tonight, I hope."

"Why not tonight?"

"I have plans for you tonight."

"Oh?"

"I'm feeling a little wild myself. After thirty-six years of marriage and five children, you still have a lot of charm and sex appeal, you're my best friend, and you're still the best dancer I know."

"That's because I've had you in my arms for more than thirty-six years. It doesn't get any better than this. I love you, Sylvia Benson Alexander."

"I love you, too, Bernard Thomas Alexander."

The party lasted well past 2:00 A.M. before they bid each other goodnight and went their separate ways in the McCoy Suites Hotel lobby.

Chuck went into the bar to have another beer. Benny noticed and followed him. Chuck didn't notice that Benny had followed him until Benny sat down across from him in the booth and passed another beer to him.

"Hey, partner. Thought you'd be headed to bed," Chuck said.

"Yeah, I'm going. Thought I'd sit a while though. You mind?"

"Naw, glad to have your company. It's been a long time."

"Yeah, we were just kids when we first met back at the Boston Shootout," Benny said, smiling. "That was a lifetime ago."

"Don't remind me. I still owe you for bowing me in my face." Chuck laughed.

"You got even with me last year when you brought Vivian home for Thanksgiving." Benny laughed, as he took a swig of beer straight from the bottle.

"Yeah, I did, didn't I?" Chuck grinned.

"Funny how things work out."

"We still talking about basketball?"

Benny smiled, sat back against the wall, and rested his long legs across the seat. "What do you think?"

"You know, don't you?"

"Yep. Sure do."

"It's for the best."

"What are you going to do now?"

"Live one day at a time."

"I'll tell you, Chuck, I wish that there were two identical Vivians. I'd be in your corner all the way. I know that she values your friendship. She loves you—she just loves Derrick a little more. You're still marketable, though." He laughed. "There are other women."

"Ha! Look who's talking," Chuck chided. "Women wouldn't kick you outta bed either, but you've taken yourself off the market. I remember how you had all the ladies back in Boston just like Gregory does now. Seems all week they've been trying to book you."

"I had your leftovers," Benny said, grinning, "and if anyone was getting booked this week it was you, not me."

Chuck laughed, his mood suddenly turning more reflective. "But it isn't anything like having the real thing, now is it?"

"You're not just talking about sex?"

"Never was about sex. I never laid a hand on your sister, but man, there have been times—" Chuck cut off his thought.

"Yeah, I know. There were times when I'd just look at Stacy without touching her and get a rush. My parents told me that I was in love with her, but I believed that her career meant more to her than I did. I guess you're right. There's nothing like the real thing. When an independent woman has a mission, you have to let go and hope that someday she'll come back to you."

"She'll be back. You just wait."

"I have no choice in the matter. It's just that I dream about her all the time. I go over every conversation in my head from the moment that we met. That's the tough part. Sometimes I wake up and expect to find her there beside me. Man! Sometimes it's pure hell!"

"Wherever she is, maybe she's having the same dreams. Thinking about you. At least you have that. Dreams are the windows of the past and open doors to the future."

A recurring dream is as hard to forget as an old friend. It comes into one's mind vividly without warning and you relive old warm memories together. Beautiful, Technicolor memories with great definition, shape, and form. Real people and real places. Shadows move in the background. Voices come from nowhere and smells recall days gone by. A sound. A whisper. Softness. Darkness, then light. A touch. A feel. Something moving close. A loud voice. Pentagon. A command. You wake.

"Incoming!"

"What? Uh, who? Would you repeat your orders, Sir?"

"At ease, Lieutenant. Take a load off."

"Yes, Sir. Thank you, Sir."

"Coffee?"

"Uh, yes, Sir. Thank you, Sir."

"So what are you doing here so late, Lieutenant?"

Officer. Captain. Handsome. Tall. Built. Brown eyes. Peanut-brown complexion. Confident. Interested.

Darkness, then light. Moving in and out. Ocean. Blue. A face. The face. Moans in the darkness. Joy. Lust. Ecstasy.

"I'm sorry that I'm late, Captain. I hope that you haven't been waiting long."

"No, Lieutenant, not long. Looks like you're catching a little flak from the Navy for having lunch with the enemy."

"They'll just have to cope. I decide who I will or won't have lunch with."

"I'm glad that you decided that it would be me. I'd hate to be in those other guys' shoes, being turned down by a beautiful and sensuous woman like you."

"Captain, I really don't have the time or the inclination to sit and play games with you. I've got about thirty minutes to eat and then I've got to get back to the Pentagon. So let's cut to the chase. Why did you want to see me today?"

"I think that you're a very attractive woman and—"

"You thought that I'd be a quick lay—another notch in your belt, huh, Captain?"

"Well, we're both adults, free, single and disengaged—"

"You're a handsome man. Built like a Greek god. Looks like you probably know your way around a bedroom, too. You're probably even a damn good lay, but guys like you are a dime a dozen in the Navy. I'm not looking for a bed warmer. My electric blanket works just fine. So if that's why we're here, you can scrub this mission, Fly Boy. You just crashed and burned. It's been nice talking with you, but I have to go."

"Go? You just got here, Lieutenant. Doesn't the Navy give their people time for a decent lunch?"

"Sure, but there's a seminar on new sonar equipment that I want to sit in on and it starts in about twenty minutes."

"You mean that you'd rather be sitting in a seminar than having lunch with me?"

"Sorry, Captain. First things first."

Dreaming. Darkness, then light. Library.

"Captain, what are you doing here?"

"Looking for you, Lieutenant. You're a hard person to catch up with. Didn't you get my messages or my flowers?"

"Yes, Captain, I got them."

"Then why didn't you call?"

"I really don't have time to spend... Look, you're a nice man, but..."

"But what?"

"I'm not interested."

"Whoa, I could begin to take this personally."

"Don't, Captain. It's business, not personal. You're the type of man who a woman could get real personal with—you're dangerous. I'm sure that you're not lacking for female companionship. Any woman in her right mind, I'm sure, would jump at the chance to spend time with you."

"You're not just any woman. I'd like to get to know you better. More importantly, I'd like for you to get to know me better."

"Why?"

"'Why'? What do you mean 'Why'?"

"Captain, I didn't stutter. Why do you want to get to know me better? And don't give me any of the usual lines. Believe me, I've heard them all."

"Options."

"All right, Captain, meet me at the Japanese Embassy at ten hundred. Wear your dress uniform and please be prompt. I've got to go now, but I'll see you."

Dreaming. Darkness, then light. Embassy.

"Are you having a good time, Captain? Where is the woman I introduced you to, Paulette Bates?"

"No, I don't know, and I don't care."

"What?"

"Lieutenant, I thought that we, you and I, were going to spend some quality time together, getting to know each other. I don't think that it's happening, do you? At least, not with five hundred other people around. So you have three options."

"Options?"

"Yes, Lieutenant, options."

"All right, Captain, what are my options?"

"You can have a lover, a friend or whatever is behind curtain number three."

"I'll take whatever is behind curtain number three."

"Good, then get your coat, say goodnight, Gracie, and let's get out of here now."

"But what's behind curtain number three?"

"I'll tell you later."

Dreaming. Darkness, then light. Lieutenant Commander Bruce Payton, USN Amphibious Base. A sailboat. Mission Bay Islands. Picnic. Scuba diving. Fishing. San Diego.

"Lieutenant, it seems that every time I see you there's a crowd of people around or you're with someone else. Can we find some time—"

"Oh no, Captain, I've seen you operate and your reputation...well, let's just say that around the San Diego area you're legendary."

"But, Lieutenant, you haven't taken advantage of all of your options yet."

"What options?"

"A lover, a friend or whatever is behind curtain number three."

"Didn't I select curtain number three before when we were in DC last year?"

"Yes, so that leaves you with two options to choose from."

"A lover or a friend?"

"Yes, it's your choice, Lieutenant."

"A friend."

Dreaming. Darkness, then light. Clubs. Parties. Military people. Dancing. Cruise. Birthday party. 0300. Condo. Innocent.

"Are you sure that this is not an imposition? I can take a cab back to base and have someone from the motor pool pick up the car for me later."

"It's late. We've been partying all night. You really put one over on me. I didn't have a clue. This is my way of saying thank you to one of my good friends for giving me a surprise birthday party."

"Okay, but if any of those women who were after you tonight come up here to your condo to give you a special present, I'm going over the terrace. They'll never tear me apart, trying to get to you."

"Maybe you didn't notice, Lieutenant, but there was only one person who had my full attention tonight."

"I noticed, Captain, but I told you long ago that I'm not looking to fall in love. You're the dangerous type, remember? The type of man who women go insane for and fall head-over-heels in love with. Insanity does not run in my family, and I'm not putting myself in harm's way."

"We've been seeing each other for some time now. I know that you're not interested in falling in love. You've made that abundantly clear, but I have to tell you the truth, I want more than just a platonic relationship with you. I have for some time. That string that you call a bikini would make a blind man see! Make the Pope give up religion! Wake up the dead and it makes me... Well, I think that you get the picture."

"I'll be truthful with you, too. I've spent more than a few nights wondering what all the women on base are talking about. When we went dancing that night on the dinner cruise, I began to feel something, and it wasn't the motion of the ocean!"

"So, why don't we—"

"Hold on, Fly Boy, I think that we've got a good relationship going. We've become good friends and I don't want to ruin that."

"I think that taking this friendship to another level can only make it better. I want to be with you, not just because you're the most sensual woman I know, but because I care about you. I respect what you're doing and I admire you and what you've accomplished. You're a very special lady, and the type of woman that I would want to take home to meet my family, if we were to get to that point. However, I know that you're not ready for that now and neither am I. I understand and respect your independence. I know that your career goals are the most important part of your life now. I would not want to interfere with that. If we take this relationship to the next level, it will be on any terms that you want. With or without the sex. I don't want to lose what we have either."

Dreaming. Darkness, then light. Colors. Bright sparkling colors. Roller coaster. Night. Relationship.

'There are places in a woman's soul that not just any man can reach; no matter how much love and attention he's willing and able to give. Men are no different. Reaching below the surface into the very soul is a scary proposition. It's not for the faint-hearted. You have to be ready and able to deal well with what you find there.'

"So now, is there any member of your family you still have to call or can we pick up where we left off?

"I still haven't talked with my sister, but what was that you were saying about 'picking up where we left off'?"

"That was then, Captain. You desert me for Christmas and fly off to San Francisco to be with your family. Okay, I say. He didn't ask me to go with him. It's his family and we've only known each other for eleven months. I can cope with that. Then you blow into town, call me up, at who knows what time of the night, and ask me to come over, and I come. Then I get here and we spend half the night talking about your family. It's now 0515, I haven't had any sleep, and I have formation at 0600. You've been on the telephone with one person or the other for over an hour."

"Well, how did you like the other half of the night?"

"I would have liked it a lot better if, after all of this time that you've been away, I could have at least gotten a whole night with you."

"Why, Lieutenant, are you trying to tell me, in your own sweet way, how much you missed me?"

"No, Captain, I didn't miss you one little bit."

"I'll make it all up to you. You can have me all night. I'll even cook, and maybe we can plan something for New Year's Eve together. How does that sound?"

"Sorry, Captain, you're too late to ask me out for New Year's Eve. I'm going out with this Marine from Camp Pendleton, Ted Peterson, who wants to put me in first place on his agenda,"

"Baby, come here and let's talk about this."

"Talk about what?"

"Let's talk about your wanting to be put 'in first place'. Isn't that what you said?"

"No. I said that I'm going out with someone who wants to put me in first place. I didn't say that it had to be you."

"Oh. Okay. Then, if I understand you correctly, you don't want me to put you in 'first place' in my life? Did I get it right that time?"

"I didn't say that either. Can't we simply drop this subject? I have to finish my shower. I've got to be out of here like yesterday."

"There's clearly something on your mind, so let me explain something to you. I have a wonderful family and I love them all very much, but I'm not putting them before my relationship with you. I had no idea that you wanted to meet my family. You hadn't said anything about this before. In fact, you've made it abundantly clear that you did *not* want to get too entangled. 'Keeping it loose,' you said. When I take someone home to meet my family, it's because I've made a commitment. There is nothing 'loose' about it. Do you think that we are at that place in our relationship to be talking about commitment? Are you ready to put me in 'first place' in your life?"

"I don't know where we are in this relationship, but one of the things that I really love about you is the fact that you do care so deeply for your family. I don't have much of a family to speak of, so I enjoy listening to you talk about your mother and father, and sisters and brothers. You should see yourself. You actually light up when you talk about them. Someday I want someone to light up like that when he talks about me, but for now, I like our relationship just like it is. It's probably just the holidays or being alone. Maybe it's PMS. Who knows! I do know that I don't want to just feel like I'm only your lover and not your friend. That I'm only one of your bed partners, whenever the mood hits you. That's not where we started from. We've both got our careers ahead of us. You're Air Force and I'm Navy. There are no strings attached to this relationship—whatever it is—but I resent not being considered your friend. Do you understand what I am trying to say to you?"

"No, but go back to that first part again."

"What first part?"

"The part about one of the things you 'love' about me."

"Sorry, Fly Boy. That just meant that you're special to me in that way."

"What way, Lieutenant?"

"You know what I mean. A special friend."

"So does that mean that you don't love me, or does that mean that you are ready to take this relationship to another level and meet my family?"

"Captain, permission to be dismissed, Sir."

"Permission denied, Lieutenant. At ease."

"Lower your flaps, Fly Boy, and find another runway to land on. This one is going out of service."

"We'll pick this up again, you know, Lieutenant. Say about 8:00 P.M. tonight in my quarters? Full dressed uniforms will not be required, and, Lieutenant, I thought that we were friends—good friends—not just lovers. Nevertheless, message received loud and clear."

Dreaming. Darkness, then light. Goodbye. Warm water rushing. Relationship. Shots. Falling in love. STOP!

"Have I done something wrong?"

"No, of course not."

"Then what gives?"

"I don't understand."

"Why haven't I seen you?"

"I've been working. You know that!"

"That didn't seem to stop you from seeing Bruce Payton, I hear."

"Only occasionally. How have things been with you?"

"You're changing the subject, why?"

"I think that—"

"I'm getting too close to the truth—"

"No, too involved."

"You know that I'm involved, Lieutenant. You won't let me fall in love with you. Now you won't let me make love to you either. Why?"

"We don't need to be in love. There's no reason to do that. Why can't we just go back to being friends?"

"It's too late for that now. You only have one option left, Lieutenant."

Dreaming. Darkness, then light. Moving. Options. Life. Career. Aircraft carrier. Admiral. Special courses. Working long. Active duty. Sleep. Stay awake! Falling. Uniform. Deserted. Command! Leap.

"Heads up, Lieutenant! Incoming!"

"Excuse me, Sir! Would you repeat your orders, Sir?"

"At ease, Lieutenant. Take a load off."

"Yes, Sir! Thank you, Sir!"

"So isn't this better?"

"Better? Better than what?"

"Isn't making love like this better than not making love?"

"You mean together?"

"Of course, together."

"You don't seem to have any trouble finding sexual partners, Captain."

"Neither do you, Lieutenant."

"So what's your point?"

"Aren't we better together than we are when we're sleeping with other people?"

"I haven't got a clue. I haven't surveyed the San Diego Standard Metropolitan Area to determine what your rating is, but the women at North Island Naval, Camp Pendleton Marine, and March Air Force base give you high marks."

"You could change that whenever you want to."

"What, and disappoint the women of San Diego city and county? Oh no, not me."

Dreaming. Darkness, then light. Advanced courses. Credentials. Challenge. Responsibility. Authority. Experience. Commission. Promotion. Pentagon. Admiral Gordon. Qualified. Influence. Aspirations. Professionalism. Impressive. Articulate. Expectations. Ready. Discoveries. An explorer.

"You've been studying all day. Let's take a break."

"I've got a ton of work to do."

"I know, but you've been at it for two weeks now."

"Okay, a short break. Why don't we go swimming?"

"That's not what I had in mind."

"I thought that we agreed to back up a little?"

"You agreed, I didn't."

"Aren't you seeing someone? Who was this exciting new woman that you were telling me about?"

"JeNelle Towson?"

"Yes, that's the one. Why don't you call her or maybe go and visit her. Cardiss was asking about you the other day. So was Regina. Oh, and Mavis left a message on your answering machine. She wants you to call her. Now, you and Mavis seemed to have been hitting it off real well a few months ago."

"That was then. This is now."

"What does that mean?"

"You know exactly what it means, Lieutenant. I don't want to be with anyone else. I'm right where I want to be."

"Do you want to go swimming or not?"

"Why do you choose to change the subject when I start talking about us?"

"Because we have an agreement."

"No falling in love."

"That's right. Now, call up that new friend of yours and do something special with her."

Dreaming. Darkness, then light. Easy. Approach. Embraced. Stars and Stripes. Mission. Agenda. Friendship. Relationship. Independence. Camp Pendleton. North Island Naval Air Station. March Air Force Base. Exchange duty. Sleeping together.

"I can't get enough of you."

"I'm here with you now."

"Yes and in a few hours you're going to be gone on another mission. How long this time, Lieutenant?"

"Same as you. Four to six weeks."

"I hear that you've been seeing Ted Peterson again."

"Occasionally. We've been working closely together."

"He must be getting to be someone who's very important to you."

"No more than anyone else."

"Including me?"

"We're going to have this discussion again? I thought that this was a done deal."

"Not when I hold you like this. Not when we make love."

"Have sex."

"You have sex if you want to, but I'm making love."

"How are things going with JeNelle?"

"They're going."

"That's great isn't it?"

"Look, couldn't we just concentrate on us for a change? I don't get to see you that often anymore. I don't want to think about or talk about anyone else when we're together."

"Why the sudden change? We always talk about everything and everyone."

"I'm ready to take this relationship to another level"

"*Whoa!* I thought that we agreed to be lovers and to leave it at that?"

"You've exhausted all of your options, Lieutenant. It's time to move on to some new challenges for us."

"I've got a career that's taking off and so do you. Let's leave this relationship where it is for the time being."

Uncomplicated. Serious. Shower. Sounds. Plans. Sound. Expected. New Year's Eve. Mission. Roses. Commitments. JeNelle Towson. Love. Family. Friendship. Unfinished business. Unguarded moment. RUSH! Impression. Dreaming. Darkness, then light.

"Surprise!"

"What are you doing here? I thought that you were still at sea."

"I've been calling you for days. The question is where have you been?"

"Restricted to base, but how did you get in without being announced?"

"The Sin Sisters. They checked with Fred to make sure that you weren't entertaining any guests. He told them that as far as he knew, you were alone and that you told him that you weren't expecting anyone tonight. The Sin Sisters told me what they did to you in the elevator and in the back seat of a car. That was terrible. They also told me that you claimed that your mother sent you *MY ROSES!* Are you angry with me for standing you up? You know that I had no control over that.

"I wasn't jumping with joy when I got your message. We have some unfinished business, remember, but I did understand."

"Our friends told me that you had two women with you when you left the club. You really do have a hell of an appetite. Two women in one night."

"That was not what it seemed."

"Do I look intimidated to you? I told you to keep it warm for me and it feels like you followed my orders, Captain."

"Aren't we going to finish our conversation? I think that we were about to discuss something important."

"Yes, I think that we should, but talking is the last thing on my mind right now, Captain, and it feels like it's the last thing on your mind, too. So let's talk in the morning, unless you have other plans that I don't know about tonight."

"Plans? Plans? I can't think when you're this close to me. Whatever plans I may have had, I've already forgotten about them."

"This must be JeNelle."

"Why did you say that?"

"Well, Fly Boy, you called her name a few times last night. You've never done that before and you've never had a picture of anyone, except your family, displayed in frames. You do the math."

"I'm sorry. I didn't mean to call . . . I mean, I didn't realize that I was saying..."

"Stop stuttering. Last night and this morning you took me—or JeNelle—to someplace I've never been before. It was a hell of a rush!"

"You're not offended by what I've done?"

"I'm not thrilled that you were fantasizing about another woman while you were having sex with me, but I have to admit, I've done the same thing from time to time myself. It happens. Sometimes a woman's got to do what a woman's got to do to get a rush."

"Even with me you've fantasized about another man?"

"Now who's getting offended? I've never lied to you; I'm not going to start now. Yes, even when I've been with you."

"Why don't you just pour a little more salt into that open wound or twist the knife a little deeper, why don't you?"

"I think that we've had a totally open and honest relationship. The most open relationship that I've ever had with anyone. Neither of us has any illusions about the other nor have we hidden the fact that we see other people. That's what I was trying to explain to you before I left. We've been sexually active a lot lately, and I do enjoy it and you, but I don't want this to get in the way of our friendship. From my perspective, we're friends with benefits. I can't even begin to see beyond that point and I don't necessarily want to."

"Why is it that all of a sudden women just want to be my friend?"

"Sounds like you haven't made it with JeNelle yet. Stop feeling so insecure. It's not your style. Half the women on military bases in this area are trying to get into your bed, including the married ones! Your reputation is legendary and your technique is lethal."

"Only *'half'* the women on base?"

"See, that's better. Now that's the man that we all know and love, but if you're really serious about this JeNelle person, we should go back to being platonic friends again. You may need to know where you stand with her. If she's been able to withstand your many charms, Fly Boy, you may really have your work cut out for you."

"JeNelle doesn't seem to want to take me seriously. I was a real jerk when we met a couple of weeks ago. I was sure that I had blown it with her."

"Look, you're the closest that I've ever come to calling someone my best friend, so let me let you in on a little secret about women."

"What's that?"

"Be yourself. Every woman that I know would kill to find an honest man like you. Someone who's not trying to run games on them all the time. Professing undying love one minute and then sneaking around knocking boots with someone else the next minute behind her back. If you can't do the time, baby, don't do the crime. If you can't give a commitment, don't ask for one."

"Commitment! I can't get JeNelle past the friendship stage. I called her 'baby' and she shot me down cold."

"Hang in there. Remember, I told you that you're the dangerous type. Don't rush her. You said that it's only been a couple of weeks."

"Well, what do you suggest I do in the meantime?"

"With your nature even cold showers aren't going to work for long. I think that you're going to have to evaluate what it is that you want from JeNelle. Is it live or is it Memorex? Is what you're feeling love or is it lust? Is it just sex, sex and commitment, marriage, what? Then you'll have to find out what she wants. If you both want the same thing, then work from there. The rough part is finding out what you both want or don't want. Getting there is the easy part if you both want the same things."

"That may be difficult with JeNelle. She doesn't give you much to go on. She doesn't talk about herself. She'll talk about her business or her family, but she holds back about her personal life. There seems to be so much there that she's not willing to reveal.

"My dear friend, you may have lucked up on a nut that you can't crack, metaphorically speaking, that is. Pun intended. There are places in a woman's soul that not just any man can reach; no matter how much love and attention he's willing and able to give. Men are no different. Reaching below the surface into the very soul is a scary proposition. It's not for the faint-hearted. You have to be ready and able to deal well with what you find there.

"And what about us?"

"We are as we have been: very good friends. Your traffic pattern is full."

"I don't want to lose what we have and I'm not just talking about what we do in bed."

"I know what you mean. You're my best friend. We won't lose that."

"Is that as far as we can go, best friends?"

"Fly Boy, you're pushing the envelope already."

Dreaming. Darkness, then light. Frustrated. Uninhibited. Pleasure. Sailing. Lieutenant Commander. Teaching. Condoms. Country boy. Attractive. Good. Sleep.

"Now what's so urgent? You sounded very upset on the telephone."

"I'm pregnant."

"Are you sure?"

"Yes, the damn rabbit died twice."

"How did this happen? We always use condoms and you're on the pill."

"We didn't use condoms the last time we were together, remember? I shipped out in a hurry for that three-day tour of duty and I forgot my pills. That's the only time that it could have happened. I told you then that you took me to a place I had never been before! And now I have a big problem."

"When did you find out?"

"Shortly after you left on maneuvers. I had to ship out the next day."

"That was four or five weeks ago. Why didn't you get in touch with me? You didn't have to go through this all this time alone."

"I tried. I called and your brother said that you were already gone. Then I tried to reach you on CommNet, but they would only permit emergency calls to go through. Even JC Baker wouldn't get a message to you. He said that he didn't want you distracted unless it was a matter of life or death. I wouldn't tell him why I needed to talk to you and he told me that your team was in the number one position and that you were in line for highest honors. I gave up trying. I know what your career and your team mean to you. Colonel Baker was right. You didn't need to be distracted. And this is a hell of a distraction."

"The fact that we're going to have a baby is a new feeling for me to digest, but I certainly would have wanted to know about it as soon as possible."

"I said I'm pregnant. I didn't say anything about having a baby."

Dreaming. Darkness, then light. Morning. Doorbell. Clock. Bed. Silk. Seductive voices. Bikinis. Jacket. Knot. Hands. Swim. Relief. Mission. Early. Morning. Position. Relationship. Unique. Sister. Shipmates. Sonar. Rumors. Love. Competent. Proud. Friend. Love. Commitment. Black Adonis. The one. Exclusive. Relationship. Mother. Father. Sister. Brother. Voice.

"Well, here it is. This is where I grew up. Thank God it never changes."

"I don't know how or why I let you talk me into coming here. What am I going to say to your family?"

"Try hello. They'll take it from there."

"I was very uncomfortable about coming here, but your son is very persuasive. I feel like I have to tell you the truth. I wanted to have an abortion, but he wouldn't hear of it."

"Unfortunately, you two don't know you're in love yet. I hope that someday you will both realize it so that you can give this baby inside of you a loving home."

"No, we aren't in love. We are just good friends who had an unguarded moment, but neither one of us is in love with the other one and we're not likely to be. I'm not ready to be a wife or a mother the way that you are. So we are not going to marry. I believe that your son is ready to be a father, so I am going to have his baby for him. I can't raise this baby, but I'm not going to deny him the right to raise it."

"Mark my words, you two are in love, but until you two figure that out, this baby will get all the love that we can all give it."

Dreaming. Darkness, then light. Backyard. Farm. Forest. Moss. White fog. Trees. Sunrise.

"Well, good morning, Sunshine. What's got you looking so radiant this early in the morning?"

"Thank you for forcing me to come here. It's a wonderful place. I see why you love it and cherish your family so much."

"Yeah, but is that why you look so radiant this morning? Didn't last night add a little gleam to all this glitter?"

"Of course, it did. It must be this good, clean, fresh country air. You were even more spectacular than usual. Even your mother and sister thought that you were in good voice."

"Oh, they did, did they?"

"Yes, and your mother sent me in here to get you to rise and shine for breakfast."

"If you keep lying on top of me like that, something's going to rise all right. I love my mother's cooking, but breakfast may have to wait a while."

"Oh, no you don't, Fly Boy. You brought me here and I'm not going to spend all of my time in bed having sex with you no matter how good it is. So fall in, Captain."

"I'll let you go for now, but we country boys go to bed early and go to sleep late. So, I'm giving you fair warning, we're going to bed early tonight."

Dreaming. Darkness, then light. Southern breakfast. Incoming!

"Fair to middlin', I think. And look at your lovely wife. My name is Caroline Ann Johnson-Plimpton. I want to tell you that you're a lucky lady to have landed this man. Just look at those broad shoulders and that big chest of his and that narrow waist. Baby's got back, too. Let me look at your hands, boy. Mmmm, I never got that far with him, but I'll bet that he's a good husband. Those big hands really tell the story about the rest of the package—you must be carrying some heavy luggage.

Dreaming. Darkness, then light. Piano. Applause. "Do You Know?" Mission. Assignment. Rushes! Fly. Sail. Quiet. Smile.

"So why are you still seeing other people?"

"You're the dangerous type—he type of man that women fall head over heels in love with and go crazy over. Let's keep it like this. Loose. No strings. No bonds. Just good friends."

"I could get real serious about you."

"I know. I get a rush whenever we're together, too."

"We've got it going on all right, but why don't you see us together?"

"A woman's got to do what a woman's got to do."

Dreaming. Darkness, then light. Rare. Speak. Decide! Promise. Fun. Sunday social. Relatives. Children. White shirts. Gloves. Simple. Joyous. Goodwill. Family. Neon. Intimate. Commitment. LIFE. Happy. Daughter. Magic. Family.

"We have a beautiful daughter!"

"You have a beautiful daughter."

"No, I said what I meant and I meant what I said. *We* have a beautiful daughter."

"Are you forgetting our agreement?"

"I thought that you would have changed your mind by now."

"I told you that I wouldn't and I haven't. Nothing has changed."

"Then you can tell me that you don't love me?"

"What's that got to do with anything?"

"You're avoiding my question."

"I'm tired and sleepy. Having your baby has worn me out."

"Rest now, but we're going to talk about this again, you know, Lieutenant."

Dreaming. Darkness, then light. Pain. Tears. Heartache. Airport. Fly. Map. Plan. Route. Detours.

"To Whitney's father and my best friend—

Only you can be there now to hold Whitney when she cries as you have held me, to feed her when she's hungry, and to teach her in the ways that you learned as a child. She is the most precious gift that I can give to you, my dear friend. I know that you and your family will love and cherish her. Teach her to be an explorer just like her dad and, most importantly, how to love family. I thank you for sharing your family with me. I will never forget them and you."

Dreaming. Darkness, then light. Career. Challenge.

"This assignment is going to be physically, emotionally, and mentally grueling. Are you sure that this is what you want to do, Lieutenant?"

"Yes, Admiral."

"Are you sufficiently recovered from your pregnancy?"

"Yes, Sir, I am."

"You understand, that this assignment means complete and total isolation from everything and everyone you love, perhaps for years?"

"I understand."

"I hope that you've thought this through carefully because once you enter the program, there is no return. Every day you're going to be putting your life on the line. This is experimental, but it is a matter of national security. No one will be able to find you."

"I am fully aware of that."

"Lieutenant, I know that this is outside...well...just let me say it. A young Air Force captain has been trying to find you. I assume that he's your baby's father, but...well, he's got some well-positioned people in the government trying to track you down. You must be very important to him. We've been able to stonewall his attempts to locate you. Shouldn't you reconsider your decision?"

"What I'm about to do goes far beyond any single relationship. This will, in a way, benefit humankind. Until now, I've lived such a little life. There's so much more. Life is immense. My daughter will learn that one day. She should have a better start at creating her universe than I did. Her father and family will make sure of that. This is the only way I think that I can help her. Her father, well, he's in love with someone else. He won't look for me for very long."

"Okay. Your orders have been cut and are sealed. You and the other women will start SEAL training next week in an undisclosed location and be deployed where needed.

"I wish you God speed, Lieutenant."

Dreaming. Darkness, then light. Screaming. Pain. Dying. Scream. Pain. Death. Death. Death.

"Benny!"

Chapter 11

"Greetings, David," Julia Carter said to her son, as he entered their home in Idaho.

"Greetings, Mother, are you well?"

"I am well. Was your journey taxing?"

"No, I found it to be most delightful. The camaraderie of the premarital festivities was quite rousing. Where is father, may I ask?"

"Yes, you may. Mr. Carter is lecturing this evening on *Hamlet* at the Shakespeare Revival Seminar. It promises to be a most stimulating event. Is there a particular reason for your query?"

"I wish to speak with you and father on a topic of importance: an affair of the heart."

Julia began to check their schedules. "It appears that we will be available on this coming Monday at precisely 2:00 P.M. until 3:00 P.M. Will that be adequate?"

"Yes, thank you, Mother. That will be most adequate. I shall retire now. Do I have your permission to withdraw?"

"Certainly, David."

David left his mother in the study and went into his bedroom. Everything was exactly as he had left it. His idols' pictures, Sherlock Holmes and Horace Rumpole, were still hanging straight on the walls in their gold and silver frames. A bust of Albert Einstein appeared freshly dusted and his collection of Wagner, Chopin, and Mendelssohn CDs were neatly shelved.

David unpacked his suitcase and put each piece of clothing neatly in its pre-designated place in a drawer. With that accomplished, he checked his notes on his laptop and entered his appointment with his parents in his iPad. There was nothing else pressing that had to be accomplished, but it was certainly too early yet to retire for the night. He fingered through his CD collection and inserted Chopin into the player. As the music began to fill the room, he reached for his violin, tuned it, and began to play along with the music. His timing was off so he stopped playing. He went to his briefcase and retrieved a small picture of Gloria, which had been taken at the wedding. He placed it on his desk and began to play again. This time he made no errors as he looked at Gloria's picture, then closed his eyes, feeling the music, seeing it in his mind's eye, and holding her in his heart.

David's interaction with his parents was limited, as they sat across the breakfast table from each other, eating in relative silence. Mealtime usually was uneventful. They raised him with no outward display of affection—publicly or privately. Quite different from his experience when he was away at law school, sitting in the kitchen of the Georgetown house, he thought. There was always vibrant and stimulating conversation there, which often resulted in uproarious laughter. Sitting at the table with his parents, whom he had not seen for nearly a year, was anything but uproarious. In fact, it was downright boring. No conversation passed between them as he witnessed in other families—particularly the Alexanders. That family he observed, during the previous week in San Diego, interacted with each other on every occasion, listening to each other and sharing their joys and sorrows together. It was an amazing, enlightening, and an incredibly enjoyable experience. His home environment seemed as empty before as it did now. He never regretted that he was an only child, but suddenly he missed being at the Georgetown house with people who had become as close as siblings, but it was summer vacation and everyone was away. Alan and Melissa in New Mexico. Vivian and Derrick on a romantic adventure. Anna, Miguel, and Angelique in Peru visiting relatives. Chuck in Pennsylvania and, most importantly, Gloria in Santa Barbara with her parents. Since she spent so much time recuperating from her injuries, she would return to Washington, DC for the summer law school session. Perhaps he would return early and assist her with her studies.

David walked across the University campus with his hands stuck down in his pockets and looking at the ground. No one spoke to him as he passed, but that was not unusual. His parents were the only professors of African American descent on campus and they were among the only Black families in Idaho. He probably would not have noticed if someone had spoken because he was deep in thought and preparing himself mentally for his meeting with his parents. He knew his parents would not have an emotional reaction to his discussion. They were devoid of that trait. Clearly, their indifference to the world outside the university campus came from living so long out of touch with the rest of the world. His parents, after all, were highly trained and well respected professors who operated within their own dense and hectic orbit.

David had walked aimlessly each day, gathering his thoughts. He had not read one *Law Review* article, watched not one episode of his favorite public television shows or even picked up his violin to play. He was thankful for the quiet time that his distance from his family afforded him, but they were his parents after all.

The large grandfather clock struck 2:00 P.M., and David rapped lightly on his parents study door.

"Enter," his father called out.

David entered the study where his parents were seated, waiting his arrival.

"Good afternoon, Mother, Father. Thank you for allotting this time. I understand that your time is limited to one hour, therefore, I will not dally, but come directly to the point."

David's parents did not respond.

"As you are fully aware, I have been away from this domicile for some time now. During my absence, I have developed a fondness— an attachment, if you will—for a young woman with whom I have matriculated over the recent past. That is to say that I have developed a deepening interest in pursuing, with some trepidation, though with careful consideration, a concentrated interaction with her. Thus far and to date, I have maintained a relatively passive position and I have been excruciatingly careful to assure, to a great extent, a distance between our academic and social activities. However, of late her presence has been, in my view, positively intoxicating. Therefore, I have come to the inexorable conclusion that I must reconcile the apparent contradictions in my own behavior. I fully expect that, at some date certain in the future, subsequent to my successful completion of law school and upon accepting a suitable position with a reputable law firm, I will explore meticulously the options available to me at that time, and if you have no objection, offer myself to her as her betrothed. My purpose here today is, of course, to inform you of these matters and to seek your guidance. Therein concludes the length and breadth of my request for this audience and I stand ready to respond to your inquires.

"I shall begin the questioning period, Mrs. Carter, with your forbearance?"

"Agreed, Mr. Carter, you may proceed."

"David, of what nationality is this woman?"

"She is American, of African descent."

"Of what social standing or position is she endowed?"

"Her parentage is of working class stock."

"Has her virtue been compromised or is it in question?"

"She is, by all accounts, a woman of contemporary tastes and standards, who has, on occasion, found herself in inauspicious circumstances."

"Does she aspire to align herself with your personage?"

"At this time, she lacks clarity of her direction and continues to be rooted in a somewhat immature and child-like mode from which, given time and proper guidance, she will emerge."

"Have you had carnal knowledge of this person?"

"To date, nothing of a physical nature has transpired between us, nor have I compromised my virtue with anyone of the opposite sex."

"Mrs. Carter, I have completed my inquiry. You may now proceed."

"Thank you, Mr. Carter. David, does this woman possess a genteel nature?"

"She possesses a robust and lusty demeanor, affable, and outgoing."

"Is this woman of light or dark complexion?"

"Her hue is comparable to nutmeg."

"Is this person accomplished in any field of endeavor?"

"As of this point, she does hold different expectations for her immediate future."

"Mr. Carter, I have completed my inquiry."

"Thank you, Mrs. Carter."

David's parents excused him from the room and spoke among themselves before they summoned him to rejoin them.

"David, we have considered carefully your dilemma and regret that we are unable to conclude that the union you propose, although it is envisioned at a point in the future, would be in your best interest. This young woman appears to be wholly unsuitable to continue the tradition of excellence that has been established and implemented. It is our decision that you sever any and all ties and associations with this young woman forthwith.

"However, we have several suitable young women in mind for you and will introduce you to them when the time is right."

David was surprised by his father's statement and his parents' unanimous rejection.

"Perhaps, I have been unclear in—"

"On the contrary. You have spoken clearly and concisely as Mrs. Carter and I would have expected. Now then, the hour has drawn to a close and you may take your leave of us."

David was perplexed at his parents' apparent inability to grasp the depth of his feelings, but he rose from his seat and left the study. He never considered that his parents would take such a harsh position as to instruct him to sever his relationship with Gloria. For the first time in his twenty-five years, he considered disobeying his parents' wishes. Gloria, after all, was too important to him to falter on his new discovery of life outside of his parents' tiny universe.

The subject was not broached again in the household over the two weeks of his summer vacation at home. Long walks, his violin and studying the law no longer consoled him. He decided to return to Washington and to the friends he had grown to respect and admire. He bid his parents farewell and felt a burst of excitement as he boarded a flight that would put him in close proximity to Gloria within a matter of hours.

Chapter 12

Alan and Melissa drove across the "Land of Enchantment." The picturesque landscape of New Mexico was carved by nature and illuminated by big, clear skies. On their way, they passed golf courses and guest ranches, pueblos and natural wonders, wineries and historic sights. It was so magnificent and grand, Melissa thought. Everywhere they stopped, Alan watched her big, blue eyes take in every one of the over nine hundred miles they traveled from Santa Barbara. They were on the road for fifteen hours in a rental car, stopping overnight at a quaint Abode Bed and Breakfast. They met an abundance of tourists, Mexicans, and Native Americans from many tribes.

"Alan, these people all look so attractive," Melissa commented.

"They're Mestiza, people from mixed marriages. Some are Genizaros, descendants of Spanish settlers whose ancestors were abducted during raids. Africanos, who escaped slavery. When the railroad came, my ancestors told me that everything changed. There was even more race mixing. Some Anglos married into some tribes and then used the legal system to rob my ancestors and the Mexicanas of the lands that they had lived on for centuries. Still, my people were patriotic despite the injustices. My great-great grandfather rode with Teddy Roosevelt's Rough Riders. My great-grandfather survived the Bataan Death March in World War II. My grandfather served in Viet Nam. When my father came home from Desert Storm, he was an activist who tried to reclaim the old land grants for our people like his father and the ancestors before him. While I was away fighting in another war in Iraq and Afghanistan to take more land from my people for the Americans."

"What happened to your father? Did he succeed?"

"He died," Alan said, quietly.

"Was he an old man?"

"No, he was young."

"How did he die?"

Alan didn't answer, but solemnness covered him as he looked ahead at the road. A slow-moving, horse-drawn wagon blocked their ride for miles.

"Blow the horn, Alan. Maybe he'll move out of the way."

"This isn't the United States," Alan said, harshly. "This is a sovereign nation. We do things differently here. From a different point of view. There's no reason to be in a hurry here. The day will still be twenty-four hours long. The sun will still rise and set and the earth will still rotate on its axis—and my father will still be dead."

Melissa was stunned and more than a little hurt by Alan's outburst. She sat quietly looking out of her window at the slowly passing scenery. Finally, the horse-drawn cart pulled out of the way and Alan picked up the pace. As they came over a rise in the road, a towering mountainous peak rose majestically and defiantly before them. Melissa sat up in her seat and reached for her camera.

"Put that away, Melissa."

"Why?"

"That's Shiprock Peak, Tsé Bit□a□í. It means rock with wings. It is a sacred place."

"Can't I even take a picture?"

"No, this isn't some desert theme park, Melissa!" Alan snapped. "You have to have permission from the tribal government."

"You're kidding, right?"

"No, I'm not. We've been on the Res for the last fifty miles. Now put that away before somebody sees you with it."

Melissa put the camera back into its bag and closed it.

The peak came ever closer as they drove. Alan pulled into an adobe village as the bright day gave way to a brilliant sunset. They were surrounded by mountains, as they got out and walked toward a crowd of Navajo people standing silently, encircling other Native Americans who were dressed in their brightly-colored regalia.

"What's going on, Alan?" Melissa asked.

"Shhh!" he hissed, abruptly.

Melissa stood silently and looked around at the faces of the Navajo, who were all focusing on the group in the center of the ring. Someone made a blood-curdling, screeching sound and the people in the center began to dance and chant in a singsong language that Melissa did not understand. Alan chanted along with them, as did all of the Navajo people, as drum cadences rocked Melissa's core. She curiously looked from face to face, but did not disturb Alan in his chant. The singing was lusty and when the dancing ended, Melissa began to applaud. Alan grabbed her hands, as the people quietly dispersed. A woman approached them and stood before Alan. Her frame was slight, but Melissa could easily see the steel in her constitution by her stride and demeanor. The woman wore her hair in two, long, thick braids that fell to the small of her back, a band around her head, and native clothing. Bright turquoise stones draped her neck and hung from her waist and wrists. She did not touch Alan, but spoke to him in native Navajo. Melissa waited until there seemed to be a break in the conversation.

"Hi, I'm Melissa Charles," she said gaily, extending her hand.

The woman and Alan looked sharply at her and Melissa withdrew her hand. The woman walked away and Alan followed. Melissa slowly walked back to the car and stood, reflecting on the events of the day. She felt helpless and out of touch, as night began to close in around her. Suddenly Alan was beside her.

"My mother and grandmother will receive you now, Melissa."

"Alan, what did I do? Why did you stop me from clapping?"

"Do you applaud in your Christian church after a prayer?"

"No."

"Neither do we."

"Oh, that was a prayer?"

"Yes, Melissa."

"What do I do, Alan? I don't know the customs here. I don't know what to say," she said nervously.

"Just respect our traditions, Melissa."

"How do I do that if I don't know what they are?"

"Suppress your Yankee ways. Don't speak unless spoken to. If a question is asked, answer it quickly, quietly, and without a lot of gesturing. My mother is accustomed to rude Anglos. She will pardon slight breaches of etiquette. I'll help you as we go along."

Alan led Melissa into the adobe, which was surprisingly cool considering how scorching hot the day and evening had been. The room was awash in Navajo rugs and other cultural artifacts, but Melissa averted her eyes and suppressed her desire to wander around the room or to touch anything.

"*Yahateeh*, my son. You have been too long away from us," Alan's mother said, as she sat in a chair in the sparsely furnished home.

An older Navajo woman spoke to Alan in his native tongue, as she fanned herself with eagle feathers.

"Thank you, Mother, I have come home to see you and the Old One, and brought a friend from the United States. Her name is Melissa Bernice Charles. Her people live on the land once inhabited by the Pequot, Mohegans, Narragansett, Wampanoags, Nausets and Nehantics, now known as Rhode Island."

"*Yahateeh*, Melissa Charles. Please be seated. I am Marina Pierro Lightfoot, mother of Mitchell, Lewis, Alan and Jeremy, wife of Keanu Lightfoot, daughter of Mexico in Amina and Ra Pierro. Granddaughter of Nimo and Kove and great granddaughter of Matese, the Spaniard, and Minnel, the Apache. Please, tell me of your people."

"My people? Well, I mean there's my mother, Marsha Charles. She's a dental hygienist and my father, Paterson Charles. He's a dentist," Melissa said and then shut up. "Oh, uh, they own their own dentistry practice in the suburbs of Providence."

Marina and Alan looked at her as if they were both waiting for more. Melissa felt nervous. The older woman spoke again and Alan and Marina listened intently and nodded their agreement with whatever the woman was saying as she continued to fan herself with the eagle feathers.

"You have a lovely home, Mrs. Lightfoot," Melissa blurted out not sure what else to say next.

Marina did not respond, but furtively glanced toward Alan.

"We will eat now," Marina said, as she began serving tacos heaped with fresh lettuce, tomatoes, refried beans, guacamole, sour cream and red chili on a piece of fry bread. A rabbit stew with Pan Dulce was also served.

Melissa waited until the meal had been served and Marina and Alan began to eat with their fingers. She watched how they handled the food and mimicked their every movement precisely not wanting to make a mistake. Suddenly her mouth was inflamed, she choked, her eyes began to water and nostrils flared. She tried to breathe, as the food scorched her mouth. She tried to act normally, but Alan noticed her pained condition and handed a glass of water to her as Marina looked on in slight amusement. The older woman's expression never changed.

"Water is precious here," Marina said, as Melissa gulped down the first glass and then reached for Alan's glass.

"Uh, I think that we have some Pierre in the car. I'll go and get it," Melissa said, starting to rise and then stopped. "Oh, uh, would you please excuse me?" she asked courteously, covering her mouth, as she looked toward Marina.

Marina nodded her consent for Melissa to leave her spot and Melissa rose and literally fled the room. She yanked open the car door and flashed open the ice cooler in the back seat. She grabbed several cubes of ice and packed her mouth. She rested against the car until the ice numbed her mouth. Alan came out moments later and smiled at Melissa's tear-stained face.

"Are you all right?" he asked.

Melissa nodded and then shook her head, unable to speak with the cubes of ice still in her mouth.

"I should have warned you about the chili peppers," Alan said.

Melissa frantically nodded in agreement.

"I'm sorry. I didn't think about it. The food does not taste that hot to me."

Melissa spit out the ice.

"Hell couldn't be that hot, Alan!"

Alan laughed and Melissa's face clouded.

"Oh, Alan, I feel like such a fool. I've probably insulted your mother and grandmother and embarrassed you."

She leaned her forehead against Alan's chest and sobbed.

"You're going to be all right, little girl from the suburbs of Providence, Rhode Island," he said, rocking her in his arms.

Early the next morning Melissa awoke on the matted floor to the smell of food cooking. Alan was asleep beside her with his broad bronze chest slowly but evenly heaving. Melissa's body ached from the night of silent lovemaking on the hard adobe floor. Marina had shown her into a room, said goodnight, and closed the rug over the portal doorway. Melissa knew immediately that Alan was not permitted to sleep with her under his mother's roof, but sometime during the night, Alan snuck into the room as silently as ants crossing a floor and cupped his hand over her mouth to keep her from screaming her alarm. They settled into a familiar lovemaking pattern, which usually had them both baying at the top of their voices, but not that time. Alan's mouth covered hers and stifled her fits of passion. She had dug her nails deep into his hard, meaty flesh until her fingers ached, as she reached the first of many climaxes before they finally reached ecstasy together and passed into a deep sleep in the silent night.

The sticky goo between Melissa's thighs and her full bladder from consuming so much water were uncomfortable, as she rolled to her side and tried to get to her knees. She stretched her back, slipped into the shorts and top that she had worn the day before, and began to search quietly for the bathroom. Her eyes met Marina's, who merely pointed toward another rug-covered portal. Marina, she noticed was dressed in rather fashionable business attire, but Melissa didn't have time to dawdle. She fled in the direction that Melina had indicated.

Melissa immediately flopped down on the toilet and moaned in relief, as the fluid poured out of her body and disappeared down a hole. She fingered herself and removed her diaphragm. It slipped out of her fingers and disappeared down the commode hole and out of sight. No handle to flush, but blue fluid flowed as she rose. She grabbed a small towel and wet it, washing her face, under her arms and between her legs. She peered into a small mirror. Her hair was a mess, she thought, as she ran her fingers through it quickly and shook it out. She dabbed some toothpaste on her fingers and into her mouth. Now, she thought to herself, she was ready to face the world.

Melissa came into the open room quietly and sat on a chair, watching Marina cook. Alan's grandmother sat quietly curing wool between two brushes. An old wooden loom sat nearby.

"Uh, Mrs. Lightfoot, is there anything that I can do to help?" Melissa asked.

"You can tell me what you want from my son?" Marina asked, not looking at Melissa.

Melissa was taken aback. "Uh, I love your son, Mrs. Lightfoot. I don't want anything from him, except his love in return."

"My son comes with a rich heritage of great ancestors. The Ancestors have smiled on him, made him aware of who he is, and strong in mind, body, and spirit. He will be a leader among our people like his father before him and his father's father before that back to the beginning of time but greater than them all. The Navajo Nation is over two hundred thousand strong. He will lead them soon and many others from different nations. He will not live in your world long and you are not prepared to live in his. You bring no history to him. No great ancestry to guide you and to mate with him and bear his children. You know nothing of him to teach his children. You only know how to coax his seed from his body to fill your needs for his flesh. You take his precious seed and discard it like so much trash. You give nothing to him in return. You only take from him the gift that his ancestors have given to him to pass on to another generation of Navajo.

"His love is not in that seed that you took from him last night. It is in this land, this air, these mountains, these streams, these forests and in his people. He has a purpose for being among us here and now. In October, he will return for nine days of *Yei-Be-Chai* to prepare him for his next task. His ancestors have sent him here to fulfill a purpose.

"He has brought you here. He is a man. I cannot guide his course for him. You must decide what is best for the common good between you: to continue to sap his seed for your pleasure or to permit him to fulfill his purpose. There are no other options." Marina spoke clearly and frankly, as she continued to cook the morning meal over an open flame. Melissa listened carefully. Marina's tone was monotone, not insulting, but directed not to anger but to inform.

"I do love him."

"To Anglos love is who you sleep with. You have not slept with another?"

"Yes, I have, but I did not love them."

Marina looked up at Melissa. "And you sleep with men who you do not love? How then do you distinguish love between sleeping with men who you say you do not love and sleeping with a man who you say you do love?"

"It's not the same thing."

Marina looked into Melissa's eyes. "For my son it is."

Alan and Melissa stayed only a few days with Marina and Alan's grandmother not sleeping together again after that first night. Melissa did not tell Alan why she would not sleep with him when he crept into her room, but she sensed that he knew the reason. When they left the adobe village, they drove to Red River to a Navajo Nation Wrangler Roundup and Concert of Western Music at the Red River Ski area. There was a taste of everything there, as they walked hand-in-hand listening to beach music, blues, Rock 'n Roll, country and western, jazz, classical, folk, and bluegrass. They tasted the huge enchilada that took ten men to prepare and looked at the huge Helium-filled balloons gliding over and around the green ski slopes. Melissa could not resist buying pottery, jewelry, paintings, rugs and other artifacts at the Native American Cultural Center. Miss Navajo Nation was in attendance at the concert and was a strikingly beautiful, young woman, Melissa thought. Melissa playfully put her hands over Alan's eyes as they watched the young woman speak to a cheering crowd from a podium. Alan put his hands over Melissa's eyes as the young, firm Navajo men performed traditional dances in their sparse native attire. Melissa managed to peek through Alan's fingers. Her jaw dropped open as the men's muscles rippled. Melissa noticed how some of the young Navajo women glimpsed Alan shyly as she and Alan walked together. She understood their interest in him. He was incredibly handsome with a thick muscular body and powerful arms and legs sculptured by his years as a Marine. His rich bronze complexion, long, black, silky hair, and finely chiseled face would turn any young woman's head.

"Hey, brother!" a handsome young man said from behind them, as they walked toward the rodeo.

Alan turned around and the young man leaped into Alan's arms. Alan let go of Melissa's hand, hugged the young man, and swung him around, kissing him on the cheek.

"Hey, brother!" Alan said, as the young man dismounted and Alan took a good look at him, beaming. "Where did you come from?"

"Been looking for you. Heard you was up on the Res." The young man beamed. "Hear you brought an Anglo home, too."

"Oh, yeah, Melissa Charles, this is my youngest brother, Jeremy Lightfoot."

"It's a pleasure to meet you, Jeremy," Melissa said, with a smile, extending her hand.

"Likewise, I'm sure," Jeremy smiled back at her. "Not bad, brother," Jeremy said to Alan, with a smile.

Melissa blushed.

"Yeah, man, where have you been?"

"On the circuit, just like you used to do."

"You know you could get yourself killed out there and Mama and the Ancient One would blame me," Alan said, with a smile to his brother.

"Come watch me ride. I'm as good as you ever were," he boasted, jokingly. "Probably better."

"What event?"

"Bronco, of course!"

Jeremy beamed, as he led them to the corral and climbed the fence.

Alan put Melissa safely up on the stands and then helped his brother mount the spotted bay horse bucking in the closed corral. Jeremy eased onto the mount carefully, pulled his hat tightly down on his head, wrapped the reins around his left hand and signaled that he was ready. When Jeremy's name was announced as riding Spitfire, the crowd cheered loudly. The gate opened and Spitfire broke loose wildly, bucking and kicking violently, trying to dislodge Jeremy from its back, but Jeremy held on fast and rode the bronco until the whistle sounded and two riders retrieved him from the horse. Once on the ground, Jeremy took off his hat and waved to the cheering crowd. None seemed more proud than Alan, who stood and smiled at his brother as Jeremy climbed the bleachers toward him and Melissa.

"Not bad for a novice," Alan teased, grinning.

"Yeah, yeah, bet I get good numbers?"

"You're on." Alan smiled.

The judges were unanimous that Jeremy's ride was the best so far in that event.

"You owe me dinner, brother." Jeremy smiled.

Alan agreed.

Later, after the rodeo, the threesome sat together with Jeremy's trophy prominently displayed on the table, as they finished a hearty meal at the Red River Inn. Jeremy told Melissa about the days when Alan rode in the rodeos around the region and made money during college to live on before Alan went into the Marines. The two brothers laughed hard and relaxed over cold beers to talk.

"Mitchell know you're home?"

"I haven't seen him. Mama didn't mention anything about him. Where is he?"

"Came up from Mexico last week. I don't know what's up with him these days. Been acting strange since you left."

"What about Lewis?"

"Up at Albuquerque, as usual. Trying to get the Navajo land back. The rest of the Tribal Council went with him this time. They should know they don't have a chance in hell," Jeremy said, taking another swig of beer.

"That's not true. That's what our father fought and died for. Lewis is doing the right thing."

"By the time he succeeds, the Anglos will have taken all the oil, coal and gas out of our lands and be gone."

"What's he talking about, Alan?" Melissa asked.

"There's a dispute that has raged for decades over the title to millions of acres of land. Back in the 1960s, Reies Lopez Tyerina tried to reclaim the old land grants and led an armed raid on the Tierra Amarillo Courthouse. My grandfather was with him during that raid. He was killed several years later. We believe that it was because of his knowledge about the old land grants."

Jeremy picked up the story and said scornfully, "The FBI investigated, as they usually do, but nobody was ever arrested for his murder either. Just another dead Indian in the dirt."

Alan's eyes narrowed, as he glared at his brother.

Jeremy threw up both hands. "I know. I know. It's our responsibility to make it right," Jeremy said. "We just have different points of view on how to make that happen."

"You learning anything? Getting your grades?"

"Yeah, yeah. GPA is 3.2."

"Oh, where are you going to school? Someplace around here?" Melissa asked.

"Stanford, third year."

"Stanford? What are you studying?"

"Women, right now I'm sure with a 3.2 GPA," Alan added dryly.

"That, too, brother," Jeremy retorted, with a smile on his youthful and handsome face, "but some of the time business and economics."

"A double major? At Stanford? You must be good!" Melissa gushed.

"The best! That's what the ancestors sent me here to do." Jeremy smiled at Alan. "Right, brother?"

Alan didn't answer Jeremy.

Later that night at the Red River Inn, as Melissa and Alan prepared for bed, she sat brushing her hair as Alan reclined on the bed, watching and smiling at her in the mirror.

"Alan."

"Yes, Melissa?"

"Your mother said that your ancestors sent you here to fulfill a purpose. That you'll come back here in October for something called *Yei-Be-Chai* to prepare for your next task. What was she referring to?"

"Not now, Melissa. Come to bed," Alan said, turning out the light beside the bed and removing his jockeys.

"I want to know, Alan," Melissa said, putting down her hairbrush and crawling onto the foot of the bed. "And what's this big mystery about your brother Mitchell?"

Alan sat up and reached for Melissa. He pulled her toward him and slipped his hands and head under her baby-doll pajama top, nibbling her fleshy breasts and pink tipped nipples.

"Are you going to talk to me or what?" Melissa said, peeking into her top at Alan.

"Or what," Alan answered, as he nuzzled her breasts with his nose and ran his hands over her bare hips and thighs.

Melissa pulled away. "Alan, I want to know," she said more forcefully.

"And I want to make love."

"Can't we talk about this?"

"Not now, Melissa. We'll talk later," Alan said, pulling her down on top of him and stroking her body.

Someone knocked on the door of the room and Alan ignored it, but Melissa didn't. She pulled her robe from the foot of the bed and started to crawl off the bed as the second knock came.

"I'll get it, Melissa," Alan said, frustrated.

He slipped back into his jockeys and went to the door.

"Yeah, who is it?" Alan asked through the closed door.

"Open up, Alan," a voice came from the other side.

Alan sighed, shook his head, and opened the door slightly.

"Yeah?" he said blocking the door with his body.

"What? You're not glad to see me?" Melissa heard a gravelly voice ask.

"I'm not alone."

"I heard," the man said, brushing past Alan and entering the room with two men behind him.

Melissa pulled the sheet up to cover herself.

The two other men came in and immediately began checking the room. They looked into the bathroom, the closets, under the bed and behind the draperies. Melissa scooted down further under the cover and frantically looked around. The first man grinned at Melissa with a cigarillo clenched between his white teeth. His hair was long, healthy looking, and jet black like Alan's and pulled back away from his deep bronze face. He was wearing all black, but very expensive-looking clothing. He turned and spoke to Alan in Navajo, but kept leering at Melissa. His glare made her very uncomfortable. Alan didn't appear at all pleased to see the man either.

"Aren't you going to introduce me?" the man asked.

"Melissa, this is Mitchell Lightfoot, my oldest brother."

Melissa nodded her head, but didn't venture to move out of the bed to greet him properly.

Alan leaned on the open door, with one hand clinching the top of the door and the other on his hip.

"Ah, Melissa," the man said, rolling her name around in his mouth and grinning widely. "What a pretty name for such a pretty lady."

"What do you want, Mitchell?"

"Can't you give your brother a hug?"

Alan reluctantly hugged him.

"That's better." He grinned with the cigarillo still clenched in his teeth. "When were you coming to see me—to pay your respects?"

"This was only intended as a short visit. Melissa wanted to see the Res. We'll be leaving in a few days."

"Yet you are here now. I have to come to find you? I have to hear from our little brother that you are here? I've not seen you in five years, but I must track you down to say hello? No! This is not right! This is not the way one brother treats another!"

"Let's not start this. I will visit you tomorrow."

"Yes! You come to the hacienda. We drink a lot, eat a lot, lie a lot. You bring your woman."

"No, just me. Not her. She is not a part of this."

"Who are you ashamed of, brother? Me or her?" Alan looked away. "You bring her, yes?"

"I'll see."

"Yes!" he said, slapping Alan on the cheek playfully, still grinning. "*Hondo lay!*" he growled at the men, ordering them to leave. "*Mañana por la mañana, hermano masculino.* You bring her."

Mitchell looked into Alan's eyes and Alan reluctantly nodded in agreement. Then Mitchell winked at Melissa and grabbed Alan between the legs.

"*Grande cojones.*" He grinned and left.

Alan closed the door and locked it. He turned out the light and sat on the side of the bed.

"Alan—"

"Get some sleep, Melissa," Alan said, as he lay down.

Melissa sensed that this was not the time for a lot of questions. She laid her head on Alan's shoulder and hugged him gently. Alan did not respond to her.

In the morning, Alan and Melissa sat at a table in the Red River Inn dining room having breakfast when a man approached the table. Alan looked up and smiled. He greeted the man warmly.

"Lewis, it is good to see you," Alan said, smiling.

"And you. I was afraid that I would miss you."

"I heard that you and the Tribal Council were in Albuquerque."

"Yes, we've just returned. We are meeting here shortly to plan a strategy. I only have a few minutes."

"Melissa Charles, this is my older brother, Lewis Lightfoot."

"A pleasure to meet you, Ms. Charles," Lewis said. "Everyone said how pretty you are and I must agree."

"Thank you, but please, call me Melissa. When you say Ms. Charles, I start looking around for my mother."

The men laughed.

"Pretty and charming, too." Lewis smiled at Alan.

"So how are things going with you and the Council?"

"Still the same problem. The state says that our fight is with the government in Washington and not with them. The state refuses to act on our behalf, saying that although we may have a claim, the state will not act on behalf of a sovereign government in any matter, which might be a disputed issue, and end up in court. The local Bureau of Indian Affairs says that it is only administering and managing our land held in trust by the United States. They continue to say publicly that their role is Indian self-determination and to encourage and support tribal efforts to govern ourselves. They also say that we need federal programs and services to develop governing and administrative skills. Who the hell do they think they are kidding? We've been governing ourselves for ten thousand years! The United States is only a little over three hundred years old!"

"I know, brother. Nothing has changed, I see."

"The struggle continues, but now you will graduate from that Eastern law school. You will know how to speak the gringo's language in court. You will soon be ready for *Yei-Be-Chai*."

"Lewis, would you explain that to me?" Melissa asked.

Lewis looked at Alan. "You have not told her about this?"

"I will, in time," Alan said, and then abruptly changed the topic of discussion. "Mitchell came to see me last night. He wants me to pay my respects at his hacienda today."

"What did the Ancient One say?"

"I did not ask."

"I see. You are full grown now, Alan. You must decide this for yourself."

"I do not hate the white man. I will not say that I do to please my brother. This was not the way of our fathers."

"He knows your mind on these matters. He is still your brother and the eldest of this family. You must pay him respect. That *is* the way of our fathers."

Alan leaned back in his chair and glimpsed Melissa's face. He nodded slowly in agreement with Lewis.

***

Mitchell's hacienda was a marvel of modern masonry and engineering in an isolated area of the Red River Valley nestled against the backdrop of the soaring mountain range. The ranch spread out in the valley and included apartment-style dwellings for the ranch hands to live in. A barrier gate surrounded the hacienda. Alan punched numbers into a box and the gate opened. Armed guards patrolled the property and accompanied Mitchell, as he came out of the front door onto the veranda dressed in swimming apparel to greet Alan and Melissa.

"*Bienvenidos*," Mitchell said, with a big smile and holding his arms outstretched toward Alan."

"*Gracious*, Mitchell," Alan replied.

"I see you bring your Rhode Island woman with you."

"Her name is Melissa," Alan responded, annoyed.

"*Si, si*, Melissa, welcome to my home," Mitchell said, putting his arms around both Alan and Melissa's waists and guiding them into the spacious hacienda. "Come, we will eat, swim and talk, we three."

Native American art from all South Western tribes graced the walls and rooms and mixed beautifully with the bright and lively Mexican flavor of the hacienda architecture. Mitchell led them through the hacienda to the grand patio and large kidney-shaped swimming pool at the rear of the house. The patio was covered with juniper, ponderosa pines and aspen trees. A desert rock garden surrounded the stone mosaic pad that led around the pool perimeter. Three buxom and buttsy young Mexican women in scant bikini swimwear lounged around the pool, applying sunscreen lotion to their glistening brown-bronze skin. The women smiled broadly, displaying their gleaming white teeth and rich brown eyes.

Mitchell seated Melissa at a patio table and snapped his fingers. A man dressed as a waiter appeared, carrying a pitcher of iced sangria and another of chilled margaritas.

"What is your pleasure, Señorita?" Mitchell asked Melissa in a deep, gravelly voice, as he hovered close to her ear.

"I'll have the sangria, thank you," Melissa said, shying away from Mitchell's invasion of her personal space.

Alan sat quietly, but stiffly, and watched, with his arms folded across his chest.

"You like it here, Melissa?" Mitchell grinned, as he handed a chilled glass of sangria to her and eyed her suggestively.

"Yes, it's beautiful," she answered without expression, glimpsing Alan's stoic demeanor.

She took a sip of the strong sangria and felt Mitchell's hand on her knee.

"Then it is settled! You will stay the night and enjoy what wildlife after dark has to offer." He grinned, still rubbing her knee and bending too close.

"We have accommodations, brother," Alan spoke, noticing Melissa's discomfort. "We are only here to fulfill a social obligation."

"It is right that you should stay here," Mitchell said, resting his eyes on Alan and leaning back away from Melissa. "Here you can sleep with your Rhode Island woman—or choose among any of these," he said, nodding toward the women by the pool.

Melissa sensed a disquieting tension between the brothers, as they both participated in an unyielding stare.

"You have known my brother long?" Mitchell asked, finally diverting his eyes from Alan. "Tell me, how did you meet him?"

Melissa smiled slightly.

"My friend—I mean our friend, Vivian Alexander, brought Alan home one night from the homeless shelter. He was living there and going to Georgetown Law—"

"*Homeless shelter!*" Mitchell exploded. "What is this homeless shelter?"

Melissa jumped at the harshness and loudness of Mitchell's tone.

"It was convenient," Alan said, still sitting stiffly.

"You lived among Anglo drug addicts and drunks? Scum?" Mitchell railed his dark eyes flashing at Alan.

"It was a family homeless center with children and their indigent parents," Melissa tried to recover.

"That is no excuse! A son of Navajo should not have degraded himself so!"

"He did help a lot of people," Melissa interjected again, trying to defend Alan against Mitchell's verbal attack.

"He has Navajo people to help—not those whining Anglos too lazy and stupid to—"

"Watch what you say, my brother!" Alan finally spoke with a deadly calm and leaning forward on the table.

Mitchell deflated slowly and signaled for the food. An uneasy calm fell among the threesome. Then Mitchell snapped his fingers and motioned for the three women to come to him.

"These are my women," Mitchell said, fondling two of them shamelessly and staring at Alan. "Beautiful, are they not, Melissa?"

"Yes, I suppose they are very attractive."

"You have women such as this in Rhode Island? Women with fire in their eyes and heat between their thighs."

Melissa did not answer as Mitchell continued to stare at Alan intently.

"Pick one and she will be yours—or take all three. They are young, ripe, and seasoned well, my brother," Mitchell grinned. "They can do more for you than this pasty, scrawny Rhode Island—"

"Let's go, Melissa!" Alan said, rising slowly from his seat. "This visit is at an end!"

Melissa rose from her seat and moved toward Alan. He reached for her hand and held it tightly.

"Wait! Wait!" Mitchell demanded.

Alan looked at his brother. "I have heard enough! I did not come here to have you insult my friend, although I expected that you would do this! She is a fine woman and does not deserve your insult!"

"She is *Anglo*! You sleep with the whore of men who raped and pillaged the land of our ancestors. Who raped our women and the barbarians who slaughtered our children in their beds while their mothers pleaded for mercy! *Insult? She* is an insult to our people! She is nothing! If you want whores—here! I offer you three of the best! More, if your *cojoneses* require it!"

"She is not the reason our father is dead! She did not do this to me or to you! She is no insult to the Navajo! What you do is!"

"You fight in their war against people of color as a Marine, yet you cannot call this land your own? Then you would take her side against *me*?" Mitchell raged.

Alan didn't answer. He turned and walked away, holding Melissa's hand tightly. Two guards blocked their departure, but Alan pushed past them and out the front door. Melissa and Alan got into the car. He jerked the car into drive, squealed the tires, and raced away without a word. Melissa sat motionless, as silent tears dripped down her face. The gulf that separated her from Alan seemed immense. First her family and now his. They were both tearing them apart.

Alan and Melissa stood at a precipice, looking out over the remains of a great abandoned adobe village. The landscape welcomed the view of the past. Warm, once rich earth with colors painted by the sun. For as far as the eye could see, the land rolled on, offering up its rich minerals to be touched and changed by the elements of the universe.

Melissa's eyes watered as she tried to capture it all. Such beauty in the land and serenity in the atmosphere. They did not speak for a long time, but simply appreciated what the quiet stillness of the view offered.

"I can't capture it all," Melissa finally said quietly. "I see so much, but I can't seem to see enough."

"I've lived here most of my life, except for my time in the Marines and away at college and law school. I still feel exactly as you do."

"It makes you want to kneel in this place."

Alan smiled and looked at the wonderment on Melissa's face. Then he looked down into the mesa and pointed to a distant riverbed.

"That's my family's summer home and up there," he said, pointing across to a plateau, "is the winter place."

"Gees, Alan, a summer and winter place, all within climbing distance."

Alan laughed. "And I had to make the trip all the time with a couple hundred sheep. Not something you'd have to do as a child in Providence." He smiled. "Come on, we'll go to the summer place and I'll show you how I spent my youth."

"Alan, what's that smoke?" Melissa pointed off into the distance.

"Mining operation."

"It seems so close."

"It is. Too close."

"Why would anyone want to destroy a land so rich in beauty?"

"You said it, 'rich'."

"Oh, I see. Isn't that still part of the Navajo Reservation?"

"Yes and a Navajo runs the operation."

"Who runs it?"

"My brother," Alan said, with disdain evident in his voice. "He does the very thing that our fathers fought against—he rapes the land for profit."

"He's very wealthy, it seems."

"I suppose," Alan said dryly. "He believes that we should use this land to buy back our rightful homeland."

"Obviously you disagree." She looked up into the fixed stare in Alan's eyes.

"He has his beliefs and I have mine."

"And that's why you two are at odds with each other."

"It goes beyond that. Mitchell and I are brothers. He was the protector when we were all small. The one who fought all the bullies when we were little children. He protected Lewis, Jeremy and me in school in the city."

"I thought you went to school here."

"No, we lived in dormitories from grade school up through high school. Our parents were farmers and sheepherders. We were with them during holidays and summer vacations, but we didn't see them during the school year."

"That must have been hard on you and your brothers at such a young age."

"Mitchell was always there for us. He took care of us, especially when my father and uncles were away in the war. He carried on the tradition. Taught us the Navajo ways that our father and grandfather taught him. In the American schools, it was forbidden to speak Navajo or to practice our own religion. They cut our hair and made us wear American clothes, eat American food, study their version of American history, Christopher Columbus and all that crap. It was as if Columbus was some great man." Alan smiled to himself. "He was a sailor who got lost and Indians found him and took care of him."

Melissa smiled. "Dumb luck," she mused.

"For the Spaniards perhaps, but not for us. We had been trading with the Africans for centuries before Columbus came. They were a gentle people, too, the Africans. Not war like. Not aggressive. We fit into each other's cultures. We had similar value systems. When the Africans were enslaved, my ancestors told me of how they used to hide escaped Africans and protect them. Some even married into Eastern tribes. Vivian's history is full of Egyptian and Eastern Native marriages in what is now South Carolina."

"She never told me that."

"Did you ever ask her about her heritage?"

"No, I guess I didn't."

Alan smiled. "Come on. Let's go. I'm getting hungry and my family is making lamb stew at the summer hogan."

"Alan, I'm not exactly a mountain climber. How are we going to get down this rock across the kiva to the bottom of the mesa?"

Alan laughed. "This kiva is a holy place, Melissa. I cannot take you through there. Don't worry, there's another way into the mesa."

They drove across the plateau and around the rugged countryside. They moved downward into a forest with green lush vegetation and cool air. As they came to a clearing, Melissa's nose caught a foul scent.

"What's that?" She frowned.

"Sheep." Alan smiled. "It's shearing time."

Alan's family was gathered there, planting and harvesting their crops. Dipping and shearing the sheep and cooking the food in the traditional way. His small army of cousins set about their tasks and the children were an integral part of the process, each knowing their function and taking on their responsibilities to the family without thought or question.

Alan moved among his family filled with energy and joy. Melissa was at his side and though they spoke often in Navajo, Alan would translate or ask his cousins to speak in English, which they did very easily. Many of his relatives, Melissa learned, were well-educated and held responsible positions in and outside of Navajo society, but they seemed to relish the times together. Alan's return, Melissa could see, sparked quite a bit of excitement among the fifty or more relatives and close family relations. He participated in each chore and activity, shedding his shirt along with his other family members and digging in to help. Melissa wandered around, helping where permitted. Carrying water, taking a turn grinding the dried corn, or playing with the babies while everyone worked.

After a while, she did not notice the smell of the sheep as the women cooking the meals permeated the air with delicious aromas of fresh breads, stews, vegetables and fruits. Melissa's eyes were never far from Alan's strong, glistening, golden body as he worked. The women, many of them young and worldly, teased her about her lustful glances and shared stories about Alan's childhood. Melissa blushed, but joined in with the camaraderie easily and felt welcomed, as the women performed cooking tasks the old way. No electricity or other modern conveniences. Just hard work with nimble fingers and confident hands, all working together and preserving the history in laughter and song.

After the evening meal, Alan took Melissa's hand and walked along the floor of the mesa to a swimming hole. The stars were bright above them as night closed in around them. They heard the laughter and saw the glow of the campfire blazing against the walls of the mesa.

Alan took off his clothes and walked into the cool waters. Melissa watched him dive in and disappear beneath the surface. When he emerged, he broke the surface with great force and energy, Melissa thought, with his black hair flooding over his face and shoulders. Water beaded up over his thick, oily skin, and running down his body, as he closed his eyes and turned his face heavenward before he slipped back below the surface. He was under so long that Melissa began to worry. She went to the edge of the water and saw the bubbles of air rising to the surface and then without warning, Alan appeared before her walking up out of the depths of the dark pool. His dark eyes fixed on her and were expressionless. A glow about him relaxed her brow. He did not speak, as he slowly approached her, but she took in the determination in his demeanor. His eyes had her fixed to her spot. Rooted in the earth beneath her feet. He was at her, on her and around her even at a distance.

He pulled her T-shirt up over her head, unbuttoned her shorts, and pulled them down, along with her panties. He removed her tennis shoes from her feet and led her into the water. He pulled her down gently into the depths, as the stars above faded from sight and the dark waters closed in around them in the silence. The chill left her body, as she felt Alan holding her. Touching not just her body, but her soul. Penetrating every fiber of her being. They touched the bottom and pushed off, thrusting upward and catapulting through the surface as the last ounce of air escaped. A great chorus of song greeted them as they emerged. Campfire flickering and forms moving against the mesa walls. As they walked out of the water, Melissa felt something around her neck. She lifted it, a necklace of turquoise beads.

"Something for you to remember me by," Alan said as they stood in the darkness with only the white, bright moon illuminating their faces.

"Remember you? You make it sound like we're not always going to be together."

Alan didn't answer. He gently feathered the hair from her face and gazed at her. He closed his eyes and traced the contours of her face with his hands.

"Something to remember you by," he said, as he finished caressing her face. "I've captured your image in my head for eternity."

"Alan—"

"Let's get back. Everyone will be wondering where we are," he said, picking up his clothes and putting them on. She did the same.

They walked back to the campsite. Everyone was inside the hogan, asleep. Alan spread the rugs on the floor and they lay down together between and among his family.

Melissa's eyes closed and she drifted into sleep, passing from one dimension into another. From one reality into another. Her dreams were troubled with uncommon sights and sounds. A bear in the distance hidden from view. Sheep unaware of the danger lurking nearby. A great wall with lights dancing against it. Falling. A clay bowl on the ground with dead creatures around it.

She felt Alan's hand on hers in the night and it brought her up to a higher place just as he had when he guided her to the surface of the water. Immersed in him and his touch, she slept.

The hot breeze blowing in through the open portals woke Melissa. Her sleepy eyes caught the glint of the sun against the turquoise necklace, as she fingered it around her neck. She looked at the space where Alan had lain, but he was gone as was everyone else. Sitting up she looked around the empty hogan.

"Where is everyone?" she asked, as she left the hogan and approached the women all seated brushing the mountain of wool from the freshly sheered sheep.

"There," Marina said, nodding toward a mound of dirt covered with blankets, heat dancing in the air above it.

Just then, the sound of a helicopter broke the silence. The sound was breaking against the mesa walls, scaring the sheep, and whipping up the dust and the water as it came into the mesa and landed in a clearing. Mitchell was the first face Melissa saw through the glass shield. He moved swiftly as he disembarked and began removing his clothes. He shoveled hot rocks into the mound of dirt, said words in Navajo, and then entered.

Melissa thought the sight was extraordinary, but the Navajo women acted as if they barely noticed. Hours passed before the mound of dirt opened and the Navajo men exited. Their skins red as boiled lobster, Melissa thought, as they rolled in the soil covering themselves and each other with dirt before heading to the river. Breakfast or brunch was served, as the men returned, but nothing was said about the strange scenes. After eating, the women went back to their work on the wool and the men to their work tending the crops and the animals.

Melissa was watching as the fresh-cleaned wool was immersed in dye pots sitting over open flames. The children strung the hot, wet wool on trees and branches to dry in the hot sun, baking in the bright man-hewn colors.

"You are still here," a gravelly voice said behind Melissa, as she sat on the ground, looking out on the wide picturesque countryside.

"Yes, I'm still here," she said, not turning to look into Mitchell's face.

"This is not like your home."

"No, it's more beautiful and alive out here in this place than in Providence."

"Providence," he smirked. "English, no doubt."

"And Irish," she said. "But you don't have to be polite to me, Mitchell," she said, standing and dusting off her bottom and her hands. "I already know quite well what you think of me."

"Think of you? I do not think of you at all."

"Then we have something in common because I don't think of you either."

Mitchell drew back, looking at Melissa's full presence. "Now you can leave my brother alone. Go back to *Providence*. Back to your own kind."

"What scares you about me, Mitchell? Is it the fact that I love Alan or the fact that he loves me, 'a pasty, scrawny, white woman'? It threatens you that despite the differences in our heritages, we can love each other. That we can get past the color of our skins and deal with each other like two adults. That we can find the positive things in our lives and focus on that. The things that bring us together. Not the things that make us different."

"Get past it?" He laughed. "You go around it. You are different. As different as the sun and moon and just as far apart. He is the sun; the center of the universe. Everything revolves around him. He lights the sky and gives you—the moon—his glow. Without him, you are just another piece of debris floating in his universe."

Mitchell turned and walked away, leaving Melissa feeling as desolate as the moon. She watched as his helicopter lifted off and flew away into the distance. The dust settled and Alan came up from the sheep pens with Jeremy, Lewis, and his cousins, laughing and wiping the sweat from their bodies.

"How about a swim?" he asked

"Sounds good to me."

They changed into swimwear and headed for the river. The heat was stifling and the cool waters felt good on her body. They frolicked in the water, with his family, until a storm rolled into the mesa. The dark clouds gathered and thunder roared loudly. Everyone ran for cover, except Alan. He stood, letting the hard rain wash over him. Melissa went back to him, slipped her arms around him and held him tight. The crack of thunder sounded so loudly that it made her shake. Alan was not afraid. He raised his arms and welcomed the fury like Moses on the Mount, turning the tide to part the sea. Again, she clung to him. He lifted her face to his and kissed her as the thunder cracked around them. He lowered her to the ground and made love to her with the booming torrents of rain drowning out their sounds of passion. The louder their lovemaking the louder the thunder seemed to be and the more the rain fell, beating against their bodies, the greater the passion.

The storm subsided as suddenly as it had started. They lay together breathless, as the now gentle rain sprayed them. The air was filled with moisture and a big, bright rainbow followed the storm.

Chapter 13

The aircraft set down at Miami International Airport. Vivian and Derrick walked hand-in-hand up the ramp to see a short, dark-skinned man wearing a straw hat and waving at them. He was smiling broadly.

"Rico," Derrick said, broadly smiling and extending his hand.

"Hey, Mon, been a long time, yes?" Rico said in a thick Caribbean accent. "You be bringing de bride witchu, Mon?"

Derrick laughed. "This is my very special friend, Vivian Lynn Alexander. Vivian, this is Rico Alevera-Vila, pilot extraordinaire."

"Hello, Rico," Vivian said curiously.

Derrick sensed her confusion.

"She pretty lady, yes," Rico said, as he kissed Vivian's hand. "She no your wife yet, Dr. DJ?"

Vivian smiled.

"Rico, are we ready to go?" Derrick asked, grinning broadly.

"Sure, Mon, I get de luggage," he said, as he scurried away.

"Derrick, where are we going?" Vivian asked in total confusion.

"Just be patient a little longer and I believe that you'll enjoy this."

Vivian relaxed. Derrick and Rico led her to a seaplane that read "Adventurer Executive Charter" on the sides. They had just gotten off an Adventurer Executive Airline private plane flight from Santa Barbara. Rico loaded the luggage and they were off on another flight. It was dark as they rose into the moonless night. Derrick was excited. He could barely wait to share his surprise with Vivian. It seemed to Vivian that they had only been airborne for a short time before Rico banked the aircraft sharply and prepared to land. Vivian peered out of the window from behind Derrick's seat, but could see nothing but darkness below. Then Rico picked up a remote control device and suddenly landing lights flickered on ahead of them. The seaplane touched down in the water between the lights on its skids and glided up to the shore on to a sandy beach. Derrick got out of the plane and helped Vivian onto the sand.

"We're here," Derrick said, as he used a flashlight to guide their way to the dock.

He held Vivian's hand, as they walked. He sensed that she was quietly curious, but trusting him unquestioningly to guide them along the sandy shore. He went to a panel box, inserted a key, opened the box, and flipped on a series of switches. Lights began to come on in sequence, moving up a winding staircase that led up a slight hill. Up they climbed until they reached the top of the hill and an octagon-shaped house loomed up before them. Vivian heard the surf pounding against the shore on the windward side of the hill. Although she was weary from the long day and somewhat jet lagged, the salt-water air was invigorating. They walked onto a smooth stone patio that surrounded the house at the lower level and past a lighted and heated swimming pool with mist rising from the clear water. A wide, stone fence surrounded the house on the outer rim.

Derrick and Rico led her into the house and up the stairs to the main level. They entered a great room with a rounded, center stone fireplace surrounded by glass and a bright red flue that went up to the vaulted and beamed ceiling, with clearstory windows high above them.

Derrick stood smiling at Vivian, as she wandered around the octagon house amazed at the contemporary interior with contiguous bedrooms, each with its own bathroom suite and independent upper stone deck entrance. The open-concept, U-shaped kitchen and adjacent large dining area were completely visible from anywhere in the spacious great room and family room. In every direction, full-view, glass doors, that led onto the stone deck, surrounded them. Vivian spotted an interior sunroom with tropical vegetation and a splash pool. She turned to Derrick, with excitement in her eyes.

"Derrick, this is unbelievable! I've never seen anything like this!"

"Then you like it?"

"Like it?" she shrieked, "I love it!"

She walked toward him and tossed the bouquet of flowers that she was carrying into the air. Derrick took the garter from his pocket and twirled it on his finger, as Vivian approached him. He took Vivian into his arms and kissed her passionately.

"Hey, Mon, de bride, she do like, I see, yes?" Rico asked, as he entered the great room carrying the last of their luggage and found Derrick and Vivian kissing.

"She do indeed," Vivian said, with her arms around Derrick's neck, resting her head on his chest.

He rocked her and smiled broadly at Rico, giving him the thumbs up sign.

Rico smiled slyly. "De luggage, it is in dare, Mon, and de food, it is in dare," he said, pointing first toward a large bedroom and then toward the kitchen. "I be gone now, yes, Mon?" he said, waving as he left by the front, glass and iron, double doors. Vivian heard a scooter start and the engine rev, as the sound sped away.

"Now, Ms. Alexander, as I was saying before we were interrupted by my nephew's illness last week, you're driving me crazy."

She kissed him and looked around furtively. "Are we alone?" she asked.

"Yes, completely."

"Where is the telephone?" she asked, with a seductive smile.

"I haven't turned it on," he said, smiling back at her.

"And your beeper?"

"I didn't bring it with me."

"And your cell phone?"

"In my car at Dulles Airport."

"Then we're completely cut off from the rest of the universe?"

"Absolutely!"

"Then, Doc, come with me," she said, leading him by the hand to one of the spacious bedrooms. "Let's see whether we can find a cure for your insanity."

In the morning, Derrick awoke to the sound of the surf pounding against the shore. One of the sliding glass doors was open and the sheer curtains blew freely in the wind. Vivian was not in the room. He got up out of bed and pulled his silk, short robe from his luggage. He went out onto the stone veranda and saw Vivian standing there with her arms wrapped around her scantily-clad body, bare-footed, eyes closed with her face to the wind. He admired her shapely body and long legs. Her broad shoulders and short stylish haircut that was so short that it did not blow in the wind, but peaked smoothly at the nape of her neck. He watched her momentarily, as she looked up to the heavens and then at the far vistas of ocean that surrounded the beach as far as the eye could see. A morning haze was lifting and the smell of salt water and mounting humidity permeated the air.

Derrick approached Vivian from behind and slipped his arms around her waist. She felt wonderful and natural in his arms, as he rested his chin on the top of her head. She leaned back against him and he cradled her in his arms. A strange excitement and simultaneous calm grew over him as he held her. He squeezed her tightly to his body and kissed her ear and neck with an open mouth.

"Mmm, that feels good," Vivian cooed, as he held her. "How's your sanity problem this morning, Doc?"

"I'm going to need a lot more of your therapy sessions, Counselor. We're going to have to schedule them on a regular basis."

"That can be arranged, Dr. Jackson."

He slipped his hand inside her scant nightshirt and massaged her breast. Vivian closed her eyes and purred with delight.

"Do you know where we are?" he asked softly.

"Heaven," she answered quietly.

"Close. This is one of the Islands of Bimini."

"That's what I said, heaven."

He turned her around and gazed into her pretty, brown eyes. Spray from the sea made her face moist and glistening, he thought, as he ran the palm of his hand over her face and brought it to his. He kissed her gently at first, but as his excitement grew, he probed her mouth with his tongue. She was responding to him, wrapping her arms around his neck, pressing her body against him. Her gold chain that read 'FAMILY' glistened against her peanut butter brown skin. He guided her to a wide chaise lounge that faced the sea. He sat, leaned back, and brought her onto his lap. She curled herself into him with her face against his bare chest. He cradled her in his arms.

They reclined, as they fondled each other and napped on the stone deck with the spray from the sea cooling their bodies, as the sun rose in the sky and the sea breeze swirled around them.

"Are you hungry?" he whispered, stroking Vivian's face.

She yawned quietly and burrowed into his embrace. "Not if it means that we have to move from this spot, I'm not," she said softly.

He kissed her forehead and hugged her. "Whatever you say, Counselor, but I'm starving," he said, feeling an alarming sensation overtaking him that he had never felt before.

She was beginning to excite him although she was only napping in his arms and on his lap.

"Okay, Doc," she said, raising her head and her body, as he slipped from beneath her.

He went inside the house and closed the door behind him. He went to his toiletry bag, pulled out an unmarked bottle and swallowed two tablets quickly. "Not now," he whispered aloud to himself, as a sensation passed over him.

He sat on the edge of the commode until the sensation subsided.

"Derrick," Vivian called from the bedroom. "I'm going to take a swim."

"I'll be down in a few minutes," he called back to her through the closed bathroom door.

"Okay."

When the sensation subsided completely, he checked his pulse and blood pressure. They were almost normal. He stowed the equipment and pills in his luggage and went into the kitchen to make a light brunch. Rico stocked the kitchen well with fresh fruits, vegetables, and fresh fish. He prepared a tray full of an assortment of fresh fruits and bagels with lox and cream cheese. He poured the iced decaffeinated coffees into glasses and carried it all to the pool.

Vivian was floating in the pool on one of the inflated pool chairs, as he came to the edge of the pool at the shallow end and sat down. He watched as she glided on the water. Her scant bikini barely covering her full breasts and round, firm hips. She was so young, only twenty-four years old, and he was thirty-five, soon to be thirty-six. They had made perfect love for the very first time in their relationship, he thought. She had thrilled him over and over again. It had been like no other that he had ever experienced before. Many years had passed since he had been sexually active. He had tried to pace himself, but his feeling for her had raced ahead. Making love with her had been everything that he had imagined that it would be and far more than he had expected. She was a full partner in their lovemaking, giving, receiving, and sharing for hours. Despite the age difference between them, she completely, naturally, lovingly satisfied him. His nature was rising just thinking about her and watching her floating listlessly in the pool.

"Vivian," he called to her, as she glided on the water, "let's have something to eat and then take a walk on the beach."

"I don't know, Dr. Jackson. I believe that it's time for your therapy session," she said, with a straight face and a gleam when she opened her beautiful, brown eyes.

He took off his silk robe and swam to her.

They made love again in the warm waters, and again on the wide chaise lounge, as they fed each other from the tray of food that Derrick prepared. Later in the afternoon, they walked hand-in-hand through the surf of the private deserted beach, talking and laughing, as was their usual custom. They reached the dock and walked far out on the pier toward a one-hundred-sixty-foot yacht moored at the end.

"Whose boat is this, Derrick?" Vivian asked, as they climbed aboard.

"It belongs to the property owner."

"And who is that?"

"Question, always questions," Derrick teased, as he went up the steps and led Vivian to the upper control deck.

"I am training to be an attorney, Derrick. Attorneys ask questions."

"Let's see how good a sailor you are."

Derrick weighed the anchor, cast off the starboard and port lines, and pushed the boat away from the pier. The boat drifted in the water and Derrick started the three engines from the control up top. He put Vivian at the controls and showed her how to steer, as they headed out to sea. They passed other boats, as they circled the largest Island of Bimini.

"Ahoy there, *The Vivian Lynn,*" one boater yelled to Derrick through a megaphone.

"Ahoy there, *The Mighty Magic Heat,*" Derrick yelled back and waved.

Derrick began to help Vivian steer toward the other boat.

"The Vivian Lynn?" she asked, astonished.

"Oh, yeah, I forgot to mention that little detail. Some coincidence, huh?"

"I should say so," she said to him, as she continued to steer close to the other boat.

Derrick went down the ladder and tossed lines across the expanse to the other boat. A couple of tall men grabbed the lines and pulled the boats together. Derrick called to Vivian to cut the engines and she watched as he greeted the men with strong handshakes and shoulder bumps. Derrick called to Vivian as the other men and their female companions climbed aboard.

"Vivian Alexander, this is—" Derrick began.

"J. Roderick 'JRock' Baylor and Kelvin 'The Count' Constantine. These gentlemen need no introduction. I recognized you both," Vivian said and smiled. "JRock plays for Miami and The Count plays for the Supersonics. You both had great years this past season."

"Beauty and brains, too," Roderick said, smiling at Derrick.

"And an Olympic gold medalist for basketball when she was still in undergrad," Derrick boasted.

"You told us that she was someone very special, but you understated the case, my brother!"

"Oh, has Derrick been talking about me?" Vivian asked.

"Has he! Can't shut the man up these days!" Kelvin said, laughing.

"And what has he been saying?"

"Oh no, none of that," Derrick said, playfully pulling Vivian into his arms. "She's going to be a lawyer real soon and a good one. So don't give her any incriminating evidence on me or I'll have to take the Fifth!" Derrick laughed.

"All I was going to say was that it's not many men who would name a boat after a casual acquaintance. You've got to be someone pretty special for that honor," Kelvin said, smiling.

"That's for damn sure," Monique Baylor, JRock's wife inserted snidely.

For ponderous moments everyone stood in uncomfortable silence.

"So, how are your daughters?" Derrick asked into the obisque.

"Three going on thirty-three," JRock joyfully said. They're spending time with my sister, Kelly."

They all laughed and spent a while getting to know each other. It was an enjoyable afternoon filled with discussions about professional basketball. Vivian was a full participant and often floored the group with her memory and knowledge of the game, and the men and women who played through time.

Of course, her younger brother, Gregory, was making a name for himself and she was pleased that both JRock and The Count had heard of her brother who the press and news media was calling Alexander the Great.

Derrick was noticeably pleased with her, as he watched her interact with his friends. As evening fell, they parted the boats and agreed to meet later and have dinner together at the Blue Water Inn on Big Bimini Island.

Vivian dressed in a colorful print strapless wrap dress with strapless open high heels. Derrick's eyes had popped wide open when he came out of the bathroom and saw her standing in front of a mirror brushing her hair and combing the mousse through it. He stood back and watched her for a while, smiling. She was a gorgeous woman, he mused, from the top of her head to the bottom of her feet. She still reminded him of the actress Jada Pinkett Smith in her younger days.

"You know we don't have to go out tonight," he said, smiling and eyeing her body, as she combed her damp hair.

Vivian smiled at him in the mirror. "What would you rather do instead?"

"Just stand here and look at you."

"Is that all?"

"I'll think of something else, but right now, I'm enjoying the view."

"While you're staring you can explain how my name got onto the owner's boat and exactly who the owner is."

"Oh, well, uh. It was a contest and I won."

"A contest?" Vivian repeated, clearly not believing this explanation.

"Yes, this island belongs to the medical practice—or at least we have a long term lease agreement. My partners had a contest to see who got to win the chance to name the cabin cruiser. I won. You don't mind do you?" he asked.

"No, I don't mind, but if you think that I believe one word of that tall tale you're nuts," she said, smiling. "Is there anything else you want to tell me?"

"Only that I feel the need for another therapy session coming on." He smiled, unbuttoning his shirt.

Vivian laughed. "We're supposed to meet your friends for dinner, remember?"

"We don't have to do anything that we don't want to do, but this is going to be the fastest dinner in history." Derrick kissed Vivian passionately and gazed into her eyes. "God, am I glad that I found you," he whispered.

"The feeling is mutual. If it hadn't been for Chuck we might have never met."

"I don't like to think about that."

"We don't have to, now, do we?"

"That or anyone else."

"No, Derrick, I'm not involved with anyone else."

"Just checking. Now, about that therapy session—"

"After dinner, baby. I'm all yours and you're all mine. Alone together on this beautiful, deserted island."

"Good because I'm a country boy, remember? I want to go to bed early and go to sleep late."

"I'm a country girl, remember? I want to wake up early and get up late," Vivian whispered, as she kissed Derrick again.

The ten days they spent on the island were blissful. They took the cruiser out a few times to go to some of the other, small, deserted islands in the turquoise sea. They went diving, snorkeling and deep-sea fishing. They stayed away from the Grand Bahamas Island and its bustling cities of Nassau and Freeport, but they dined at small community restaurants on the smaller islands or on the yacht, as they whiled away the hours together.

Chapter 14

"Welcome to Alaska," Mr. and Mrs. Alexander," the desk clerk said, as Kenneth signed the guest register. "Your honeymoon suite is ready."

"Thank you," Kenneth said, with a broad smile.

A bellhop showed them to and through the spacious accommodations. A large fruit, cheese, and wine basket sat on the coffee table in the living room. Fresh flowers were strategically placed and a magnum of sparkling cider sat waiting in an ice bucket near a candlelight buffet. A table for two was well decorated and the food service staff was finishing the final dish. A fireplace roared, as they entered the bedroom. Kenneth looked around the well-appointed suite and approved. The maid service began hanging the couples' clothes and putting away their other belongings. Kenneth tipped the headwaiter as he and the rest of the staff quietly left the suite.

"Alaska," JeNelle said, amazed. "I've always wanted to visit this state, but I never found the time. How did you know?"

"I didn't, but I've always wanted to visit here, too. So now for the next three to four weeks, we're going to tour the state."

"This is wonderful, Kenneth." JeNelle hugged him. "Where are we going?"

"Well, Mrs. Alexander, we'll discuss that in the morning, but tonight I have something else in mind." He held her smiling face in his hands. "Now, how about modeling a few of your bridal shower gifts over dinner?"

JeNelle blushed. She went to the closet, opened it, and walked in. She chose two outfits and returned to the living room.

"Well, Mr. Alexander, where do you want to begin?" She held up two different negligees, one in each hand.

"In the middle." He approached her and began to undress her.

"I thought that you wanted me to model these for you over dinner?"

"I do." He continued to undress her, kissing her bare skin as he removed every stitch of her clothing.

"Which one do you like better?" she asked, as Kenneth kissed her abdomen and removed her garter belt, stockings, and panties.

"The left one," he said, as he rubbed her shoulders.

"Okay, why don't you get comfortable, open the sparkling cider, and I'll be right back."

JeNelle went into the bathroom and let down her hair. Her makeup still looked fresh, she thought. She spritzed some water on her face with an atomizer and dabbed perfume behind her ears, between her breasts, and behind her knees. She slipped into the dark blue, silky, floor-length negligee with spaghetti straps and open back. She fluffed her hair, refreshed her lip-gloss, and slipped into the matching short jacket that fell to her shapely hips. She dusted herself with powder.

Then it occurred to her that she had gone through the same ritual before on her wedding night with Michel San Angelo. They had a simple wedding at his father's compound in The Hamptons in New York. Only his father, Millos, his uncle Milo, his sister Maria, his younger brother, Antonio, and her parents and Gloria were there. No other family or friends. She had worn a short, winter-white suit and carried a small corsage that they had picked out on the way to the compound. No wedding reception. Just a quick helicopter trip to his family's Lear jet at Kennedy Airport and they were off to Cancun.

She had wanted a romantic honeymoon with Michel. He was an older man twice her age and quite worldly. They had not had sex before they married and she was totally inexperienced, she recalled. She had not dated heavily in high school. Her music had been her romance since she was old enough to climb onto a piano stool. She was then barely seventeen, in her first year at Julliard and far away from home.

Her first night with Michel had not proven to be at all what she envisioned. Even on that night, he was holding informal meetings in their hacienda with frightening-looking men who only spoke Spanish. Michel's bodyguards were always close at hand and stopped her when she wanted to spend time with him on their wedding night.

She waited in their bedroom for hours until his meeting finally broke up well after midnight. He came to their bedroom noticeably drunk and angry about how the meeting had gone. He did not compliment her on her attire after all the preparation she went through. He poured a couple of shots of Vino and drank them down rapidly. He did not offer her anything to drink to celebrate their union. His body was tense when she approached him. He grabbed her hair and buried his face under her chin biting hard into her neck. He pulled her down onto the hard, cold floor and pulled her gown up over her face as he roughly entered her, probing her first with his fingers. He kept repeating, "You are my virgin! My Madonna!" in Italian, delighting in show of blood as proof positive of her innocence as he violently entered her.

"JeNelle," she heard Kenneth call to her, snapping her from her trance. "Are you all right?"

"Uh, yes. Yes, Kenneth, I'm fine." She gathered herself and went into the living room.

"I have something for you."

"Not another gift, I hope."

"Just a small one." He reached into his pocket and handed a small box to her.

"What's this?

"Open it and see."

JeNelle opened the box and found a gold chain, which said FAMILY. She smiled, as he put it around her neck.

"It's beautiful," she said, fingering the piece.

Soft lights and the flickering flame from the fireplace cast a warm glow over the living room. Music played softly in the background. Kenneth had changed into a silk, paisley night jacket and matching solid black, silk pajama bottoms tied loosely at the waist. He uncorked the sparkling cider. She saw his face grow into a broad smile, as he looked at her. His eyes scanned her in a warm and admiring way.

"Simply stunning, Mrs. Alexander," he said, as he looked at his bride. He poured the cider and handed one glass to her. "To you, Mrs. Alexander. I love you." He toasted her. They drank the cider and Kenneth took the glass from her hand. "May I have this dance?" he asked, as the music played.

"You certainly may, Mr. Alexander," she said, with a warm smile.

As Kenneth took her in his arms, she closed her eyes and swayed with him to the music. He let her hand go and slipped both arms around her. He kissed her gently on her neck. It was more romantic than she imagined it would be. Kenneth was always so attentive and loving, she thought. So different from Michel. She felt that she wanted to make him as happy as he made her. To love him and make love to him with complete abandon.

They danced slowly several times and ate the scrumptious repast that was prepared for them. After dinner, they sat on the sofa, cuddling and talking about their wedding day in great detail and the many happy family and friends who had attended and made the day more inspiring for them.

Kenneth was gazing at her, she knew. She wanted to reach out to him and touch his muscular body. She caressed his face with the palm of her hand.

"I love you, Kenneth," she whispered.

She could feel the emotion beginning to well up inside her, as he kissed the palm of her hand.

"I know that you do, JeNelle. It's all right, honey. You can touch me. I'm here for you. I'll always be here for you," she heard him saying.

He was guiding her hand over his body as he lay back on the sofa. His body felt warm and inviting. His gold chain with the word **FAMILY** was bright against his skin. He closed his eyes and put his hands behind his head. His breathing was slow and steady, as she felt the curvature of his arms and shoulders. Rubbing her hands over his chest and abdomen, she could see the shape of the rock-hard bulge in his pajama bottoms. Her hands began to shake and she began to tremble as she recalled how Michel San Angelo had forced himself into her mouth. Holding her head fixed and forcing her to perform oral copulation on him over and over and over. She thought that she would choke or pass out from asphyxiation. He had smacked her when she didn't perform exactly as he had instructed. Then he sodomized her, grabbing her hair and forcing himself inside her. Their wedding night was an unspeakable horror. She had screamed in pain and agony, but no one came to her rescue. Michel swore that he would train her to perform as a woman before the week was over. There was no one that she could turn to for help. He never approached her in any way but brutality from that very first night. He brought other women and, sometimes, young men to their bed and forced her to watch as the women or young men had sex with him. She cried almost every day when he was with her for nearly two years, but her tears meant nothing to Michel. *"Virgins should cry from the pain,"* he said as he performed yet another atrocity on her body. *"That way you know that they're still virgins and not whores."*

"Honey, it's okay. Please, don't cry," Kenneth was saying to her softly, holding her in his arms. "I don't want you to do anything that makes you uncomfortable. I love you, JeNelle."

Her body was trembling. She didn't realize that she was crying until Kenneth was holding her in his warm, gentle embrace and her tears dripped down his chest.

"Make love to me, Kenneth," she sobbed. "Please make love to me."

"Honey, you're upset. We don't have to—"

She tried to gather herself. "Please," she begged, "this is our wedding night. I don't want to disappoint you."

"JeNelle, it's okay. You haven't disappointed me. I love you. I want you to be happy. We can just hold each other like we're doing now. We'll have the rest of our lives together. We have our baby to look forward to. I don't want to put any pressure on you."

"Kenneth, please. Please make love to me."

"Shhh, JeNelle," he said, trying to calm her. "Okay, honey. Don't cry. It hurts me to see you so unhappy."

"I love you, Kenneth," she said, gazing into his eyes, with tears streaming down her face. "You don't make me unhappy. Please. Make love to me."

Kenneth complied with her pleas, but he was very cautious in his approaches to her, she felt. He did not let himself go freely and completely. She ached in her heart that she was not able to make love to him. That she was not being a full partner in their lovemaking. That the man she loved slept beside her unfulfilled again, as he was every night from the beginning.

Kenneth thought it odd seeing his former friend Colonel John Calvin Baker, out of his military uniform, coming toward him in the park for a prearranged meeting, but it had been many years since Kenneth called JC a friend. Baker hadn't changed much. He still had that crisp military step, Kenneth thought. When they first met, it was on one of Kenneth's trips to see Benny while Benny was still at the Air Force Academy in Colorado Springs. Baker was a Major then. One of a few Black training officers who, unlike others of his peer group, was a rising military star. Now, he was his own worst enemy destined to live out the remainder of his military career in relative obscurity at Eielson Air Force Base twenty miles outside of Fairbanks in Alaska.

It was a breezy, sixty-one degrees as Baker approached Kenneth in the park at 10:00 P.M. The midnight sun was still bright and Kenneth could see the traces of premature gray hair below the ski cap of Baker's head. Baker checked the area carefully before he approached, passed Kenneth, and beckoned him with a nod of his head to follow to a more secluded spot in the park. Kenneth complied and the two men walked behind some thick evergreens out of sight of passersby.

"All right, Baker, what's this about?" Kenneth asked when they were finally alone.

"You're looking good, man," Baker said, trying to break the tension he was feeling and the impersonal expression on Kenneth's face. "Life must be treating you well."

"It always has, Baker."

"Hear you got married, too."

"Yes, I did. I'm on my honeymoon, so make this quick and to the point."

"You haven't always been this hard on your friends, KJ. Back in the day we were aces, remember that? We went skiing a lot together. Had some good laughs—you, me, Benny and some of the old crew. Your family still have that big reunion on the fourth?"

"You didn't get me to come all the way to Alaska to reminisce about the good ol' days," Kenneth said, still keeping his impersonal distance.

Baker looked away. "I'm sorry, KJ," he said rather quietly. "I'm sorry for getting you involved in that whole scene. I mean, we were friends and I let you down. I don't know how I got us into that mess, but you seem to have come through this unscathed. Prosperous, too, I hear. I've been keeping up with you in the newspaper and on line. I've got plenty of time to read up here. It's not like being in Washington making things happen."

"Baker, you've got five minutes to tell me why it was so urgent for me to meet you here alone and what you want from me."

Baker looked back into Kenneth's face. He knew that Kenneth's patience was wearing thin. "All right, so I blew it. You're never going to forget what I did, but you were so damned principled—"

"Four minutes," Kenneth said.

"All right, all right. It's about Sandoval Anniston and those contracts. I wasn't just trying to get myself on the fast track for five stars. I kept my eyes and ears open, too. I could tell you things—"

"Three minutes."

"Hold on, man! I'm trying to tell you what's going down! Damn! It's hard to lay all this out in a few minutes. It's complicated. There are a lot of irons in the fire. I just don't think you've got the whole picture—damn! I know you don't."

"Two minutes."

"All right! Someone is trying to get to you! You've put yourself in the line of fire! You've got to work with me on this. I think I can help you out."

"One minute."

"You're not listening, KJ! I'm trying to tell you that I may be your only way out of this. I've got some inside information that could make you a big man or break you—"

"Time's up," Kenneth said, as he turned and started to walk away.

"Do you know who your wife is?" Baker called after Kenneth.

Kenneth stopped, turned around and looked at Baker. "What's my wife got to do with this?" he asked, walking back toward Baker.

"Do you know who she was married to?"

"This had better not be another one of your sorry ass excuses for your own stupidity!" Kenneth said sternly.

"It's not. I swear."

"What is it that you think you know?"

"I know that JeNelle Towson used to be JeNelle San Angelo, married into the biggest and most influential mafia families in the country. You know, La Costa Nostra. Her former father-in-law is Don Millos Giovanni Santangello, self-made multi-billionaire. The Godfathers' Godfather. Head of one of the richest families in the world."

"So what? What's that got to do with JeNelle? She hasn't been married to Michel San Angelo in over eleven years."

"Not San Angelo—Santangello. Look, I'll tell you, but I need your help."

"To do what?"

"To get out of Alaska. You've got friends—powerful friends. Even more important, you've got family in the right places."

"And you want me to get people I know and respect involved in something that *you've* dreamed up? Save it," Kenneth said, putting up one hand.

"I'm not feeding you some line of bull, KJ! I swear I'm not! This is the truth. Besides, you owe me."

"Now I know you've lost it! You try to coerce me into taking inflated government contracts to bilk the government out of millions of dollars and I owe you?"

"You're wearing a wire, aren't you?"

"Recording every word."

"I should have known," Baker said, as he thought for a moment. "I've got to trust you. I've got no choice."

Kenneth listened for over an hour to Baker layout what he knew or suspected.

"I'll talk with Vivian, but I can't promise you anything."

"That's good enough for me, KJ. You've always been straight up."

"I want to keep JeNelle out of this though."

"But she could be the key. The old man, Millos, would do anything she asked him to."

"He doesn't run the government."

"The hell he doesn't! He snaps his finger and half the congress snaps to attention! You still don't know what you're dealing with here. Who do you think got the word that JeNelle needed help to clear your name? And how do you think JeNelle was able to divorce Michel? The old man. He's protected her for years. Like I said before, he'd do anything for her."

"JeNelle is out of this!"

"All right, all right, I hear you, but—"

"No buts!"

Kenneth entered the suite and walked into the bedroom. JeNelle was still asleep. He closed the bedroom door and went back into the living room, took out his laptop, and plugged it into his cell phone. He began dialing several numbers and sending messages. Just as he finished, he heard JeNelle come into the room.

"Are you working again?" she asked, with a sleepy smile.

"Just making a few notes. Did I disturb you?"

She walked to the cell phone, disconnected the laptop and held up the connector.

"A few notes, huh?"

"Well, maybe just a little work."

"Not on this honeymoon, Kenneth Alexander," she scolded jokingly.

"All right, Mrs. Alexander, no more work." He rose from his seat, took her in his arms, held her close, and stroked her hair.

"Is something wrong, Kenneth? You seem to be a million miles away." JeNelle felt the tension in his embrace.

"No, I'm here with you." He kissed her long and gently. "What would you like to do tomorrow?"

"We've already talked about this, remember? We were going to the Mayor's Summer Solstice Festival and you were going to participate in the Midnight Sun 10K run. I thought that you were out running, getting prepared for tomorrow while I was taking a nap. It's nearly midnight. Where were you?"

"It's hard to think of this as midnight when it's broad daylight outside," he said, changing the subject for his sake as well as hers.

Chapter 15

Weeks after returning from Bimini, Vivian sat in the living room watching a television news program on MSNBC while Gloria sat painting her toe nails. They heard commotion at the front door entrance of the Georgetown house and saw Melissa carrying, unsuccessfully, an arm full of books.

"What is all this?" Vivian asked, as she rose from the sofa to help Melissa pick up books that had fallen to the floor. Gloria didn't budge. Vivian began to read some of the titles.

"*Handbook of North American Indians: The Southwest Edition; The People: Indians of the American Southwest; Pueblo Nations: Eight Centuries of Pueblo Indian History.* Do I need to ask why you're doing all this reading and research?"

"I need to know so much more than I do about...things," Melissa said, cutting her thought short.

"From the look of *'things'* this has something to do with Alan. Is he starting that research project on the old land grants already?"

Melissa looked up at Vivian in surprise. "You know about that?"

"Yes, Alan told me about it."

"He didn't say anything to me," she said, somewhat taken aback. "Why would he tell you?"

"I asked him about his family and his heritage because I have a friend from undergrad, JaiHonnah Hawkins, who is also part Navajo and both she and he told me. Actually, his mother and her grandmother are related."

"When did he discuss this?" Melissa asked, as she sat down with a thud and with a perplexed expression on her face.

"Oh, I don't know. Many times over the last few years. It's no secret or anything, Melissa."

"Then why didn't I know?"

Vivian shrugged and started to leave the study room.

"Vivian."

"Yes?"

"Do you know who your ancestors are?"

"Sure, why?"

"How did you learn about them?"

"From my older brothers, parents, grandparents, uncles, aunts, cousins, why? What's this about?"

"Alan's mother said I have no ancestry to give to Alan."

"Oh, I see"

Melissa looked up at Vivian. "You know what that means?"

"Well, yes, I suppose."

"How do you know?"

"Alan told me about the Navajo culture. Ask him about it sometime. You'd probably learn more talking with him about his ancestry than you could learn reading all of those books."

"Do you know about *Yei-Be-Chai?*"

"The cleansing and healing ceremony?"

"How did you know? Never mind. Alan told you, right?" Melissa sighed in frustration.

Vivian smiled.

"I guess I've been more interested in Alan's present than in his past and his family history. I didn't think that much about it until Alan's mother brought it up. It must be very important."

"To most people, yes, but to any member of the Native American Nations, it's crucial. You have to know *'whose'* you are to define *who* you are. It's that way in most ethnic groups."

"Geesh, Vivian, I don't even know who my grandparents were."

"Ask your parents."

"We're not on good terms right now."

"Why, what happened?"

"My parents made a few very derogatory and racist remarks to Alan."

"Oh, I'm sorry to hear that. How is Alan handling it?"

"He says that it doesn't bother him, but I think it does."

"You're getting serious about Alan?"

"Well, yes. I think I'm in love."

"Oh," Vivian said dryly.

"What does that 'oh' mean?"

"Melissa, I can't keep up. Last winter, I could have sworn that you and Chuck had something serious going on. Before that, you were head-over-heels in heat for Stan Cavanaugh, not to mention a few other less notable relationships. Now it's Alan Lightfoot. I don't mean to be critical, but do you know what love is?"

Melissa propped her head up on her hands and stared at the books spread out on the table.

"I know how Alan makes me feel when we're—well, you know—making love."

"That's not the same thing as 'being in love', Melissa. It's not what you two do between the sheets."

"That's what Alan's mother said."

"Sounds like a wise woman."

"I'm lost. I just don't know what to do. What do you think—"

"Oh no, Melissa, I'm not in the Dear Abby business."

"But you and Derrick seem to be in love. I mean, you're always together even when you're apart. Just like you and Derrick, Alan is older than I am. What makes your relationship work with Derrick?"

"Yes, Derrick is more than ten years older than I am, but the age difference has nothing to do with our relationship. What works for us is that we talk with each other a lot about everything, particularly our family histories—the people who molded and shaped our lives. The values that we both have and our dreams for the future. Neither one of us has declared that we're 'in love'. That's not our objective. That's why we held off having sex for so long. We needed to see what we had in common before we considered adding sex to the equation. If, or when, we do feel that there is enough between us to declare that we're *in love*, we'll both know it and why it exists."

"That could take forever."

"What's the hurry? There is no 'use by' date stamped on our foreheads. We're not on some time schedule. We don't want sex to be the only thing we have going for us. That's like putting the cart before the horse. You can't get anywhere from there like that."

"So you think that I should start with who I am?"

"That's as good a place to start as any. Maybe you can figure out why your parents said those things to Alan while you're at it."

"Talking to my parents isn't as easy as talking to your parents, Vivian."

Vivian smiled. "That's because we've had a lot of practice. We've been talking all of my life. It gets easier the longer you practice it."

Melissa looked up at Vivian. "Can I have a hug?"

"Anytime, Melissa." Vivian smiled, as they hugged each other.

"You want to make this a *ménage à trois*?" Bill asked, as he returned from his trip and saw Vivian and Melissa hugging.

"Come here, you sexy stallion," Vivian said, laughing.

Bill came into the study and hugged both women together.

"God it's good to be home and find two of my women waiting for me," Bill said.

"Don't start getting any ideas, Bill Chandler. I'm already a ball of confusion," Melissa said, laughing.

"Yes, and as of two weeks ago, I'm a one-man woman," Vivian added.

Bill moved Vivian's head from side to side, looking into her eyes as she beamed.

"Yep, looks like Derrick has you all lit up," Bill smiled.

Vivian blushed and Melissa laughed.

"Hey, good lookin'," Gloria said, entering the study. "What did you bring for me?"

"Me," Bill said, as he hugged her.

Gloria pursed her lips and rolled her eyes.

"Where were you this time, Bill?" Vivian asked.

"France. Paris to be exact."

"You really do get to go to some exciting places, Bill," Melissa said. "Is there any place in the world that you haven't been yet?"

"Providence, Rhode Island," Bill teased.

Melissa rolled her eyes. "Consider yourself lucky," Melissa said sarcastically.

"Okay, Bill, who was your client this time?" Gloria asked.

"It's a new designer—Pegasus. The company hasn't been around that long."

"And they can afford someone like you?" Gloria asked.

"Hey, I give discounts sometimes."

"What's the product?" Vivian asked.

"A full line of men's clothes and fragrances. You probably haven't heard that much about them."

"I sure haven't," Gloria added. "Did you get paid?"

Bill laughed. "My agent handles that, Gloria. I just go where I'm told to go, and do my thing."

"And you must do it very well, too. You got a lot of other calls for jobs while you were away," Melissa said. "One company called quite a bit."

"Yeah, I'll get around to it, but right now, I'm just glad to be home with my family."

The women all smiled.

Chapter 16

Melissa packed a small overnight bag, wrote a quick note to her housemates telling them that she was going home for the weekend, and grabbed a taxicab to Reagan National Airport. She had not called her parents in advance and they were surprised when she came into their posh dentistry offices in the upscale suburbs.

"Melissa, dear," Marsha Charles smiled, as her daughter walked through the door.

"Mother, how are you?" Melissa asked unemotionally.

"Fine, dear. I'm glad you're home. Arrington Prescott has been asking—"

"I didn't come home to talk about Arrington Prescott!"

"Melissa Charles, you keep a civil tone when you speak to me! I knew it! You've been living in that cesspool with those perverts and Negroes too long! It was bound to rub off on you! And that Indian! How dare he think that he could climb out of the gutter and touch... I don't even want to think about it!"

"Those are my friends that you're talking about, Mother, and I'll be damned if I'm going to stand here and listen to you speak like that about them!"

"You're too insolent for your own good, young lady. I think you should go home and straight to your room immediately until you learn how to behave!"

"Marsha! Melissa! What is going on out here? We have patients! We cannot have chaos in the office with patients and employees here!" Paterson Charles chastised his wife and daughter. "I had to leave my patient in the middle of a root canal!"

Melissa turned on her heels and walked out of the office. She was still angry when she slammed the front door of her parents' home and paced, seething. Her bedroom was just as she had left it. Pink! Baby dolls with white, porcelain faces and pink cheeks were everywhere. Soft, fuzzy white stuffed rabbits with pink noses and ears. Everything about the room was infantile, she thought, as she sat in a white rocking chair with pink cushions and looked around the room. She wondered how she could have lived in this dollhouse. Nothing about the place said that an adult lived there. It was a child's room. What did she expect? She was still a child to her parents. They had been overprotective of her all of her life. Babying her. Coddling her. Controlling her. Dictating with whom she could and couldn't associate. This had to end! She wasn't a child anymore. She was twenty-four years old and she wasn't going to live a Pepto-Bismol existence or permit her parents to treat her as if she were.

She went to the attic, grabbed empty cardboard boxes, and began packing the dolls and trinkets away. Hours passed before her father knocked on her bedroom door. He seemed to ignore the packed boxes, as he entered.

"Melissa, your mother and I are most distressed over your behavior. We did not raise you to go cavorting around with people of that ilk. Now, we believe that it is in your best interest to move out of that place where you have been living and move back into the house with your cousin, Jenny—"

"No way! I am not a child anymore, Father. I will be twenty-five years old on my next birthday. I am going to graduate from law school this coming spring."

"I do not know what has gotten into you, but this behavior is totally unacceptable. Now, I have already called your cousin and she has agreed that you can—"

"Father, you must not have heard me. I am not moving, so you can call Jenny back and tell her and her family thanks, but no thanks."

"Young lady, I warn you that if you persist in this behavior, I will be forced to cut off your allowance and then we will just see how your tone changes!" he said angrily, leaving the room and slamming the bedroom door behind him.

That was the last straw. Melissa picked up her purse and overnight bag, took one last look at the denuded room, and headed out of the bedroom door. Her parents heard her and came to the staircase, as she descended the wide circular stairway. Melissa stopped and stood before her parents.

"I came home to talk with you both about our family, but I see that that was a mistake. We do not have a family. So I'm going back to where my family is."

She took her house keys off the ring, placed them on a table in the entrance hall, and walked out of the front door.

❂

It was late when the taxicab let her out in front of the Georgetown house. The house was dark, but she spotted Alan's Jeep parked at the curb. The house was cool and quiet, as she entered. She put her overnight bag on the floor, disrobed, and crawled into bed with Alan.

"That was a quick trip," he said, yawning, as she slipped into his arms.

"Let's just say that it was a trip and leave it at that," she said, as he held her in the dark.

"You want to talk about it?"

"Not now, no," she whispered, as she kissed him on the cheek.

They fell asleep in each other's arms.

For the next couple of weeks, Melissa searched for jobs to support herself. In her spare time, she read everything she could find on the Navajo Nation and the history of Native Americans in the United States. The more she read, the angrier she became. She did not discuss her project with Alan, but shared her findings with Vivian. They talked extensively about what Melissa had read and Vivian gave her other sources to check, including sources in Mexico and Spain that Vivian found over the Internet. Anna was becoming a fountain of information about the Natives of South America. In all of her private school education, Melissa never studied about the Aztecs, Toltecs and Mayans. She was fascinated with all that she was learning. Melissa began compiling the information she found in a notebook. She had old newspaper and magazine accounts of the struggles that Native American tribes endured for over three hundred years.

Vivian arranged for Melissa to work in one of the law libraries at Georgetown Law Center and to do some legal research for the Senate Commerce Committee. When Melissa got her first paycheck, she was ecstatic. She raced home after work and bought Sparking Cider that she chilled and served to the other housemates. She was very happy with her newfound independence. It would be tough not going shopping at the high-priced shops and boutiques or spending lavishly on jewelry or at the salon, but she would just have to cope. She had her family—Bill, David, Angelique, Vivian, Gloria, Anna, Miguel, and especially Alan.

The doorbell rang and Melissa got up to answer it. "Yes," she said to the man standing at the door, holding a folder.

"Mrs. Menendez-Gaza live here?"

"Yes, but she's not here at the moment. She's at the grocery store. Would you like to wait for her or leave a message?"

"I just wanted to give her husband's property to her."

"Oh."

"I'm Officer Andre Hays from the DC Fire Department."

"Has the case been closed?"

"No, but we know that it was arson. Miguel Menendez-Gaza certainly didn't start it, so we're returning his personal effects. It's not much, but it may mean something to his wife and family."

"Thank you, Officer." Melissa accepted the envelope. "I'll be sure to give it to her."

"Have a good day, Ma'am."

The officer started to leave.

"Officer Hays?"

"Yes."

"Did you say that the fire was deliberately set?"

"Yes, Ma'am."

"Do you know why?"

"If we knew why, maybe we could find out whom, but all of our leads were dead ends."

"Thank you," said Melissa before she closed the door and returned to the study.

When Anna returned from the grocery store, Melissa gave the envelope to her and sat with her while she went through the wallet and other personal effects. Anna told Melissa that her husband had left Peru just after little Miguel was born. Miguel was nearly nine years old now and had never known his father. Anna talked about what a hard worker her husband was and how he hated to leave his family. He had only left to find work in the States. He had written a letter or sent a postcard every week and sent money as often as he could. Anna said that she sensed that something was wrong when six months passed and she had not heard from him. She sifted through his belongings and found a postcard with a picture of Shiprock Peak on the front and the beginning of a note to her on the back. He was writing to tell her that he was herding sheep for men of respect and he thought that he might be able to come to get his family and bring them to live on the Reservation. Melissa noticed the postcard and mentioned that she had seen the peak when she and Alan visited the Navajo Reservation. Inside the change compartment, stuck in the lining of the wallet, was a small, gold cross. Anna said that it looked Spanish to her, not Mexican. On the back of the cross, etched into the metal, were: *Diega* and *1500*. Anna said that she did not recognize the piece of jewelry, but thought that it would make a nice gift for her son, Miguel, for his birthday. Anna and Melissa sat and talked about Anna's life in the small Peruvian village where she and her husband had made a home. Melissa enjoyed listening to Anna talk about her family and history in Peru and what she knew from her husband's letters and cards about Mexico. Anna gave life to the textbooks that Melissa had been reading. Such a rich history passed down through the ages just like Alan's, and Vivian's, too, for that matter, Melissa thought. She was learning a lot and enjoying the process.

Chapter 17

The taxicab pulled up in front of the Santa Barbara beach house and Kenneth got out. He helped JeNelle to her feet.

"Welcome home, Mrs. Alexander," he said, holding her in his arms. He kissed her gently on the lips.

"Thank you, Mr. Alexander. It's good to be home."

They stood for a few moments and looked at the newly completed addition to their home. What was once a bungalow was now a modern, three-story California-style with upper decks, turrets, and porches. The storage units were gone and the landscaping restored.

Kenneth lifted his bride in his arms and carried her across the threshold, and into the house. He returned to the cab to help the driver with the luggage. Two men sitting in a car across the road got out and approached him.

"Mr. Alexander?" a short, stocky-built man with graying hair asked, as he approached Kenneth.

"Yes, I'm Kenneth Alexander."

"Mr. Alexander, I'm Special Agent Brosnan and this is Special Agent Torrack," the man said, displaying his CIA badge and Identification Card. "Could we speak with you for a moment…privately?"

Kenneth asked the cab driver to take the luggage into the house and then paid him. When the taxicab drove away, Kenneth turned to the two men.

"Now, gentlemen, what can I do for you?"

"Mr. Alexander, you once worked on a frequency surveillance system for the Naval Air Warfare Center."

"I don't understand what this is all about. Would you explain exactly why you're here?"

"The government needs your help."

"To do what…exactly?"

"To complete the project that you designed."

"I've just returned from my honeymoon. My wife and I are a little tired from our trip. So, if you'll excuse me—"

"Mr. Alexander, we've been told that you'd probably be unwilling to discuss this matter or even lend any support for the project, but let me assure you that this is a matter of national security…"

"Good evening, gentlemen," Kenneth said, as he picked up his briefcase and went inside the house.

"Honey, who were those men?" JeNelle asked, as Kenneth came into the house.

"I'm not sure, but what I'm sure of is that I want another kiss from my beautiful wife," he said, taking her in his arms.

She smiled and complied with his request.

"Now, what do you want to do about dinner? How about Citronelle or the Cold Spring Tavern? We could hop in the car and drive up to Montecito and go to Pane e Vino or The Stonehouse or Ristorante Piatti. We haven't been there lately," he said, still holding her.

"How about we stay home and have a salad, some French bread and you can have a carafe of Sauvignon Blanc," she suggested, smiling broadly.

"JeNelle, we don't have any food in the house, remember? We've been away for four weeks. And you can't have wine in your condition."

JeNelle smiled and led Kenneth to the kitchen.

"*Voila*," she said, as she opened the side-by-side, stainless steel refrigerators and displayed their fully stocked condition.

"Okay, I know that you're always working your magic on me, but how did you manage this?"

"Magician's helper. Mama. I called her from the airport while you were checking the airplane and asked her to do a little shopping for us. Now, let's take our luggage into the new bedroom, get comfortable, and raid the kitchen," she said, folding herself into his arms.

"Let's just stop after the 'get comfortable' part of the evening," he whispered in her ear, while holding her. "Dinner can wait."

The telephone rang.

"I'll get it," JeNelle said.

"Let it ring," Kenneth said, still holding her. "No one knows that we're back yet."

He kissed her.

"Kenneth. Johnston here. Would you pick up the telephone, please? It's very important," Judge Worthington's voice came over the answering machine.

Kenneth sighed and picked up the telephone.

"Johnston, what's the problem?"

"Kenneth, I need to see you right away."

"Can this wait? JeNelle and I just got back—"

"I know, Kenneth. I wouldn't disturb you if it wasn't urgent."

He sounded stressed. "Okay, Johnston, come on over."

"Would you mind meeting me at home? At my place?"

"Now?"

"Yes, Kenneth. There's a car waiting for you outside your door."

"Johnston, what's this about?"

"I'll tell you when you get here. Please, Kenneth, this is vitally important," Johnston pleaded.

"All right, but this had better be."

"Thanks, Kenneth."

They hung up.

"What's that about, Kenneth?" JeNelle asked. "What did Johnston want?"

"I'm not sure, honey. He wants me to come and see him."

"Now? Tonight?"

"Yes, but I'll be back as soon as I can and then we can 'get comfortable'," he said, holding her and kissing her gently on the lips.

Kenneth left the house and Agent Brosnan opened the car door for Kenneth to get in. The agent slid into the back seat with Kenneth and Agent Torrack drove them away. As they approached Johnston's estate in Montecito, Kenneth noticed the extraordinary amount of security surrounding the estate. From the demeanor of the security agents, this could only be one thing, Kenneth thought. He entered the ten-foot hight, eight-foot wide glass and iron doors of Judge Worthington's mansion. The Judge was waiting for him and escorted him to his private study and then left.

"Good evening, Mr. Alexander, it's good to see you again."

"Good evening, Mr. President."

"Did you and your bride have a good visit in the great State of Alaska?"

"Yes, Sir," Kenneth said, dryly.

"She's a beautiful woman, your wife. Quite bright and dynamic."

"Yes, Sir, she is," Kenneth said, folding his arms across his chest and staring at the President of the United States of America.

"Please. Relax, Mr. Alexander. Have a seat."

"Thank you, but no. I prefer to stand."

The president laughed. "I knew that this wasn't going to be easy, but do you have to make it this tough on an old man?"

Kenneth relaxed and took a seat in Johnston's study across from the President.

"Thank you. I sense from your demeanor that you want me to come straight to the point."

Kenneth didn't answer. He sat and waited, looking directly into the President's eyes.

"All right, I understand that you were the lead engineering specialist on a NSA frequency survcillance system for the Naval Air Warfare Center when you were at Sandoval Anniston."

"That's correct."

"Tell me about it."

Kenneth's perplexed expression caused the President to chuckle. "I assure you, Mr. Alexander, I do have the highest security clearance authority. You can tell me how this works."

"This technology, improperly deployed, could have global implications. This isn't a political issue to be used to gain an advantage for your party's upcoming elections."

"I'm well aware of that fact. That's why I'm meeting with you alone. I'm not treating this as some political football. We believe that a multinational corporation has access to your research, your system, and created a prototype."

Kenneth was visibly distressed. "You understand what this means, don't you?"

"Yes, Mr. Alexander, I do. It means that the world's entire defense systems could be compromised and destabilized, including everything in the United States. We, along with every other nation, would be defenseless. That someone with enough resources could literally hold the world hostage. We've already witnessed some acts of tyranny and terrorism. We believe that we know who's behind it."

"Who?"

"I can't give you that information, but I can say that our enemies in the Middle East are trying to get at this project. There's been quite a bit of industrial espionage uncovered. We believe that there are many facets to this, but someone has built an empire on contraband—drugs, guns—you name it, they've done it. Someone who is feared because he is the personification of evil and presents a clear and present danger to all of us. Now will you tell me about your frequency surveillance system?"

Kenneth sat back in the chair and thought a moment.

"The code name for the project was ALACE: Autonomous Lagrangian Circulation Explorer. High-tech drifter buoys were to be deployed in the ocean and tracked by satellites to observe surface and subsurface movement. The buoys float at a preset depth down to 2,000 meters and can be programmed to rise to the surface where NOAA's or NORAD's polar orbiting satellites can locate their radio signals. The drifters then re-submerge and continue to collect data. Altimeters send out microwave radar and sonar signals that bounce off the ocean floor and return to satellites. Precise calculations of the signals return times allow the altimeter to measure differences in anything that passes through the web, creating a three-dimensional map of the world, everything flying around the globe, moving under the sea or across land. I designed it for defense purposes. A sea-based, defensive shield. ALACE can be programmed to detect objects the size of a gnat, destabilize guidance, tracking any on-board system and shut it down."

"Including stealth technology?"

"Everything. Anything airborne would simply fall out of the sky and anything on or under the sea would be dead in the water if used improperly. All computerized systems would stop working. Banking, industries, television, radio, airports, street lights, microwave ovens, all systems."

"What about AWACS?"

"Neutralized."

The President took a deep breath. "Can your system monitor, reverse and/or block another system of a similar nature? Neutralize it?"

"Yes, if properly deployed. ALACE can work on a random and intermittent pattern so swiftly as to be undetectable. There's some additional technology that's needed to cause the system to work in reverse."

"When you left Sandoval Anniston, the project folded because you had designed and engineered the system, but no one else knew or could figure out how you made it work."

"I left all of my notes and tests results for my successor to follow."

"We know, but they still haven't been able to make it operate with the same efficiency that you demonstrated in the prototype. Believe me, they've tried. We need you back on the project. NSA tells me that your design is uniquely one of a kind."

"No, Mr. President. I have a business to run and a family to take care of."

"Hold on, Mr. Alexander. I know what you're thinking. That this is some type of veiled attempt on the part of my party to get you on our side. To try to use you the way that...well, regrettably, the way that some of the military leaders and the people at Sandoval Anniston tried to do. They're not involved with this anymore. After the Congressional investigation, which you had a large part in setting on the right track, I removed a number of...well, it was in the newspapers and on television. I'm sure that you must have seen it."

Kenneth didn't answer. He had seen the press accounts of the shakeup at the Pentagon and at Sandoval Anniston. He thought about JC Baker.

Much had been put right, he thought, but the fact remained that much of his work for the Sandoval Anniston Corporation had been used in ways that he did not intend. Projects that he designed and engineered were used as weapons of war, not for peaceful purposes. He knew that if he permitted himself to become involved again there was no guarantee that the same thing might not reoccur again.

"I can appreciate your position, but at the risk of repeating myself, I do have other commitments."

"Hold on, Mr. Alexander. We're prepared to compensate you generously for your service. Name your price."

"If that's all, I'll say goodnight. I have a wife waiting dinner for me and some unpacking to do," Kenneth said, as he began to rise from his seat.

"Okay. Okay. You are unyielding, aren't you, Kenneth?"

"No, I just have another point of view about my priorities."

"That's not what you said in your closing comments before the Congressional committee. As I recall you said, *A nation is formed by the willingness of each of us to share in the responsibility for upholding the common good. A government is invigorated when each of us is willing to participate in shaping the future of this nation and our world. We must define the common good and begin again to shape a common future. Let each person do his or her part. If one citizen is unwilling to participate, all of us are going to suffer. For the American ideal, though it is shared by all of us, is realized in each one of us. Let there be no illusions about the difficulty of forming this kind of a national community. It's tough, difficult, not easy. But a spirit of harmony will survive in America only if each of us remembers that we share a common destiny. If each of us remembers when self-interest and bitterness seem to prevail that we share a world community'."*

Kenneth sat back in his seat. He cupped his hand over his face and rested it on his chin. The president had recited his words verbatim. He rubbed his face again, as he pondered his own statements. The president waited patiently as Kenneth thought.

"I'll finish the project on one condition," Kenneth said, looking directly into the president's eyes.

"Name it."

"I won't take any money for this, but I want Lieutenant Stacy Greene, US Navy, back from wherever she has been deployed."

The President shifted in his seat. Kenneth waited. The President rubbed his face and pondered Kenneth's request.

"You have my word that I'll extract Lieutenant Greene at the earliest possible moment, but we never had this conversation about her or her mission and you cannot divulge to your family or anyone else that she'll return. Especially not to your brother, Benjamin."

"Agreed." Kenneth extended his hand.

"You'll be working with someone you know and trust on this project. Our best invisible agent. The agent will be authorized to reveal to you everything. Code name: Delta Dawn. The agent will fill you in on the plan. You tell the agent what you need and you'll have it. We'll use our SEAL teams, who specialize in new and unique communications technology, to deploy your system worldwide once it's ready."

"Mr. President, I'll redesign and engineer the system, but if I find that it's being used for offensive rather than defensive purposes, I'll shut it down."

"We know. I understand that you're quite a basketball player. Now, I see that you know how to play hardball, too. Johnny Worthington told me that I was up against it, trying to get you to help. Integrity. I like that quality in a man."

"It seems that you've learned a few things about playing hardball, too, Sir. I wasn't sure that anyone was listening to my comments before the Congressional committee."

"Everyone was listening, Mr. Alexander."

The special agents drove Kenneth back to his home. JeNelle had finished unpacking their clothes, had started the laundry, and was setting the table on the deck for dinner when Kenneth came in.

"What was going on with Johnston, Kenneth?" JeNelle asked, as she folded the cloth napkins and placed them on the table.

Kenneth leaned against the door jam, folded his arms across his chest, and smiled as he eyed her body while she worked. When he did not answer her, she looked up at him and caught a gleam in his eyes.

"Oh, no you don't. I know that look in your eyes. We've got work to do tonight."

"I wouldn't call it work. It's more like—"

"Oh no, I mean the gifts. Right after dinner, we're going to get started on opening and acknowledging that mountain of gifts we received."

"Couldn't we hire someone to do that, JeNelle? It's going to take weeks to go through everything and I can think of a few other ways that we can spend our time," he said, grinning.

"Oh no. We, you and me, Kenneth."

The gleam left Kenneth's eyes. He knew that he was going to have to work late on the frequency project and he had a short turnaround time for completion.

"Please, Kenneth," JeNelle cooed, as she slipped her arms around him and looked up into his eyes. "I don't want to hire someone to do this. I want to share this with you. It means a lot to me. We've both got to go back to work and we really won't have this special time to share with each other except when we get home at night. So can we please do this together?"

How could he deny her? He couldn't share with her what he had to do.

"All right, honey." He kissed her gently and held her in his arms. "We'll do it together."

After they cleaned the kitchen and started the dishwasher, they went into one of the spare bedrooms and carried loads of brightly wrapped wedding gifts into the living room. They began opening each gift separately and writing a special thank-you message to each person. Kenneth got up from the floor where they were sitting to pour more brandy into his glass while JeNelle opened gift number forty-one.

"Who's it from, JeNelle?" Kenneth asked as he finished pouring the drink and returned to her.

She did not answer him. He looked at her face. Tears were streaming down her cheeks and dripping on the gift in her hand.

"What is it?" he asked, concerned.

She did not answer, but handed the gift to him and wept. He gathered her in his arm and looked at the gift. It was a pure gold Florentine double picture frame. It contained a picture of her and Michel San Angelo smiling together on their wedding day and a copy of their marriage certificate. Kenneth closed the double frame and rocked JeNelle in his arms as she cried.

"How could he be so cruel?" she sobbed.

"I don't know," Kenneth answered as he held her. "We'll find a way to put a stop to this harassment. I promise you that. I'll speak with Johnston about it tomorrow. That's enough gift-opening for tonight. Let's get a good night's sleep and you'll feel better in the morning."

"No, no. I don't want to get you involved in this. Michel can be a violent man. I couldn't bear it if anything happened to you," she sobbed.

"I won't tolerate anyone harassing you like this."

"I'll handle it. Please don't do anything. Promise me?"

"I'm sorry. I can't do that. I won't make a promise to you that I know that I can't keep."

JeNelle wiped her eyes and hugged him. "I'll handle this myself. Please let me do this my way," she pleaded. "You're right. It's late. Let's go to bed. I promise that I'll feel better in the morning."

In their darkened bedroom Kenneth held his wife in his arms as she slept restlessly. He was wide awake. She whimpered in her sleep, tensed, and woke with a start.

"I'm here, JeNelle," Kenneth soothingly whispered as she began to tremble.

She buried her face in his chest.

"You were dreaming again. You're all right."

JeNelle composed herself. "Make love to me," she whispered slipping her arm around his neck and moving closer to him.

"I love you, but that's not going to help us solve your nightmares."

"I'll be fine. All that I need to know is that you love me," she said as she kissed him and he complied with her request.

In the morning, JeNelle cried quietly in the shower. Kenneth, she knew, was in the kitchen making breakfast. Michel terrorized her many times after their divorce, but she had taken no action against him. This time she would. She tried to compose herself, but the tears would not stop falling. She held her face under the shower as if the force of the water would wash away her agony. She knew that she would have to control herself and prevent Kenneth from discovering how deeply she ached in fear of Michel's terrorism. She felt her abdomen where she knew that new life lay growing inside of her. She couldn't afford to let anything cause stress on her body and the new life inside her. She composed herself and dressed. She took a deep breath before she went into the kitchen. Kenneth was taking the breakfast trays to the deck, as she entered.

"Are you hungry?" Kenneth asked.

"I could eat." She managed to smile back at him.

"Good. Everything is ready."

They had breakfast on the deck, talked about the improvements to their home, and listened to the surge of the ocean tide break loudly against the beach. They talked of what they expected the day to bring and agreed to have lunch together at 1:00 P.M. They drove to work together, pausing for a long farewell kiss in the car.

Kenneth grabbed his suit jacket and briefcase, as he watched JeNelle unlock the door to INSIGHTS. He winked at her, as she entered and locked the door behind her. He crossed the street and entered CompuCorrect's Southern Division offices. He looked around the office briefly. Things appeared to be shaping up nicely, he thought. He flipped on the lights, headed to his office, and noticed a light in Joe Grayson's office. When he knocked at the open door, Joe looked up from his desk and smiled.

"Welcome back, boss!" Joe rose from his desk and extended his hand. "What are you doing here so early?"

"Me? I should be asking you that question." Kenneth looked at his watch and then shook Joe's hand.

"I don't have a beautiful new bride to keep me at home in the morning," Joe joked.

"Neither do I, Joe. After a month-long honeymoon, JeNelle's already at work. So I thought that I'd come in and see whether you and Sara left anything for me to do."

Joe laughed. "We can find a few things around here to occupy your time. I'm sure that we can have you back home, say about midnight."

"Oh, no. I've got strict orders that my new bride issued personally. Dinner is at 6:00 P.M. sharp and she's driving. So unless I'm prepared to handle a divorce action, and I'm not, I'll be at the car waiting for Mrs. Alexander at 5:00 P.M."

Kenneth and Joe laughed.

"Already got you tamed, does she?"

"I wouldn't have it any other way," Kenneth said. "So tell me, what's on today's agenda?"

Joe began rattling off the status of each project. They talked for nearly an hour.

"That's about it, Kenneth. Forty employees have transferred or are in the process of transferring in from the Northern Division. Here is a list of the new employees. Sara told me that you would like to meet with them personally, so everyone will be in the conference room at 9:00 A.M."

Kenneth looked over the list of existing employees and the thirty new names, but stopped at one name. "Lisa Lambert?" he asked in disbelief.

"Oh, yes. Dr. Lambert. She said that she knew you. She's got impeccable credentials and comes highly recommended. I interviewed her twice. Very bright and aggressive. I was surprised that she submitted her resume. She seems overqualified for this position, but everyone has to eat. I know that you don't like this kind of talk, but man is she gorgeous! The governor wrote a letter, too. It's all in her file on your computer and—" Stopping mid-thought, he paused. "What's wrong, Kenneth? Why are you looking like that?"

"Joe, do you remember how we met?"

"Sure, Kenneth. We met in the hotel bar in Sacramento. That was the luckiest day of my life meeting you."

"Do you remember why I was in the bar?"

"You were trying to decide what to do about two women that you were involved—" Joe stopped short. "Oh no! Please don't tell me that one of the women was Dr. Lambert!"

Kenneth nodded in the affirmative.

Joe slumped in his seat. "You'll have my resignation on your desk in five minutes and I'll be out—"

Kenneth laughed. "Hold on, Joe. It's not that bad."

"Oh, hell yes it is! You can't be expected to have to work with a woman that you were once in love with now that you're married to JeNelle!"

"We weren't in love, Joe."

"I hope that JeNelle knows that!"

"JeNelle knows about Lisa. They were once business associates and friends."

"Saints have mercy on my soul!" Joe exclaimed. "I'm gone! I'm out of here!"

Kenneth laughed. "No, you're not, Joe. Just as I expected, you've done an excellent job for this company. You're not getting any pink slip or walking papers from me."

"It's not you that I'm worried about, Kenneth. It's JeNelle! She's going to kill me for hiring Dr. Lambert! Has JeNelle ever shown any homicidal tendencies?"

"No, not lately, but this may do it." Kenneth laughed.

"I'm dead!" Joe said, rolling his eyes back in his head.

"I'll talk with her, Joe. Maybe she'll give you a reprieve."

"Not likely! Stick a fork in me somebody, please! I'm done! Or maybe I can fire Dr. Lambert before JeNelle finds out about this."

"Hold on. Let's just see what's going on here. I'm curious about why Lisa would even apply for a position with this company after what she tried to do to us. Moreover, with her credentials, she could work anywhere she chose to."

"What did she do? I don't understand."

Kenneth explained to Joe about the contracts and the Congressional investigation. He also told him about the State Attorney General's decision, clearing Lisa of criminal charges, but that federal conspiracy charges were still pending. Joe's face dropped as Kenneth talked.

"I remember now. That's when you were on television. No wonder she couldn't get a job," Joe said in disbelief. "What do you want to do about this, Kenneth?"

"Nothing for now. I'll handle it."

Later, Joe sat in Sara's office still dazed by the morning's experience. Sara was busily working on the payroll, but finally looked up at Joe's blank expression.

"Joe, you've been sitting there for more than thirty minutes, staring into space. What's the problem? Just because Kenneth's back doesn't mean that we can take a vacation."

"I don't get it," he said in a daze.

"You don't get what?" Sara asked, as she continued to work.

"Kenneth. I don't understand him."

"What's to understand? What you see is who he is. You should know that by now. He's great! He's wonderful! He's the best boss anybody could have."

"You don't understand, Lass."

"Okay, then explain it to me," Sara said, putting down her pencil and folding her arms on the desk.

"I just made, what most people would consider, a career-ending decision, but Kenneth isn't even angry with me."

"That's not his style, Joe. He doesn't fix blame. He fixes the problem. That's the way that he operates. There's no mystery there."

"Yes, but how in the world is he going to fix this?"

"All right, Joe, I wasn't going to ask, but what did you do?"

"I hired Lisa Lambert."

Sara's soft green eyes widened. She rose from the desk slowly and menacingly.

"You did *what!*" Sara shrieked.

Joe cringed in his seat. "Now, Sara, please don't look at me like that."

Sara gritted her teeth, as she placed her palms on her desk and leaned forward even more. "Do you know what you've done? Have you any idea what that woman almost did to this company and to Kenneth?"

"I do now," Joe said, still cringing, "but I didn't know when I hired her."

"Then you can just go unhire her!"

"I can't do that. Kenneth's in there meeting with the new employees now, including Dr. Lambert."

"She's *here*? In this *building*?" Sara shrieked.

"Calm down, Sara. Kenneth knew that she was coming. He seems to have it under control."

"Of course, he does! I'm wondering whether I should murder you or her! It would be justifiable homicide either way!"

"If you don't then JeNelle certainly will."

"Oh my, *God!*" Sara said slowly, but expressively. "I forgot about JeNelle! As if Kenneth didn't have enough to contend with!"

They heard loud applause and hurrahs coming from the conference room.

"Meeting must be over, huh?" Joe asked sheepishly of Sara.

She cut him with a cool gaze and bared her teeth.

Kenneth sat in his office on the sofa making notes on a laptop. Lisa knocked on his open door. Kenneth looked up at her.

"Come in, Lisa." He stopped what he was doing. "Please have a seat."

"Thank you, Kenneth." She seated herself in a chair across from him.

Kenneth took a relaxed position on the sofa. "Well, Lisa, have you settled in yet?"

"Settled in?"

"Yes, is your office comfortable? Did you select an administrative assistant to work with you? Have you had a chance to go over your tasks?"

"I thought that you might want to fire me. I mean, yes, the accommodations are fine, but are you saying that I'm staying?"

"Yes, Lisa. I have no reason to fire you. You've got impeccable credentials and I'm sure that you'll be an asset to the company, but if you're uncomfortable with the arrangements, I'll understand. I'll certainly help you find another position with some other company."

Lisa sat back in her seat and searched Kenneth's face, her eyes probing. "You want me to quit then. Don't you?"

"No. Joe hired you to do a job. I suspect that you're more than capable of doing just that. No less. No more. Now, if we're clear, I want you to go to San Francisco and work with Tom for a few weeks. Sara will arrange your travel and per diem. As you know, Tom's one of the best sales and marketing men around. You'll be working in his department. With your background in economics and business, your marketing strategy will help this company focus on the industries that we need to concentrate on. Do you have any questions?"

"Why are you doing this for me, Kenneth? I mean we were lovers. You must realize that I'm still under suspicion for federal charges. My name is mud in this state and in Washington, DC. None of the other companies would touch me with a ten-foot pole."

"What you, JC Baker, and others did or tried to do is reprehensible, but I'm not a judge or jury. Joe hired you based on the merits of your resume and interviews. That's his job. I'm not going to second-guess him. As long as your relationship with CompuCorrect is mutually beneficial, then we don't have a problem."

"And what about our personal relationship? You were the most fantastic lover I've ever had, Kenneth. Surely you haven't forgotten the times that we spent together."

"We ended that part of our relationship a little less than amicably, I believe. Still, it's a closed matter as far as I'm concerned."

"And what about JeNelle?"

"I won't discuss JeNelle with you. She's my partner for life and I love her completely. Now if you choose to renew or revive your relationship with her, that's your decision. I'll abide by any decision that JeNelle chooses to make."

"Just like that?"

"It's the KIS method, Lisa. I'm keeping it simple. Now, if you have no other questions, let's get to work. We have clients to serve," Kenneth said, rising and extending his hand.

Lisa rose from her seat, shook his hand, and left Kenneth's office. She paused outside Kenneth's office door momentarily and smiled to herself. *He hasn't forgotten what we did for each other,* she mused. *He'll come back to me. I'll see to that.*

"How was the honeymoon, Kenneth?" Tom asked jovially via Skype.

"Great, Tom. How are things in the Northern Division?"

"I don't want to talk about the company yet. Tell me about the honeymoon. Tell me about Alaska. Tell me the good news. Can we expect a new addition to the Alexander household—say in about nine months?" Tom laughed.

"The honeymoon was great. We had a wonderful time in Alaska and can recommend it highly. I'm enjoying being JeNelle's husband, and as for a new addition to the family, well, we'll keep you posted. Now, how's the Northern Division?"

"All right, Kenneth, if you insist. We'll talk about business."

Tom began to cover the events that occurred in Kenneth's absence. He flashed the sales and marketing report over the screen. Kenneth studied it, pushed a button, and copied it into his computer. Then they discussed the budget, cash-flow projections and their profit and loss statement.

"Looks like you need some help in the Northern Division, Tom."

"I'm swamped, Kenneth. With the mass exodus of employees moving to the Southern Division, I'm working with a skeleton crew."

"I'm not surprised. I did an orientation with the new staff this morning. I've also met with the staff that moved here while I was away. I didn't realize that so many people would accept the offer to transfer. I'll send some help up to you, but it looks like we're going to have to hire another thirty or forty people according to Joe's report."

"Thanks, Kenneth, and by the way, you were right about Joe. He's done a great job for the company. I like his style. Good man! Works real well with people. He'll go far in this company."

"I'm glad to hear you say that because he's hired Lisa Lambert."

Tom's face came up close to the video screen. "*What!* Fire him *now!* Get him out of there and her too!" he demanded.

Kenneth laughed.

"This isn't funny, Kenneth. That woman is a Piranha! Fire both of them!"

"Tom, do you trust me?" Kenneth asked calmly.

Tom sat back in his chair and rubbed his face with the palms of his hands.

"I do, yes, Kenneth," he said slowly, but skeptically.

"Good, Lisa's coming to work with you for a while. She's in your department."

"*What!*" Tom screamed. "You're kidding, right?"

"No, Tom. It's no joke. I'm putting her on the sales and marketing team. She's a known entity with large-scale businesses not only in California, but also elsewhere."

Tom collapsed on his desk and bounced his head. He finally looked up and reached for a large box of headache tablets and swallowed some without water.

"Kenneth, you're going to drive me to an early grave or an insane asylum. I think that it's time to start talking about taking CompuCorrect public. We're growing too fast and I'm struggling to keep up," Tom said seriously. "I have no life anymore. I can't even find time to spend with my children or Shirley. She's swamped, too. And what about you, Kenneth? Now you're a married man. I'm sure that you and JeNelle want to have a family. Some semblance of a private life."

Tom really looked stressed to Kenneth. "Tom, I don't believe that it's time to take CompuCorrect public, but I'll consider it."

"There's been a lot of interest in us lately. Our exhibit at that Small Business Expo was very impressive. People think that we have something good going for us and investors have been talking some pretty impressive numbers. We could open a chain of outlets across the state. Maybe even take the company nationwide."

"We'd also lose control of our integrity, but let's talk about it again in a few weeks. Get Lisa and the other new employees in your department acclimated to the operation, and then you and Shirley take off for an extended holiday. I'll send Joe up to put him on hiring new staff for the northern division. With him there, I'll handle things from here."

"How are you going to manage running both offices while we're away? I saw your calendar. You've got speaking engagements coming up all over the state, the Youth in Business and Industry Project, plans for the next Small Business Expo, and probably a lot of other things that I don't even know about."

"Don't worry about that, Tom. You and Shirley just start looking at travel brochures," Kenneth said and disconnected the contact.

⊶

"Where's Kenneth, JeNelle?" Canty asked her daughter.

"At the office," she answered, chopping the vegetables frantically, as her mother looked on.

"Will he make it home for dinner?"

"Yes," she said somberly.

Her mother noticed her mood. "What is it, JeNelle?"

"Nothing!" she snapped.

"Don't take that tone with your mother, JeNelle. I know that you're pregnant and pregnant women have mood swings, but you've been in a snit for weeks now," Harvey said firmly.

Tears began to roll down JeNelle's face. Harvey noticed and moved to gather his daughter in his arms.

"I'm sorry, baby. I shouldn't have spoken so harshly to you."

"It's not you, Daddy. It's me," she sobbed.

"I don't understand. What's got you so upset?" Harvey asked, sitting JeNelle down at the kitchen table. "Is it Michel again?"

"No, I haven't heard from him since I spoke to Milo San Angelo."

"Is it this Lisa Lambert?"

"She's still in San Francisco, but Kenneth's been flying up there once or twice a week to work with Joe since Shirley and Tom have been on vacation."

"And you think that something's going on between Kenneth and Lisa?" Canty asked, frustrated.

JeNelle didn't answer. She stood up, wiped her tears, and started chopping the vegetables again.

Canty shook her head. She stood next to JeNelle and grabbed her shoulders, turning her daughter to face her. "Kenneth loves you, JeNelle. He's not the type of man who plays around. A wise woman knows the importance of speaking life into her man. If you love him, believe in him, encourage him and be his peace."

"He's been working day and night," JeNelle answered. "He's home for dinner and then he either works here in the study or he goes back to the office. Sometimes he doesn't come to bed until two or three in the morning. Then he's up and out by 6:00 A.M. He's been working on the weekends, too. We never spend any time—" she cut off her thought.

"Making love," Canty added. "And you think that he's fooling around because he's not sleeping with you."

"The man runs a company," Harvey said, "but that doesn't mean that he doesn't love you. He's a busy man. You should understand that. It wasn't too long ago that you were doing the very same thing at INSIGHTS."

"Have you read those books that I lent to you?" Canty asked.

"No, Mama."

"What books?" Kenneth asked, as he entered the kitchen and smiled at his wife and in-laws.

From behind his back, he revealed two bouquets of flowers and gave one to Canty, with a quick kiss on the cheek. She beamed. The other flowers he gave to JeNelle. He kissed her and held her tight. He felt her burgeoning baby mound and smiled at her.

"What books are you talking about?" Kenneth asked again, picking up a piece of cut carrot and popping it into his mouth.

"Oh, just some books about how to—"

"Uh, Mama," JeNelle interrupted.

Kenneth looked at Canty quizzically. "How to what?" Kenneth asked.

"Uh, Son, your mother-in-law is being nosey," Harvey said, laughing.

Kenneth caught his drift. "Uh, please don't give my partner any more ideas. She's still got all of those bridal shower gadgets and gizmos in our bedroom and she's got my tongue hanging out all of the time as it is. Lovemaking lessons she doesn't need!" he said. "She could write a book!"

Canty and Harvey laughed and JeNelle smiled slight, but she knew better.

Later that night after her parents left, Kenneth was working in the study when JeNelle came in and stood by the door.

"Honey, it's late," he said with concern, looking at his watch. "You should have been asleep hours ago."

"I don't sleep very well when you're not with me," JeNelle said softly.

Kenneth pulled JeNelle onto his lap, pulled her head onto his shoulder, and stroked her belly.

"Little people keeping you awake?" he asked.

"No, not tonight. One big person."

"I'm sorry, honey."

"Kenneth, what are you working on so hard that's keeping you up until all hours?"

"I have an outside project and I can't use anyone else to finish it, but it won't be long now. When Tom and Shirley get back things will ease up and we can spend more time together."

"That's not how you operate and you know it. You've been in overdrive non-stop since we met. I'm worried about you. You're not working to secure our future or build a business anymore and it never was about making piles of money. We've got more resources than we'll ever use in three lifetimes and you're not even thirty-five. What's driving you to work so hard?"

"You're right, it's not about money. It's about making things better. It's about fulfilling the investment that our ancestors made in us. The investment that we'll make in our children and that they will make in their children. I was blessed to have ancestors who believed in the future. A future without racism, hatred, war, discrimination, starvation, helplessness or homelessness. They looked forward to a place in time when life was a positive and not a negative. A time when people would enjoy each other and accept each other without question or forethought. Without pretense or prejudice. That's what I'm working for. That's what my family has always been about. Working for the common good."

"I love you most for that very reason, Kenneth, and I share your dreams for our future. I'm just not willing to sacrifice as much now as you are. I'm not willing to sacrifice the time we have together here and now. I know that I'm being selfish, but I want us to be together. I don't want you working so hard. Perhaps it's time for you to give Tom's suggestion, about taking CompuCorrect public, some serious thought."

"This is an important time for this company. There's a lot going on right now. Taking CompuCorrect public could mean leaving us open to potential takeover attempts. That could mean the loss of our integrity. Our employees count on that integrity and support to do their jobs. They're the ones who have gotten us to where we are now."

"I know that, but it's also an important time for us, too. I'm not going to interfere with how you run your company. I just want you to know that I love you, trust you, and support you. I also want you to know that I need you, too. I know that I haven't been the sexual partner that you had hoped for—"

"JeNelle," Kenneth interrupted, "we're fine. There's nothing to worry about on that score. I love you completely."

"Let me finish, please."

"All right."

"You've tried everything possible. You've been creative, spontaneous, loving, affectionate, patient, giving, fun, and more than what any woman would have expected and you haven't complained once about my lack of experience in showing you how much you mean to me. You even covered for me with my parents tonight for the sake of my ego. You've gone to sleep unfulfilled more nights than I care to even think about."

"Honey, you don't have to be an aggressive or even an assertive partner when we make love. You turn me on just thinking about you or holding you like this. Like we are right now. I'm yours no matter what. Body, mind, soul, and spirit. Everything that I am or ever hoped to be is because you love me. I can survive without an interactive sex life, but life would almost be meaningless without you in it."

"You love me and I know that with clear confidence, Kenneth, but it's not enough and I know that, too. It's late now and I want to go to bed—but not alone. Not without you next to me."

"Uh, JeNelle, what books were those that your mother was talking about?"

"Why?"

"I believe that maybe I should be the one reading them."

"Oh, no you don't. You're already at the pro level. I just need to catch up," she said, smiling at him, as she turned out his desk lamp and led him to their bedroom.

⚎

"How was the vacation, Tom?" Kenneth asked via Skype.

Tom beamed. Shirley blushed.

"Man, Derrick Jackson's place in Bimini is incredible! Thanks for arranging it with him for us."

"More than that," Shirley said, wiggling her finger in front of the camera in her office.

"Way to go, Tom!" Kenneth yelled, as he spotted the diamond engagement ring on Shirley's finger.

"Man, two people who hated each other could go to Derrick's place and fall in love with each other overnight!"

Kenneth laughed. "Yeah, I've heard. Vivian seems to have enjoyed the experience tremendously."

"Are they announcing something, too?" Shirley asked.

"Derrick tells me that he's ready, but he doesn't want to put pressure on my sister. She'll be finished with law school in the spring. She's already working on getting her career going, working on Capitol Hill part time, and he doesn't want to interfere with that."

"Career! You mean that Vivian would work if she married Derrick?"

"You know Vivian. She was born to practice law."

"Derrick's well off. I've heard that he's worth billions—"

"Yeah, a lot," Kenneth said, "but Vivian Lynn Alexander is still the daughter of Bernard and Sylvia Alexander, Granddaughter of—"

Tom and Shirley laughed. "We get the picture," Tom said.

"I've thought about your suggestion, Tom, to take CompuCorrect public."

"And?"

"We will do it."

"Great!" Tom shouted.

"Wait a minute, you two, I'm not on board with this idea," Shirley interjected. "I know that this will mean a lot of investors will be lining up at our door, but I'm not ready to go that route yet and I thought that you weren't sold on the idea either, Kenneth."

"I have some other reasons for changing my perspective on this, Shirley."

"Do you mind sharing your thoughts with us?"

"Not now, but I will as soon as some things clear up."

"All right, Kenneth. I trust you. You know that."

"Yes, I do. Don't worry. I won't let you down."

"So when do we go public, Kenneth?" Tom asked.

"Vivian's working on it now. She'll have the new corporate platform worked out soon and then we can be listed on the stock exchange if we're all agreed. I've made some inquires about board members. I definitely want Johnston Worthington, Derrick Jackson and Chuck Montgomery on the Board of Directors. I have a few others in mind also. I'm looking at selecting members from foreign markets particularly. Shirley, I'm going to need a financial statement from you and a new annual report before the end of the year. Tom, work up a prospectus on the company."

"This is going to be a lot of work, Kenneth," Tom said.

"Yes, it is, but what's new about that? We've been doing that for nine years now."

"Kenneth, you are going to stay with the company if we go public, aren't you?"

Kenneth didn't answer immediately, but Tom and Shirley saw the faint change in his expression.

"Kenneth," Tom said, suddenly quite concerned, "did you hear what Shirley asked you?"

"Yes, Tom, I heard her."

"Well?"

"Well what?"

"Are you thinking about leaving CompuCorrect?"

"I've not made that decision yet."

"Kenneth, you can't!" Shirley insisted, concerned. "The company would fold without your leadership! You know that!"

"Shirley, calm down. I said that I haven't decided, and, after all, there are three of us running this company, not just me. Either one of you could step into the position of Chair of the Board and President of the company and take it to greater heights."

"No way, Kenneth!" Tom said adamantly. "This company was your idea from the beginning. Your dream and it works well because of your leadership. Not because of me or Shirley, so if you're thinking of leaving, we're not going to go public!"

"Tom's right, Kenneth," Shirley added.

"Hey, you two. I didn't say that I was leaving. Let's just keep this simple for the moment, but understand that at some point things could change. We have to be prepared for that possibility. Now, let's get going on our projects. I'll come up to San Francisco next week and we can talk about this in a little more detail. In the meantime, Tom, get Lisa Lambert involved in the planning phase. I want to keep her in the loop on this."

"Sure, Kenneth, but why?"

"I have my reasons, Tom. Thanks, I'll see you both next week."

Chapter 18

"Hey, playa, playa how's it going?" Cecil Jordon asked, as she stepped down into the kiddy pool in the condo complex and joined Benny Alexander and his daughter, Whitney.

"It's going, Cecil," he answered with a slight smile, keeping his eyes on his toddler and kicking water on her as she played.

Cecil noticed his melancholy though. There were times since Stacy left that Benny bore her sudden and unexplained departure better than at other times, but Cecil suspected that this was not one of those occasions. She watched him as he sat on the edge of the pool, playing with his toddler, and splashing water on her as she played with the other children. He was smiling, as his baby girl tried to navigate around the other babies to capture a red ball that kept eluding her. She was an independent little thing, Cecil thought, sitting quietly next to Benny, watching Whitney. The two-year-old always made him smile. Her fat little legs churned up the water and she made a big splash, as she lost her balance and plopped butt first. She grinned at Benny and squinted up her pretty face, but then she was off again after her ball.

"I'll watch Whitney for you if you want to swim, Benny."

"Thanks, but no, Cecil. Whitney and I don't get to spend a lot of quality time together. She's growing up so fast. Seems like just yesterday that I brought her home from the hospital. Now she's walking and talking up a blue streak. Next thing you know she'll be off to nursery school."

"She's a sweetheart, Benny."

"Yeah." He smiled. "I knew she would be. She's quick, too. Doesn't miss a trick. She's learned how to climb out of her crib already. Yesterday, I thought that she was napping so I took a shower. Next thing I knew she was crawling around on my shower floor in her nightgown, dumping my plants out! She had muddy dirt everywhere. She told me 'Let's make pies, Daddy.'"

He laughed and Cecil smiled.

"You two make some pair, Benny. It's good to see a brother taking care of his responsibilities."

"Yeah, that's my girl. She's not just a responsibility. Just look at her with that determination in her eyes. Same fire that Stacy has. She's a blank page. Innocent and ready to start writing her own story, just like her mother."

"She's a lot like you, too, Benny."

"Thanks, Cecil. I like to think so, but the older she gets the more she reminds me of Stacy."

"Everything reminds you of Stacy, Benny," Cecil said, putting her arm around him and giving him a quick hug.

She leaned her head on his shoulder and he briefly leaned his head on hers.

"Think I'll take you up on your offer, Cecil," Benny said, standing up.

He pulled his USAF T-shirt up over his head, exposing his tight six-pack abs and concaved abdomen, and headed for the pool. He had thick thighs and long leg muscles, too. Brotherman was ripped. Cecil watched Benny walk to the Olympic-sized pool and dive in. Other women sitting around the indoor pool were watching him, too, she noticed, but Benny didn't. He lapped the pool full out, extending himself, as he usually did, far beyond his endurance. His tall, solid frame and muscular body reminded Cecil of Donald Dixon, but why shouldn't it? Benny and Don were first cousins, after all. They seemed to be good friends, too, but that's where the similarity seemed to end, she thought. Benny had a free and easy spirit that endeared him to everyone he met, but Don had an edginess about him. A kind of reluctance to know people too well or to let them know him. Nothing got by him either. He could laugh heartily like Benny, but with full awareness of everything going on around him. She noticed how his eyes were always scanning his surroundings almost imperceptibly. Never at ease or at rest. He kept his energy banks in reserve. Mysteriously controlled behavior even while he carried on a lively repartee. He seemed to notice the slightest movement, smell, or sound. Indeed, he was an interesting study, she thought. Very suave and debonair, too. He turned women's heads, just like Benny, but unlike Benny these days, Don always seemed to look back. Don flashed a killer smile that would melt your heart or break it into a million pieces. Only a fool would trust him with something as breakable as her heart or let herself get caught up in his web, Cecil concluded. If she did, she'd never be able to escape.

"Thanks, Cecil," Benny said, coming back to the kiddy pool.

He was breathing hard, as he sat down, wiping the water from his head and face with a big, fluffy, white towel. She noticed his FAMILY gold chain around his neck.

"That was quick."

"Only felt like thirty laps today. How's Miss Whitney Ivy doing?"

"She's fine. See, she finally captured that ball." Cecil laughed.

"You ever going to do this?" Benny asked.

"What? Have a baby? Naw, I don't think so. That's not me. Little people take a lot of care and attention if you're going to do the job right."

"You'd make a great mother to somebody."

"Ha! You're a better parent than I could ever be. Nah, too much ugly in this world for me."

"Ah, Cecil, you can't reject the idea of parenthood just because of the negative things that go on in this world."

"Oh, yes I can." Cecil laughed. "I didn't grow up in the rarefied air of Goodwill, South Carolina, like you did, my friend. A lot of people I started growing up with just aren't here no more. Too many babies dying and too many mothers crying. Stacy and I used to talk about that. She lost her twin sister to drugs. I've lost people too and I've got nieces and nephews who I'm worried about, especially after what happened to Travon Martin and others. Can't bring nobody in this world and then watch some stranger take them away over a pair of shoes or a shirt or a stick of chewing gum."

"You're forgetting about all of the good stuff, Cecil. Like sitting here watching that little comet of mine soar and explore. All anybody can do is to be the best parent that they can. Expose little people to every positive opportunity that this universe has to offer and support them every step of the way."

"You can say that now, Benny, but if you could have your life back the way it was before Whitney was born, I'll bet that you'd take it."

"You'd lose that bet." He laughed. "Can't imagine life without my little comet. Sure it was a rush before Whitney Ivy, but now she's my rush."

Cecil shook her head. "Benny, you sure have changed."

"I hope I've improved, Cecil. I still like to party and hang out, but it's different now."

"Well, my friend, I loved you like a brother before and I love you even more now."

"Me and who else?" Benny asked with a sly smile.

"Oh, I guess you're referring to your cousin?"

"Seems you've got the boy's nose open to me."

"Ha! You must be confusing us with James and Janice."

"Nah, now, I know that Don gets around, but—"

"Don't even try it, Benny. I've seen his type too many times before. They ought to call him Don the Wand! He's the love 'em and leave 'em type."

"That's not him," Benny protested. "It's his lifestyle. He's always on the move. The man hasn't been able to live anywhere long enough to develop a relationship."

"And why not?"

Benny got suddenly quiet. "He'll have to tell you about it."

"That's just it. He hasn't said a lot about what he does for a living. All he said is that his job requires a lot of travel."

"Yeah, but he's legit...I mean, he's not doing anything illegal."

"I believe you, Benny. It's not that important anyway."

"Oh, so my cousin hasn't got a chance, huh?"

She smiled. "Sure, he's been calling. Says that he's going to stop through again sometime real soon."

"You going to see him again?"

"We'll see. Depends on my schedule."

"Don't go breaking the man's heart, Cecil. You could scar him for life," Benny joked.

"Right!" Cecil said, rolling her eyes and sucking her teeth.

"So what does that mean? You don't think that men can hurt when a relationship doesn't work out?"

"I don't have a clue about what men feel or don't feel. It's not something that I focus on."

"Let's focus on it now."

"Why?"

"Just humor me."

"Benny, this doesn't make any sense."

"Just answer my question."

"What was the question?"

"Do you think that a man can hurt?"

"As compared to what?"

"As compared to what a woman feels."

"Some men, perhaps. Some men take relationships seriously and make a commitment, but not most men. They're looking for the next goodbye."

"And you believe that Don falls into the category of men who don't hurt?"

"I don't know, Benny, I mean, I barely know the man. We've only been out a handful of times. He doesn't strike me as the commitment type, but this is all purely academic. It's like trying to believe in one religion. There's too much to choose from. I'm not looking for a full-time relationship, but if I were, it certainly wouldn't be with your cousin."

"Give the man a chance, Cecil. I think he's very interested in you."

"A chance to do what?"

"A chance to show you what he's made of."

"Uh, Benny, I've already tasted the forbidden fruit, sweet and tart, but I'm not going to make a seven course meal out of your cousin."

"A chance, Cecil."

"I'll see him, but—"

"You're not going to take him seriously."

"No way!"

Benny smiled and shook his head. Cecil noticed.

"Okay what does that mean?" she asked.

"It means that relationships get so screwed up before they even get a chance to get started.

"Are we talking about me and Don or you and Stacy?"

"Both, I guess. I know that I screwed up by not letting Stacy know how I really felt about her earlier in our relationship. We were friends and we were both focusing on our careers. I was focusing on the sex. Stacy was focusing on our friendship. The sex for her was secondary. Neither one of us focused on whether we had something to work toward. I never knew where I stood with her and I never told her where I wanted the relationship to go. You and Stacy are a lot alike. You've focused on your career to the exclusion of everything else. Love, commitment, marriage aren't even in your vocabulary. Just career and occasionally sex."

"And you think that Don is like you?"

"Sure he is. I've been with a lot of women, but I didn't make a commitment to anyone until I thought that I was in love with JeNelle and you know how committed I was then. The only reason that happened in the first place was because I didn't believe that Stacy was willing to commit to a future together. Those were the signals that I was getting from her. All that she was willing to commit to was a friendship. I think that's where Don's going. You're not open to a commitment no matter what Don does or says. It's hard for a man to know what to do, or say, or feel in a relationship anymore. Women have changed over time more than men have."

"You're probably right. That's why I'm not going to get into anything heavy with Don or anyone else for that matter."

"So you're going to live your life without someone special in it?"

"What's wrong with that? Having a man in my life doesn't guarantee happiness. Even with a man like you or even Kenneth. Both of you are the type of men that some women dreamed of when they were little girls, but your type are few and far between. What's left out there are men who can only give bits and pieces of themselves. A woman either accepts a little bit of many men or not a whole lot of any one man. Either way, what's the difference?"

"Don's a whole person, Cecil. He's got a lot to offer a woman like you on a lot of levels, but you're right, no relationship comes with a built-in guarantee that it's going to work out. No relationship is bullet proof. Still, you have to have the relationship first to see whether it works."

"Like you said, Benny, women have changed. We're not looking for love in all the wrong places anymore or waiting to exhale. Don's been interesting. Certainly unique in many respects, but that wears thin after a while. All that fun and fury doesn't last. When it's gone, you have to just keep moving."

Benny just shook his head. "I'm glad that my parents were born before women became so self-sufficient."

"What?" Cecil laughed.

"Oh, you can laugh, but some women, present company included, are making male partners obsolete."

Cecil laughed loud. "Benny, I'm not a lesbian. I enjoy being with men. Your cousin included. I'm just not looking for some fictional Prince Charming to come and rescue me. I can take it or leave it. Either way, I'll live."

"Don't women dream about love and marriage anymore?"

"I sure can't tell you what women want, but if Janice and I are considered typical women in today's society, we have vastly different views on what's necessary. She left last night to go clear across the country to visit your cousin James. I wouldn't go across the street to visit most men I know."

Chapter 19

James Dixon had a broad smile on his face as he craned his neck, looking for Janice to come toward the airport security exit. The Columbia, South Carolina airport was busy even at that early hour in the morning. Janice, he knew, had taken the last flight out of San Diego to Chicago and then a connecting flight from Chicago to Columbia. It was nearly 6:30 A.M.

She was finally there, Janice thought to herself, as the aircraft touched down at Columbia airport. She wondered whether James would be waiting for her. It was awfully early in the morning. Maybe he had forgotten how early her flight got in, she thought, as she struggled to pull her carry-on baggage from the overhead compartment. The line to get off the plane was beginning to move slowly. She waited for the woman ahead of her to put her child in the stroller and gather her many baby bags.

Janice was anxious to see James in his own surroundings, but the baby was a sweet diversion. Janice couldn't tell whether it was a boy or a girl, but she smiled and wondered how she would feel if it were her baby.

She finally stepped off the aircraft and started up the ramp to the security gate. She braced herself against the disappointing possibility that James wouldn't be waiting for her. She'd been disappointed by men she'd dated before. Each time she'd swear to herself that she'd be more like Cecil and just move on, but it never worked out that way for her. She'd look forward to the next man and hope that that time would be better than the last.

Janice raised her eyes and saw the tall, male figure smiling at her. He was wearing pleated, khaki slacks, a powder blue, pinstriped, short-sleeve shirt and loafers. No gold draped anywhere except the simple

248

FAMILY chain around his neck and no earrings in his earlobes. A plain watch with a plain, black, leather strap was the only adornment with the exception of his award-winning smile. His smile broadened hers, as he moved toward her before she was even out of the security gate.

"Hi, James," she beamed.

"Janice, you look wonderful," he gushed.

"Thank you, but I must look a hot mess after traveling all night."

"No, no," he protested sincerely. "You look great. Let me carry those bags for you." He took her luggage.

Then James did something that surprised her. He kissed her gently on the lips, smiled broadly, and reached for her hand.

James felt his six-foot, five-inch frame grow to ten feet as he held Janice's hand and walked on air through the airport to the baggage claim area. It was so exciting being with her again. He wondered whether she would turn down his invitation to come to South Carolina to visit him. He was prepared to pay for her airline ticket, if she would agree to come, but then she mentioned that she would be in Columbia lecturing for a week at South Carolina University and asked what his schedule was during that time. He told her that no matter what his schedule dictated, he'd be there whenever she arrived, but hoped that she'd come to South Carolina early and visit him and his family on his farm. He couldn't believe it when she accepted.

"How was your flight, Janice?"

"I guess it was fine. I really didn't notice. I was so excited about coming."

She noticed how James' whole demeanor lit up and he squeezed her hand a little tighter.

"I'm sorry that you had to come out so early in the morning to meet me."

"Early?" James laughed. "This isn't early for me. Actually, I couldn't sleep last night. I was looking forward to seeing you again."

He noticed how Janice's face lit up and she held his hand a little tighter. It made him feel special.

As they left the baggage claim area and exited through the sliding doors, a light rain was falling.

"Wait here, Janice, and I'll get the car. I don't want you to get wet and catch a cold on your first visit to South Carolina." He smiled.

He released her hand, kissed her again gently, and dashed toward the parking lot, carrying her luggage. How sweet and thoughtful he is, she thought as she watched him dash away. Moments later a shiny, blue SUV pulled up and James got out. He opened the door for her and helped her inside. He reached across her and fastened her seatbelt for her.

"Thank you, James."

"What are you thanking me for?"

"For being such a gentleman."

"You're welcome, but I haven't done anything extraordinary, Janice."

She smiled at his confused expression. Here he was making her feel like a princess, someone special, and he didn't even realize it.

"That will be six dollars," the tollbooth attendant said, as they exited the airport.

"Six dollars? I didn't realize that a short stay in a parking lot would cost that much in South Carolina," Janice said.

"I got here a little early. It's only two dollars an hour," James said shyly.

Janice felt the tingle go from her head to her toes. James had been waiting for her for three hours!

The drive to Goodwill would take over an hour James said, but he took a route that took them past some of the sights of Columbia. He drove through the University of South Carolina campus, pointing out the different buildings and giving her a little history behind some of the sites they passed. Then it was on to Goodwill in Summer County. The misty fog hung like white broken clouds, as they sped through the dense, green countryside. Janice opened her window, sniffed the lush honeysuckle and pine fragrances and felt the heavy humidity that saturated the air. A few cars passed them speeding down the narrow roadway. However, James didn't seem to be in any hurry to get to Goodwill and Janice wondered why.

"Janice, I have to admit that I'm a little nervous about bringing you to Goodwill. I mean, it's not that I'm ashamed of where I live or anything, but it's very different from San Diego."

"I was hoping that it would be very different, James. Benny talks about Goodwill all the time. I'm looking forward to it. So far what I've seen of South Carolina is more beautiful than I expected."

James glanced at Janice and sped up. When she saw the sign that read WELCOME HOME, she really felt as if she was coming to a special place. The bright sunlight broke through and Mother Nature began to sparkle. There were no stoplights in town. No frantic traffic jams. No looming buildings or trendy shops. There were brightly painted framed stores with real wood structures. Flower boxes hanging from shop windows and screened doors and windows opened to let in the fresh air. A wide, long town square divided the roadway that contained gazebos, brick paver pathways, flowers, trees and water features. A few people sweeping off the sidewalk waved as they drove by. James spoke and waved back. They stopped for a tractor to slowly cross their path and Janice noticed a mailman smiling and talking with his customers, as they entered the post office in the town hall. Women with young children walked around the open market, feeling and smelling the fresh produce and chatting with the store owner and other customers.

"Well, this is Main Street, Janice." James smiled.

"It's great, James, but I thought that you lived on a farm."

"I do, but I wanted you to see the town first."

"Are you still nervous about my visit?"

"Well, yes. I mean, you're from a big city...a metropolis and Goodwill is far from that."

Janice smiled. "All right, James. No more sightseeing. Take me to your home."

James drove out of town and shortly turned into a narrow lane. Janice saw workers constructing a new house on a slight hill.

"That's the home that Kenneth and JeNelle are building," James pointed out, "and over there is Uncle Bernard and Aunt Sylvia's home. On this side is my parents' home. Down the road a little further is—"

"And where is your home, James?"

"I guess I've stalled long enough, huh?"

Janice nodded and James drove into the long, circular driveway leading to an impressive, long, brick rambler. Flowers and trees were strategically placed around the lush green, well-manicured lawn. Big, beautiful weeping willows and pink dogwood trees swayed gently in the thick breeze. Azaleas and morning glories, peonies and roses fought for prominence in the gardens. Butterflies flitted around from bloom to bloom.

James drove under a carport next to a black Ford pickup truck. The carport was attached to a side, screened-in porch that occupied bright yellow lounge chairs and a hot tub. James got out of the car and came around quickly to open Janice's door.

"It's beautiful, James," Janice said, sincerely as she took in the serene surroundings. He opened the screened door for her and she stepped inside. He opened the door to the house, which led past a laundry room, a powder room, and then into a large country kitchen neatly arranged and scrubbed. The modern, stainless steel appliances gleamed and Janice could see an enclosed breakfast room with a glass-topped, wrought iron table with four chairs. Neatly arranged fresh, garden flowers were on the table that was already set for two. It was perfect, she thought.

James watched Janice's expression nervously, as she wandered through the kitchen, then the dining room and living room. Her smile seemed to brighten as she walked around, he thought.

"What's in there?" She pointed toward his bedroom.

"Oh, uh, that's where I usually sleep, but, uh your room is through here," he said nervously.

He opened a door to a hallway that had a bedroom on either side. He led her into one of the rooms that he worked so hard to make look attractive. His mother helped him and so had Aretha and his Aunt Sylvia. They assured him that Janice would like it. The fresh flowers that he placed in vases around the room didn't seem to be enough to him.

"Uh, I know that this isn't what you're used to. I mean, it's not very elegant or anything, but if you tell me what you'd like changed—"

Janice kissed him. "Not a thing. Don't you change anything about this wonderful home of yours. It's perfect just as it is," she said sincerely.

James exhaled slowly and shook his head. "Wow, I was really worried that you wouldn't like it."

"I love it, James."

"Well," he said, gathering himself, "I guess I'll get your luggage out of the car now."

"Oh, so what were you going to do, take me back to the airport if you thought that I didn't like your home?"

"No, I hadn't thought that far ahead. I just kept trying to think positively." James smiled.

Janice just shook her head. No man ever treated her with such warmth and respect. James wasn't even expecting her to sleep with him. That was a true novelty. With other men, even complete strangers, if they paid for your drink at a bar, they expected you to be grateful enough to sleep with them the next minute. James was very unique, she thought. He assumed nothing and didn't take anything for granted.

That was very different from the way Cecil described Donald's—James' twin brother's—behavior. Not that he was crass or anything. Just that he was very direct. The perfect match for Cecil, she told her. Cecil was direct, too. Cecil would cut through all the courting phase of any relationship and go straight to the heart of the matter with her suitors. She could be very intimidating to most men she dated. Cecil didn't pull any punches either. If she saw a man that she liked, she usually took the offensive, captivated him in no time, and walked away, leaving the man in a daze, wondering what had hit him. Don had not been an easy conquest for Cecil. They were very much alike.

James and Janice shared a leisurely breakfast together, while he explained that the house was powered by solar panels and geothermal energy, propane, and operated on a well-and-septic system, but Janice was yawning and James insisted that she take a nap and relax. He closed the heavy blinds in her room and covered her with a fluffy sham.

"I won't be far if you need me," he said, as he kissed her lightly on the lips and left the room, pulling the door closed behind him.

Janice couldn't believe how James was so caring and considerate. No grabbing at her, trying to seduce her. No overt sexual suggestions. No callous comments. Instead, he was just the opposite. He was a gentleman. A Southern Gentleman with old fashion charm.

Later, James returned to the kitchen where she was standing, looking out of the patio door at the backyard swimming pool. She had been watching him riding around the farm on a big palomino horse.

"Oh, you're awake already," James said with a big smile. "I thought that you'd still be sleeping. I'll just take a quick shower and then I'll make lunch and start dinner. My parents are coming over later this afternoon."

"It's early yet, James. Why the rush?"

"I wanted to make sure that everything was just right."

"What time are your parents coming?"

"They'll be here at 6:00 P.M. sharp."

"James, it's only 1:30 P.M.," she said, moving toward him. "Couldn't we just spend some time together?"

James backed up. "I've been working outside in the fields, Janice, helping my people to move the cattle to a different pasture. I'm full of sweat and dirt—"

Janice stood on the tips of her toes and kissed him gently on the lips.

"You look real good to me." She smiled. "Smell like a man whose been doing his job. Nothing wrong with that."

"But I don't want to get this funk on you. You look so fresh and clean. Let me just get out of these clothes and take a quick shower."

"Okay, if you insist." She smiled at his discomfort.

James rushed off to his room and turned on the shower. He could not believe how Janice was so even and easygoing. She took everything in stride. She wasn't even offended that he had work to do. She was his guest, but she wasn't demanding.

Later, when James returned to the kitchen, she was sitting in his den reading a copy of *Black Enterprise* magazine. There was a copy of *Jet* there, too. In it, she found pictures of Kenneth and JeNelle's wedding. There were a lot of books and picture albums on the shelves. All kinds of books: poetry, literature, text books, financial exposés, novels. Someone had been doing a lot of reading, she thought.

"Can I get anything for you, Janice?"

"I'd like a glass of white wine, if you have it."

"Sure, foreign or domestic? I have some Santa Barbara County wines that Kenneth sent to me."

"I have California wines all the time. What do you usually have?"

"I have some Zinfandel from South Carolina's Montmorenci Vineyards," he said, opening his wine cabinet and pulling out a bottle.

"I didn't know that South Carolina had vineyards."

"I'll have to take you there and to some of the other places around the state."

"I'm not sure that I'll have the time to visit the whole state this week, James." Janice chuckled. "And next week I'll be lecturing on campus."

James smiled, handing the glass of wine to her.

"I hope that this is the beginning of many trips that you'll make to the Palmetto State."

Janice blushed. "You do a lot of reading it seems," Janice said, accepting the glass of wine.

"Yes, I particularly like poetry."

"I see that you have a lot of books of poetry on the shelf. What's your favorite poem?"

"'The Phenomenal Woman,'" he said shyly, but then he began to recite it to her. Then another and another. For the rest of the rainy afternoon they sat in the comfort of his den having a light lunch and reciting poetry to each other. James had never thought that such an attractive and intelligent city woman would enjoy reciting poetry for entertainment, but Janice seemed to be enjoying herself. She had beautiful, dark green eyes, he thought, as he looked into them, and butter-biscuit brown complexion. A cute, heart-shaped mouth and oval face. Her hands were small and well-proportioned to her body size, which was a trim frame of average height. Her dark, sandy-colored hair was in a crinkle-cut style over her ears usually, but she had it pinned back and rolled at the ends. Her cream-colored cotton blouse was tucked inside her matching shorts. No hair on her slightly bowed legs and strapless sandals on her small feet. She was perfection in his eyes and a rare delight. Soft spoken, yet with a magical lyrical flare when she spoke. He knew that she would be an excellent speaker or lecturer. People would listen to her naturally, just as he was listening to her now reading Maya Angelou's poetry with such soft passion.

He kissed her before he realized what he was doing. He had done that a lot. She was so kissable. Sweet like a ripe, juicy peach at its peak of flavor.

"I like doing that with you," James said.

"You do?"

"Yes, why do you sound surprised? Surely you know the effect that you have on me."

"Well, it's only a kiss. I mean, I'm enjoying it, too."

"I hope you don't mind if I hold you in my arms."

"Mind? Why would I mind?"

"I don't want you to think that I'm trying to take advantage of you."

"Advantage?"

James laughed.

"What's so funny?"

"You. You seem so surprised at everything I say. Why is that?"

"I guess it's because you're so sweet to me and considerate."

"I am?"

"Yes, didn't you know that?"

"No, I mean, I haven't done anything out of the ordinary. It's just real nice being around you. You deserve to have very nice things done for you. Much more than I can do."

"Like what?"

"Like having flowers sent to you every day or limousines taking you wherever you want to go or beautiful clothes and jewelry delivered to you from world-famous designers or tickets to anywhere in the world—"

"Whoa, James. I don't need all of that stuff. You've got beautiful flowers in your guest room that you cut out of your own garden with your own two hands. There's nothing wrong with your car. I like wearing jeans and tennis shoes and the only airline ticket I'm interested in brings me to South Carolina."

"Uh, Janice, may I have that hug and a few more of those kisses of yours?"

"On one condition."

"What's that?"

"That I can hug you and kiss you, too."

"Agreed!"

⌐══⊸

"How do you like South Carolina so far, Janice?" Romelo Dixon asked, as he passed the butter beans to her across the nicely-decorated dinner table.

"I'm enjoying it a lot," Janice said, blushing.

James blushed, too.

"My son has been looking forward to your visit. Can't keep his mind on anything these past few weeks."

"Stop teasing James Edward now, Romelo," Olivia Dixon said playfully. "You remember how you were when you first brought me home to meet your family."

"What do you mean, Libby, I wasn't nervous. Not like James Edward has been."

"Oh, yes, you were." Olivia laughed. "You were shaking like a leaf. You couldn't even pronounce my name for fifteen minutes because you kept stuttering."

"Go way!" He blushed. "Wasn't like that atall. It was cold that day. That's all."

"Ha! It was ninety degrees in the shade, I tell you, and Romelo's parents thought that he would pass out. James Edward hasn't been acting nearly as strange as you did." She laughed at her husband's chagrin.

"So James was nervous, huh?" Janice asked with a sly smile.

"Sure was. I thought that he'd never be satisfied with fixing up your room for you. He bought six of everything! Sheets, spreads, draperies, comforters, rugs…all in different colors. He decorated and redecorated that room at least six different times in the last week!" Olivia laughed.

"Mom, I just wanted to make sure that Janice would be comfortable and like it here. You know that." James shifted uncomfortably in his chair.

"And I do, James, very much." Janice smiled at him and brushed her hand over his on the table.

"James Edward, where are you taking Janice while she's here?" Romelo asked.

"That depends on her schedule. Although she's here a week early, she still has to do a lecture tour," he said, turning his attention from his parents. "Of course, there is Grand Aunt Hanna Ivy in Atlantic Beach. She hasn't met you yet and Uncle Rufus and Aunt Gladys want you to come over to Santee to go fishing. You might enjoy the Bellefield Nature Center and the Baruch Institutes for nature research or the Brookgreen Gardens; it's a wildlife park and aviary." Cousin Ruth Benson-Smith and Cousin Rosalyn Benson-Styles in Charleston called and asked if you'd like to come there for a few days."

"James, you don't have to go to all of that trouble for me. As far as I'm concerned we don't have to leave Goodwill." Janice smiled. "I'm enjoying being on the farm and watching the grass grow. It's so peaceful here and I can get a ton of reading done. In fact, I may even do some writing, so we really don't have to go sightseeing. Besides you and your father are running a large working hydroponics business. I'd like to see more of that operation."

James smiled broadly at Janice.

"Gee whiz, Libby. Look what time it is. We'd better get a move on if we're going to make it to town for the dancing tonight."

"All right, but do you kids need any help with the dishes?"

"No, Mom, you and Dad go along. I can handle this."

"Thanks, Son. You did a real good job on that dinner."

"I used your recipe, Dad. It had to be good."

Olivia hugged Janice. "I'm so happy that you agreed to come and visit. Your presence here means a great deal to all of us and we hope that you'll want to come back often."

"Thank you, Mrs. Dixon. You have made me feel very welcomed here. I'd like to come back and visit whenever James has the time."

"Oh, James Edward will make the time for you, Janice," Olivia said, smiling.

James and his parents embraced and they left. He started clearing the dishes from the dinner table.

"I can do that, James."

"Oh, there isn't that much to do."

"I'd like to help. You cooked a great dinner. The least that I can do is to help you clean up."

"I thought that you had some reading that you wanted to do?"

"Oh, that can wait," she said, as she kissed him on the lips.

They finished cleaning up and Janice browsed through James' music collection. She put on several selections of Barry White and turned down the lights while James took out the trash. Janice was smiling at him broadly when he came into the cozy family room.

"What?" He smiled.

"May I have this dance?"

"Oh, uh, sure," he said, as Barry White's deep melodious tones filled the room.

They danced slowly together and James began to hum along with the music. Janice took his lead and began humming the tunes, too. Before long they were singing to each other as they danced together into the darkening evening. James lit candles around the room and put on more music. They talked, sipped wine, and listened to the sounds as night closed in around them. Janice snuggled into James' arm on the sofa and laid her head against his shoulder. She could feel his heart beating strongly as he stroked her hair and they intertwined their fingers.

"Janice?"

"Yes."

"I want you to know that I don't do this all the time. I mean, you're the first woman who I've invited to stay here."

"Why did you want me to know that?"

"I don't want you to get the wrong impression. I mean, I know that my brother and Benny have reputations as, well, you know—"

"Yes, I know, but you're very different from your brother."

"My brother and I are twins, but we live very different lives. He probably would know all the right things to say to you."

"You're doing just fine, James. This has been the most romantic evening I've ever had."

"But all we did was stay here and listen to music. I'm enjoying it, but I thought that you might find it boring. I thought of taking you into town for the dance, but I was feeling selfish. I wanted you to myself."

"Are you confusing me with Cecil?"

"Well, you two do lead very different kinds of lives in San Diego. I don't imagine that you just sit around the house playing cards. I mean, both of you are independent, attractive, self-sufficient women. There aren't a lot of places in South Carolina like the ones in San Diego that you took me to. Like that club, uh..."

"Jason's?"

"Yes, that's the one. You and Cecil knew a lot of people there it seemed."

"You mean a lot of men, don't you?"

There was a long pause. Janice raised her head and looked at James' face. He did not look at her. She wondered what he was thinking.

"Yes," he answered without expression. "Men who have a lot going for them. I mean, the parking lot looked like an expensive foreign car dealership. Jag, Maserati, Benz. I didn't see one Ford or Chevy truck anywhere."

"Why are you letting that kind of stuff bother you?"

"It's hard to compete with that. I mean, I don't exactly live on the fast track. I'm a country boy. I've lived in big cities, but I like things a lot slower and easier. I like to enjoy myself. I like to go out and have a good time, but most of the time I'd rather be here in Goodwill working the farm or running the family business with my father."

"Are you trying to compete with the men in San Diego?" Janice asked, still looking at him.

"Couldn't you tell?"

"But why?"

"Because of you, Janice. I've made no secret about my feelings for you, but I'm not sure that I've even got a chance. I mean, your condo looks like it was the prototype for *Architectural Digest*. So does Benny's. You drive a Jaguar. You work for one of the top organizations in the world and you're a part of their leadership team. People at SCU tell me that they're surprised that you even agreed to come and lecture here. They also tell me that you're one of the foremost biochemists in the country."

Janice put her soft fingers to his chin and turned his face to hers. She gazed into his eyes. He felt a rush of anxiety at how she might be receiving his confession of his insecurities and shortcomings. She was, after all, a very confident woman, he thought. She was also beautiful. Not just her face and body, but her spirit. He was awestruck when she stepped out of the Cessna at the Santa Barbara Airport the first time he met her. He focused his attention on her at the first rehearsal even before they were paired together for Kenneth's wedding.

Janice and Cecil were both very attractive and all week at the different parties and events that they attended he noticed how men flocked around both of them. Men of every type and description, but he knew, almost the very moment he first laid eyes on her, that he had more than just a physical attraction to her. That's why he extended his trip to California for two extra weeks. He and Benny had fun in San Diego, but it was Janice that he waited each day to see.

"James, you don't have to compete with anyone ever, but if you did, there would be no contest. You'd win hands down!"

She kissed him gently on the lips. He wanted more and pulled her across his lap into his arms. Kissing her felt so natural. She tasted sweat and warm and giving. She thrilled him to his very core. He fought to keep his body in check. To not let his hands roam freely over her body. To not touch her breasts, her hips, or her thighs. He heard her moan quietly and felt her soft hands manipulating the back of his head, pulling him into her. He couldn't prevent his tongue from searching for hers.

Someone cleared his throat and Janice and James looked up suddenly and began to untangle themselves.

"Uh, hey, excuse me, little brother," Donald Dixon said, with a sly grin on his face.

"Hey, yourself. When did you get in?" James asked, releasing Janice and regaining his composure.

He stood up and embraced his brother.

"Oh, a little while ago. How are you, Janice?"

"Fine, Don," she said, as she hugged him. "It's good to see you again."

Don looked at their faces. They seemed to be blushing for being caught in such a passionate moment.

"Uh, maybe I'd better stay over at the folks' house."

"Nah, you don't have to do that," James said, wiping the perspiration from his brow.

"Are you sure? I mean, it's no trouble for me to—"

"No, it's not a problem for me if it isn't for Janice."

"Me? Oh, James, this is your home. You decide. I'm comfortable with Don here."

"Well, actually, Don and I built this place together. He has the north wing while I have the south wing. We share the common areas. The house belongs to both of us. It's just that he's not here most of the time."

"Oh, I didn't know that. Then there's no question. You've got to stay, Don," Janice smiled.

"All right, but I'll make myself scarce. I'm only going to be around for a few days."

"Oh, are you on vacation or something?" Janice asked.

Both men looked at her.

"Uh, yes. Something like that," Don said without expression. "Anything left to eat?"

"Yeah, look in the refrigerator and there's pie on the counter."

"Okay, uh, you two hungry?"

"Uh, no, we ate a little while ago with the folks."

"Where are they? I stopped by the house to see them, but they weren't at home."

"They went to the dance in town."

"Oh, yeah, Friday night. I forgot. Well, you two can get back to your, uh, conversation. I'll grab something and head into town."

Janice and James blushed.

"Yeah, you do that, big brother," James said, with a bashful smile. "It's good to have you home again." James hugged Don again.

"It's always good to come home."

Don left the family room and went into the kitchen. James and Janice heard him opening the microwave, as they both tried to mask their amusement at being caught like teenagers in the back seat of a car.

"I'm sorry about that, Janice. I didn't mean to embarrass you."

"Embarrass me? I wasn't embarrassed." She chuckled.

"I never know when my brother might show up. Usually it's not a problem."

"I see that he doesn't call to let you know when he's going to be in town either. Drives Cecil crazy when he just shows up out of the blue like that."

"He usually doesn't have the time to plan ahead like most people. He just comes whenever he can."

"What does he do, James?"

"Uh, he's a lawyer. More wine, Janice?"

"Oh, I see. The silent treatment."

"No, it's not that. It's just that I don't know a lot about Don's life outside of here."

"That's curious. Don't you two talk?"

"All the time about the important things, like family."

"I see. Well, if you're comfortable with whatever it is that he does, then that's not a problem for me and, yes."

"Yes, what?"

"Yes, I'll take another glass of wine." She smiled. "I'm beginning to appreciate more than just your South Carolina vineyard."

"You working?" James asked Don across the kitchen table early the next morning before Janice woke up.

"Don't know yet. I'm waiting for a call, but what's up with you and Janice?"

"What do you mean?"

"Brother, this is a first for you. Bringing a lady to stay with you here. You know the family tradition. You only bring home someone you intend to marry."

"So?"

"So, what's up? Is that your intention?"

"I don't know."

"Looked like you knew last night."

"You noticed, huh?"

"Like I could miss it?"

"Janice and I are just getting to know each other a little better, that's all."

"Oh, okay. I see. You really don't want to talk about this with me."

"It's not that. I mean, there's not much to say."

"What's the 'not much' part?"

"I like her...a lot, but man, I can't compete with those guys in California."

"Sure you can! You've got a lot going for you."

"Yeah, right!"

"James, there's no difference between you and any of those other people in San Diego. You have a double doctorate, a tenured professorship, run the family farm and the Alexander-Dixon hydroponics business with dad. You're no country hick. I've told you that before. If you want her, take her."

"That's not me, Don. You know that. As much as I like Janice, and I do want to be with her, I'm not going to 'take her'. She has to decide whether I'm someone she wants to be with. She's not some one in a million kid of girl. She's a once in a lifetime kind of woman."

"Man, if you wait for her to decide you could end up losing her."

"I'm not just looking for a one-night stand," James said, as he got up and poured another cup of coffee for himself. "You want some more coffee?"

"Yeah."

James poured another cup for Don.

"I'm looking down the road."

"Then you are that serious about her?"

"I don't know, but I think so, yes."

"Then you'd better put a lot more pep in your step, my brother. Janice and Cecil are both very dynamic women. You're going to have to handle the situation."

"Handle it? You handle it with Cecil, but Janice is a different type of woman. She can't be 'handled' and even if she could, I wouldn't try that approach with her. You're just asking for trouble."

"I don't have a lot of time for the soft approach."

"You're going to have to or you're going to be handling yourself by yourself. Cecil's not going to take 'handling' either, I'll bet. She's too smart for that."

"Oh, is this advice from the world-class lover, little brother?" Don joked.

"Don't hand me that 'little brother' stuff." James laughed. "You just happen to be born five minutes before I was."

Don laughed. "Still qualifies."

"Yeah, right."

"So, have you done your duty yet?"

"Man, you're a trip sometimes, you know?"

"You didn't answer my question."

"No, I didn't."

"You didn't what?"

"Answer your question."

"You mean you haven't…"

James cut his eyes at Don.

"Man, what are you waiting for? Life's short! It could be over in a flash!"

"Oh, as if I didn't know that?"

Don sunk back in his seat. "I'm fine, James. You worry too much about me. I know what I'm doing."

"We're not going to have this same argument again. You're my brother and I love you, but every time you leave I wonder—"

"I know. That's what I mean, James. You can't live your life like tomorrow is promised to you. You've got to live every day as if it's your last, so if you want to be with Janice, you'd better get a move on."

"I have a different point of view. Anything that's worth having, takes time and a lot of hard work. From my perspective, Janice is worth it. I'm willing to put in the time and work hard to earn her respect and her affection if she's willing to do the same thing."

When Don's phone sounded, he checked the text message and then dialed one number. "What's up?" he asked of the voice on the other end of the line. "Yeah, the New York family... San Diego?... They called us? That's a switch... Didn't we hear something about an offshore connection? What new equipment? Is it in place? When? Who's taking it in? SEALs? What's my cousin got to do with it? No, I'm on it! Uh, ETA four plus...Yeah, out!"

"Sounds like you've got to roll out again."

Don sat, perplexed, but didn't answer James.

"Don, did you hear me?"

"Yeah, little brother," he said slowly.

"What's this about a cousin?"

Don looked at James and James knew that he wasn't going to get an answer.

"Okay, so when are you leaving?" James asked.

"Now."

"Now? It's only 5:30 A.M."

"Yeah, I know. Tell Janice that I'll see her soon."

"You're going to San Diego?"

"Eventually, I've got a few stops to make before I get there though."

"Should I tell Janice to warn Cecil? I hear that Cecil doesn't appreciate your pop calls."

"Warn her? You make it sound like Hannibal at the gates of Rome."

"I intended to."

Don laughed. "You're right, little brother!"

⚬➤

"Good morning," Janice said, as she stood by the kitchen door admiring James' tall, muscular and agile body moving effortlessly around the kitchen cooking what smelled like a hearty breakfast.

James turned to look at her over his shoulder. *Wow! She is even more beautiful in the early morning light.*

"Good morning," he said.

"Uh, do I have time for a run before breakfast?"

"You jog?"

"Yes, every day."

"So do I."

"Great! Do we have time?"

"Yes," James said, turning off the flames on the stove and the oven.

They went outside into the morning mist that was beginning to rise with the sun. They stretched and peeked at each other's bodies as they limbered up. Then they were off jogging down a grassy path through the trees and across the road. They waved at people they passed who smiled and waved back.

On and on they went through town, around the track at the high school and through another route that brought them back to the farm. They walked around as they cooled down and Janice felt that tingling sensation flooding over her. She took off her running shoes and sox and headed for the pool. She dove in and started lapping the pool. James followed suit and dove in after her. The water was cool and refreshing after their morning run. They climbed out of the pool and James lay on a wide chaise lounge breathing deeply. Janice pulled a fresh towel from the clothesline in the yard and wiped her face. She looked at James' body dripping wet with his jogging shorts clinging to him and forming around his ample pubic area. His gold FAMILY chain glistened against his beautiful brown skin. She stood over him and shook her hair until the droplets fell on him.

"Hey!" James laughed, as he felt the water falling on him.

He opened his eyes and saw Janice giving him the once over with a devilish smile on her face. He noticed how her T-shirt clung to her and her nipples protruded through and stood at attention. He reached up and pulled her down on top of him.

Janice felt James' body beneath her as she lay on top of him and between his legs. She laid her head on his chest as he unplaited her hair and spread it apart. His thick chest was still heaving and she felt the muscle in his jock strap move against her abdomen.

"I like this," James said, as he held her gently.

"I do, too," she said, raising her head, stacking her hands under her chin to look into his eyes.

"I could get used to this very easily."

"I hope so. I truly hope so, James," she said, as she kissed him.

Then she suddenly stopped and looked around.

"Uh, James, where's your brother?" she whispered.

James laughed. "He's gone. He left hours ago."

"Then we're alone?"

"Just you and me in the universe," he said, as his passion for her grew with their kiss.

Janice's response was equally as passionate.

Chapter 20

A few weeks later, Cecil was working in her office when her telephone rang.

"Dr. Jordon, you have a delivery in reception," Loris Campbell, Cecil's administrative assistant, said with a light sing-song voice.

"Sign for it, please, Loris."

"Sorry, Dr. Jordon, only you can accept this delivery."

"All right, Loris, send the delivery person in," she said, as she continued working.

The door to her office opened and a huge bouquet of flowers came in. Cecil didn't look up immediately until the delivery person cleared his throat a few times.

"Yes, what is it?" she finally asked. She looked up and gasped. "What in the world—" She got up from her desk. She approached the bouquet. "Who died?"

"Now is that any way to treat a gift from an admirer?" a deep-throated, melodic voice asked from behind the flowers.

"Depends," Cecil answered dryly, as she crossed her arms across her chest, stood hip shot, and pursed her lips.

"On?"

"On who the admirer is," she said to the flowers.

"Well, how many admirers would be sending flowers to you in the middle of the week?"

"All of them," she quipped.

"Anyone special?"

"All of them."

Don placed the flower stand on the floor and stepped out from behind them.

"All of them?" he asked with a sheepish grin.

Cecil didn't answer him. She just gave him a Mona Lisa smile. "Don, what are you doing here?"

"I was in the neighborhood and thought that I'd pop in to see Benny."

"Oh, so you didn't know that Benny was out of town, I suppose?"

"Again? My timing must be off, but since he's not around how about me and you," Don said, slipping his arms around her waist and pulling her close for a little slow dance, "tripping the light fantastic tonight? I've got a set of Benny's keys to his condo and his car. We could…" he whispered something in her ear.

"You sure don't waste any time," she said, rubbing her body against his and then slipping quickly out of his embrace.

"Oh, come on, Cecil, I don't have a lot of time to waste. I mean, let me cut to the chase. You're a brilliant, gorgeous, and sensual woman who has a dynamic personality and a fantastic wit. Not to mention a body that would make any strong man weak. Now, I don't know what's wrong with the men in San Diego, but I feel like their loss could be my gain," he said, slipping his arms around her again and guiding her into another slow dance.

Cecil was feeling a devilishly amorous twinge, but decided not to let that affect her better judgment about getting further involved with Donald Dixon. She was already too interested in him as it was, she thought. "There's nothing wrong with San Diego men. In fact, I have a date tonight," she lied, as she turned on her heels and started to walk toward her desk.

Don grabbed her from behind and pulled her close to him, still swaying to the silent music.

"Break it," he whispered in her ear, enveloping her in his arms. "I'll see you at six."

He kissed her neck and headed for the door.

"Don! You can't just—"

"Six, gorgeous," he said with a wink, as he walked through the doorway and left.

"Well! If he thinks that he can just waltz in here!" she fumed aloud, but then caught sight of the flowers. They were spectacular, she thought. "But that's not going to get Don the Wand into my—"

"Dr. Jordon?" Loris asked, "Are you talking to me?"

Cecil hadn't heard Loris come in. She felt suddenly embarrassed. "Oh, no, Loris. I'm just thinking about how some men think that you'll just drop everything and...oh, never mind," she said, as she spied the flowers again. Loris followed Cecil's line of sight and looked at them too. "Do you like these?" Cecil asked, lifting the flowers and handing it to Loris.

"Sure, Dr. Jordon, and that fantastic deliveryman, too, but didn't he give these—"

"You take these flowers and you can have the deliveryman, too, with my blessing."

"Okay, Dr. Jordon," Loris said, puzzled. "Oh, by the way, Dr. Atterly called and said that she has a meeting tonight and wondered if you'd mind taking a cab home?"

"Call her back for me, please, Loris. Tell her that I'll manage. I'm working late tonight anyway."

"Oh, and Mr. Easton called while you-know-who was here. I told him that you were unavailable. He wants you to call him ASAP."

"Thanks, Loris. Enjoy the flowers and hold all calls this afternoon. I have a project I'm trying to finish."

"Yes, but if you don't want that deliveryman, would you write out instructions on how I can get him?"

"Just stand still, Loris. He'll find you." She smiled back. "He's got woman radar."

Loris smiled and closed Cecil's office door as she left. Cecil picked up the telephone and dialed Charles Easton's number.

"Hey, baby, what time are we on for tonight?" Charles asked.

"Tonight? I don't think so. Did we have something planned? There's nothing on my calendar."

"I thought we were beyond that scheduling stuff, Cecil. Can't I just expect my woman to be available when I want to be with her?"

"I don't know. Give me her name and number and I'll call her and ask her for you."

"Just whisper, she'll hear you."

"Sorry, it loses its flavor in the translation."

"Come on, baby. I need you tonight. It's been a hellacious week and it's only Wednesday. I want to kick back, ya know? Get some dinner, hit a few clubs, maybe go to the beach, lay on the sand, and count stars or something. Maybe catch a movie—"

"Sorry, pal, I've got to work, but Loris is free." She laughed.

"Are you really working or is that guy in town again?"

"I'm really working and yes he's in town again, but I'm not going to see him tonight either."

"You still working on that special project?"

"Yes, I've got to finish this underwater calculation for currents in different parts of the world. I just got the plans and the prototype. The client needs a quick turnaround on this."

"If this is how it's going to be after we're married, then I may have to reconsider my options."

"Don't even go there, Charles. I'm not hearing that marriage stuff from you."

"Don't work too late, baby. Give me a call later when you get home. I'll hang out until I hear from you."

"Charles, I told—"

"Bye, baby."

He hung up.

"Men!" Cecil said, frustrated.

She went back to work.

Later, Cecil stood up to stretch. She paced her office and glared at the coffee pot because it was empty. The reception area was full of the cleaning crew, but there was no coffee there either and all of the employees were gone. Her watch read 8:35 P.M. She was beginning to get weary and decided to pack it in for the night. She slipped some papers into her briefcase, slipped her feet into her high-heel shoes, laced the straps around her ankles, and grabbed her purse. Maybe she'd stop at Michelangelo's and pick up something to eat, she thought, as she rode down in the elevator. She said goodnight to the security guards, as she signed out of the building. Out of the front doors and to the curb she walked looking for a cab. Nothing in sight. Lights flashed in her face, as a car pulled up to the curb in front of her, and screeched to a halt. Benny's Mercedes Benz 500 SL with the top down and Don in the driver's seat.

"I see you didn't break your date," he said sarcastically, getting out of the car and escorting her to the passenger side.

It all happened so fast that Cecil didn't recover until she was seated and Don slid into the driver's side.

"I didn't have a date," she said defiantly.

Don didn't speak, but he just drove to the condo. He parked, took Cecil's briefcase out of the back seat, and escorted her to the elevator. The doors opened and they went inside. She started to push the button for her floor, but Don grabbed her hand and pulled her toward him. He kissed her hard and with such force that she found herself gasping for air wedged against the corner of the elevator. His body had her pinned in with no room to move. Not that she wanted to necessarily, but he was overwhelming. His hands were spread apart above her against the wall and he nuzzled her neck with his nose and open-mouth kisses as he whispered in her ear.

"Don't ever lie to me, Cecil, and I won't ever lie to you. Now, this is how I see things," he continued in a whisper-soft voice while still pinning her into the corner. "You've already wasted what little time we have together. I'm not asking for a commitment or a long-term relationship and neither are you. I planned this nice little romantic dinner for two in Benny's condo. We'll wine and dine and chit and chat for as long as you want, but it's all going to end up the same way. We're going to make love tonight. All night. In the morning I'll be leaving early. If it works for you, then call me. If it doesn't, don't. Now you push any button on the panel you want," he said, moving away from her to the opposite side of the elevator. He crossed his arms across his chest and fixed his stare on her.

Cecil caught her breath and pondered her options. She faced his unyielding stare and that twinge of damnable lust began to rise in her.

All she had to do was push the button for the twenty-third floor, her floor, and get out of the elevator. Don, she knew, would not try to stop her. His bold moves had her fixated though. She pushed twenty-three and the elevator began to rise. They defiantly stared at each other without expression as the elevator ascended. Finally, the elevator stopped and the doors opened. She stood there ready to move, but unable to do so. Don's expression never changed as the doors closed. He pushed the button for the 28th floor and the elevator continued to rise. The doors opened and he waited. Her feet moved effortlessly as she walked down the hallway to Benny's door, 2814. Don opened it and she walked in.

In the morning when Cecil woke, Don was gone. She lay in the bed alone looking up at the mirror above the bed. A business card lay on the pillow next to her with Don's name on it and a telephone number. At least he had been true to his vow, she thought. They had made wild, passionate love everywhere in the condo from the moment they walked in the door. No holds barred, she recalled with a smile. She stared at the card, wondering what she was afraid of. A man who was clear and direct about what he wanted? Wasn't that what she was looking for? Not someone who was professing love and commitment. How much involvement could there be between them? He wasn't around that much. Hit or miss once in a while. That was more than enough. She picked up the telephone and dialed the number.

"Yes," Don answered.

"It works for me," she said.

"See you soon," he answered.

They hung up.

"You must have had your freak on last night!" Janice chided, as Cecil dragged into the condo. "Do tell! Do tell!"

Cecil slumped against the kitchen door frame. "Is that fresh coffee?" she asked, as she unlaced her heels, kicked off her shoes, and traversed the kitchen to the coffee pot.

Shaking her head, Janice waited for the news. "Knocked you to your knees, huh?"

"At least," Cecil groaned, stretching her neck from side to side. She sat at the kitchen table with her head on her hand, sipping the hot coffee.

"Mmm, that country boy must have been serving you a little somethin', somethin'," Janice teased.

Cecil cut her eyes in her best friend's direction. "Could we skip the press conference, Janice?"

"All right." Janice laughed, as she watched Cecil devour the hot liquid and lay her head on her folded arms on the table. "Charles called half the night. Didn't you have your cell phone?"

"Don turned it off and took my pager, too."

"Let's get you into a hot tub."

"Been there, done that," Cecil said, her words muffled by the table top. "All I need is some sleep."

"Well, sleep fast. Don left a message on your answering machine. Seems that he's had a change in plans. He'll be here at 1:00 P.M. for lunch."

"Lunch!" Cecil squealed. "Uh uh! No way! I've got to work on this project."

Janice laughed. "Sure you're right," Janice said, placing her juice glass and coffee cup in the dishwasher. "I'm outta here."

Janice left for work and Cecil climbed into bed. She slept soundly until she heard the doorbell ringing. She dragged out of bed and grabbed a robe. When she opened the door, Don came in carrying two bags of food. She smelled the familiar aroma of Michelangelo's' cuisine. A distinctive Italian scent, but she also caught sight of a gun holstered under Don's armpit. Don saw her glance at the weapon and closed his jacket.

"Hungry?" he asked, kissing her on the cheek.

"Don, why are you carrying—"

"Cecil, there are some things that we can't talk about. Now, here's how I see things—"

"Whoa," she said, putting up both hands in a stop-sign motion. "We've been there already today."

Don pulled her toward him. "It's not about sex. It's about having lunch together. I've got a 4:00 P.M. flight. Now, can we eat?"

"So I can't ask you about that—"

"You can ask me about anything, but there are some answers that I won't give you, and I told you, I don't want any lies between us," he said, looking into her eyes, "but if it will make you more comfortable, I'll take it off and put it away."

She nodded in the affirmative and Don took off his jacket and holster. He loosened his tie and unbuttoned his shirt at the neck. They sat at the kitchen table and ate. Cecil didn't ask about the weapon and Don offered no further explanation. The issue hung in the air like a wet blanket covering every conversation they had over lunch.

"This is very good," Don said, finishing his second serving of half cheese and half meat manicotti.

"Michelangelo's has very good food," Cecil said blithely.

Don's demeanor changed almost imperceptibly, but Cecil noticed.

"Michelangelo's?" Don asked. "You think that this food came from there?"

Cecil quizzically looked at Don. "Of course. Are you saying that it didn't?"

"Have you been to Michelangelo's before?"

"Sure, lots of times. The food is great, the atmosphere is charming, and the entertainment is enjoyable."

"So you're one of those women who like to party a lot?"

Something in Don's question struck a nerve in Cecil. "*Those* women?"

"Yeah, you know, a party girl," he said off handedly

"Is that synonymous with body by Fischer, brain by Mattel?" she snapped.

Don looked up from his plate and sat back in his seat, measuring Cecil's demeanor. He folded his muscular arms akimbo. "Is this PMS or didn't you get enough rest?" Cecil's eyes narrowed and Don saw the rage swelling. "Oh, so now you're angry? I swear a man just can't catch a break. Mention PMS and you women go berserk, but I'll bet that you analyze that topic of PMS to the nth degree in the ladies room."

"You must be an expert if you've made a survey of topics that women discuss in the ladies room!" Cecil said, flashing gritted teeth. "Is that what you do for a living? Hang around ladies' rooms eavesdropping on women's conversations? If so, let me let you in on a little secret among us women. You only need a gun when your asinine surveys come up with the wrong result, but we women have learned to overlook these little skewed results! After all, you're only men. Your anatomy is different. Your brains are in your other head!"

Don's eyes searched Cecil's carefully. He liked what he saw. A side of his mouth hitched up. "Maybe it was too much caffeine."

Cecil leaned menacingly forward on the table. "Haven't you heard? All women drink decaf."

"Passionate, too, huh?" Don asked, warming to the irate woman across from him.

"It's a female thing. Don't try to understand it," she snapped.

"Oh, I understand it, all right. Haven't you heard? That's what I do for a living. Hang around ladies' rooms eavesdropping on women's conversations."

"Was that a representative statistical sample, empirical study or did you use a rule of thumb up your ass?"

"Are we having our first argument or is this your version of foreplay?"

"*What?*"

Don's face grew into a broad, smug grin.

Cecil suddenly realized that Don was purposefully baiting her. Her adrenalin was pumping through her body. Her temples were pulsating, but Don was sitting across from her perfectly cool, calm, and collected. No man had taken her through that kind of mental obstacle course before. He knew all the buttons to push. She felt herself becoming entangled in his unorthodox, but charming web.

"What didn't you understand? Either it's an argument or it's foreplay?"

"Which head are you thinking with now?"

"Both. It's a man thing." He grinned, as he checked his watch. "I think that I only have time for a quick—"

"In your dreams, Don Juan!" Cecil snapped.

"I was going to say a quick trip to the airport, Cecil. Which part of your beautiful anatomy were *you* thinking with?" He rose from the table and leaned over her. "Dr. Jordon, you're the quintessential woman. Unique among all others. Body, beauty, and brains," he whispered and kissed her cheek. "Now give that beautiful body and electrifying brain a rest. I'll be back real soon."

He rubbed his mouth across her mutinous one until the taste of her seeped into his system and he was forced to pull her up against him. His kiss was passionate and disarming. Cecil could not hold back the tide of her emotions that flowed into it.

"Mmm," he whispered, "sure wish that I didn't have to go. This could have developed into a more interesting afternoon."

When Don was gone, Cecil went limp after she crawled back into her bed, but her brain would not rest. She thought of Don and how he cleverly took her through a range of emotions in the space of less than twenty-four hours. She had a happy little hum in her blood. That web was closing in more tightly around her. Don was no ordinary man, she thought, as she drifted into a twilight sleep, and far too dangerous to her resolve.

Cecil sat at the large, highly polished oak conference table with the other department heads and professors for the monthly Oceanography Department's meeting. All department projects were displayed on a video screen in a power-point presentation and discussed in their entirety. The Scripps Institute of Oceanography was involved in many high-priority and important projects, among them Cecil's project to locate sites in the oceans for the deployment of weather tracking equipment or at least that's what the proposal had called it.

The meeting was already into the second hour and Cecil was still feeling weary from her last all-night experience with Donald Dixon. As the meeting drowned on, her mind drifted back to that night and the exhilaration she felt with him. He was certainly a skillful and ardent lover, she mused. Benny had been right, as she recalled what he had said about Don after Kenneth and JeNelle's wedding, there was more to

Don than what he had revealed. How they carried on a lively repartee the whole night all through their lovemaking. She had talked about her projects while he caused her to have multiple orgasmic reactions. How he could remember the details of her projects while simultaneously in the throes of lust was positively awe inspiring. How she could even form coherent thought with Don's skillfulness had even surprised her. Most of her lovers could walk and chew gum at the same time, but Don operated on multiple levels simultaneously and had brought her to new heights of consciousness. No other lover had done that. He seemed to be in total control when she panted the theory she had been working on about the deployment of a new weather monitoring system called ALACE. He had been relentless in his passion, but she had caused his heart to skip a beat or two also. He knew his family history well, she recalled, as he recited the family tree, but she had caused his memory to falter when trying to recall his parents' names. All night they had both called for divine intervention.

"Dr. Jordon, are you with us?" Director Henson asked her, as he snapped her out of her erotic daydream.

"Of course," she said, gathering her notes to speak. "Scripps portion of the ALACE project is complete. As you will find on the monitor, we were asked to identify site locations in bodies of water around the globe for the deployment of submersible weather stations. The currents in the areas, as well as the temperature fluctuations, were of concern to the client. Moreover, motion objects of the size and description of the prototype buoy could attract sea animals. In my research, I have devised a plan to compensate for any eventuality. Now, if you will..." she continued.

Chapter 21

Benny lay in his swimming trunks on the hammock that hung between two big Live Oak trees at his parents' home in Goodwill, Summer County, South Carolina. The hot September breeze blew across his body. He and Whitney had been swimming and he had put her to bed for a nap. He looked up through the branches of the trees as the sun passed over his head. Birds sang sweet songs and Stacy's face and voice were still vivid in his mind. He closed his eyes and laced his hands behind his head, saying a silent prayer. He felt the presence of someone standing beside him.

"Hi there, Fly Boy," a female voice said. "Are you awake?" the voice said.

He prayed that when he opened his eyes, Stacy Greene would be standing there. Still, when he opened his eyes, he tried to conceal his disappointment. "Oh, hello, Caroline Ann. If you're looking for my mother, she went into town."

"No, I was looking for you, Fly Boy."

The reference jabbed into his heart. Only Stacy had called him Fly Boy.

"I thought that you would be here for the Labor Day weekend so I took a chance and just stopped by."

Benny put one hand up to shade his eyes from the sun.

"You came here to see me?" he asked confused.

"Sure. Where is that wife of yours? I heard in town that she's not here with you this trip."

"*Wife!*" Benny said emphatically then caught himself. "Oh, you mean Stacy?"

"Yes, how many wives do you have? I know that you Fly Boys get around, but I hear that only sailors have a wife in every port." she said, giggled.

Benny sat up on the hammock and put his feet on the ground.

"What did you want to see me about, Caroline Ann?" Benny asked not wanting to talk about Stacy.

"You didn't answer my question, Benjamin Staton."

He took a deep breath. "She's been deployed."

"And she left you all alone on a holiday? Seems like she's been doing a lot of that lately. Anyway, why aren't you wearing a wedding ring?"

Benny was becoming annoyed with all of the questions about him and Stacy.

"Why did you want to see me?"

"I thought that if your wife wasn't with you, we could take the children to the Labor Day parade in town tomorrow."

"Thanks, but I'm going to the parade with my family. Maybe the next time I'm at home—"

"Then why don't I come by and go with you and your folks. My mother isn't going to the parade. It's just me and my boys."

"I have no objection to you and your boys going with us, but you live on the other side of town. You'd have to pass the parade route and go five miles out of your way to get here. That seems to be unnecessary to me."

"If you're sure that you don't object, I'll be here at 8:00 A.M."

"Eight o'clock! Caroline Ann, the parade starts at noon."

"I thought that we might spend some time together, Benjamin Staton. I haven't seen that pretty little girl of yours since Independence Day. I'm sure that my boys would love to spend some time swimming with you and your daughter in your pool."

"Sure," he said, not wanting to carry on a lengthy conversation and beginning to figure out what Caroline Ann was up to. "We'll see you at eight tomorrow."

Benny rolled back onto the hammock and closed his eyes. He wanted to get back to his dreams of Stacy, but he realized that Caroline Ann was still standing beside him. He opened his eyes and found her scanning his body.

"Was there something else that you wanted, Caroline Ann?"

She smiled and winked at him. "Yes, but I'll tell you about it later."

She walked away and he cupped his hands over his face. "Damn!" he said in a low annoyed voice. "Not again!"

He was frustrated with the number of aggressive passes that women were making toward him. He hoped that he was not going to be subjected to that while he was in Goodwill. Everyone there believed that he and Stacy were married and he had done nothing to correct that impression. That's what he wanted anyway. He wanted Stacy to marry him. To love him as much as he loved her. He had not slept with another woman since she left. He didn't even have the desire to be with anyone else but her. The press of his military responsibilities kept him busy, leaving little time to focus on anyone other than his daughter. Watching Whitney grow up recalled Stacy to his mind though. When he could manage it on lecture or recruiting tours, he would take Whitney with him and always had pictures of Stacy with him, too. He loved them both and wanted to have a family. He sat up suddenly on the hammock.

"A ring!" he said aloud to himself.

He went into the house and showered. Aretha agreed to babysit Whitney for him and he headed into Columbia. He went from one jewelry store to the next. Finally, he saw what he was looking for, a marquis diamond engagement ring. He didn't know the size that he needed, but he'd worry about that later. He bought a set of matching gold wedding bands and slipped one on the third finger of his left hand. He hoped that would be enough to ward off the unsolicited advances women were making toward him.

The next morning, Whitney climbed onto his bed before 8:00 A.M and gave him a big sloppy kiss. He awoke looking into his daughter's beautiful face, with a head full of dark blond crinkly hair and big, light crystal brown eyes. He cradled her in his arms and glanced at the clock. Whitney was giggling and pulling at the hairs on his chest. He thought that she must be masochistic and loved to hear him say ouch. She had a hearty laugh and a beautiful smile for someone with only four front teeth. They played together until Aretha came to his door.

"You've got company," Aretha said in a sing-song manner. She noticed the ring on his finger, then came and sat on his bed. "Big brother, uh, is there something that you want to tell me?" Aretha asked, resting her head on her hand.

Benny reached for the blue velvet box on his nightstand and handed it to her. She opened it and smiled broadly.

"Spent a pretty penny on this," she said, lifting the diamond ring from the box.

"It doesn't matter about the money. I just want to make sure that I'm ready when Stacy comes back."

"She'll love it. She'll be back, Benjamin Staton, and this ice won't melt or spoil in the meantime." She kissed him and lifted Whitney from the bed. Then she turned around and looked at her brother. "You stay put for as long as you need to, Benjamin Staton. I'll handle your light work for you." She winked at him and closed his bedroom door.

He lay on his side and ran his hands over the spot where Stacy once slept beside him. He closed his eyes and remembered. Someone knocked softly on his door and broke his concentration on his dream. "Yes. Come in."

Caroline Ann stuck her head inside and smiled broadly. She came into the room and sat on his bed. "I hear that you're not feeling well today, Benjamin Staton. I came in to see what I could do for you."

He noticed her eyeing his body and pulled the sheet up over his chest. "I just need some rest, Caroline Ann. You and the boys are welcome to swim in the pool."

"No, I'll just stay here and keep you company. Aretha Grace is outside with your daughter and my boys."

She saw the blue velvet box on his nightstand in front of the picture of Stacy. She reached for it.

"Ooh, what's this? Can I see?"

Benny beat her to it and picked it up. "It's a gift for Stacy, Caroline Ann. A very special gift. I'd rather that Stacy be the first one to see it, if you don't mind."

"Gee, Benjamin Staton, it's not like I'd steal it or anything," she said, seemingly annoyed.

"I know that you wouldn't, but like I said, it's for Stacy."

She picked up the picture of Stacy and looked at it. "Do you have any wedding pictures of you and Stacy?"

"Look, I really need to catch a nap. I'll talk to you later."

He took Stacy's picture from her hands and she saw the wedding band on his finger.

"I see you're wearing your ring again. Gee, it looks new. Did you—"

"Carolina Ann," a voice came from the doorway.

"Oh, hi, Mrs. Alexander, I just came in to see how Benjamin Staton was feeling. How are you?"

"I'm fine, Carolina Ann, but Aretha needs your help with your boys out at the pool."

"Oh, oh sure, Mrs. Alexander. I'll check on you later, Benjamin Staton," she said with a broad smile, as she left the room.

Sylvia Alexander made sure that Caroline Ann had gone to the pool and then she returned to Benny's room. She sat on the bed beside him and stroked his face.

"Looks like the hounds are on your scent again."

"Still, you mean, don't you, Mom?" Benny said blankly.

"Aretha tried to cover for you. She asked me to come in here and rescue you."

"Thanks. I'm really not up to the challenge when I'm at home. There are so many good memories of Stacy here that I just want some quiet time."

Sylvia picked up the picture of Stacy from the bed. "I know, Son. I miss having Stacy around, too, but I'm still confident that she'll turn up some day."

"I pray that you're right. I'll be ready when she does," he said, handing the blue velvet box to her.

Sylvia opened it and tears formed in her eyes. "It's beautiful, Benjamin Staton," she said, with a watery smile. "Stacy's going to love it."

"The question is will she love me? It's been over three years since she left. Maybe she's found someone else. Maybe she's forgotten all about me and Whitney."

Sylvia caressed her son's face and smiled. "She couldn't love anyone else, Benjamin Staton. She's in love with you. Believe what I'm telling you, Son."

"It's hard sometimes, Mom. I miss her so much."

"Has her father heard from her?"

"I don't think so. He said that he would call me if he did, but he doesn't have a telephone in his house. I've called him at the garage where he works, but that was several months ago."

"You have a few days. Why don't you just fly up to Asheville, North Carolina, and see the man, Benjamin Staton? It's certainly better than sitting around here dodging Caroline Ann, don't you think?"

Benny smiled at his mother, sat up, and gave her a tight squeeze. "Has anyone told you lately that you're the best mother in the universe?"

Sylvia laughed. "Every minute of every day, Benjamin Staton, but I never get tired of hearing it one more time."

She kissed her son and left his bedroom.

⊙═‹›

The wheels of the twin engine Cessna touched down at the Asheville Airport. Gregory Alexander scrambled out of the aircraft over the wing and his sister, Aretha, handed their niece, Whitney Ivy, to him once he was on the ground. They insisted on accompanying Benny to Asheville, so that they could baby sit with Whitney. Benny suspected that their hidden agenda was to get him to give them flying lessons. Aretha had been after him for four years to teach her. He knew that sooner or later he would have to comply, but the thought of his younger, teenage sister making solo flights around the country sent chills up his spine. She was as independent as any adult and he knew that she would not think twice about a solo cross-country flight if the spirit moved her to do so. The spirit seemed to move Aretha to do a lot of unconventional things.

They rented a SUV at the airport and drove through the narrow mountainous streets of Asheville until they reached College Avenue where Stacy's father and younger brother lived in a small two-bedroom house. The grassy lawn looked as if it needed cutting and an old Ford Fairmont with patches of rust stains sat in the yard. The front door was open when Benny knocked. After the second knock a man appear from around the side of the house. He was wearing a stained T-shirt over his dark bulky build and blue coveralls with motor oil stains. He wiped his hands on an oily cloth and then wiped the sweat from his brow with his forearm.

"Can I help ya?" he asked, seeing the three people with a baby standing on the porch landing. "Oh, dat must be you...uh...Alexander... uh...Capn' Alexander, ain't it?"

"Major Alexander, Mr. Greene, but please just call me Benny."

"Oh, yeah, didn't quite recognize ya out of ya uniform," the man said, as he extended his hand to Benny.

"This is my brother, Gregory Clayton, and my sister, Aretha Grace, Mr. Greene."

"How y'all doin'?" He shook their hands. "And who dis lil' lady?" He looked at Whitney.

"This is my daughter, Whitney Ivy."

"Pretty lil' thing, she be," he said, smiling at her.

Whitney lifted her head from Benny's shoulder and reached for the man. He wiped his hands again and took her from Benny. His smooth, charcoal complexion lit up.

"You folks come 'round back here wit' me. It be too hot to sit in de house."

They followed the man, as he carried Whitney around to the back of the house. The yard was rather unkempt there too, but it was clear that the man used it primarily to repair cars. Tool boxes sat on a concrete pad next to a car that was rolled up on red ramps. He led them to some chairs in the yard under big sheltering elm trees. He grabbed a clean towel out of a basket of freshly washed clothes and placed it on his lap before he put Whitney on his knees.

"Sure be a friendly lil' girl, Major. Pretty eyes, too. Nice smile she got," he said, admiring Whitney.

"I know, Mr. Greene, she looks just like Stacy. Whitney Ivy is your granddaughter."

Mr. Greene looked at Benny in disbelief. Then he looked at Whitney for a long while. He reached into his back pocket and pulled out his flat, weather-worn wallet. The plastic pages in the old wallet were yellow with age and stuck together, but he found the picture of Stacy and her twin sister, Casey, when they were babies. He held the picture up to Whitney's face. The picture and Whitney were almost identical. Whitney had Stacy's honey-toned completion. The eyes were and identical light crystal brown with long feathery lashes.

"My granddaughter," he said, looking at Benny as a smile grew across his craggy face. "I have a granddaughter," he said still trying to take it all in. He laughed loudly. "I have a granddaughter!" he said, still louder as he held Whitney against his chest. Tears formed in his eyes. He looked at Benny with such appreciation in his face.

Whitney giggled and cooed while wiping the tears that rolled down her grandfather's face. He could not speak. Aretha reached into her purse and handed a few tissues to him.

"Thank ya, lil' lady," he said, as he wiped his eyes.

"Mr. Greene, I was wondering whether you've heard from Stacy."

"Please, Major, calls me Willis. Dat be my given name."

"Sure, Willis, but about my question."

"Oh, oh no. I ain't hear-ed much from Stacy since de day she got on dat dere bus and left fo' dat Naval Academy in Napolis. I gits a call from her ere now and again, but I ain't hear-ed from Stacy goin' on five year now. She be all right though 'cause ere first of the month, money gits put in dis here savings account at de bank. 'Cordin to de bank, it be havin' my name on it. I sure didn' open no 'count wit dat dere bank."

Benny's excitement grew. "Do you know where the money comes from? Who's sending it?"

"No, it be one dos 'lectonic things...you know...uh..."

"Electronic funds transfer?" Gregory offered.

"Yeah, yeah, dat be it. 'Lectonics funds. Boy, uh...you go in dere in dat kitchen and look on dat dere table. It be dat envelope with dat star on it and bring it here."

"I'll do it for you, Mr. Greene," Aretha offered, as she hopped up from her seat and headed into the back screened door and into the dark humid kitchen. She searched around on the red Formica-topped table sitting against the wall. She heard someone move on the sofa in the living room. The figure stood up, came forward and leaned against the door.

"Whatchu doin' in here?" a gruff voice asked.

Aretha turned and saw a boy of about fifteen years old standing bare-chested with jeans hanging low on his waist. The top of his underwear could be seen riding his narrow hips, but Aretha was more concerned with the gun that he had in his hand. She looked up at his chin. His complexion was honey toned like Stacey's and scraggly hairs grew in places around his jaw. His eyes were light crystal-brown and he had a blue rag tied around his dark brown curly hair.

"You hear me, bitch! Whatchu doin' in here!"

Aretha's eyes narrowed. She balled up her fist and walked up to the boy who towered over her by at least five inches. She got directly in his face.

"You don't know me and I don't know you, so I'm going to excuse your bad manners this time! But don't you *ever* call me anything other than Aretha Grace Alexander again!"

The boy was stunned. He backed away from her flashing dark eyes.

"Yeah, and they be callin' you a dead whatever your name be," he said, holding the gun up and sliding the chamber back.

"Before you kill me, would you mind telling me your name?" Aretha asked, without any note of concern in her voice.

The question startled him. "Streetwise!" he said, with a scowl.

"Is that your name or your condition?"

"Whatchu talkin' 'bout! Dat be my name!"

"All right, Mr. Streetwise. I apologize for barging in here and interrupting your nap, but Mr. Greene asked me to find an envelope for him. So if you don't mind, I'll be about that business and trouble you no further."

"Mr. Greene? You mean Willis? He sentchu in here?"

"Yes, we brought his granddaughter to see him. We're trying to locate his daughter."

"Stacy? Stacy had a baby?"

"You all right, Aretha Grace?" Gregory asked, as he came in the screened door.

"Who dis?"

"This is my brother, Gregory Clayton Alexander. Gregory Clayton, this is Mr. Streetwise," Aretha said.

"Hey, man, how ya doin'?" Gregory started to say, as he extended his hand and then spotted the gun. He pulled Aretha behind him. "Uh, we got a problem here, my brother?" Gregory asked.

"No, no problem, Gregory Clayton," Aretha answered, coming out from behind him. "I must have frightened Mr. Streetwise when I came in. We've just been having an interesting conversation."

"Yeah, right!" the boy said, looking at Gregory's size and build. He put the gun into his pocket. "Conversation, it be like dat."

"Oh, right!" Gregory said. "Do you mind if we find that envelope?" Gregory asked, looking at the boy.

"Fuck do I care!"

"Thank you, Mr. Streetwise," Aretha said, as she found the envelope and pushed Gregory out of the door ahead of her.

They crossed the yard and handed the envelope to Mr. Greene. He in turn handed it directly to Benny and gestured for him to open it. Benny looked at the information and disappointment crossed his face.

"What does it say, Ben?" Gregory asked.

"Payroll, US Treasury," Benny answered, as he handed it to Gregory.

"Pentagon," Gregory said. "This came out of the Pentagon."

"How do you know that, G?" Benny asked.

"Remember, I worked there the last couple of summers. I did some computer work and I saw a lot of these. This comes out of a special fund," he said, pointing to encrypted codes on the paper. "Stacy must be into some top secret stuff!"

"That I already know," Benny said. "Can you tell anything else from that, G?"

"No, I'd have to get an encryption code book and they keep that in a vault somewhere in the Pentagon."

Aretha looked up and saw the boy's shadow standing back away from the screened door. Mr. Greene saw it, too.

"Russell! Russell Greene, git out cheer and meet yo niece!" Willis Greene bellowed.

Aretha and Gregory looked at each other and simultaneously mouthed the name *Russell*.

The boy sauntered out of the house and over to where they were sitting. Benny stood up and extended his hand.

"Hello, Russell, my name is Benjamin Alexander. This is my younger brother, Gregory Clayton, and my youngest sister, Aretha Grace. It's a pleasure to meet you."

"Yeah, whatever," Russell said, folding his arms across his bare chest not even looking at Benny.

Benny looked at the boy, and then withdrew his hand.

"We've already met. I interrupted Russell's nap, Benjamin Staton. I'm sure that he's not fully awake yet," Aretha said by way of apologizing for Russell's rudeness.

Willis Greene noticed it, too. "Man 'stended his hand, Russell! Don't makes me gits ugly on you front of—"

"That's all right, Mr. Greene," Benny said, reaching for Whitney. He pulled a business card from his pocket. "My address and telephone number are on this. If you hear anything from or about Stacy, I'd appreciate a call."

"Sure, Major, but does ya haves to be a goin'? I means, couldn't I offer yous somethin' to drink? I means, I just found this pretty lil' granddaughter. A man don't learns dat ere day," Willis said, almost pleading.

Aretha and Gregory looked at Benny. He relaxed and sat down again.

"All right, Mr. Greene. We can stay a little longer, but my family is having a picnic in Goodwill, South Carolina. We've got to get back for that."

"You drove here?" Willis asked.

"No, I flew us up here in a small rented airplane..."

"Get outta here! Ain't no Black man flyin' no airplane!" Russell said, rolling his eyes.

Everyone looked at him.

"I suppose that you've never heard of the Tuskegee Airmen. They were the first. I'm an Air Force pilot, Russell. I'm stationed at March Air Force Base outside San Diego, California."

"Now I 'spose you gonna say dat you fly jets!"

"As a matter of fact, I do."

"Yeah, right!"

Benny pulled his Air Force identification card out of his wallet and handed it to Russell. The boy reluctantly took it, scanned it quickly, and handed it back to Benny.

"Yeah, probably got dat at Target!" Russell grumbled.

Benny laughed. "No, I graduated from the Air Force Academy in Colorado Springs, Colorado, then flight training school in Enid, Oklahoma. My first year out of flight school I flew every jet that the Air Force and Navy have on the runway, including the F-15 Eagle fighter, F-14 Phantom fighter, the EF-111 Ravens and A-6B Prowler. My team flies F-14s."

"Your team? You tryna tell me dat de white man be lettin' a black man lead a jet fighter team? Man, you be trippin'!"

"No one *let* me do anything, Russell. I learned to fly an old crop duster when I was younger than you are now. I worked and trained a long time. I'm not in uniform today, but as you can see from my ID I hold the rank of Major in the United States Air Force," Benny said calmly. "Maybe the next time that I'm in this area, you and your dad can fly down to Shaw Air Force Base with me. I'd be happy to show you around."

"Dad? You sound like a white boy comin' in here with dat 'dad' shit! Dat be Willis!"

"Boy, I ain't but two second offa you!" Willis scowled.

"Mr. Greene, could we have something to drink please," Aretha suddenly asked to deflate the growing confrontation.

Willis calmed himself. "Sure, sure, lil' lady. Russell, go fix some of dat lemonade for us."

"May I help?" Aretha asked.

Gregory grabbed her arm.

"I'm all right, Gregory Clayton."

"Uh, I'll help, too," Gregory said, rising from his seat.

"Would you lead the way, Russell?" Aretha asked, smiling at him.

Russell sauntered toward the house and into the kitchen. Aretha and Gregory followed.

"Russell, where are the glasses?" Aretha asked.

Russell pointed to the cabinet and Aretha took an assortment of glasses out of the cabinet while Gregory got ice out of the freezer.

"Your brother really be a jet pilot?" Russell asked suddenly, as he leaned against the door jam.

"He is, yes," Gregory said. "And he's great at what he does. He's going to teach me and Aretha to fly."

"Yeah, right! A girl flyer! Sure you're right!"

"There are hundreds of women who have a pilot's license, Russell. Where are the lemons?"

Russell pointed to another cabinet and Aretha opened it and saw powdered lemonade.

"Do you have any real lemons?"

"Lemons? Naw, ain't got no lemons! Dats got lemons in it, and sugar, too! Ain't dat good 'nough for you?"

"It's fine, Russell. It's just that it has chemicals in it that aren't good for you and especially not for Whitney Ivy."

"So dat ain't good 'nough 'cause it got chem…whatever you said?"

"We'll make this work out. Whitney still has some juice boxes in the car."

They made the lemonade and returned to the yard. Russell didn't return with them, but Aretha sensed him watching them as they talked with Willis. Whitney went exploring in the yard under her family's watchful eyes. They talked for several hours.

When they were leaving, Benny gave some pictures that he had in his wallet of Stacy and some of Whitney to Willis. Gregory put Whitney in her car seat and got in beside her. Aretha went to the front door and knocked until Russell came to the door.

"Yeah?" he scowled at her.

"I just wanted to say goodbye to you, Russell. We're leaving now. It was nice to meet you," she said, as she extended her hand.

He opened the screen door and barely touched her hand, then quickly drew it back. Aretha went to Mr. Greene, smiled at him, and hugged him. They all waved at Mr. Greene as they backed out into the street and drove away.

"Ben, did you know that kid was packing a nine?" Gregory asked, with his eyes open wide.

"Yes, I saw it in his pocket. I've seen gang bangers before in East LA. You two handled yourselves real well. I'm proud of both of you."

"Be proud of Aretha, Ben. I was ready to clock the little brother! He had that nine on her when I went into the kitchen."

Concerned, Benny asked, "Are you all right, Aretha?"

"Sure, Benjamin Staton. I'm fine. It's Russell Greene we should all be worried about," she said wisely. "Living in the city isn't easy on a young brother like him."

Months later, Benny was back in his condo in San Diego making dinner while Whitney played on the floor at his feet. She pulled metal pots and pans from the cabinet banging them together or beating them with his long-handled wooden mixing spoons. She giggled with each clang and bang and sang a tuneless song. Benny laughed at his daughter's antics and talked to her as he tossed a salad for their dinner. He was barechested and barefoot wearing a pair of cutoff USAF sweats when the telephone rang.

"Hi there, Fly Boy," a female voice said on the other end of the telephone.

Benny's heart leaped.

"Stacy!"

"No, this is Caroline Ann. Caroline Ann Johnson-Plimpton from Goodwill."

"Oh. Hello, Caroline Ann. How are you? What can I do for you?"

"Fine, just fine. Your wife's not back yet, I see. She's been away for years."

"Stacy's still deployed, but what's the reason for your call? Is everything all right in Goodwill?"

"Well, I was in the neighborhood and I thought that I might just stop by and say hello."

"In the neighborhood? You mean that you're in San Diego?"

"Better than that. I'm in the lobby of your building, but this man won't let me come up to your condo without your permission. Tell him that it's all right, Benjamin Staton."

"Major Alexander, this is Fred. Were you expecting Ms. Johnson-Plimpton?"

"No, I wasn't, but it's all right, Fred. Send her up."

Benny sighed and mashed his teeth. "Why me, Lord!" Benny said aloud to himself. He went to the closet, pulled out a robe and wrapped it around his body.

When the door bell sounded, Benny picked up Whitney and went to answer it. Caroline Ann stood there with a large, rolling suitcase at her feet smiling at Benny.

"Hi, Fly Boy," she said as she came in and gave him a quick kiss on the cheek pulling her luggage behind her.

Oh no, he thought to himself. She's got to be kidding. "Caroline Ann, what are you doing in San Diego?" Benny asked, as he closed the door.

"Oh, I had to drop the boys off at their father's house in Salt Lake City, Utah, so I thought that I'd come spend a few days in San Diego before I go back to South Carolina," she said, as she browsed around the condo marveling at it's high-style decor.

"Oh, I see," Benny said dryly. "Where are you staying while you're in town?"

"I thought that you and your wife might put me up for a few days. Looks like you've got plenty of space," she said, as she roamed around the bi-level condo.

"I'm not so sure that this is a good idea. I mean Stacy's away and I have to be away for long hours every day."

"Oh, that's okay. I can find my way around," she said still scoping out the condo. "You know it's probably not often that you get visitors from home out here. Especially ones whose mothers are as close as ours are. I'm sure that your wife wouldn't mind you putting me up for a few days, seeing that our families are so close and all."

Benny gave up. It wasn't the Southern way to be inhospitable to friends from home.

"All right, if it's only for a few days, you're welcome to use a spare room."

"Great! So where are we going tonight?"

"Tonight? I didn't plan to go anywhere. I was making dinner and planning to make an early night of it. I've got to be on the flight line at 0500."

"Can't we just go out for a little while? Maybe to a club to do a little dancing?"

"I told you that—"

"Please, Benjamin Staton," Caroline Ann purred.

"All right, just for a few hours if Mrs. Tyler doesn't mind sitting with Whitney. I'll put your bag in one of the spare rooms down here."

Benny started toward one of the two spare bedrooms on the first level of the condo.

"What's up there, Benjamin Staton?" Caroline Ann asked, pointing to the balcony level.

"Oh, Whitney's nursery and my bed...Stacy's and my room. I'm sure that you'll be fine down here in one of the guest rooms," Benny said. "Make yourself comfortable. I'll make a few calls and I'll be right back."

Benny rushed up to his bedroom and pushed the speed dial for Cecil and Janice.

"Help," he said dryly when Janice answered.

"Benny, what is it? Is it Whitney?" she asked, concerned.

"Whitney's fine. I need you and Cecil on a mission of mercy for me tonight."

Janice laughed. "What? A mission? What's going on, Benny?"

"Come up, you'll see when you get here," Benny said dryly.

They hung up and Benny called Mrs. Tyler, his next door neighbor who was his daughter's regular caretaker. She agreed to sit with Whitney for the night. Cecil and Janice rang the doorbell and Benny went to answer it. Caroline Ann was lounging on the sofa.

"Cecil! Janice! What a wonderful surprise. Please come in. It's good to see you lovely ladies!"

They looked at him quizzically.

"Benny, what are you—"

"Let me introduce an old schoolmate of mine from home," Benny said, leading them into the living room. "Caroline Ann Johnson-Plimpton, this is Dr. Cecil Jordon and Dr. Janice Atterly, two very close friends of mine and my wife's."

Both women looked at Benny as if he had lost his mind.

"Your wife," Janice said quietly.

Cecil caught on. "Yes, Janice, you know, Stacy, right, Benny?"

"That's right. Uh, Caroline Ann will be spending a few days here and if you ladies are not too busy, why don't we all go out for a while tonight after dinner?"

"Sure, Benny, we'd love to help you entertain a friend of yours and Stacy's," Cecil said.

Janice was still confused, but she smiled at Benny who she thought was uncharacteristically nervous.

Later that evening they went to Jason's, a club in the Gaslight District, and one that Benny frequented often before Whitney was born. He hadn't been there since Stacy left, but a number of his old friends and acquaintances greeted him warmly as he entered, escorting the three women.

"Good evening, Captain Alexander. It's been a long time. It's good to see you."

"Good evening, Ray, but it's Major Alexander now. It's good to see you again, too."

"Seems like old times. Some things never seem to change. Are there *four* in your party tonight?"

"Yes, Ray, four," Benny said dryly.

Ray led them to a table. Some of Benny's friends yelled to him as he passed by. Women openly flirted even though he was escorting three women and wearing a wedding band. Benny spotted someone at the bar that he had not seen in a long time. He excused himself and approached the man.

"Bruce," Benny said, extending his hand.

"Benny. Benny Alexander. How you doin', my man?" Bruce Payton asked, shaking Benny's hand.

"Fine, Bruce, long time no see."

"Yeah, I haven't seen you since you stole my lady from me."

Benny laughed. "It's not like that, Bruce. You know Stacy and I were just friends. That's all."

"Right, Alexander!" Bruce laughed. "That's why she called me by your name when I took her sailing. Whatever happened to her? Did you two finally get hitched or something? I see that you're sporting a wedding band."

"Oh, no, this is nothing, but I was going to ask you whether you've seen or heard from Stacy lately."

"Naw, man. After you and she got tight, Stacy dropped out of sight. I tried calling her a few times, but she never called me back. Someone said that she was pregnant and then left the area. A buddy on mine saw her getting on a military transport with a bunch of other military women, but that's the last I heard from or about her."

"Thanks, Bruce. If you hear from her, would you let me know?"

"Hell no, Alexander! You fly boys must be sucking in too much pure oxygen. If I hear from Stacy I'm not mentioning your name!" He laughed. "You stole her away from me once. I'm not letting you get a second chance at that beautiful woman."

"It's important, Bruce. Very important."

Bruce scrutinized Benny for a few seconds. He obviously saw something in his eyes and shrugged. "All right, Alexander. You've always been a stand up kind of brother. If I hear from Stacy, I'll tell her that you've been asking about her, but I don't think that I'll be the first person that she'll call if she hits town again."

"Thanks, Bruce."

They shook hands again and Benny returned to the table.

"Wasn't that Lieutenant Commander Bruce Payton that you were talking with, Benny?" Cecil asked.

"Yeah," Benny said, "Stacy's...sailing teacher," he said, catching himself.

"Sailing teacher? I thought that Stacy was in the Navy. Why would she need a sailing teacher?" Caroline Ann asked.

No one answered. Benny signaled the waiter for drinks. Cecil and Janice engaged Caroline Ann in conversation. They sensed what their friend was going through. They had seen that familiar pain on his face before.

Benny sat quietly at the table watching the condensation run down the outside of his glass of mineral water. Cecil and Janice had taken Caroline Ann and introduced her to every eligible man that they knew in the club and gotten the men to keep her busy on the dance floor. Caroline Ann, however, kept watching Benny. She excused herself in the middle of a dance and scooted into the booth next to him.

"This is a great place, Benny. You seem to know a lot of people here. Do you and Stacy come here a lot?"

"Sometimes, Caroline Ann. Stacy loves to dance and she's great on a dance floor. She used to do this—"

"Could we not talk about Stacy tonight?" Caroline Ann interrupted in a snit.

"Sure. Are you having a good time?"

"I'd have a better time if you'd dance with me."

"I haven't been doing any dancing since Stacy...I mean for a while. I'm a little rusty."

The band started up a slow tune and the vocalist began the song, *Missing You*. Caroline Ann grabbed Benny's hand and pulled him to the dance floor. He reluctantly agreed and held her away from his body. She moved in close to him and wrapped her arms around him burying her face in his chest.

"Mmm, I love that cologne, Benny," Caroline Ann said, as she hugged him and swayed to the music. "It's getting me excited."

Benny didn't answer. He was thinking about the words that the vocalist was singing and about Stacy. He and Stacy had often danced close to each other to that tune. He could still feel her in his arms.

Cecil noticed Benny's face. "Rescue 911," she whispered to Janice. Janice got up from the table, approached Caroline Ann and Benny on the dance floor, and tapped Caroline Ann on the shoulder.

"My turn," Janice said, with a smile as Caroline Ann released Benny and she slipped into Benny's arms.

Caroline Ann frowned as she left the dance floor.

"That woman's on a mission of her own, Benny, and you're the target!" Janice said, as she and Benny danced.

"I know. She showed up out of the blue today with no warning. What could I do? I couldn't just send her to a hotel."

"No, that wouldn't have been like you at all, but you're going to have to be on alert status with her around."

"I know. I appreciate you and Cecil for bailing me out tonight."

"We'll be around if you need us, but we're beginning to worry about you, Benny. Even when Stacy was around you two dated other people. Since she's been gone, you haven't dated anyone at all."

"I'm in love with Stacy, Janice, and I miss the hell out of her. It's been like living in purgatory since she left."

"It's about time that you admitted that. You and Stacy were driving me and Cecil crazy!"

"Why?"

"Because neither one of you would admit that you were in love!"

"Was I that obvious?"

"Damn straight!"

"Then why didn't you tell me?"

"Neither you nor Stacy would have believed us. You two were too busy giving each other the ultimate rush and living free and single. Stacy's career was on the top of her agenda and trying to forget about her childhood in Cabrini Green."

"Then you think that she cares for me?"

"Wake up, Alexander! The girl is a goner! I think that she was afraid to stay here and love you the way that she wanted to, especially when you went on that all-out mission trying to fall in love with JeNelle."

"Did she tell you that she was in love with me?"

"No, not once, but I'm a woman. I know these things. Look, I'm your friend, Benny, and I love you like a brother, but I'd be damned if I'd spend nine months giving you a baby that you wanted, just because you asked me to. It would take a whole hell of a lot more than just friendship for me to do that. Believe me!"

The music ended and Benny kissed Janice lightly on the lips and hugged her tightly. "I don't know how I got so lucky to find two friends like you and Cecil," Benny said, as he hugged Janice.

"You deserve us, Benny," Janice said, laughing. "You've been like a kid brother to us, putting up with every gag and stunt that we've played on you. We're proud to be your friend, too. A man like you, Benny, and that good looking, phine cousin of yours, are rare. JeNelle took Kenneth off the market and Stacy's got your heart with her, wherever the hell she is. Now that only leaves James."

"Hold on, Janice, the man's a country kid. Give him a break. He's not ready for a prime-time sister like you all at once."

"From what I've seen of James, he's dinner time!"

They were laughing and hugging, as they walked back to the table where Cecil sat talking with Bruce. Caroline Ann sat watching Janice and Benny on the dance floor. Bruce looked up as Benny approached.

"Hey, my man! I hope you don't mind me sitting here trying to steal one of these lovely ladies from you. You always did travel in the best of company!" Bruce said, eyeing the three women. "Which one can I steal a dance with?" he asked with a smile.

Cecil, Janice, and Benny all looked at Caroline Ann, but Caroline Ann's eyes were on Benny.

"Caroline Ann Johnson-Plimpton this is Lieutenant Commander Bruce Payton, US Navy. He was my wife's sailing instructor."

Bruce's neck snapped and he looked at Benny quizzically.

"Wife?" he asked.

Cecil pinched him under the table.

"Ouch!" he yelled.

"Weren't you going to ask Caroline Ann to dance, Bruce?" Cecil asked, grinning through gritted teeth.

"Oh, oh yeah," Bruce said, as it began to dawn on him what was going on. He stood, helped Caroline Ann to her feet, and he leaned toward Benny. "That's two you owe me, my brother," he whispered.

Benny smiled. "You got it!" Benny said, as Bruce led Caroline Ann to the dance floor.

Later that night, Caroline Ann and Benny returned to his condo. She was quiet on the drive back.

"I hope you enjoyed yourself, Caroline Ann," Benny said, as they came into the living room.

"Stacy's not your wife, is she, Benjamin Staton?"

Benny stopped in his tracks. He knew that his little subterfuge was over. He turned and looked at Caroline Ann. "Yes, she is, Caroline Ann, in every way that's important to me except legally and I intend to change that as soon as possible."

"So you'd marry a woman who would run off and leave her baby and you?"

"If that woman is Stacy Greene, I'd do it at the speed of light."

"What kind of woman would do that?"

Benny didn't answer her immediately. He didn't feel it necessary to explain his relationship with Stacy to her. "It's late and I've got an early start in the morning, so I'll say goodnight."

He turned and climbed the stairs to the balcony, went into his bedroom, and closed the door. Caroline Ann stood and watched him until he was out of sight.

In the morning Benny shaved and showered. He came out of the bathroom and found Caroline Ann lying across his bed in a very provocative position wearing a negligee.

"What are you doing in here?" he asked, as he quickly covered his nude body.

"I thought that I'd make breakfast for us before you left. I wanted to know what you'd like to have to eat. It's the least that I could do, but I could do more. Much, much more," she said suggestively. "I knocked on your door, but apparently you didn't hear me."

"I appreciate the offer of breakfast, but I'm in a hurry. Maybe we can have breakfast another time, so if you'll excuse me," he said, opening his bedroom door.

Caroline Ann got up and sauntered toward him.

"A growing boy needs nourishment," she said, as she ran her fingers lightly across his broad bare chest.

"Have a good day, Caroline Ann," he said, still holding the door open.

Caroline Ann left his room; he closed the door behind her, and locked it.

"Why me, Lord," he said to himself. "I asked you to bring Stacy back, Lord. Remember? Stacy Greene, not Caroline Ann Johnson-Plimpton," he said dryly.

Months after Caroline Ann left, Benny bathed Whitney and put her to bed for a nap. He watched her sleeping in her bed for a while and then went to his room and lay across his bed. He looked at the picture of Stacy on the nightstand and picked it up. He recalled how he met her and later the times that they spent together. Stacy, he recalled, had just graduated from the Naval Academy in Annapolis, Maryland, with high honors and received her commission assigned to Admiral Gordon at the Pentagon in Washington, DC, as one of the Admiral's liaison officers, but she wanted to be assigned to active duty aboard a ship. She took special, advanced, and top-secret telecommunications courses outside of her regular duties as a liaison officer to the Japanese Embassy. He spotted her in a dimly lit Pentagon cafeteria. She was studying late and battling to stay awake. Even in the poor lighting she was a very attractive woman who looked like the songstress, Alisha Keys, he had thought,. He had approached her with the expectation that he might be able to seduce her while on his brief trip to Washington, but they began to talk together about her professional goals and experiences. As he sat with her, listening to the excitement in her commentary about the unlimited possibilities of a career in the Navy, she stirred something within him. Something that was very familiar. In many ways she was very much like him. She had electricity that ran through her, he thought. Even though he was going out that night with his friend and commanding officer, JC Baker, and some women he knew, the young, attractive Lieutenant Stacy Greene had shocked him with her electrifying energy and her goals and objectives.

The next day she agreed to meet him for lunch. He saw how truly beautiful she was when she entered the restaurant. Her clean, crisp smile and light brown eyes were mesmerizing. Other military men in the restaurant had approached her and invited her to have lunch with them, but she came straight to him with such eagerness to continue the conversation that they had begun the night before. He had something else in mind, however, and when he made several passes at her, her interest in continuing their conversation had disappeared.

Benny's thoughts were interrupted when he heard a key in the door and someone entering into the condo.

"Hey, Cousin, you here?" Don Dixon's voice called out.

Benny left his bedroom and went to the balcony.

"Yeah, man. You and Cecil just getting back?"

"Yeah, just dropped her off at her place."

"So, how was the trip?"

Don smiled broadly.

"Like that, huh?"

"Man!" Don said, shaking his head expressively.

"I hear that Cancun is nice this time of the year."

"I suppose that it is," Don said, smiling. "I was working on something and the rest of the time Cecil had me under water all week!"

"That's what the good doctor does for a living."

"I know. I got to see her at work. The lady knows her stuff. The expedition that she led knew it, too."

"A lot of people, huh?"

"Scientists from around the world. About twenty-five of them. They were hanging on every word she spoke. They collected a couple hundred samples from the area. I've never been diving that deep before."

"You look like you had a good time."

"I learned a lot, too," he said, grinning.

"Cuz, are we talking about oceanography?"

Don smiled. "Yeah, that, too. You got any beer?"

"Yeah, I just got some Coronas. There're in the bar refrigerator."

Don went to the bar, grabbed two bottles, and opened them. He handed one to Benny as Benny came down the stairs. They went into Benny's media room to relax.

"So, Cuz, what did you do while I was away?"

"I took Whitney to the zoo and a few other places. She's getting pretty big now. She's even talking like a grown person. Tickles me to see her smile."

"I know. She's got Stacy's smile. You've told me before, Cuz."

Benny laughed and took a long swig of the beer. He stared at the bottle and fingered the condensation that ran down the label. "I guess I have, huh?" Benny said reflectively.

"Yeah, but you never told me how you and Stacy hooked up."

"Funny you should mention that. I was just thinking about it."

"You're always thinking about Stacy," Don said before turning the beer up to his mouth. He sensed a melancholy mood in his cousin's demeanor and it tore at his gut that he could, with a phone call, end his cousin's suffering.

"Yeah, you're right. I do think about her a lot."

"All right, I'm waiting. Tell me about this lady that's got you in cold storage." Don laughed, trying to lighten Benny's mood. He wanted to tell his cousin and friend the truth and ease his mind, but duty came before family.

Benny described how he and Stacy met at the Pentagon. He spoke in slow reflective tones as if he did not want to leave out one detail. He was expressionless. No excitement in his voice or demeanor. Almost a solemn mood of someone in mourning at the loss of a loved one.

Benny got up from the sofa and got another beer for himself and Don.

"I've learned a lot about myself. I know that I haven't handled the truth very well, especially when it hurts. Life is about growth and sometimes growing up hurts. I never realized how fragile my ego was until I met Stacy. I've always been eager to explore life and live it to its fullest, but we all have defense mechanisms that come into play when someone gives us another point of view that's contrary to the ones that we hold. Stacy did that for me. She forced me to grow up a little more and to deal with the real world.

"I didn't want to deal with the fact that Stacy still wanted to have the freedom to have a career other than being a wife and mother. That she had a special dedication to duty and honor or that she wanted to see other men while we were together. Or the fact that I was not the only man who could sexually or emotionally satisfy her. Stacy operated on a different level though. She is always honest with me, but she is never condescending or denigrating. She told me how much she valued my opinion and our relationship. She made me feel good all the time. We worked on our platonic relationship for a long time first and that made it easier to work on all of the other aspects. We helped each other reach for and achieve our goals. That made me feel useful to her. You know, not in the traditional ways, but important.

"We talked about sensitive issues and gave each other permission to give feedback even when we may not have liked what was being said. It was an unwritten agreement between us and we realized that our relationship had a purpose; not just something that we stumbled into and took for granted. I broke the agreement between us without even realizing it. Stacy tried to warn me that I was taking our friendship for granted. That I was focusing too much on our sexual relationship. I told her about JeNelle and Stacy was very supportive. She even suggested that we go back to having a platonic relationship. I wasn't willing to do that, but Stacy began to make herself scarce. That was a direct kick in my gut. She was taking on more difficult and challenging assignments. I had to support her views on what she was doing and the goals that she had set for herself. We had a powerful and strong relationship because we could share each other's points of view even when they were vastly different. The only argument that Stacy and I have ever had was over whether to have Whitney. We gave each other permission to disagree. It wasn't about winning or losing. It was about sharing.

"I know a lot of women, Don. They all have special qualities and talents, but you don't meet a Stacy Greene every day. She's years younger than me, but very mature for her age. We got below the surface and I like what I found there. We reached new heights and I liked what I found there, too. I love Stacy on more than just a sexual level, but she's not here for me to tell her that."

"When did you realize that you loved her?"

"When it was too late. When she was gone."

"Man, that's rough. You spent all that time together even through the pregnancy and it didn't hit you until she had already split?"

"That's when I admitted it to myself, but Stacy meant a lot to me long before that."

"She must have if you didn't even question whether she was pregnant with your baby or not."

"Never entered my mind that Whitney Ivy wasn't mine."

"Man, you must be in love or crazy. The first thing I would have done was a DNA test."

"For what?"

"*For what!* To see if she was my baby, that's for what."

"You don't know Stacy. She wasn't about playing any games. The night that she told me that she was pregnant we argued all night. She was determined to have an abortion; worked it all out, set a date, and paid for the procedure. All she wanted from me was my moral support, but I was just as determined that she wasn't going to and that we were going to be parents."

"But look what you had to give up."

"What? What have I given up?"

"Your freedom, man! Your life! You're an ugly brother, but the women you had!" Don said jokingly. "Living large out here in California. Black book thick as a New York City telephone directory. Career rising to the top. Man, don't get me wrong, I love Whitney Ivy, but you had it all big time!"

"Man, nothing's stopping me from going back into the life but me. Whitney's not only my responsibility, she's also my joy. I haven't given up anything. My life's not on hold. I'm just living it from another point of view. It was nice running with the ladies. Obeying my thirst. Feeling the rush, but Whitney makes all of that unnecessary."

"All because of Stacy."

"One day, Don Juan, it's going to hit you, too," Benny joked.

"Not likely. I like it just like it is."

"What about Cecil?"

"What about her?"

"She could be the one. You never know about these things."

"Cecil's cool. She knows what time it is."

"Looks like more than just a booty call to me."

"Yeah, well, even if I was to look at this from 'another point of view' like you did, the good Dr. Jordon ain't about hearing it," Don said, laughing.

"Defense mechanism. Sounds real familiar to me. Sounds like me and Stacy all over again."

"Cecil's not into laying any traps for me by getting pregnant."

"Neither was Stacy, but what happens if you do accidentally get Cecil pregnant? You know, you two have an 'unguarded moment' like Stacy and I did. What happens then?"

Don looked at Benny. "Damn, man! Don't even joke like that!"

"So she could go have an abortion?"

"Hell no! No abortion! No way!"

"Just what I said to Stacy, but she was still determined to have the procedure."

"So what happened? What changed her mind?"

"I took her home with me. I let her see up close and personal what family means to me. Why we all have this chain and what it means. While we were there, she decided to go through with the pregnancy. That wasn't an easy decision for her to make and I knew it. She sacrificed her career for nine months to have Whitney for me because first and foremost we are friends. My family told me then that Stacy and I meant more to each other than either of us realized.

"My father told me to figure out where I was going and then to plot my course to get there. I didn't have a clue then what he was talking about. I was too busy trying to get next to JeNelle. If I had only known then what I know now."

"Yeah, that sounds like Uncle Bernie, all right. Always has a way of putting you on the right track."

"Yeah, if I had only really listened to him maybe Stacy would be here now with me and Whitney."

"So what are you doing with that overactive libido of yours?"

Benny made a gesture with his hand.

"All this time? Man! You've really got it bad! You better come on and hang out with us at Derrick's resort and chalet in Lake Tahoe."

"Who's going?"

"James, Chuck, Bill, Derrick, David, Alan, Joe, and me. We're trying to get KJ to come, too."

"Sounds like a real stud weekend."

"Everybody's kind of hooked up, you know, except you and me."

"I didn't know that Chuck was seeing somebody. I talked with him last week."

"I saw him for lunch in DC. I think the man has something fierce going on for your sister. He didn't admit it to me though, but he's been seeing this nurse at the hospital."

"Yeah, no I don't think that Viv's got a clue. She's got this thing for Derrick."

"I know. We've been out a few times together. It ain't one-sided. Derrick's hooked on Vivian," Don said, laughing.

"How is KJ going to manage to get away? JeNelle's due sometime in November."

"That's where you come in. JeNelle told me that he's been working day and night and that KJ needs a break."

"That's nothing new. KJ always works like that."

"This must be different because JeNelle is worried about him."

"Why? What's going on?"

"His company is attracting a lot of attention. A lot of off-shore attention."

"That's good, isn't it? I mean, getting more investors into the company could eventually put him up there with the Fortune 500."

"This isn't just about investment. The kind of attention he's attracting could mean a hostile take-over attempt."

"You mean someone wants to take CompuCorrect away from KJ, Tom, and Shirley?"

"It's not clear what's going on or why, but something is happening. That's for sure."

"KJ hasn't said anything to me about it."

"You know your brother. The man moves in mysterious ways," Don said.

"Yeah, he does. Count me in on the ski trip. I'll work on getting KJ there."

⚬

"So I can count on you, big brother?" Benny asked.

"This may not be the best time for me to leave town."

"JeNelle's doing fine, I hear, and Tahoe's got some good powder early. It's the best time before those babies come. Come on, KJ, the slopes are calling us. We haven't been skiing together in years. This is going to be a real male-bonding weekend."

"All right, Benny. I can't argue with you and JeNelle. She's nearly kicking me out of the house. Says that she needs her space because she's so large," he said, laughing. "Count me in. I'll get my ski gear ready tonight."

"Great! I'll fly up there and pick you up. Meet me at General Aviation, Hanger 2, at about 7:00 A.M. tomorrow."

"You got it!"

They hung up the telephone.

"Going skiing?" Lisa asked, as she stood at Kenneth's open office door.

He looked up at her. "Were we scheduled to meet about something?" he asked, ignoring her question and refocusing on the work stacked on his desk.

He picked up his pen and began to review and sign contracts. Lisa came into his office, closed his door, and perched on the side of his desk beside him.

"I have a few more contracts for you to review," she said, bending toward him.

Kenneth didn't look up or stop reviewing or signing. "Have those contracts been through the accounting, scheduling, or equipment departments yet?" he asked.

"No, I thought that you'd want to look at them first."

"Lisa, you've been with this company long enough to know the protocol around here. Before any potential contract from the sales and marketing department reaches my desk, the department heads and their staffs perform their analysis, due diligence, and Joe does a quality control review. This company doesn't sign off on any potential contract to perform unless or until we're all clear that we are in a position to do the job to the customer's expectation and satisfaction."

"That's such a long process Kenneth and we haven't been able to spend any time working together," Lisa said.

Kenneth looked up briefly and shook his head. "Lisa, the process usually takes less than four hours. Joe can usually tell a potential client whether we are able to do a job on the same day that the contract is submitted. Now I suggest that you get the process started on those contracts you want to give to me so that the potential clients aren't inconvenienced."

Lisa noticed Kenneth's indifference to her and slid off his desk. He didn't look up as she left his office.

"Going skiing?" she said aloud to herself, "And without JeNelle."

She went to her office, submitted the contracts over the internal office network as was the usual process and then made a few telephone calls.

Chapter 22

Snow was falling heavily as the airplane touched down on the runway at the airport in Lake Tahoe, Nevada. The mountains were thickly covered and the passengers, most of whom were skiers on the flight, marked their excitement with cheers and loud laughter. The taxicabs were plentiful, as they rolled up to the cab stand to whisk skiers to different resorts.

"Havenhurst Resort," Lisa Lambert said, as she piled into the cab.

A man stuck his head into the window.

"Did I hear you say Havenhurst Resort?" the tall, Black man asked.

"Yes," she answered.

"That's where I'm staying. Mind if we share the ride?"

"No, I don't mind," Lisa said, as she slid over in the back seat of the taxi.

The man smiled broadly at her and she felt something familiar about him. He was certainly a handsome man, built well, and had an air of confidence and sophistication about him. When they reached the resort, the man paid the cab driver and helped her from the taxi. He thanked her for permitting him to share her taxi, but then he disappeared into the crowded lobby of the resort. Lisa went to the desk where a long line of registrants stood patiently waiting to check in. She spotted the man at a different counter reserved for VIP registrants.

"Jackson party," she overheard him say to the desk clerk.

"Yes, Sir," the desk clerk beamed, as he handed the man his keys. "You're in..."

"Thanks, but I already know where it is," the man said.

"Yes, Miss," another desk clerk was saying to Lisa. "Can I help you?"

"Oh, yes, I'm Mrs. Alexander. I believe that my husband is registered here. His name is Kenneth Alexander."

The desk clerk checked his computer and looked at her quizzically.

"Yes, Mrs. Alexander, but was he expecting you to join him?"

"It was a last minute decision."

"Well," the desk clerk hesitated.

"Either he's registered or he's not!" Lisa snapped.

"Certainly, ma'am, he's registered. He's already checked in, but..."

"Fine! Just give me a key and have someone take me to him!"

The desk clerk consulted with another clerk and then retrieved a key and called for a bellhop. The bellhop took Lisa out of the Registration Pavilion to a mobile tractor and drove her to a secluded villa near the North Slope. She tipped the bellhop and looked around the large plush villa. She could hear the sound of someone in the shower of one of the bedrooms, as she tiptoed toward the door. The telephone rang and Lisa picked it up.

"Hello," she said quietly.

"Lisa?"

"Yes."

"This is JeNelle."

"Yes, JeNelle, what can I do for you?"

"What are you doing at Lake Tahoe?"

"Working with Kenneth, of course," she answered smugly.

"Kenneth didn't say anything about taking staff with him this weekend."

"It was a last minute decision."

"Is he there now?"

"He's in the shower now, but I'll be sure to tell him that you called."

JeNelle hung up.

Lisa grinned to herself, disrobed, closed the thick draperies in the bedroom, and slid between the sheets. She listened, but could not hear the shower water running. The bathroom door opened and she saw a man's figure standing in the doorway with something shinny in his hand.

"Surprised?" she asked.

"Is this some new form of room service?" the man asked.

The voice was not Kenneth's. Lisa flicked on the lamp on the nightstand. "*You!*" she shouted and then noticed a gun in the man's hand. It was the same man with whom she had shared the taxi ride from the airport. She was stunned and afraid as the man approached her.

"Yes, but the question, my dear, is who are you and why are you in my bed?" the man asked, pulling back the covers and searching the bed for a weapon.

Lisa tried to cover her nakedness with her hands.

"I'm Lisa! Dr. Lisa Lambert! Isn't this Kenneth Alexander's villa?"

"Uh huh," the man said still holding the gun, but not pointing it at her. "Was he, uh, expecting you?" the man asked, surveying Lisa's body.

"Well, no," she said nervously. "I work for him at CompuCorrect's Southern Division."

"And just what do you do for him—at the company, Dr. Lambert?" he suggestively asked.

"Sales and marketing," she answered, still keeping her eyes on the gun.

"I'll bet," he answered, as they both heard voices in the great room and the sound of skis being racked.

"Hey, KJ!" the man shouted. "In here!"

"Yeah, what is it?" Kenneth Alexander asked, as he came through the door unzipping his heavy parker coat.

"You've got company, Cousin," the man said to Kenneth.

"Cousin?" Lisa said aloud.

Kenneth came into the room followed by Benny Alexander, Derrick Jackson, Chuck Montgomery, Alan Lightfoot, David Carter, Tom Jenkins, James Dixon and Joe Grayson. They all looked at Lisa lying in the bed, as she pulled the cover up over her body.

"Lisa," Kenneth said dryly.

"Kenneth, who are all of these men?" Lisa asked defiantly, looking from face to face.

Kenneth shook his head, he did not answer her.

"Let me speak with you, Cousin," Kenneth said, as he led Donald out of the room.

The other men shook their heads and left the bedroom, too. Lisa could hear them talking in the great room, as she quickly dressed.

"Lisa," Kenneth said, as he reentered the bedroom with the man, "This is my cousin, Donald Dixon. I think that we should have a little talk, don't you?"

⚬━◦

"Here! Put him over here," Joe Grayson said hurriedly, as David Carter, Alan Lightfoot, Benny Alexander and Kenneth Alexander carried Bill Chandler into the villa.

"I'll get some ice," James Dixon said.

"You bring your bag?" Derrick Jackson asked Chuck Montgomery.

"Yeah. It's in the room," Chuck said, as David and Alan lowered Bill onto the sofa.

Bill winced in pain as Tom Jenkins lifted his leg to a stool.

"It's all my fault," Tom nervously admitted. "I never should have been up on the North Slope. I can't ski that well."

"Let's get his pants off," Chuck said, taking off Bill's ski boots.

Benny took Bill's ski jacket and goggles, as Alan and Joe lifted Bill while Tom and David removed Bill's ski pants. Derrick returned with Chuck's medical kit and Chuck began examining Bill's rapidly swelling knee. James brought in the ice in a Ziploc bag.

"Doesn't look that bad," Chuck said.

"No, it's not broken," Derrick added, flexing Bill's knee.

"You ought to feel it from my side. Hurts like hell!" Bill said, wincing.

Chuck and Derrick continued to examine Bill's knee.

Tom looked on and winced in sympathy with his hands on his head. "Is he going to be all right?"

"Yeah, I think so," Chuck said, pulling a hypodermic needle from his bag. "I'll give him a shot of cortisone."

"Damn, I hate needles," Bill said, looking away.

Derrick cleaned the knee with antiseptic as Chuck filled the syringe.

"Hold him steady," Chuck said, as he began to insert the needle. "This is going to hurt like hell."

Alan and David each grabbed an arm while Kenneth and Tom held Bill's leg steady.

"Oh *shit!*" Bill yelled, as Chuck inserted the needle under his kneecap.

"Hold on, buddy," Chuck said. "Don't move. I'm almost finished."

Derrick held the antiseptic over the syringe, as Chuck removed the needle.

"There. That ought to do it," Derrick said, reaching for the ice pack from James and placing it on Bill's knee.

Bill leaned his head back against the seat and closed his eyes. Everybody relaxed.

"Damn! That could have been a disaster," Tom said.

"Next time you'll have to zig instead of zag," Donald commented, laughing.

"No next time for me! You guys are crazy to ski that North Slope!"

"It's the rush, Tom!" Benny said.

"You call it a rush. I call it crazy! Man, nobody is supposed to move that fast or jump off a cliff that high off the ground!"

Everyone laughed.

"You okay now, Bill?" Derrick asked.

"That depends on what you mean by 'okay'."

"You hurt anywhere else?"

"I feel like I got run over by a Mack truck!"

"Nah, it was an evergreen you were dancing with. You gave a whole new meaning to the term 'pole dancing'. A good massage will do the trick," Derrick said.

"Now that sounds like something that I can take lying down," Bill quipped, the pain beginning to subside. "You guys go on and get out of here. Get back on the slopes. I'll call and get one or two of the resort masseurs to come over."

"Sounds like he's back to normal," Alan said, with a wry smile.

"Let's take his advice and get back on the slopes," Donald said.

"Keep that ice on for twenty minutes and then off for twenty."

"Yeah, and keep your leg elevated," Derrick added.

"I'll stay with Bill. You guys go on," Tom said.

"Let's head 'em up and move 'em out," Chuck said.

"Don't do anything that I wouldn't enjoy, Bill," Benny added.

The other men left and Tom took off his ski gear. "Can I do anything for you?" Tom asked.

"Yeah, you can put more wood in that fire," Bill said. "It's freezing in here."

Tom loaded more logs and stoked the flames.

"That was a real bad spill you took."

"I'll be fine, Tom. Don't worry about it."

"Yeah, but I could have caused you to end your career!"

"You mean modeling?"

"Yeah, that and your movie career. It would have been all my fault if you did."

"Modeling and acting don't last forever. I don't have to smile in a courtroom," Bill said, trying to reposition himself on the sofa.

"Here, let me help you," Tom said, lifting Bill's legs as Bill lay down.

"Would you see whether anyone is available for a massage?" Bill asked.

Tom picked up the telephone and called the ski lodge concierge. The clerk said that it would be hours before anyone could come because their masseurs were booked solid.

"No luck, Bill. Uh, maybe I could do it."

"You know how to give massages?"

"Better than I know how to ski," Tom said, smiling.

"Okay, I've got some stuff in my bag."

Tom brought Bill's toiletry bag into the great room and handed it to him.

"You look, Tom. It's in a blue bottle."

Tom began taking out bottle after bottle of scented or flavored jells and placing them on the coffee table.

"You've got quite a collection: banana, peach, strawberry. What's all this for?"

"You never know what flavor somebody wants."

"Flavor?"

"Never mind, Tom."

"Oh, I get it."

"Sure you do."

"Really. I understand. Uh, what flavor do you want me to use?"

"None, just use the oil."

Tom reached for the bottle and poured some on his hands. He began rubbing Bill's shoulders and arms and then massaging deeply. He removed the ice pack and had Bill turn over while he massaged his back and legs. Bill removed his jock strap while Tom massaged his lower back, butt, and thighs.

"You didn't tell me."

"What?"

"What flavor you like."

"Coconut."

Bill drifted between sleep and consciousness as Tom worked on him.

⚬══✦══

"Man, you took that run like a champ!" James said, as they lined up to get on the ski lift.

"Felt good to be on the slopes again," Benny answered. "I want to take on those hills in Vail again."

"Never been there. I usually just go up to North Carolina, Virginia or West Virginia."

"You haven't lived until you've skied Vail and Aspen."

"Does Janice ski?"

"Yeah," Benny smiled. "You ought to go with her sometime."

James smiled. "I intend to."

"So, David, where did you learn to ski so well?" Joe asked.

"Idaho. My parents are both professors. We used to live in Boise before they moved to Minnesota."

"A lot of good skiing out there?"

"Yes, where did you receive your training? Where did you learn to ski?"

"Right here in Tahoe. I used to live in Sacramento. Easy to get here from there. Used to hear about this place from people who came into the bar where I was working. Didn't have much else to do on my days off, so I used to come up here. Never could stay at a resort like this one though."

"The accommodations are above the norm. I'ts hard to imagine that Derrick owns a part of the resort and chalet where we're staying."

"Man, this is living! You see all these jetsetters? Millionaires and billionaires."

"Certainly. One might aspire to this lifestyle. Personally, it is my considered opinion that the ostentatious display of wealth only serves to heighten the expectation of the ruling classes rather than benefits the societal ethos as a pejorative psyche."

"Huh?"

"He means that the rich get richer and the poor don't get anything," Alan interjected.

"Oh."

"Just like old times, huh?" Derrick asked Chuck.

"Yeah, like when we were kids and I taught you how to ski," Chuck said.

"You taught me?" Derrick laughed. "You were scared as shit to get on skis."

"Nah, man. You were this big-time jock. Afraid you'd mess up your game!"

Derrick laughed. "Actually, I think that it was Bob who taught us both."

"Yeah, back in the day he'd do anything to get next to Sheila. Sheila sure didn't trust you being around white folks. You remember how she used to follow us around everywhere?"

Derrick laughed. "Frankly, I think that she was more interested in Bob than she was in what we were up to."

"Man! Did we get into some shit back then?"

"Yeah and I was always having to save your ass! Thought you could come up in the hood and rap to the sistahs. Man, you were one crazy white boy. You nearly got me killed more than a few times!"

Chuck laughed. "I knew you had my back! And what about you? Big time high school jock! You could book anything in a skirt!"

"Man, my head wasn't there. You know that. I had to do work to get my buzz on. Besides, Grover Jackson didn't play that!"

"Yeah, you're right. Remember how he used to be there in the gym watching us practice? Then he'd take us straight to the library until it closed."

"Yeah, then he'd take us to your house so Esther could make us study some more!"

"Harriet would come get us and take us to museums and parks or concerts. Anything to keep us out of the street."

"Yeah, my mother thought we needed culture," Derrick said, laughing. "Those were the days all right."

"Nothing's better than it was back in the day."

"I don't know about that," Derrick said, musing to himself.

Chuck noticed the gleam in Derrick's eyes. "Oh, you thinking about Vivian?"

"Always."

"You got it bad, huh?"

"This ain't puppy love like that crush I had on…uh…Damn! What was her name?"

"Trina."

"Yeah, Trina Morse. Man, did I think I was in love or what?"

"Couldn't tell you anything after she gave you that blowjob. Had you walking in space."

"I got the message loud and clear when Grover found that hickey on my neck!"

"So did I. I couldn't sit down for a week after he whipped both our butts. And I hadn't even done anything…yet."

"Yeah, he was mad all right. Then we got it again from Steven and he didn't catch us doing anything."

"He knew, all right. Talia gave me that rosy lipstick print all around my—"

"Oh yeah, I forgot about that. The rainbow party. God were we young and dumb!"

"Grover and Steven bought those condoms when you were what—twelve?"

"Nah, I was fourteen. You were twelve."

Chuck laughed. "Yeah, I'd rather take a whipping rather than those lectures we used to get every day."

"We still get those lectures, Chuck."

"Yeah, but now they don't know whether we're guilty of anything or not," Chuck said, laughing."

"Grover knows I'm guilty. Sheila told him that I took Vivian to Bimini."

"What, no lecture?"

"Not this time. Not yet at least. All he asked was when was I bringing her home to meet the family."

"What did you tell him?"

"Soon." Derrick looked into Chuck's eyes. "Very soon."

"This is a surprising development," Donald said.

"I suspected something like this might happen. Lisa and I had a relationship before," Kenneth said.

"Apparently an intimate one by the look of things."

"Purely sexual. Not emotional."

"You sure?"

"Oh yeah. Lisa is known as the Black Ice Queen. Talk about frozen. She earned that title honestly. We slept together for about five or six months."

"Looks like she knows how to handle the rock."

Kenneth grinned at Don and shook his head. "Like a pro!"

"So what happened?"

"My heart wasn't in it and neither was hers. We called it even and walked away. I suspected that her hidden agenda was those military contracts that JC Baker was pushing."

"Yeah, I remember the Congressional investigation. Sandoval Anniston took a big chunk of those military contracts, didn't they?"

"Who didn't? Everybody had their hands in the public's wallet."

"You didn't. You blew the scheme wide open."

"I was lucky. I worked for Sandoval during the Bush-Cheney eras, remember? Baker and I were friends back then. I didn't know about him and Lisa until the investigation. They had known each other in DC when she worked for the Heritage Foundation."

"He never told you that you were sleeping with his woman?"

"Lisa's not anybody's *woman*, including JC Baker's. What I later learned was that she was sent to do a job on me and she did it."

"That's where I think you're wrong. I don't think that it's over."

Kenneth looked at Don quizzically. "No way!"

"Man, you must have been serving her something!"

"Purely physical, no substance and she know it. She knew what JeNelle meant to me. That's how we got together in the first place."

"You sure you don't still feel something for her?"

Kenneth looked Don in the eyes. "Not a thing."

"All right. We've gotten a lot accomplished. Your plan is workable. Then we're clear?"

"Very clear."

"You want a brandy, Bill?" Tom asked, as Bill awoke from a long nap.

"What time is it?"

"About four o'clock."

"Where is everybody?"

"They went to dinner early. They're going on the night run."

"Yeah—wish I could join them."

"How are you feeling?"

"Better, but not great. You give good massages."

"You've got nice skin—. Uh, I mean your body is soft—. I mean, you feel like a man with muscles and all, but—"

"Don't sweat it, Tom. I know what you mean."

"So you work out?"

"Yeah, I have to if I want to keep working. The camera picks up everything."

"I've seen your pictures in *Esquire*."

"That must have been the Polo ad."

"Yeah, but this guy in the office had your autograph on a spread in this other magazine."

"What issue?"

"January or February."

"Oh, you mean in the gay trades."

"Yeah, you do let it all hang out, so to speak, don't you?"

"I'm not ashamed of my body, if that's what you are talking about."

"Uh, I didn't mean to offend you. I was just making conversation."

"We don't have to talk about gay issues, Tom. I'm not one dimensional."

"You're right. Uh, but I was just curious."

"About what?"

"When did you know that you were gay?"

Bill laughed. "I still don't know it."

"What do you mean? You do sleep with men, don't you?"

"And women, too."

"Then you're not gay after all."

"Thanks for solving that issue for me, Tom. I was really beginning to be confused about my sexuality," Bill said, with tongue in cheek.

Tom flushed. "I do say dumb shit sometimes, don't I?"

"Let's just say that you're not well informed and leave it at that."

"Uh, how about that drink?"

"Yeah, I guess one wouldn't hurt."

"You don't drink?"

"Not usually, and before you ask I don't do drugs or smoke."

Tom laughed and poured the brandy. He handed it to Bill and sat down beside him on the sofa. "You know, I didn't think that I would, but I like you, Bill."

"I'm happy for you, Tom." Bill laughed, as he sipped the brandy and settled into a comfortable position.

Tom laughed. "You know what I mean. You're a regular guy."

"Yeah, thanks, but don't tell my clients that or I'll be out of business."

"You get a lot of good ads."

"I'm working. In fact, my agent tells me that I have a contract pending to do a television ad for a soap company."

"Soap?"

"Yeah, they're filming it in LA next month."

"Oh, I've never seen a film crew at work before. When is it? I might come and watch you work."

"Sometime during the Christmas holidays. That's the only time that I can get away to do a commercial. I'll let you know when."

"Yes, do that," Tom said, taking another sip of brandy. "You want another brandy and another massage?"

Bill leaned back, laced his hands behind his head, and watched the fire flicker in the roaring fireplace.

"I can't move, now can I?"

Chapter 23

"Hi, honey, I'm home," Kenneth called out, as he came into the house and placed his skis in a closet. "JeNelle, are you here?" he called again.

There was no answer. Kenneth picked up the mail and fingered through it. Then he noticed how quiet the house was. He went up the steps to their new master bedroom and noticed that the bed was made. He unpacked his bag and looked at his watch. It was late and JeNelle was still not at home. He picked up the telephone and dialed her private line at INSIGHTS. The answering machine picked up. He hung up and dialed Canty and Harvey. He got their answering machine as well. He looked at his phone on his belt. No messages. He opened the doors and walked out onto the deck and watched the tide roll in. He heard the telephone ringing and picked it up.

"Kenneth," Joe said.

"Yeah, man, what's up?"

"Your time."

"What?"

"I'm on my way to pick you up."

"Why?"

"I just left Sara's. JeNelle's in labor. I'm a block away."

Kenneth raced to the front door just as Joe pulled into the driveway. They sped toward the hospital and Kenneth got out of the car before Joe stopped. He raced through the halls to the labor rooms and saw JeNelle's Aunt Bessie in the hallway.

"Where is she?" he demanded.

"In there," Bessie said.

Kenneth went into the room and saw Canty and Harvey holding each of JeNelle's hands, as she screamed in agony. Kenneth went to her side.

"How is she?"

"She'll be better now that you're here."

"Why didn't someone call me?"

"JeNelle called you a couple of days ago, but that was false labor that time. This is the real thing," Canty said.

"I didn't get any message and I told the resort to find me if she called."

JeNelle screamed again in pain.

"Won't be long now," Canty said. "Contractions are about three minutes apart."

"How was the trip," JeNelle asked.

"We can talk about that later, JeNelle. Right now I want to know—"

"*Oh God!*" she screamed.

"Breathe, honey. Come on, just like we practiced." He took a breath, coaching her to mimic his action. She finally settled into his breathing rhythm.

Harvey and Canty left the room as Kenneth, the nurses, and doctors took over. Hours passed, as Canty and Harvey waited for news of the birth of their grandsons. Finally, Kenneth came out of JeNelle's room with a big smile on his face.

"Well?" Harvey asked.

"Healthy twin boys," Kenneth said, on an exhausted exhale of breath. "Mother, Kevin Harvey and Kenneth Bernard are doing fine."

"Praise be," Bessie said.

"We're grandparents," Canty smiled, as she gazed up into Harvey's eyes.

"Kevin Harvey and Kenneth Bernard Alexander," Harvey said, as he kissed his wife and tightly hugged her.

"You can see them in a few minutes," Kenneth said. "I'm going to call my family."

Kenneth called the operator for a conference call. It was 3:00 A.M. on the East Coast when Sylvia, Bernard, and Aretha Alexander picked up the call in Goodwill. Vivian Alexander in Washington and Gregory Alexander in Charlottesville, Virginia came on the line. Then Benny Alexander, who had just gotten into bed in San Diego, picked up on the call. They talked for nearly an hour. Kenneth gave them all the details.

Sylvia said that Bernard had tears in his eyes, and Bernard didn't deny it.

"I'm on my way," Benny said. "Whitney and I will be there in a few hours, KJ."

"Benny, you've been flying all day. Flying everybody to San Francisco, then Santa Barbara, then yourself home to San Diego."

"See you shortly, big brother," Benny firmly said.

"We'll come there for Thanksgiving this year," Bernard said.

Kenneth smiled to himself. "I love you all," he said to his family.

"We know, Kenneth James. See you in a few days. We love you, too," Bernard answered.

They all hung up.

It was almost exactly two hours later when Benny came in carrying Whitney. He handed her to Canty and he and Kenneth embraced for a long time.

"Now where are my new nephews?" Benny demanded, wiping his eyes.

Kenneth led him into the nursery to the glass partition; they gazed at the boys and hugged each other. A nurse beckoned them inside, covered them both with sterile gowns, and handed one of the twins to each of them. The brothers sat for a while just looking at each of the boys and then at each other. They smiled broadly.

"You know, I have you to thank for these two golden nuggets," Kenneth said, looking at Benny.

"I never laid a hand on JeNelle, I swear!" Benny joked.

Kenneth laughed. "Thank God for that, but if anything were to happen to me, I want you to—"

"I know, KJ, but nothing is going to happen."

"Yet, if it did."

"I know what my responsibilities are. Your boys will be fine and so will you and JeNelle."

"Thanks, little brother."

Chuck Montgomery put the van in park and helped David Carter and Alan Lightfoot to get Bill Chandler into the house and up to his bedroom. Derrick Jackson brought in the luggage and put it by the front door.

"You need a ride to your place?" Chuck asked Derrick.

"Nah, I'm going to stay here. Be with Vivian when she wakes up."

"You sure you're not too tired? That was a long flight back from San Francisco."

"Yeah, and a long weekend away from Vivian. Too long," he said, smiling.

"You take it easy, DJ."

"I hear you, little brother. I'm doing fine."

They embraced and Chuck left.

Derrick slipped carefully into bed with Vivian so as not to wake her.

"Now if I was a jealous woman I'd be raising cane about you coming to bed at this time of the morning," Vivian joked, looking at the clock.

"Hey, baby, did I wake you?" Derrick said, hugging Vivian. "I'm sorry. I was trying to be quiet. Did you miss me?"

"I'm not sure. Who are you?" Vivian joked.

"I wasn't gone that long, Vivian," he said, as he kissed her back.

"Still don't know who you are."

Derrick kissed her with desire evident in his touch.

"Oh now I recognize you," Vivian said, as he released her. "You were in my sixth grade class at Goodwill Institute."

"I got your sixth grade," he joked, as he rolled on top of her.

Chapter 24

"Tom, did you hear the news?" Shirley Taylor asked.

"No, what?"

"Kenneth and JeNelle. Twin boys. Kevin and Kenneth, Jr. Kenneth just called."

"That's good."

"Tom."

"Yes."

"Is something wrong?"

"Wrong? No what could be wrong?"

"I don't know. Didn't you have a good trip?"

"Yeah, it was great, but—"

"But what?"

"Bill wrenched his knee."

"Is he all right?"

"Yes, Chuck and Derrick said that he'd be fine."

"Then what's the problem?"

"It was my fault. I skied right across him and he fell—ran into these trees."

"Still you said that he's going to be all right."

"Yeah, I mean, yes, he is."

"Tom, are you sure that you're all right?"

"Yes, yes. I'm fine. Just tired."

"You want to come over?"

"There? Your place?"

"Yes, you've been here before."

"No, I, uh, I'll see you in the office later. Goodbye, Shirley."

"Tom—"

Tom hung up and covered his head, as he tried to go back to sleep.

Chapter 25

Chuck walked into the surgical wing of Georgetown Hospital and stepped behind the nurses' station to check his patients' charts.

"Good morning, Dr. Montgomery," Dr. Mindy Burke, a neurosurgeon, said.

"Good morning," Chuck answered not looking up.

"A little early even for you, isn't it, doctor? I didn't see your name on the Emergency Room surgical rotation list for this morning."

"No, I'm not scheduled to perform any miracles today. I just came in on the redeye from San Francisco. Thought I'd check on a few patients before I go home."

"What time are you on duty today?" she asked.

"Not until 3:00 P.M.," he answered still not looking up.

"Was it a good trip?"

"Yeah, it was great. Look, how is Mrs. Fulton doing? Her chart says that her blood pressure was abnormally high."

"Oh, yes, well, uh, the dietician didn't know that she was supposed to be on a salt-free diet."

"Damn! Is she stable now?"

"Yes, but I'll check her again before I go off duty at seven o'clock."

"Never mind, I'll do it myself. I wanted to discharge her before Christmas if she's up to it. She's a nice lady."

"So where did you go?"

"When?"

"This weekend?"

"Oh, uh, Tahoe, skiing."

"You went alone?"

"No, eleven guys."

"Sounds interesting. No women?"

"Not this trip."

"You meet anyone?"

"Wasn't looking to."

"Why, are you seeing someone?"

"What's with all the questions?"

"Thought you might want to go out or something."

Chuck finally looked up, pushed his cowboy hat back further on his head, and leaned back in his seat.

"Dr. Burke, are you asking me out on a date?" he asked, with a questioning smile.

"You noticed?"

"Aren't you married to that—"

"He's out of town for a couple of weeks."

"Uh, I'm flattered but—"

"How about your place? Say about seven-thirty?"

"Yeah, no I don't think so. Not this time."

"You don't know what you're missing."

"Uh, yes I do," Chuck said, with a wink and a smile, as he rose to go and check on his patients. Mrs. Fulton's condition was stable and he sat and talked with her about her family and the fact that she was looking forward to spending the holidays with her children and grandchildren. She told him that she had two granddaughters about his age that she wanted him to meet. She blushed when he told her that he preferred more mature women—well seasoned, around seventy years old or so. He checked on his other patients and left the hospital.

Dawn was breaking as Chuck entered his condo. He spotted the picture of Vivian and picked it up. "I know what I'm missing all right," he mused aloud.

The telephone rang.

"Hello, I'm not here so don't leave a—"

Vivian laughed. "Hey, cowboy. Did I catch you at a bad time?"

"Uh, no, I just got in.'

"Are you alone?"

"I think so."

"Don't act the innocent with me, Charles Montgomery. Derrick told me how those women at Tahoe were checking you out on the ski slopes and how the women at the hospital are always hitting on you—even the married ones."

Chuck laughed. "He told you that, did he?"

"Yes, so what's her name?"

"Whose name?"

"The woman you've been with for the last two hours. I've been calling you all morning."

"Mrs. Fulton."

"She's married?"

"Happily."

"And you're seeing her?"

"Regularly. Every day in fact."

"You've been intimate with this Mrs. Fulton?"

"Very." Chuck started laughing.

"I don't think that's funny, Chuck."

"Mrs. Fulton gets a laugh out of it."

"Are you serious about her?"

"Very."

"Does she have children?"

"Yes."

"Chuck, don't you need to think about this? I mean, a married woman with a husband and children. You could be wrecking her family."

"She can handle it. She's been around the track a few times," he said, laughing. "We won't be seeing each other as much."

"How do you feel about that?"

"I'm going to miss her. She told me that she loves me though."

"I'm sorry, Chuck. Is there anything that I can do?"

"Do you know any eligible men?"

"What?"

"Eligible men—you know—free, single and disengaged."

"Yes, but why?"

"Either I find young men for Mrs. Fulton granddaughters or I'm going on the auction block."

"Granddaughters? How old is Mrs. Fulton?"

"Seventy."

"Chuck, you're wicked!"

Chuck roared. "All right, Annie, what's up? I need some shuteye."

"Oh, I almost forgot the reason I called you. Kenny Bernard and Kevin Harvey Alexander put in an appearance this morning. Kenneth called just before you got in from San Francisco.

"That's great. How is JeNelle?"

"Fine and very happy. Kenneth tried to call you."

"I went to the hospital after I dropped Derrick by your place. You've told him the news, of course. Is he still there?"

"Yes, he's taking a shower."

"You two spending the day together?"

"Derrick's planning something. How about you? Want to come by? You haven't been around much."

"I'm on duty later."

"Chuck."

"Yes."

"I do miss having you around. We all do. I mean, I wouldn't want you to stop coming by because of me and Derrick."

"I've got to sleep, Annie. I'll see you and the posse soon."

They hung up and Chuck picked up Vivian's picture again.

"Damn! Damn! Damn!" he said, airing his soulful guilty desire to be with Vivian.

He put her picture face down and climbed into bed. "Vivian," he whispered, as he drifted off to sleep.

Chapter 26

Kevin and Kenny had just finished their 2:00 A.M. feedings. JeNelle sat by their cribs while they slept. She had been home from the hospital for a week and Kenneth was with her every minute. He was great with the boys. Then she thought about Lisa and Kenneth at Tahoe. Kenneth did not mention it once since he came home. He only mentioned Bill's injury as if nothing else significant had happened, but she remembered how smugly Lisa had behaved a few weeks before Kevin and Kenny were born. That day was vivid in her mind.

She had just looked up from her desk in her office overlooking the floor of her store and quickly scanned the area. The store was relatively full of shoppers in the book section. A few customers in the art exhibit area and more people in the card and gift sections. She thought that she glimpsed a familiar face in the book section. *No, it couldn't be,* she had thought before she turned on the security monitor and scanned more closely. Lisa! Lisa Lambert was in the store! Her heart had tripped at the sight of her. She had sat thinking and watching as Lisa browsed through some books, made a few selections, and then went to the service desk for Wanda to ring up the purchases. Then she noticed that Wanda Willis picked up the telephone and her telephone rang.

"Mrs. Alexander?"

"Yes, Wanda."

"I need your authorization on a check for over $200.00."

"All right, Wanda. I'll be right there."

Gathering herself for what was to come, she went to Wanda's station. She had not seen Lisa since that December meeting of the Blue Ribbon Panel on Youth in Business and Industry. Lisa had been chairing those meetings in Sacramento for the Governor and simultaneously having an intimate affair with Kenneth. Kenneth had not said much about why he and Lisa had broken off their relationship. He had only assured her that it was over. That he and Lisa were never in love, but that they had been lovers. She had not pressed him for details since it was later disclosed that Lisa had an ulterior motive for starting the affair with Kenneth in the first place. That was behind them now. Or at least it was until Lisa started working for CompuCorrect. Kenneth had told her about it. That he had not made the decision to hire Lisa. That he and Lisa would not be working closely together or, at least, no more closely than he worked with any of his other employees. She trusted Kenneth and knew that, if he told her that there was nothing between himself and Lisa, it was the truth.

"Hello, Lisa," she had said as politely as she could.

"JeNelle," Lisa had responded without expression in her usual business persona.

"Wanda, Dr. Lambert's check is cleared."

"Thank you, Mrs. Alexander," Wanda had said, initialing the check.

As she turned and started to walk away, Lisa had called to her.

"JeNelle."

"Yes, Lisa. Was there something else?"

"Yes, in fact there is. I'm chairing the Business and Industry Program for the Business and Professional Women's Legislative Agenda Convention in Chicago. As the President of the California Chapter of the League, I thought that perhaps we should get together for lunch and discuss any ideas that you might have for our program and workshops. I'd like for you to be on one of the panels also."

"Certainly, Lisa. What did you have in mind?"

"I'm free for lunch today, if you're available."

"Let me check. Kenneth and I usually have lunch together."

"He's tied up today. He's meeting with some new clients for lunch."

"Oh, he didn't mention it to me."

"I'm sure that his secretary, Patricia, can confirm that for you."

"That's not necessary, Lisa. I believe you."

"Then shall we say 1:00 P.M. at Maison's?"

She had felt uncomfortable about meeting Lisa. Perhaps she was just overreacting, she had thought to herself at the time.

The telephone rang. *"Hi, honey, how's your day going?"* Kenneth had asked.

"Not bad. How about yours?"

"A little hectic. How about an early lunch today? Say about 11:30?"

"Don't you have a lunch scheduled with some new clients?"

"Yes, but how did you know about that? I just scheduled it two hours ago?"

"Lisa Lambert told me."

"Lisa? How did that happen?"

"She was in the store. We're having lunch at Maison's at 1:00 P.M. There's no reason for you to have to eat two lunches," she had said, laughing. *"You don't even like to eat lunch most of the time. Why don't you use the time to work out?"*

"JeNelle, I enjoy having lunch with you. I look forward to spending that time together. Is the honeymoon over already?" he had joked.

"Not a chance, Mr. Alexander."

"That's good to hear. You had me worried."

"You can take me out to dinner tonight. Say 6:00 P.M."

"Or I could cook at home and we could make an early night of it. Just you and me and babies."

"Okay, you're on."

"Great. I love you."

"I love you more."

They had hung up.

"Good afternoon, Mrs. Alexander," Jerrod, the Maître d at Maison's had said as she arrived, *"And how are we doing today?"* looking at her rotund belly.

"We are fine, Jerrod. I have a reservation for 1:00 P.M."

"Certainly, I have it here on the computer that your husband's company installed. It's a party of two. Your guest is Dr. Lisa Lambert, correct?"

"Yes, Jerrod."

"Well, Mrs. Alexander, why don't you make yourself comfortable in the sitting room? I'll inform you when Dr. Lambert arrives."

"Thank you, Jerrod."

Maison's was reportedly one of the finest restaurants in Santa Barbara. JeNelle recalled, as she sat in the over-stuffed wingback chair leafing through the newspaper, that she had been the one who introduced Lisa to Kenneth in that same restaurant. Little did she know then that her introduction would lead to an affair between Kenneth and Lisa. She shook off her thoughts of the past and focused on the newspaper articles. Then she spotted a horrifying account.

The Post, New York, New York

The streets of the city's Little Italy ran red today with the blood of wealthy, restaurateur, industrialist and financier, Millos Giovanni San Angelo. The Don, as he was called in certain circles, was shot to death on the city streets as he left one of his restaurants. The killing smacked of the old gangland style hits of an earlier period in La Costra Nostra's brutal history. It has long been rumored that Mr. San Angelo is a member to the Santangello dynasty of Italy. A blood feud started over a purported affair between his mother, Angelina Maria Giovanni, and Tommaso Cascioferro. Because she refused to leave her husband and children Don Tomas swore vengeance on the entire Santangello family. According to witnesses, both Millos and Milo survived a brutal attack on the Santangellos and were sent out of Italy to save their lives. Perhaps an old vendetta has caught up with Millos San Angelo.

Eyewitness accounts say that four Black men in a BMW sped by and a hail of bullets from automatic weapons rained down on San Angelo, hitting him several times. No one else was injured and Mr. San Angelo was pronounced dead on the scene.

The police have no clues as to a motive for the deadly attack. The Mayor is demanding a full-scale investigation.

Wall Street is expected to react negatively to the death of one of the most powerful men in the world today. His vast empire spanned not only the United States, but also substantial holdings worldwide.

Mr. San Angelo is survived by two sons, Michel and Antonio, a daughter, Maria, and a brother, Milo San Angelo of San Diego, California. It is widely believed that Maria San Angelo, a New York City resident, will be chosen to head her father's vast empire rather than her older brother, Michel, who is thought to have amassed vast wealth far greater than his father's. Michel San Angelo spends little time in the United States and prefers the jet-set lifestyle in Europe, particularly Spain, much more to his reported exotic tastes. The youngest son is a student at a university in Virginia.

Funeral arrangements have not yet been announced, but it is expected that he will be laid to rest at a private ceremony at his compound in The Hamptons.

Few men have...

JeNelle's heart beat faster as she read the gruesome details of her former father-in-law's death. She had thought about how kind Millos had been to her and how close she still was with his brother, Milo, and his daughter, Maria. Millos' youngest boy, Antonio, was in college now, she mused. She believed that Millos had been the one who helped her when she was desperate to find a way to help Kenneth during the Congressional hearings.

"JeNelle," Lisa had said suddenly, standing beside the chair where she was sitting. *"Jerrod told me that you were in here. Our table isn't ready yet."*

"Fine, Lisa. May I order something for you to drink?"

"Yes, thank you. A Stoli neat please," Lisa told the waiter who JeNelle had summoned.

"And for you, Mrs. Alexander?" he had asked.

"Spring water with a twist, please, Milton."

"Very good, Mrs. Alexander."

Lisa, JeNelle knew, was watching her closely. She could feel her stare.

"Well, JeNelle, Kenneth tells me that your baby will be born soon," Lisa said.

"Babies. We're having twins, but that shouldn't interfere with my participation in the Legislative Agenda Program. What topic do you want me to address on the panel discussion?"

"I haven't worked that out with the other members of the planning committee yet."

"Then perhaps this luncheon is a bit premature."

"No, we can discuss other conference matters over lunch, but I'm curious."

"About?"

"How you took the news that Kenneth had hired me to work for him?"

"With a grain of salt. That's how much it meant to me. Kenneth makes his own decisions about who works for his company. We often talk about it; however, I don't interfere in his decisions."

"Considering that Kenneth and I had a very fulfilling and active love affair not that long ago, I would have thought that you would have at least discussed it."

"Love affair? I don't think so. Let's call it what it was, Lisa. It was an affair. Period. Love had nothing to do with it. If it had, he would still be with you because that's the kind of guy he is. Therefore, it was of little or no consequence."

That comment had seemed to have rocked Lisa's smug demeanor somewhat, she had thought to herself. The waiter returned with the drinks.

"Mrs. Alexander, may I say that you look marvelous today! Simply marvelous!" Milton had gushed. *"I trust that you and Mr. Alexander will be dining with us again very soon?"*

"Perhaps, Milton. Mr. Alexander and I do tend to enjoy dining alone at home together, but I'll mention it to him tonight."

"Thank you, Mrs. Alexander, and if there's anything else that you desire, please don't hesitate to call on me."

"Thank you, Milton."

"So, you and Kenneth don't go out much? As I recall, Kenneth enjoyed trying different restaurants and then going to bed with a glass of wine or liquor."

"That was then, Lisa."

"Your table is ready, Mrs. Alexander," Jerrod interrupted.

"Thank you, Jerrod."

That night Kenneth never asked about her luncheon with Lisa and she never brought it up. After dinner, Kenneth sat in the study concentrating on his project. He told her that he would need to spend every evening working to finish a project so that they could spend more time together. She was looking at the progress that the workmen were making at finishing the construction of their new home in Goodwill, Summer County, South Carolina. She looked at the video that Gregory e-mailed to them and she and Kenneth selected fabrics for the nursery and for their bedrooms. The house was beginning to take shape, but Kenneth had not spent a lot of time talking with her about it or about anything else, she thought, including his special project. Perhaps she misunderstood him when he said that he did not personally hire Lisa. Or that he and Lisa were not working closely together. Could she have misunderstood Lisa, though, when she said that she and Kenneth had a "very fulfilling and active love affair?" That was quite a different point of view from the few words that Kenneth had used to describe his relationship with Lisa, she thought. Could Kenneth describe their love life as 'fulfilling' or even 'active'? She had peeked into the study and noticed that Kenneth was still working intently. She had not want to disturb him so she had found other things to occupy her time while she waited for Kevin and Kenny to be born.

"Hi, Mama."

"JeNelle, what a surprise. Why are you calling so late? Are you all right?"

"Yes, I'm fine. Kenneth's working again."

"He's in the office at this time of the night?"

"No, he's here. He's in the study."

"And you're feeling a little lonely," she had said, with a knowing tone in her voice and calm manner.

"Who's that, Canty?" she had heard her father ask.

"It's JeNelle, Harvey. She's all right."

"Mama, did I catch you at a bad time?"

"Well, your daddy and I were, you know, uh, reminiscing," she had giggled.

"I'm sorry, Mama, I didn't—"

"Don't worry about it, baby, we can get back to it..."

"No, Mama. This call wasn't important. I'll stop by the shop and have lunch with you and Daddy sometime this week. We can talk then."

"Did you read about Millos San Angelo in the newspaper?"

"Yes and it was all over the television news tonight."

"Are you worried about what Michel might do now that his father is dead?"

"No, why should I?"

"He's a crazy man, JeNelle. Regardless of the newspaper's speculation about the Cali—whatever's role in his murder, I wouldn't put it past Michel to have been behind this whole thing. You know he hated his father for backing you in the divorce."

"That was ages ago."

"Michel's not the type of man who'd forget something like that."

"I don't want to talk or think about Michel. You and Daddy have a good night."

"Well, if you're sure, baby?"

"Yes, Mama. Goodnight."

When she hung up the telephone and leaned back on the sofa pit in the living room, her thoughts had raced. Even her parents were having a very fulfilling and active sex life. Her mother could always make her father smile. She had even heard them 'reminiscing' a few times herself.

Kenneth's parents were no different. Kenneth and his brothers and sisters had teased their parents openly about their father calling for divine intervention late at night or early in the morning. She had not been able to do that for Kenneth. To give him the type of sexual experience that would make him call out in ecstasy. Michel had only taught her how to endure pain not pleasure. Agony not bliss. The thought of him ordering someone's death was not that hard for her to imagine. She had thought him capable of anything.

Then the telephone rang again.

"Hello."

"JeNelle, have you read those books that I gave you?"

"Good night, Mama!" She had smiled.

"Read, baby!"

They had hung up.

The telephone rang again.

"Mama, I haven't—"

"Mama? It's me, JeNelle, your sister, Gloria. Remember me?"

"Oh, hi, Gloria. I'm sorry. I just got off... oh, never mind. How are you? How are your classes going?" She had looked at her watch. *"It must be pretty late there in DC?"*

"Yes, we just finished a study session. How is that phine stud of a husband of yours?"

"He's fine. He's working in the study."

"And what are you doing these days? Are you gaining a lot of weight?"

"No. Not a lot."

"You know, with that Lisa Lambert around, you need to get your figure back real soon after you drop this load."

"I'm not worried about Lisa."

"You ought to be. I overheard Benny and Vivian on the telephone a few times when Kenneth was with Lisa, laughing about how Lisa was knocking Kenneth to his knees! A man doesn't forget good action like that overnight. You'd better be serving something he can't find anywhere else or old Lisa will be back in his saddle again. I know! I've pussy whipped a few myself and I'm aiming to get in the saddle again!"

"That's not all that's involved in a marriage—just sex. Besides, I trust Kenneth," she had said confidently.

"God! Are you behind the times! Men don't just love a woman because she can smile pretty or hold a tea cup the right way or use the correct fork at a formal dinner! Kenneth is not Michel. You better be giving him something that he'll be dying to come home to 'cause love don't love nobody. You better be knocking his boots off every day all day! You've already lost one husband. Don't be foolish and lose another one."

"I'm sure that you didn't call me at this time of the night to discuss sex. What else is on your mind?"

"It's related, in a way. We're going on this ski trip and I want a few new things to knock someone's eyes out! I mean, I need to buy some ski equipment and Bill's going to take me to these couture houses so that I can pick out some new designer threads. I want this new man to know that I'm in the house!"

"How much do you need?"

"Three thousand ought to get it."

"Dollars?" she had shrieked. *"American money?"*

"It's for a worthy cause, JeNelle. Besides, you and Kenneth can afford it. You're probably in old Millos San Angelo's will big time, too."

"That's not the point, Gloria!" She had ignored Gloria's mention of Millos.

"Please, JeNelle. I really want to look good," she had begged.

"All right, Gloria, I'll deposit it in your account tomorrow. Who's this new flame of yours? Somebody at Georgetown Law?"

"Derrick Jackson."

"Derrick?" she had shrieked. *"I thought that he and Vivian were still together. Kenneth talks to Derrick all the time. He didn't say that Vivian and Derrick weren't seeing each other anymore. When did it happen?"*

"It hasn't yet, but when Derrick gets a load of me in my new threads, he and Vivian will be history. I know how to make love to a man like him!"

"Don't do this! Don't set yourself up for a big disappointment and don't interfere in Vivian's relationship with Derrick. From what I've seen and heard about them, they're falling in love."

"I don't see any rings on anybody's finger, not that that matters. Derrick's a man. Free, single, and disengaged."

"And Vivian's your friend and a part of our family."

"All's fair in love and war," Gloria had flippantly said.

"Gloria, you'll get no support from me if that's what you're up to."

"You'd take sides with Vivian against me, your own flesh and blood? I should think that you'd be giving me encouragement. I mean, Derrick's very well off. He's reported to be a multi-billionaire. He could take care of me with no sweat. What does Vivian care about being financially well situated? She wants to work for a living. I don't!"

"Forget it. I'm not sending a dime to you. Now if you want to ruin your relationship with the Alexander family, and that includes me, I can't stop you, but I sure don't have to pay for it. Your regular allowance will be in your account as usual next month."

"So, you are taking sides! You're choosing Vivian over me?"

"Think what you like. Now it's late. Good night!"

She had slammed down the telephone.

The nerve of that girl, she had thought to herself. She felt two hands on her shoulders, massaging her neck and back.

"You're too tense, JeNelle," Kenneth had said, as he massaged her. *"What's our sister up to now?"*

"No good, I'll tell you!"

"Sounded like she's still making a play for Derrick."

She had turned and looked at Kenneth, surprised. *"You knew about this?"*

"Vivian told me and so did Derrick. We talked about it up at Tahoe a lot. They've been trying to handle the situation without hurting Gloria. Derrick wants to lay it on the line with Gloria, but Vivian doesn't want him to do that. My sister thinks that Gloria's been hurt enough," Kenneth had said, still massaging her.

"Why didn't you tell me about this?"

"Vivian and Derrick didn't want to upset you, especially not while you're carrying our babies."

He had kissed her on her neck and she had relaxed. He sat on the sofa and began massaging her feet, ankles, and legs.

"Is there anything else that you're keeping from me?"

"No, nothing of any importance," he had said nonchalantly, not looking at her as he worked on her knees.

"You wouldn't lie to me about anything, would you, Kenneth?"

He didn't break his concentration on what he was doing.

"No," he had answered, *"but enough, Mrs. Alexander. It's late and you and our babies should have been asleep hours ago and I'm sure that although you haven't said anything, the death of your former father-in-law is probably on your mind."*

He had taken her by her hands and led her to their bedroom. He had helped her undress and they had showered together. He had washed her back and massaged her shoulders. She could see that he was weary, but he brushed her hair and led her to bed. He had held her close.

"Kenneth," she whispered when they were finally nestled in bed, *"I didn't mention anything about Millos because I didn't want you to worry."*

"Why should I be worried about some lunatics killing Millos San Angelo? Is there something you haven't told me? Has Michel been harassing you again?"

She had felt his body tense. *"No, no, nothing like that,"* she had lied.

Michel had called her many times since she and Kenneth married. She simply hung up the telephone when she heard his voice.

"Then I don't understand."

"That part of my life is over. The newspaper article mentioned something about an inheritance and I didn't want you to worry that I would accept anything from the San Angelos."

"Are you sure that's it, JeNelle, or were you worried about Michel coming after you now that his father wasn't there to stop him?"

Kenneth as usual, was right on target, but she didn't want to vent her fears.

"Michel and I are through, Kenneth. It was over long ago," she had said, not wanting to sound worried.

"He's still in love with you, JeNelle, as much as a man like him can be in love. I'm in love with you, too, and he can't have you back. No matter what it takes. You and I are going to be as happy as two people in love have a right to be."

Kenneth had said those words with such steel and confidence in his voice that it chilled her, but they went to sleep without further discussion.

That had happened weeks before Kevin and Kenny were born. Now as she sat watching their baby boys sleeping in their cribs, she tried to dismiss her concerns about Lisa and Kenneth, and about what Michel was capable of doing, but she couldn't shake the feeling that Kenneth was keeping something from her. He had not mentioned the fact that Lisa had answered the telephone when she called him in Lake Tahoe. Kenneth had not mentioned that Lisa was even there although he constantly talked about what a great time the eleven men had on the trip. They conducted some business, too. Chuck and Derrick had agreed to be board members for CompuCorrect Interconnect, the new public company Kenneth was planning. She had even overheard him telling two of her store managers, Barry Kennedy and Felix Olson, that they were certainly welcome to join them the next time that they went skiing, but even with them Kenneth never mentioned Lisa.

She looked at their boys and decided to disregard all thoughts that Kenneth and Lisa were still intimately involved with each other. She and Kenneth were a family now with their babies and there was nothing that Lisa or Michel could do to change it. She wouldn't let them.

"JeNelle, I don't know how I let you talk me into this," Janice Atterly fussed. "You know that I'm not a joiner."

"You have a lot to offer the Business and Professional Women's League. You'd be perfect in our career counseling program for high school youth. We don't have a lot of biochemists in the organization and—"

"Enough already, JeNelle," Janice said, putting up both of her hands in mock defeat. "I said that I would do this. I've paid my dues. Are they tax deductible, do you know?"

JeNelle laughed. "Probably, this is a professional woman's organization. Where is Cecil?"

"She'll come to Los Angeles later tonight. Don's been in town."

"Again?" JeNelle laughed with surprise.

"Oh, yes. This time she took an expedition up to Seattle around Puget Sound. Don met her there and as usual, decided to fly back with her through San Diego for a few days before he went wherever else he had to go. I still don't know what the man does for a living, do you?"

"No, I never thought to ask. I'm sure that it's nothing illegal, if that's what you're worried about?"

"No, I'm not worried. Cecil's no fool. She knows what time it is, but tell me, how is married life?"

JeNelle beamed.

"Oh, okay. That good, huh?"

"Perfect! Or at least almost perfect."

"What's the 'almost' about?"

"Nothing, really."

"JeNelle," Janice coaxed.

"Well, Lisa Lambert's dropping these hints about her and Kenneth and—"

"Hold it right there!" Janice said sternly. "No way! No how! Kenneth isn't the type! It's not in his DNA to be unfaithful."

"I know that."

"Then what?"

JeNelle could not tell her friend that Lisa had been in Lake Tahoe with Kenneth.

"Let's get back to these plans for the National Convention. We can talk about this other stuff later."

Chapter 27

"Tom, what's going on?" Shirley Taylor asked, as they ate dinner at the Equinox Restaurant.

"I don't know what you mean," he said, picking at his food.

"Ever since you got back from Tahoe you've been...well...distracted."

"It's your imagination, Shirley. Uh, what do you want for desert?"

"We just started dinner, Tom, and we've already ordered desert," she said and put down her fork. "Now I want to know what's bothering you."

Tom Jenkins looked up into her eyes. "I uh... well... uh... you see...," he said, struggling to get it out. "It's nothing," he finally said, frustrated.

"Is it us? I mean, are you having second thoughts about us?"

"No... we're fine, Shirley."

"Apparently not."

"I don't understand."

"Tom Jenkins, when was the last time you kissed me?"

Tom's eyes widened. "Uh, yesterday or maybe the day before. I don't... well, let me think. It must have been... uh..."

"Before you left for Tahoe and that was nearly three months ago."

"It couldn't have been that long ago," he said, becoming visibly nervous.

"Am I suddenly unappealing now that we're supposedly engaged? Have you lost interest in me? Did you meet someone else while you were away or since you've been back?"

"No, of course not," he said confidently. "What gave you that idea?"

Shirley took her napkin out of her lap and put it on the table. Frustration was getting the better of her. "Look, Tom, maybe what we need to do is take a break and look at our relationship again. I'm no fool. Something has changed between us and I haven't got a clue what it is. I care a hell of a lot for you, but I can't help if I don't know what's going

348

on. You're going to LA tomorrow for a few days. When you get back, I'll be in Chicago for a week at the Business and Professional Women's Convention. That ought to be enough time for us to sort out what we want to do about this relationship, but one thing is certain. I can't keep pretending that everything is fine between us when I know it's not." She rose from the table. "I'll skip desert," she said, as she turned on her heels and walked out of the restaurant.

Tom sat with his fingers partially covering his face. He could not focus. Everything was getting out of hand, he thought. He had to pull himself together. His work was suffering. His children seemed distant from him and now Shirley. He signed for dinner and left the restaurant. His car was parked only a few blocks away. He started walking and passed his car without even noticing it.

An icy February wind whipped past him and caused him to shiver. His fingers were cold and he realized that he was not wearing an overcoat or gloves. He noticed a limo parked in front of a bar. He figured that if the rich drank there it was relatively safe for him to duck in for a minute. He went into the bar to warm up before starting back to his car. It was dark inside, but it was fairly crowded. He only planned to stay for a moment or two. Just long enough to get warm again.

"What'll it be?" the bartender asked, as he sat down on a barstool.

Tom craned his neck around the bartender at the array of liquor on the bar.

"Stoli," he said.

The bartender placed a napkin on the bar and soon returned with his drink.

"That'll be twenty dollars," the bartender said.

"*Twenty?* For one damn shot?"

"Yeah, cover charge included."

"I've got it," Oscar Booth said to the bartender sitting down next to him. "He's a friend of mine."

Tom looked up at Oscar and smiled. "Hey, man. I didn't see you there."

"No problem. Looks like you need a friend. You want to talk about it?"

Tom smiled to himself. Even Oscar, who he didn't know very well, had spotted his depressed state. They had worked together on CompuCorrect's deal to install a new computer system at the Presidio a few years earlier. Tom had not seen much of Oscar since then, but he did enjoy working with him. Oscar was very bright and knew a lot about computers and computer networks. They had gone out a few times for a beer. Oscar was also politically astute and had introduced him to other business associates who had subsequently become clients of CompuCorrect.

"Nah, I'll get it together," Tom said, taking a drink and feeling the rush as the alcohol traveled to every part of his body.

"I'm a good listener," Oscar said, smiling. "We can keep this in the family. How about another drink?"

"Nah, I got to get going. Got to get up early and go down to LA."

"Just one more, Tom. We can talk about more business for your company, if you like."

"Well, maybe one more wouldn't hurt," Tom said, looking at his watch. "Besides, I'm always interested in new clients."

Oscar signaled the bartender and Tom downed the drink that he had in front of him. He was beginning to feel a buzz by the time he finished the second one and Oscar ordered a third.

"How's Alexander doing? Hear he had twin boys."

"Kenneth? Yeah he and JeNelle are doing just fine. Their boys are three months old now. Getting to be pretty big, too," Tom said, smiling.

"Seen Bill Chandler lately?"

The question startled Tom. It seemed to have come from out of nowhere.

"Uh, we, uh yeah. Went skiing together a while back and uh. As a matter of fact, I'm going to see him in LA tomorrow, but how did you—"

"The bachelor party, remember?"

"Oh, oh yeah. Whew! Some party that was... I mean, did you know?" Tom leaned in, looked around cautiously and whispered, "Those entertainers weren't women?"

Oscar smiled. "Oh, uh, when did you find that out?"

"Uh, shhh," Tom said, beginning to be a little inebriated. "Oh, uh, I knew it all the time," he lied.

"You did?"

"Sure, man!"

Tom felt a hand on his knee rubbing him. Something about it didn't feel like just a friendly gesture, but he didn't know quite what to do.

"Uh, uh, better go to the men's room," Tom said, sliding off the barstool and away from Oscar.

Tom found his way through the crowd that filled the bar and went into the men's room. When he opened the door, the soft lighting made it more difficult to see, but he made out that there were two set of feet in the same stall. Both were wearing men's shoes. His vision was a bit blurred so he bent over to be sure that he was seeing correctly when a hand cupped him from behind. He shot straight up, turned quickly, almost losing his balance, to see Oscar's smiling face.

"What the fuck are you doing?" Tom railed.

"Calm down, man. I thought—"

"You thought wrong!" Tom flashed.

"What are you here for?" Oscar asked, grinning broadly. "Didn't you just say to come in here?"

"No! I was talking about me!"

"Sounded like an invitation to me, especially here in this bar. Why did you come in here if you weren't looking for a date?"

"A date? It was cold... I mean... I was cold... I just came in here to warm up!" Tom said, trying to get his thoughts together.

"That's what I thought. I can warm you up," Oscar said, smiling and moving toward Tom.

"Hell no!" Tom said, pushing Oscar aside and bolting from the men's room.

Tom pushed his way through the crowd and noticed for the first time that there were no women in the bar, just men in business suits.

"What the fuck is this?" he said, wheeling around, as he clawed his way past the men.

"Let me help you," Oscar said, grabbing Tom's arm as he began to fall.

The next thing Tom remembered was being loaded into what he thought was a limousine and then being helped into his house and placed on his bed. He remembered someone undressing him and flashes of light. Oscars face was blurred as it moved away from his, but the kiss that he had just responded to suddenly didn't feel like Shirley's.

Chapter 28

"What's in LA?" Don asked, as Cecil rose from the kitchen table.

"A couple of things. I let JeNelle talk me into joining her Business and Professional Women's League. Their convention starts next week in Chicago. JeNelle's planning the California reception and wants me and Janice to help. So we are meeting with JeNelle and other League members to prepare for the Chicago convention," she said, pouring another cup of coffee for herself and Don, "and Bill Chandler called to say that perhaps he knew of a few ways to help. He's going to be in LA to shoot a commercial. Wants me to meet him there.

"Then there are some potentially hefty endowments." Cecil continued, yawning. "Scripps needs money to fund its expeditions. There are some very wealthy contributors and investors in LA."

She picked up the dishes from the table, scraped them, and put them into the dishwasher.

"Are you going to be there long?"

"A couple of days."

Donald stood up and trapped her against the sink. He kissed the back of her neck and then nibbled on her ear.

"When do you have to be there?" he whispered in a low voice.

"I should have left already," she said, as she closed her eyes and leaned back against his chest.

"Then there's no hurry," he whispered. "You're already late."

Cecil felt Don's body pressing against her.

"The sooner I get out of here the better," she haltingly said.

"I agree," he said, as he unbuttoned her slacks and slipped his hand inside. "I was supposed to be somewhere else yesterday."

"Then we'd both better get a move on."

"Yeah, soon. Real soon," he whispered, as he unbuttoned her blouse.

"What about your coffee?" she asked, as Don's mouth covered her ear.

"I'll drink it cold."

"You want cream and sugar?"

"You could say that," Don laughed softly, as he continued to mesmerize her with his skillful foreplay.

"Let's not start something that neither one of us can finish."

"Never crossed my mind," he whispered, slipping her breasts out of her bra.

Cecil turned and Don kissed her deeply. She undid his tie and unbuttoned his shirt. She released the hook on his slacks, unzipped them, and reached inside his briefs. His kiss became more intense. He lifted her onto the kitchen counter and magically removed her slacks and panties. Her chest was heaving, as she removed his shirt and felt the muscles in his arms flex, as he pulled her toward him. He moaned lowly as she touched and caressed him. He nibbled her breasts, mounted her thighs on his shoulders and buried his head between them. She grabbed the cabinet doors and hung on trying to get a hold on her breathing.

"Tell me about your projects," he said, causing her to nearly lose all conscious thought.

⌖

He had done it again, she thought later on her drive to LA. He caused her to operate on several levels at once while he took her body on a roller coaster ride. And what was this fascination he had with her projects? she wondered.

Chapter 29

The sun broke into the limousine as the chauffeur opened the door for Tom Jenkins. He blocked the sun with his hand and fumbled for his sunglasses.

"What do I owe you?" Tom asked the chauffeur.

"It's already been taken care of by Mr. Chandler, Sir," the chauffeur said.

The chauffeur led him to a door of a large building on the movie lot and opened it. Tom walked in and saw people hustling and bustling around.

"Mr. Jenkins for Mr. Chandler," the chauffeur announced to the guard at the door.

"This way, Mr. Jenkins," the guard said, as he led Tom to a director's chair that surprisingly had his name already stenciled on the back of the seat. Next to it was a chair marked "Cecil Jordon."

Tom sat down and watched in amazement at all of the activity.

"Get the talent!" one woman yelled out.

Bill Chandler and Cecil Jordon emerged from a trailer parked inside the large sound stage, smiling and laughing and approached him.

"What's with the shades, Tom?" Cecil asked, smiling broadly.

"Lights bothering my eyes," Tom slightly grinned.

Bill lightly laughed. "Get some seltzer, water, and a couple of aspirin for Mr. Jenkins," Bill ordered to an aide who was hovering nearby.

"We're ready for you, Mr. Chandler," another aide said.

Bill took off his robe and handed it to Cecil. She perched in the director's chair next to Tom and watched as Bill entered the hot movie set with bright lights and the director began to coach him on what she wanted him to do. Bill took his position in the makeshift bathroom setting.

"Quiet on the set!" someone yelled.

"Chic Soap Commercial, Take One!"

"We're rolling!"

"And action!" the director yelled.

The shower water started and Bill began to perform. He spoke his lines as he began to lather up. He played to the camera. His incredible blue eyes, dark hair slicked back away from his face, and charm made him a natural. His finely sculptured body alone would sell ice to Eskimos. Two takes and it was over.

"Cut! Print! That's a wrap!" the director yelled.

"Is that it?" Tom asked, surprised.

"I suppose so," Cecil answered, shrugging.

A stage-crew member handed a towel to Bill, as he left the set after shaking hands with the crew, agents, director, and other cast. He joined Tom and Cecil.

"That was quick," Tom said.

Bill laughed. "It wasn't *Gone With The Wind*, Tom. It was only a soap commercial."

"Thanks again, Mr. Chandler," the account executive said to Bill, shaking his hand. "We're glad you finally agreed to do this ad. We know that you're in high demand. You have a very high Q rating. We'll send the one hundred fifty-five thousand to your agent by overnight mail."

"That should make my agent very happy," Bill smiled, as he shook the man's hand.

"You made one hundred fifty-five thousand dollars for fifteen minutes work?" Tom asked in amazement.

"Twice that. The first part was a signing bonus, but I'm worth it," Bill said, smiling.

"Mr. Chandler, you're a real professional," the director said, shaking his hand. "I always enjoy working with you. I hope that we'll be on that European car ad in a few weeks."

"I haven't made a decision about that yet. I've got an active law school schedule that needs a little attention."

"I hope that you'll do this anyway. You have a fantastic body in European clothes, I hear."

"I'll send the name of my tailor to you," he said.

The director walked away and a while later after Bill dressed, he, Cecil, and Tom left the movie studio by chauffeured limousine and headed into the city.

"Where to, Mr. Chandler?"

"The Chelcier," Bill said.

"What now?" Tom asked.

"Celebrity fashion show for charities," Bill said, as he opened the bar in the back seat of the stretch limo. "Want some of the hair of the dog?"

"I don't think so," Tom said, removing his sun shades and rubbing his eyes.

Bill and Cecil snickered.

"Must have been some party," Cecil teased.

"I guess so. I don't remember much after the first drink."

"It's always the first one that gets you," Bill said, smiling. "Don't worry, Tom. The next one will be painless."

Tom raised an eyebrow at Bill, but didn't say anything. He put on his shades and leaned back against the seat.

Bill led Tom and Cecil to the lavish buffet luncheon and then he went to change for the fashion show. Tom and Cecil mingled with the other guests and spotted quite a few actors, actresses, and other wealthy and influential patrons. Top models, both male and female, from around the world were participating.

Bill was a big hit, as he modeled seven different outfits. People in the audience were bidding outlandish amounts of money anonymously for the clothing. Bill's last ensemble received rave reviews, as he emerged from backstage wearing a formal period outfit from the 1920s. He performed like a true renaissance man with a touch of Fred Astaire as "Putting on the Ritz" was played by the orchestra. The audience clapped and cheered and bid handsomely on the attire. No one was surprised when Bill's seven ensembles received the highest bids—three million dollars and change was the total. When Bill was asked which charity should receive the donation, he smiled broadly at Cecil.

"Make the check out to Scripps Institute of Oceanography," he said, "earmarked exclusively for the use of Dr. Cecil Jordon."

He blew a kiss to her and Cecil rose from her chair and blew a two-handed one back at him. Bill invited her on stage and she thanked Bill and the patrons for their generosity. She spoke briefly about Scripps' mission and accomplishments and applause punctuated her remarks several times. She smiled broadly as Bill accompanied her to her seat. Tom was still applauding when Bill and Cecil joined him at the table.

"Very impressive,"Tom gushed, kissing Cecil on the cheek.

"Thanks, Tom, but Bill deserves the credit. He just funded my next expedition single-handed."

"Rovers, right?" Bill asked.

"Yes, now I can have the prototype go into production. I don't know how to thank you."

"Don't try," Bill said. "It ain't over yet."

"Telephone for you, Mr. Chandler," a waiter said.

Bill excused himself and left Tom and Cecil while other patrons surrounded Cecil and asked questions or offered assistance with her projects. She was prepared with pledge cards, which the patrons took or simply made out checks and handed them to her. Tom sat and watched in amazement. He made a sizable donation of his own and pledged an additional amount on behalf of CompuCorrect.

Tom noticed a strange expression on Bill's face, as he stood talking on the telephone. Bill's eyes were scanning the room and then landed on a distinguished, but disconcerting looking man across the crowded room who was talking on a cell phone and seemed to be looking at Bill. Bill ended his conversation and walked back toward him and Cecil.

"Problem?"Tom asked.

"Uh, no. No problem," Bill distantly commented and then his mood seemed to change and he smiled broadly. "Next, dinner and the revival of *Bubbling Brown Sugar,*" he said.

"Oh no, not for me,"Tom said, putting up both hands. "I'm going to catch a flight back to San Francisco."

"Later," Bill smiled, as he clamped a hand on Tom's shoulder and looked directly into his eyes. "There's no real hurry, now is there?"

"No, but I'm not prepared for tails and tux tonight."

"Not a problem," Bill said, as he motioned for two of his outfitters to join him. He whispered to them and then turned to Tom again. "Go with these gentlemen and they'll take care of you. The chauffeur will bring you to my hotel later."

Tom agreed and followed the men. Bill and Cecil headed back to the hotel in a cab.

"Bill, something's wrong, isn't it? You've seemed preoccupied since you got that telephone call."

"No, everything is working out just fine," he said, smiling at her. "I had hoped that we could have some time together later tonight, but something has come up."

"Umph! Umph! Umph! William Anthony Chandler, you are a man of many talents," Cecil said, provocatively. "You look fantastic in those outfits today—the soap suds, too."

"Oh, you like the suds, did you?" he asked, mischievously grinning.

"I may even buy some myself."

"I have a case of it in my suite. I'll share it with you," he grinned, with a gleam in his eyes.

Later that evening, the limousine lined up behind a long line of other expensive transports and finally pulled up to a wide, red-carpeted entrance before a palatial theater. Reporters and photographers aggressively asked questions and frantically snapped pictures. As the doorman opened the limo door and Bill and Tom got out amid a hail of flashing lights, Bill turned, reached in and helped Cecil to her feet.

"I feel like Cinderella," Cecil whispered to Bill, as the cameras continued to flash.

"You look like a new and improved version of her, too," Bill whispered, as he offered her his arm. "You're stunning, Dr. Jordon."

Cecil smiled and took Bill's arm, as he walked slowly up the long, red carpet, waving to the cheering people lining both sides of the walkway. Bill signed autographs and consented to have an on-camera interview with Cecil on his arm. He introduced her and mentioned her work for Scripps. The interviewer for an entertainment channel asked her several questions and then turned to Bill again.

"Can we report that you and Dr. Jordon are an item?"

Bill merely grinned, as he winked at the interviewer before whisking Cecil off into the theater. During the cocktail hour, Bill, Cecil, and Tom were kept in constant conversation as they toured the room.

"Man, this is the life!" Tom gushed. "Look at all the stars and megastars in this place! It looks like an Academy Award production!"

"Just people with the same hopes and dreams and fears that anyone has," Bill said.

"You can say that because you're one of them."

Bill laughed, self-deprecatingly. "If you only knew, Tom," he mysteriously said.

The seven course dinner was fabulous and so was the show. Bill took them backstage to meet the cast, some of whom were very close and personal friends and lovers of his. Later he walked with Tom and Cecil to the limousine at the stage door and said their good nights there.

As the limousine pulled away, Tom looked back and saw Bill getting into another limousine. He could not quite make out the face of the man in the back seat, but Tom thought he resembled the man at the charity fashion show.

The next morning, Cecil packed her clothes and sat talking with Tom over breakfast in Bill's suite.

"Well, Tom, I've got to get a move on. I've got to see my family and pick up Janice. Then we're heading back to San Diego and off to Chicago. Any message for Shirley?"

Shirley, Tom thought to himself. He had not thought of her once since he left San Francisco. "No, no message," he said dryly. "It's been great, Cecil. Put me on your mailing list for future projects."

"I will, Tom, but is everything all right with you? You seem a little out of sorts."

"I'm fine. Thanks for asking."

Cecil was not convinced. Tom, she thought, had a forlorn look on his face. She decided not to pry.

"Would you tell Bill that I'll talk with him soon?"

"Yes, I'll tell him."

Cecil and Tom embraced and Cecil left. Tom thought about Shirley and their last conversation flashed in his mind. He could not focus on that now. The pressures at the office, the new corporate platform, his relationship with his children, with Shirley, were more than he wanted to think about sitting in Bill's lavish suite. He settled in to read the newspaper on the terrace. When he got to the society columns in the Style Section there was a picture of him, Cecil and Bill at the theater. The columnist was very flattering about the threesome and Tom smiled to himself as he read several different articles about both the charity fashion show and the theater presentation. He was finishing his third cup of coffee when Bill came into the suite with his tie undone, shirt unbuttoned at the collar, and his tuxedo jacket slung over his left shoulder.

"What happened to you?" Tom asked with concern, as he rose and went toward Bill.

Bill waved him off, sat down at the table with his face buried in his hands. Bill energetically rubbed his face and then his shoulders.

"Any breakfast left?"

"Yeah, I'll get it."

Tom rose from the table and went to the buffet. He could see that Bill was in some discomfort. He returned to the table with two plates of food and poured coffee and juice for Bill.

"Did you rest well?" Bill asked, stretching his neck and arms.

"Yeah, yeah. Cecil and I sat up for a while waiting for you, but we weren't sure how long you were going to be, so we went to bed—in separate beds that is," Tom said, smiling weakly.

Bill smiled at Tom halfheartedly and ate a few mouthfuls of food.

"Man, am I beat!" Bill said.

"Heavy date, huh?"

"A killer date." Bill stretched. "I'm going to soak and relax."

"Sure, Bill. Looks like you need it."

Bill rose from the table and went to his bedroom. Tom heard the water running in the Jacuzzi and saw Bill moving around the bedroom through the slightly open door. He continued to read the newspaper and peeked over the top when he noticed bruises on Bill's once flawless body. He put down the paper and went to Bill's bedroom door.

"Bill, do you know an Oscar Booth?" Tom asked through the partially open door.

"Works at the Presidio in San Francisco. Budget analyst, I think. I met him at Kenneth's bachelor party. Why?"

"He asked about you."

"Yeah, he would. What did he do, make a pass at you?"

"Well, yeah, I think—I mean—man, I don't know. By the time I figured out that I was in a gay bar I was too ripe to care. I think he took me home though."

"Your place or his?"

"Mine!" Tom shouted.

Bill laughed. "Then you don't have to guess about it. He made a pass."

"How do you know that?"

"If he wasn't making a pass, he would have taken you to his place. He's married. Two or three kids, I think."

"But he's gay!" Tom flashed.

"His equipment still works," Bill said.

"But how—"

"His wife knows that he's not heterosexual. He said he told her before they started seriously seeing each other, but he wanted children of his own, so they married."

"What? And she still married him?"

"Like I said, they've got children together. Been married about ten years, I think."

"So you can be gay and marry a woman?"

"Some men can, Tom," Bill said, wrapping up in the hotel's terrycloth robe and opening the door to the bathroom.

Bill lathered his face and began to shave while Tom looked on. He noticed Tom's reflective mood, as he looked at him in the mirror.

"Don't worry, Tom. One encounter doesn't make you gay or even bisexual."

"One?"

Bill smiled at Tom and continued shaving.

Chapter 30

"It's been eons since I've been in Chicago," Janice Atterly said, standing with Cecil Jordon and JeNelle Towson Alexander in the huge McCoy Chicago Hotel lobby.

"I never expected so many women to be here, JeNelle," Cecil said, as they registered.

"Me either," Janice added, as she looked around the lobby at all of the red, white and blue name tags pinned to the clothing of the Women's Business and Professional League members.

"Oh, this isn't everyone," JeNelle answered. "We're registering early because I needed to help Wanda and some of my other staff members set up my store's booth in the exhibit center, but many more will probably be here in time for the opening ceremony. The convention doesn't really get started until then."

"Look at all these sessions," Janice gasped, as she flipped through the thick program guide. "I'll never get to all of the ones that I'm interested in."

"Don't worry. All of the sessions are videotaped. You can select the ones that you missed at night over the hotel's video system or purchase them from the League," JeNelle said.

"Janice, look at all the women's groups, associations, and organizations that are participating. Not only lawyers, doctors, economists, and teachers, but also sororities, congresswomen, military, government, and even truckers! There are even ethnic women's groups! There must be well over a hundred different organizations!"

"Two hundred. We're an all-inclusive league, Cecil. Not an exclusive one."

"You're all signed in, Mrs. Alexander," the registrar said, as she pinned JeNelle's tag to her suit.

"What's this?" Janice asked, looking at the special ribbon that hung from JeNelle's badge.

"Honors," the registrar said, with a smile. "The women who have received special commendations display their awards on their badges. Mrs. Alexander is not only the League's California State President, she's also on the national board, a member of the elite Women of Distinction group, the—"

"That's only to say that I had a little extra time on my hands, Janice," JeNelle interrupted.

"Right, JeNelle," Cecil chided. "We know who's the real mover and shaker in the California business community. Entrepreneur Extraordinaire, JeNelle Towson Alexander."

JeNelle pursed her lips and the women all laughed as she blushed.

"Let's find that suite and get settled in," JeNelle scoffed.

The bellhop rolled the carrier off the elevator at one of the VIP floors and up to double doors with a gold plate affixed to it. He opened the doors and JeNelle, Janice, and Cecil went in.

"Well, it's about time you all got here," Vivian said, smiling as they entered. "Melissa and I were beginning to wonder where you all were."

"Down in the jam-packed lobby trying to tear your sister-in-law away from one crowd of people after another," Janice said, as she hugged Vivian.

"Yes, with the most highly decorated member of the League," Cecil added. "Those people stopped JeNelle fifty times before she got to the elevator!"

"I know," Vivian said, embracing JeNelle. "I've been to these conventions with JeNelle before. Don't expect to get anywhere fast with her around."

JeNelle sucked her teeth and rolled her eyes.

"Look who's talking." JeNelle fingered Vivian's honors badge. "The President of the District of Columbia League and Chairwoman of the Legislative Foundation."

"You, too, Vivian?" Janice asked.

"Yeah, how do you say no to an overachiever like JeNelle, especially when she's your sister-in-law?" Vivian rhetorically asked. "She's even gotten our mothers involved—my mother and JeNelle's mother. She'll be after Melissa's mother soon."

"They're professional women, too. My mother is part owner of Towson & Towson Couture. Melissa's mother is part owner of the Charles Dental Clinics, and Vivian's mother is Secretary of the South Carolina Nurses League."

"Heavens! Don't mention this to my grandmother," Janice lamented. "She and my grandfather own a little variety shop in East LA!"

"You should have brought her along," Vivian said. "A lot of good networking goes on at these conventions."

"That's what I'm afraid of. My grandmother is more active than I am."

The women laughed and began settling in.

"We've got to hustle, JeNelle," Vivian said. "The President's Reception starts in another thirty minutes."

"Ah, no rest for the weary," JeNelle jokingly sighed.

"What's that about?" Janice asked.

"That's where all of the League State Presidents formerly greet and welcome the Presidents and other leaders of all of the women's organizations," Melissa answered. "I hear that the First Lady is going to be there today."

The receiving line was long when Vivian and JeNelle entered the hotel's luxury penthouse and took their places in the line. They chatted with the other representatives while they stood greeting the other guests. The First Lady was at the head of the line, along with the President of the League. The State Presidents stood in alphabetical order, according to the state they represented. JeNelle and Vivian were near each other and noticed that the First Lady seemed to be glancing at them.

Later, as the receiving line was dismissed, the First Lady approached Vivian and JeNelle followed by her entourage.

"Mrs. Alexander."

"Good afternoon, it's good to see you again," JeNelle said, shaking the First Lady's hand.

"And you, too."

"Thank you, may I present the President of the Washington, DC, Chapter of the League, Ms. Vivian L. Alexander."

"It's a pleasure to meet you finally," the First Lady said, extending her hand. "Your brother, Kenneth, speaks highly of you. I've been expecting a call from you."

"Oh?"

"Yes, you haven't called me about membership in the organization?"

"Membership is certainly open to all who want to join us. If you'd like, I'll ask our membership chairperson to send an application to you. I believe that we already have your address."

The First Lady stared at Vivian for a moment and a broad smile grew on her face.

"That will be appreciated, Ms. Alexander. I've been informed that you're quite a good attorney and that you've done some splendid work with the homeless and with placing children from the orphanages with good families. I'm particularly interested in the work that you've been doing with teen pregnancy. The preteen workshops you started seem to be having a good result. I hear from the Mayor that in the three years that you've been working on this project, none of your focus group members have had or fathered children. They seem to have higher expectations for themselves now. I also understand that you're chairing a committee on domestic violence. Professor Fehey speaks highly of you, too. He says that you're one of his brightest students and biggest challenges. He and my husband grew up together."

"Thank you, but I haven't done anything alone. There're many people working to improve the dire situation that homeless people find themselves in. As for the orphaned children, I've been fortunate. My teen leaders' group is meeting with great success. They're mentoring the preteens now. They deserve the credit for their success not me. As for the domestic violence issue, that was my brother's, Kenneth's, idea," she said, not wanting to look at JeNelle at that moment. "He thought that it was an issue that needed special attention and I agreed."

"You know I have this interest in health care reform. I believe that you could be a tremendous asset to our efforts in that regard. Let me tell you what I have in mind..." the First Lady said, guiding Vivian to a secluded spot to chat.

JeNelle smiled, as Vivian, escorted by the First Lady, strolled away.

"JeNelle," a voice said with an Italian accent behind her.

JeNelle turned and saw her former sister-in-law, Maria San Angelo wearing a New York State President's badge.

"Maria." JeNelle smiled, as they warmly embraced.

Maria and JeNelle were close throughout JeNelle's short-term marriage to her brother Michel. They were close in age and Maria developed into quite a business woman in her own right, running several legitimate companies of her father's vast empire. She attended Vassar and Cornell and was a PhD candidate in business and economics at Columbia. Maria was not only a scholar and entrepreneur, she and JeNelle worked together on many projects over the years to assist young people with scholarships and other assistance to go to college.

"Antonio, he is well?" JeNelle asked.

"He's away in college now. He is an angry young man because—"

"Maria, I was sorry to hear about your father," JeNelle said sympathetically. "I would have come to the funeral—"

"No, you should not have come. My father loved you like a daughter, JeNelle. He would not have wanted you to subject yourself to the stress during your pregnancy and Uncle Milo insisted that you needed to take care of yourself and your family."

"Your father was always good to me and your Uncle Milo has been my protector for many years now."

"We owed you a great debt, JeNelle. We still do." Maria's face darkened. "Perhaps my father would still be alive if—"

JeNelle hugged her. "It was a horrible tragedy." JeNelle whispered in their embrace. "Your father did not deserve to die like that. I hope that the authorities find the people responsible and bring them to justice."

Maria smiled at JeNelle. "The person responsible will be punished."

JeNelle knew what Maria's cryptic remark meant in Italian families.

"Don't worry though. Michel will never hurt you again. I promise you that on my father's grave." The mention of Michel's name made

JeNelle shake slightly and Maria noticed it. "He still frightens you, even now."

"I have a new life, a wonderful husband, and raising twin boys and I'm expecting again. Michel is in the past."

"Yes, JeNelle, he is. He is my brother, but he should never have been your husband. Let us not speak of him. He does not deserve your consideration."

Something in Maria's tone caused JeNelle to notice her steely demeanor. A knowing smile then crossed Maria's face and the two women chatted about their families and the convention.

⚬━◦⊷

"We can count on the support of Congressman Briggs in the House and Senator Mitchell in the Senate," Vivian was saying as the legislative session she was chairing continued. "We will have to work with the uncommitted congressmen and women on the list on page twenty-two to demonstrate the need for their support for these bills."

"This will not be an easy task," one of the legislative members remarked, frustrated at the number of uncommitted votes.

"Just keep in mind what these bills are designed to accomplish, JoBeth," Vivian said. "What we have developed is a national coalition against domestic violence. There are nearly three thousand shelters and service programs nationwide providing safe environments for women and children. Congress and state and local governments aren't going to continue funding these programs forever and private donations are insufficient for the long term. We must get to the core of this growing problem. The US Commission on Civil Rights will be holding hearings across the country on the problem of battered women and addressing common problems that these three thousand programs usually face. We will continue the work with our state task forces in their efforts to lobby state and local governments to promulgate state laws that support our programs involving battered women of all social, racial, ethnic, religious, and economic groups, ages, and lifestyles. This League has gone on record as being opposed to the use of violence as a means of control over others, and to support equality in relationships and strategies for helping women assume control over their own lives, but we can't handle this problem alone for long."

"The national information and referral centers are established on a regional basis," JoBeth added. "And our public policy office is scheduled to provide testimony for the Attorney General's Task Force hearing on Family Violence. Melissa Charles is heading that effort."

"Who's working on special events and activities under the Family Violence Prevention Services Act?" another woman asked.

"Maria San Angelo is heading that up," Vivian answered. "She'll have a report at the plenary session later today."

The women all smiled and nodded in support.

"Remember, battered women come from all rural and urban areas and from all religious, ethnic, economic, and educational backgrounds, and from varying ages, physical abilities and lifestyles. Over fifty percent of all women will experience physical violence in an intimate relationship and up to thirty percent of those women will be battered regularly. Every fifteen seconds a crime of battering occurs. Women suffer for years after the battering stops. Some reach crises periods and are able to begin to heal while others go into denial and don't get the help they desperately need to cope. The numbers are staggering, but so is the effort of this League. We are women from across this nation and around the world that are dedicated to the eradication of the battering and abuse problems and to helping women heal. We've got an eminent expert from San Diego who's going to address this issue at the breakfast session tomorrow."

⊙═◄►

In another session, Janice Atterly was giving her presentation, complete with slides, on the status of another of Saulk Institute's programs before a large group of female scientists and other interested women.

"Well, if it isn't Annie Oakley," the blonde haired woman said to Vivian, as she left a planning and strategy session.

Vivian looked up at her quizzically.

"Have we met before?" Vivian asked.

"You don't remember me?"

"I'm sorry, but no I don't."

"I'm Shelly Davis." She smiled. "You and I met during that blizzard in DC several years ago. Chuck Montgomery gave us both a ride."

"Oh, yes, now I remember." Vivian laughed. "We were waiting for a taxi."

"Yes." Shelly smiled, as Vivian shook her hand. "How is that hunk?"

Vivian laughed. "You mean, Chuck?"

"Sure." She leaned in close. "Tell me, did you two ever get it together—get married, I mean?"

"Married? What gave you that idea?" Vivian asked, surprised.

Shelly laughed. "That man was crazy about you. I used to call him whenever I was in DC and we would go out together, but it never failed. Sooner or later he'd end up talking about you."

Vivian laughed. "No, Chuck wasn't romantically interested in me. We're friends, but he introduced me to a friend of his, Derrick Jackson."

"That's hard to believe. I didn't think that Chuck would let any man give him competition for you." Shelly laughed.

"Shelly, I'm surprised. Chuck and I have only been good friends. He's a very special man though. He's still single if you're interested."

"Oh, I'm interested all right. I'll have to call him and see whether he's mentally single before I invest any more quality time in him. This Derrick Jackson must be something awesome."

"Oh, yes. He's definitely that." Vivian smiled broadly. "In fact, Ahkmed Sudah-Ryheme—you remember him, he was the other passenger—works with Derrick. He's a fine physician."

"I know. Chuck told me about Ahkmed. I see that you're heading the DC delegation."

"Yes, what about you?"

"I'm the Chicago Chapter President. This is some turnout, isn't it?"

"It's just great. What do you do, Shelly?"

"How soon we forget. I own a furniture manufacturing company, remember? We talked about it the night Chuck drove us through that blizzard. My father left the business. I've been running it ever since. We have a lot of government contracts, mostly military. We're small, but we're growing. I sold some furniture to a friend of yours, Bill Chandler, because of Chuck, but recently I almost lost the business."

"Why, what happened?"

"Congressional investigation. This man from California—I forgot his name—blew the whistle on an inflation conspiracy. Awesome speaker. Good looking, too, but it nearly wrecked my father and bankrupted the business."

"You wouldn't be referring to Kenneth Alexander would you?"

"That's him. You must have seen it in the newspaper."

"Kenneth is my brother."

"No *shit?*"

"Yes."

"Isn't this a coincidence? It's a small world."

"How is your father doing now?"

"Just great! After your brother blew the whistle, my father got real angry. He's a former military man and a real patriot. He walked into my office one day and said that he quit. That he was going to teach high school ethics."

"Just like that?"

"Yep. He said that Kenneth Alexander made a lot of sense to him and that it was everybody's duty to teach young people right from wrong. He loves what he's doing now."

"That's great. I'm glad to hear that something good came out of Kenneth's efforts."

"A lot of people appreciated what he did. He's a very special person. I hope that you'll tell him that for me."

"I will, but why don't you mention it to his wife, JeNelle Towson Alexander? She's here at the convention."

"You mean the President of the California Chapter? She's married to that hunk?" Shelly smiled.

Vivian laughed. "Yes and they have twin boys."

"Damn, the good ones are always taken."

Vivian laughed again. "Not always. Chuck's still single, remember, and I think that he's one of the best men I know—and he's still a 'hunk.'"

"Hmm, you sure you're not romantically involved with him? Your face sure does light up when you talk about him."

"I'm sure. He and Derrick are best friends."

"Maybe I'll call him after all."

"Only if you promise to treat him as something other than 'a hunk'. He's got a lot more going for him than just good looks and an exciting body."

"I'll remember that."

The two women sat together and talked for quite a while.

⚬══⊹⊱

JeNelle was leaving one session where she had listened to a discussion by young women who were members of the League's College Division. She was talking with some of the student members when she spotted a familiar face smiling at her from across the concourse. JeNelle excused herself and approached Dr. Beverly Carson, a psychiatrist, who helped her through one of the worst periods of her life. They were fellow classmates in college.

"JeNelle Towson," Beverly smiled, "or I should say JeNelle Alexander."

"Beverly, it's good to see you again after what, ten years?"

"It's been at least that long. I've been reading about you in the newspapers though. You've been doing a lot of good things and I hear that your company is setting all kinds of records as a successful small business. Excellent idea to get that Youth In Business and Industry Project underway."

"My best career is as a wife and mother of twin boys, Kenny and Kevin," JeNelle said, "and we're expecting again."

"Yes, I read that you got married again. It was in all of the society columns. You seem very happy. You married Kenneth Alexander if I remember correctly."

"I did, yes and he's wonderful. I never thought that I would ever marry again, but I'm very happy that I did."

"Does your husband know about—"

"Yes, I told him all about Michel."

"You told him everything?"

"I told him the relevant facts."

"JeNelle—"

"Don't start, Beverly. I know that tone."

Beverly smiled at JeNelle, locked her arms with hers, and guided her away to a more secluded spot in the lobby.

"JeNelle, when you left therapy you had made progress, but I felt then that we had more work to do together."

"That's all over with now. As I've said, I'm remarried to a wonderful man, I have wonderful children, my in-laws are great, and my partnership in my parents' business is doing very well. What more could a woman need?"

"You tell me. Are you still having nightmares?"

JeNelle didn't answer. She looked away from Beverly.

"Uh huh. Look, I have the name and address of a therapist in Santa Barbara—"

"I don't think that it's necessary for me to see another therapist, Beverly. My God, it has been a very long time."

"But you're still having nightmares."

"Sometimes, but I'm usually so exhausted by the time that I go to bed that I sleep right through the night."

"And how is your sex life?"

"Kenneth is a very affectionate, creative, and loving husband."

"And what about you? Have you been able to—"

JeNelle looked away and spoke to a passerby, ignoring Beverly's question.

"We're friends, JeNelle, not just doctor and patient. We were in undergrad together."

"I know and I appreciate that. Why don't I call you for lunch or dinner the next time that I'm in San Diego? My husband and I are there frequently to visit my brother-in-law, Benny Alexander."

"Then you're not going to consider going back into therapy, I take it?"

"With my schedule? I'm lucky if I can schedule time to breathe."

"This is important, JeNelle. Women who have been battered and brutalized the way that you were don't just 'get over it'. You were a young, innocent, and inexperienced girl, barely seventeen when you married Michel. What you went through for nearly two years was criminal. Now I know that you have worked hard to build your business and that you have a new life now, but you seem to have some unresolved issues that need to be addressed. You know that my doors are always open to you and I want to help. I'm also leading a breakfast session on this topic tomorrow. I hope that you'll come."

"Thanks, Beverly. It was really good seeing you again. I'll call you about lunch."

They embraced and JeNelle quickly walked away. She hurried back to the suite and felt relief that Vivian, Melissa, Cecil, Shirley, and Janice were not there. She hurried into her room, closed and locked the door, and fell to her knees. Seeing Beverly Carson again brought the whole sordid and ugly details of her marriage to Michel vividly back to her mind. She closed her eyes and thought of Kenneth. She tried to visualize his face, but Michel's face blocked her.

"Good afternoon, CompuCorrect, Southern Division, Mr. Alexander's office."

"Patricia, this is JeNelle, is Kenneth there?"

"JeNelle, are you all right? What's wrong?"

"Kenneth, is he there?"

"He's in a conference with some clients. Hold on, JeNelle, I'll get him."

JeNelle waited for what seemed to be to her an eternity.

"Honey, what is it?" Kenneth's concerned voice came over the telephone. "Pat says that you're crying. What's happened?"

"Kenneth..." she sobbed.

"JeNelle, please tell me what's wrong?"

She tried to compose herself.

"JeNelle? JeNelle? Honey, look, I'm leaving now. I can probably be in Chicago in a few hours. Are you at the hotel?"

"Yes, but don't come...I mean, I just needed to hear your voice." She took a deep breath. "I just miss you. My hormones are at it again. You know how I am when I'm pregnant. I'll be fine."

"No, JeNelle, you're not fine. I can hear it in your voice. It's not just your hormones acting up, is it? Now please, tell me what's happened to you or I'm on the next flight out of here!"

"I just miss you and the boys. I'm being foolish. Patricia told me that you were in a conference—"

"To hell with the conference, JeNelle! Now tell me what happened! Is it Michel? Is he there? Did he try—"

"No, no, Kenneth. Michel hasn't done anything."

Kenneth didn't say anything for a moment.

"Kenneth, are you there?"

"Yes."

"Look, you go back to your conference. Now that I've talked with you and I know that everything is all right, I'll be fine. I love you."

"I love you more, JeNelle."

They hung up and JeNelle collapsed in tears on the floor beside her bed. She cried into the carpet until she fell asleep. She had been asleep for some time when she felt herself being lifted from the floor. The room was dark, but she caught the scent of familiar cologne and she could feel masculine arms around her. When she came to her senses, she was laying on the bed. Someone was removing her shoes. Her eyes became accustomed to the dimness in the room.

"Kenneth?"

"Yes, honey. It's me. Get some sleep."

She turned on the light by the bed. Kenneth was removing his suit jacket and loosening his tie. He sat down beside her and removed his shoes.

"Kenneth, what are you doing here?" JeNelle asked, sitting up in bed.

Wearing a T-shirt and Jockeys, Kenneth got into bed beside her, cradled her in his arms, and turned out the light.

"Couldn't sleep," he said. "Never can when you're not there. Now close your eyes so that I can get some sleep."

JeNelle tightly hugged him and buried her face in his chest. His arms were around her, protecting her from her nightmares. He was kissing her forehead and caressing her face just as he always did.

"Kenneth, you didn't have to do this. I told you that I was fine," she whispered. "I wasn't in any danger or anything. I was just missing you."

"You're talking, JeNelle. How can I sleep when you're talking?" he whispered.

"The boys! Where are the boys?" she said, as she suddenly sat up.

"Probably being spoiled by your parents or sleeping like you and I should be doing," Kenneth said, pulling her back into his arms.

Kenneth, she knew, was not sleeping. He was holding her, but she could sense by his breathing that he was awake.

"You want to fool around?" JeNelle whispered.

Kenneth turned on the lamp, turned toward her, and looked into her eyes. "I want to know why you have nightmares. I want to know why you tremble and cringe whenever I touch you. I want to know why you cry in your sleep. I want to know why you can't make love to me. I want to—"

JeNelle put her fingers to his lips and looked into his eyes. "Make love to me..."

Kenneth sat up and put his feet on the floor. He buried his face in his hands momentarily. JeNelle rubbed Kenneth's back.

"No, JeNelle, we have to talk about this and find a way to work through it. I love you, but we can't keep pretending that everything is fine. We have to do—"

"Not now, Kenneth, please," she began to cry. "I just need you to hold me."

⚬━◦

"What happened to you last night, Cecil," Melissa Charles asked.

"Oh, nothing," she said, grinning, as she read the morning newspaper and finished her breakfast.

"Six-foot-seven, brown eyes, big thighs, ready, willing and able. That's what happened to Cecil, Melissa," Janice Atterly said, with a smirk.

"You don't mean that hunk at the club last night, do you?"

"That's the one, Melissa."

"Who is he, Cecil?" Vivian asked.

Cecil rolled her eyes at Janice. "Troy Ellerbert. We were in undergrad together at UC-San Diego. He's one of the assistant coaches for the Chicago Bears now."

"And another one that Cecil left eating her dust," Janice dryly said.

"Nice body on the brother," Vivian noted.

"His friend looked real good, too," Melissa added.

"He's a player, Melissa," Cecil dryly said.

"Oh, what position?"

"Half-ass husband."

"Oh that kind of player," Vivian knowingly said.

"So if he's married why was he trying to get Janice's number?"

Vivian, Janice, Shirley, and Cecil stared at Melissa.

"Dumb question, huh?" Melissa shyly asked.

"Not your best effort, Melissa," Vivian said.

"My Alan isn't going to be like that," Melissa confidently said.

"Any man is capable of being like that Melissa, including *your Alan*," Cecil said, still reading the morning paper.

"Any man who's insecure and immature," Vivian retorted, sipping her orange juice.

Cecil cut her eyes at Vivian briefly, but didn't answer her. Vivian noticed.

"Cecil, is this another one of those 'black things' that I'm not supposed to understand just because I'm not black?" Melissa asked.

"What do you mean?"

"It seems to me that every time we get together, no matter what we start talking about, the conversation always gets around to the male/female relationship. Then it's always about how Black men are such dogs. They can't be trusted. They're shiftless no-accounts. They run away from responsibilities for their actions. I don't know, but I don't believe that Black men are any different than white men or a man with any particular skin color, but I don't think that every white man that I meet in a club is a dog."

"They are different, Melissa," Cecil dryly said.

"I don't agree with that, Cecil," Vivian interjected. "Remember, I live with three men and four if you count Chuck Montgomery. David is the only Black man in the house and he doesn't fit the 'dog' mold. When I was in undergrad at Spelman—just to show you how naive I was—I didn't think that Black men and women had any greater problems than anyone else. I figured that since I had known good men—and women for that matter—that there had to be more good men out there. Okay, so I didn't have the complete view coming from a small town in Summer County, South Carolina, but I'm not into the blame game. I've learned that there are clearly lots of problems that Black men have and there are many brothers that I wouldn't even think of trying to defend, including my former fiancée, Carlton Andrews. However, I still believe that the vast majority of Black men are trying and doing the right thing when it comes to relationships with females. I just think that sometimes we believe that white people's lives are easier than they really are, and if you believe that then just look at the Susan Smith trial in South Carolina or even the number of Catholic priests who have been indicted for child molestation, or Buttafucco, or the men who blew up the Boston Marathon, the man who killed those babies and teachers or Anthony Weiner, or Jeffrey Dahmer: incest, adultery, social climbing, minimum wage jobs, denial, and, of course, murder. They are no more representative of white people than OJ Simpson or Clarence Thomas or Tiger Woods is of Black men. You have to address each one of them—Black men, I mean—as individuals."

"Maybe I'm naive then, too, Vivian," Shirley added, "and I haven't had a lot of male role models in my life like you have, but it seems to me that everyone—men and women—just seem to be afraid of relationships, afraid of looking at each other on anything other than a surface level."

"That's me all right," Melissa added. "At first—with Alan, I mean—I thought that loving him was about having good sex—me and Dr. Phil, right," she said, chuckling, "but it's not—I didn't really know him like I should have. He's the sum total of a lot of evolution and history that I didn't know anything about. Look at me. I don't even know who I am. How could I begin to know who he is? My parents brought me up in a world where men and women got together because it was the politically correct thing to do. You only associate with 'your own kind', but they didn't have a clue who they were, so how could they teach me who I was, and how could Alan be expected to love this one-dimensional, incomplete person?"

"What does your background have to do with it, Melissa? It's not your history that he's sleeping with."

"Oh, yes, it is. Our histories are real dichotomies. White, Anglo Saxon, protestant princess meets mixed Navajo Native American and Mexican, Shaman leader with brains and body. We're living in distant and different realities. Now I believe that if a relationship is going to have any chance at all to survive, you've got to dig deep into each other's realities one-on-one. I keep hitting rocky soil every time I dig into my history, but Alan's is fertile ground."

The other women laughed.

"Relationships don't have quick fixes even after you've dug deep one-on-one—take me and James for example," Janice opined. "Here's a man who knows who he is and isn't afraid to let me see him for what he is. He has two PhDs, lectures at a university and runs a farm and product export business, yet he thinks that I'm some kind of superwoman just because I sacrificed to get to where I am professionally. I've had to fight to get respect from my peers and in relationships—especially with men. He doesn't blame me for getting to where I am, he respects me without question or reservation, but he thinks that he has nothing to offer me on a social level and now I've got to work to make him understand that I'm not some type of Black female Einstein—too erudite to operate on any other level but stellar. Now ain't that the shit? Here I find a man with all the qualities that I've been looking for in a relationship in this one and I may not be able to hold on to it because he's put me on some damn pedestal! He thinks that I can rock the world with one hand tied behind my back and all I'm thinking is that all I want to do is be the hand that rocks the cradle—not the movie version, of course."

The women laughed.

"I know a whole lot of sisters who would severely beg to differ with you," Cecil said. "I'll take the weight when it comes to a choice between being loved or respected. I'll take respect any day of the week. Women haven't had that *carte blanche* option of respect before. Just look at the women who are at this convention. They didn't get to where they are because they were loved. They got here because they were respected—because they took control of their lives—not because someone controlled them. Black women particularly have to run faster, climb higher and reach further just to stay even and then you find out that you're a day late and a dollar short. Personally, I like James, but if a man can't deal with a successful woman then tough! He can go find some country bumpkin just so he can feel like a man. We are strong. We are independent. So what? I'm entitled to be anything I want to be regardless of who the sperm donor was. A man can either deal with who and what I am today or not. I'm not going to bend and twist myself around to be what any man wants me to be—I'm no contortionist. I'm not the same woman I was when I was twenty and I'm not going to be the same woman I am today when I'm forty. None of us are. People change over time and so do their tastes and needs. Sometimes men and women in a relationship can change together—move in the same direction—but that's not guaranteed to happen. I like to keep it brief and to the point—nothing long term. Brothers can't seem to deal with that. One-on-one or as a group, Black men are at the bottom of the emotional involvement totem pole—no pun intended for *your* Alan, Melissa."

"I try to listen to make sure that I understand what women are saying, but I guess that I have too many men in my life who have done the right things in their relationships over the long haul far more than the wrong thing. I'm not ready to sign any woman's proclamation that says that brothers are the worst thing going, short or long term, and I don't believe that they're the dregs of society," Vivian said.

"I'll drink to that," a male voice said from the alcove leading to JeNelle's bedroom.

"KJ!" Vivian yelled, as she leaped from her seat and jumped into her brother's arms. "Where did you come from?"

She noticed something in his eyes.

"Well, originally, the union between Bernard and Sylvia Alexander," he teased. "Sounds like you did, too, little sister."

"I didn't know that you were here?"

"Apparently not, but I'm proud of you. I overheard your conversation. For brothers everywhere who are trying to do the right thing, I thank you," Kenneth said, as he kissed her hand.

"Kenneth Alexander, you know that you're the exception to the rule," Cecil said, as she hugged him. "They made you and broke the mold."

"I beg to differ with you, Cecil, but I haven't finished collecting hugs yet," he said, as Janice, Melissa, and Shirley lined up for their hugs.

"All right, Kenneth, give us a man's perspective on the state of the relationship between the Black man and the Black woman," Janice said.

"Not when I'm surrounded by all of these dynamic women, I won't." He laughed. "This hotel is loaded with women who are representative of women at large—I'm with my sister on this issue. We've both been subjected to people who have influenced us and created different expectations, which weren't optional. Bernard and Sylvia were clear and precise over the long haul—totally unambiguous about what they expected from us and how we were expected to relate to each other and other people, especially in relationships, one-on-one or as a group— with love, respect and integrity."

"Must be a Southern thing," Cecil commented.

Everyone laughed.

Later, Vivian and Kenneth sat alone in the suite talking over a cup of coffee. Vivian looked at the furrows in her brother's brow and the concern in his eyes and knew that the burdens he carried were heavy. He had been quiet for a while and seemed lost in his thought.

"You know a family is a wonderful thing to have," Vivian said quietly. "I'm looking forward to having one someday."

Kenneth looked up at his sister's face.

"I was thinking the same thing. Remembering what it was like when we were children and our parents and grandparents showed us how to protect ourselves and each other from harm. We have to unravel the past buried within us to solve the problems that face us today. No one can escape the past. The hurts lie just below the surface."

"Love doesn't always make the hurt go away. It doesn't rescue you from the past. A partner can be supportive, but he or she can't be responsible for the trials in his or her partner's life."

"Doesn't sound like we're talking about the same thing."

"Yes we are, Kenneth. We were taught to be responsible to each other, but not necessarily for each other. You can't wave a magic wand and make the hurt go away. You can be there, the way that you've been for me many times, to help me find my way. The being there was the part that helped me the most. That helped me—the moral support helped me unravel my life myself. You couldn't do that for me."

"You've always recognized it when you've had a problem and you've always wanted to solve your problems. You were open and honest with yourself and you gave yourself permission to feel vulnerable. To let it all out aloud. You didn't bury anything deep inside."

"Then perhaps that's the answer you're looking for."

"What is?"

"Digging up the past. Unearthing the problems and any secrets—all of the secrets."

Kenneth looked at his younger sister and realized exactly what she meant. Instantly, a plan came together in his head. Perhaps it would help. He had to at least try.

"By the way, as of tomorrow, Baker is out of Alaska."

"You were able to do it then."

"Took a little longer than I had hoped, but it's done. He's being transferred to—"

Kenneth put up one hand. "I don't want to know."

"What was this all about, KJ?"

"Do you mind taking this one on blind faith?"

Vivian searched her brother's eyes. "No questions," she agreed. "Anything else you need?"

"Not now. Maybe later."

"Just let me know."

"Thanks, Viv."

Chapter 31

"This was a great idea, Kenneth, to steal a weekend alone together."

"We haven't had much time to just enjoy a leisurely weekend and, although we both love the boys, we need a break."

"Yes, but why San Diego?"

"It's convenient. It's also a good excuse to visit Benny and Whitney. We're not too far from home and you've never shown me the city before."

"Oh, so I'm going to be the tour guide, huh?"

"You went to school here and you lived here for a while. I guess you learned something about this city."

"Okay, today we'll play tourist and tour guide. First we'll go to the San Diego Zoo. Then we'll go to hear the carillon at Balboa Park. Maybe a game of tennis at the Sports Club and then hang out tonight at Jason's. How does that sound?"

"I suppose that you're not going to feed me on this grand tour. When do we eat?"

JeNelle laughed. "Kenneth, you usually don't eat that much."

"I'm hungry today. Where should we eat after the zoo?"

JeNelle looked at him quizzically. "There are a lot of great restaurants. What do you have a taste for?"

Kenneth eyed his wife suggestively and JeNelle blushed.

"Let's skip the zoo," he grinned, as he took her hand and led her out of Benny's kitchen onto the terrace. "We can have lunch later."

They stretched out on a chaise lounge together and held each other, as they looked out over the city. They necked and talked quietly together, relaxing for hours. Later they dressed and strolled through the Gaslight district near the wharf. They bought a few trinkets—mostly for their sons—and Kenneth spotted a men's tailor shop that he wanted to stop in. JeNelle was a little reluctant, but Kenneth insisted. Once inside, Kenneth browsed through the array of fabrics and styles of suits. Kenneth held her hand and asked her opinion. A man came out of a fitting room and stood before a mirror.

"Milo?" JeNelle questioned, walking toward the man in the mirror.

"*LaBelle*," he gushed in Italian. "You are here?"

"Yes, Kenneth is with me. He's looking at having some suits made," she answered in Italian, as they kissed each other on both cheeks.

"You remembered this place?"

"Yes, Michel owns it, but it wasn't my idea to come here. We were just in the neighborhood."

"Have you had lunch yet?"

"No, we've just been lazy today."

"Come then. I'll fix personally," he said, enthusiastically smiling. "You and Kenneth, you come to the restaurant and eat."

"No, I don't—"

"Of course you can, *Bella*. You not been there in long time now."

"Yes, honey, why don't you go with Milo," Kenneth suggested, suddenly standing beside her. "I'm going to be fitted for a few suits. I'll join you shortly."

"Yes, yes. We go now," Milo said definitively.

"All right," JeNelle relented.

She and Milo walked the short distance to the restaurant and sat in the kitchen while Milo made lunch. They spoke in Italian to each other.

"You look very happy, JeNelle," Milo said, as he started to pour a glass of wine for her, but she stopped him. "Kenneth Alexander, he is a good man I believe."

"He is, Milo. He's so different from Michel. I'm pregnant again that's why I can't drink the wine."

"We should talk about Michel, *Bella*. It is important that you know something."

"I know more than I care to about him."

"It's not enough."

Chapter 32

"So how was the convention, Shirley, and the business trip for the company?" Tom asked cheerfully, as he met her at the airport.

"It was fine," she said slowly, quizzically looking at him.

"Great! That's just great!" He joyfully smiled.

"Tom, have you been drinking?"

"Nope, not a drop."

Shirley wasn't convinced. She kept staring at his jovial manner. "Are you sure?"

"Of course, I'm sure. I'm just very happy to see you, that's all."

Shirley quickly shook her head. "Maybe I should have had a V-8," she said sarcastically. "I don't think that I can match your energy level."

"That can be arranged." He beamed. "Your place or mine?"

"I just got back from a long trip. Why don't we just postpone this—"

"Can't. Got an itch that I gotta scratch."

"Your jock strap too tight or something?"

"That too," he said, smiling.

Shirley just stared at him.

"Aw, come on, Shirley. Let's pretend that we're back in Bimini. You remember…just you and me on the sand with the waves washing over our bodies and the sun in our faces—"

"Hold it, Tom, you have been drinking? We're in the San Francisco Airport and it's cold outside."

"We can pretend though and I swear I haven't had a drop. I just want to be with you. You were the one complaining that our relationship wasn't working. We haven't seen each other in nearly two weeks. Can't we just have a little private time to ourselves?"

Shirley looked at Tom's almost pleading expression. This was certainly out of character for him, she thought.

"All right, Tom, but I can't promise that—"

"That's fine. I've got enough of a head of steam going for both of us! I'll get your luggage."

Once they arrived at Shirley's townhouse, Tom took her luggage directly to her bedroom. Shirley stopped to look through her mail.

"Shirley," Tom sang. "I'm waiting for you."

Shirley rolled her eyes and took a deep breath. She wasn't feeling amorous at all and this rush to ecstasy wasn't helping her dispassion any. Tom had not proven to be a very creative lover either. That was something that she thought they would have to work on, but tonight wasn't the night to start, she mused. She climbed the stairs and found Tom already in bed broadly smiling. His clothes were strewn everywhere in the room, but he seemed so anxious to make love that she ignored the disarray.

"Tom, how are things in the office?" she asked, as she began to disrobe. "I mean, with the take-over attempt."

"Oh, uh, Kenneth seems to have it under control."

"Isn't he worried at all?"

"Doesn't seem to be."

"He came to Chicago. Showed up on the spur of the moment."

"He and JeNelle are in San Diego for the weekend. Couldn't be but so much of a problem if he's on a weekend getaway."

"Still seems to be something happening though. Showing up like that. You think everything is all right with him and JeNelle?"

"Shirley, would you stop talking and come to bed?" Tom whined.

Shirley sighed. "All right, Tom, but can't I just take a shower to help me relax?"

"No, come on. I'll relax you. We can take a shower together later."

Shirley shook her head and climbed into bed. Tom was immediately all over her. No foreplay, straight into action he dove frantically. He had barely started when suddenly it was over. Tom slumped on top of Shirley and momentarily buried his face in a pillow. He rolled off Shirley and lay on his stomach, turning his face away from her. He didn't say anything more. Shirley gently stroked his back.

"Goodnight, Tom," she whispered.

Tom laid awake feeling total failure and frustration overtake him. He waited until he knew that Shirley was asleep, dressed, and left.

Chapter 33

"So have we got everything?" Chuck Montgomery asked, as he came back into the Georgetown house.

"We're all ready," Bill Chandler said, as he and the rest of the Georgetown crew waited patiently in the living room for Derrick Jackson and Vivian Alexander to arrive.

"They're still not here yet?" Chuck asked, surprised.

"Vivian just called," Alan said. "She's on her way. Derrick's got an emergency. He's going to come up later."

"Maybe I should wait and come up with Derrick," Gloria Towson suggested.

Everyone cut their eyes at her.

"That's not necessary, Gloria. Derrick knows the way to the Poconos. Our families don't live that far from where we're going skiing. He's been there before," Chuck said, noticing Gloria's interest.

"He might want to have company on the ride. It is snowing outside. He shouldn't travel alone on a day like this," she said.

"If Derrick wanted company, I'm sure that he would have asked Vivian to wait for him," Melissa Charles interjected. "They are seeing each other, you know."

"Nobody asked you, Melissa," Gloria sniped. "Derrick and I are friends, too. He came to see me all the time while I was in the physical therapy hospital."

Melissa just shook her head.

"He had patients there, Gloria," Bill added. "That's the type of man that he is. He stopped in to see you because you're a friend of his lady's. Don't go reading anything else into his visits."

"Huh, that's what you think," Gloria retorted.

The front door opened and Vivian detoured into the front living room. Everyone was quiet. Vivian noticed that something was amiss, but decided to ignore it. "Well, crew, are we ready to hit the slopes?" she cheerfully asked.

"Yeah, let's go before this snow really gets us socked in," Melissa said, rising from her chair.

Everyone got up at once and grabbed their gear. The Georgetown crew piled into the trucks. Chuck was leading with Anna, Miguel, and Angelique Menendez-Gaza. Vivian was next in her 4Runner 4X4 with Bill Chandler, Gloria Towson and David Carter. Alan Lightfoot and Melissa Charles were in his Jeep bringing up the rear. The streets of Washington were beginning to fill with snow, as they headed toward I-95 North. They communicated with each other over CB radios in each vehicle, they talked among themselves and/or listened to music and the weather report as they drove along. Gloria was quiet.

"It's getting pretty dicey out here," Bill said, as the snow came down more heavily.

"We should be all right. We've all got four-wheel-drive vehicles and emergency equipment if we need it. Chuck wouldn't take any risks with Angelique and Miguel in the truck," Vivian confidently answered.

The further north they drove the heavier the snow fell. They saw several accidents along the highway and the news bulletins were cautioning everyone to stay off the roads. The conditions were getting worse.

"Vivian, Alan," Chuck said over the CB radio. "I think that we'd better hole up at my parents' place for tonight. It's only about forty miles from where we are now, over."

"Do you think that will be all right, Chuck? I mean, there are three carloads of people, over," Alan asked.

Chuck laughed. "I'm sure that it will be fine, Alan. I'll call ahead and let them know that we're coming, over."

"What's so funny, Chuck? Over," Alan asked.

"You'll see, Alan. Over and out," Chuck confidently answered.

They slowly trudged through the deepening snow up into the mountainous terrain of the Pocono Mountains. The scenery was breathtakingly beautiful, they all voiced as the snow blanketed the landscape in quiet splendor. No noise of the bustling city life. Trees bent under the weight of the ice and heavy snow and roadways disappeared. Chuck confidently led the way. His truck, loaded with luggage and skiing equipment, forged a trail that Vivian and Alan followed with ease. It was afternoon when Chuck pulled into a roadway between two pillars with **Welcome Home** etched into the cement. A winding road led to a large farmhouse with smoke billowing out of several chimneys that looked like it should be in a Currier and Ives picture. A big red barn sat inside a large corral. Grain silos stood with ice sickles hanging around the perimeters. The landscape was vast with fields that stretched out so far that they were indistinguishable from the grey, snow-filled sky. The crew marveled at the beauty of the surroundings in every direction as they pulled up in the large driveway and parked their vehicles. Chuck got out and they all helped each other plow through the snow up onto the front porch. The front door opened before he could reach for the knob.

"Chucky Pie!" Esther Montgomery shrieked, as she saw her son standing there with his friends. "I knew you'd make it! Steven! Come quick! Chucky Pie is home!"

"Hi, Mama," Chuck said, as he tightly hugged her.

"Come on in, everybody," Esther insisted excitedly, "it's cold outside and we're all ready for you."

Esther Montgomery was a small woman with blond hair and blue eyes who made bold demonstrative moves. The crew was surprised at her enthusiasm, but felt welcomed by it as they looked at each other with curious smiles, shrugged their shoulders, and entered the farmhouse.

"Charles, is that you at last?"

"Yes, Pop," Chuck said, as his father, Steven Montgomery, a tall, lanky man with bright brown eyes and electric smile, hugged him.

"And these must be your 'Georgetown Posse'," Steven said, smiling at the crew as he pumped everyone's hands enthusiastically, led them into an enormous family room and started introducing themselves.

"Hi, I'm—"

"Oh, you don't need an introduction," Esther said, standing next to her husband, "you're Chucky Pie's Annie Oakley, Vivian Alexander, aren't you?" she asked enthusiastically. "She's prettier than Chucky Pie said, isn't she, Steven?" Esther gushed.

"She sure is," Steven Montgomery beamed, as he hugged Vivian so tight that he nearly knocked the wind out of her.

Chuck flushed and buried his face in one hand. He shook his head.

"Chucky Pie, you didn't tell us how really beautiful this girl is," Esther scolded.

Vivian was taken aback. She had not really thought that Chuck would have said that much about her to his parents. She looked at Chuck quizzically; he averted his eyes, and briefly covered his face.

"Ah look. We're embarrassing Chucky Pie." Esther gushed. "You all just make yourselves at home. Everybody will be here soon. I got some good, hot, homemade soups on the stove and some fresh bread baking in the oven. So when the families get here—"

"Ah, Mom, you didn't tell everybody that we were coming, did you?" Chuck lamented.

"Only your sisters and brothers, Chucky Pie. Everyone wants to meet Vivian and the rest of your friends. I just got off the phone with Harriet."

"Oh no," Chuck lamented.

"What's wrong, Chuck?" Bill asked. "You look like you've been hoisted on your own petard."

"I have." Chuck sighed. "I'm in for it now."

The telephone rang and Steven went to answer it.

"Vivian, honey, it's for you. It's DJ," Steven said, handing the cordless telephone to her.

"Derrick?" Vivian asked, still surprised by the reception that she received.

"Thank Heaven you made it safely, baby."

"Yes, we're all here. We're fine, but where are you?"

"I'm still in DC. The roads were too bad and the weather reports are saying that it's not safe to travel."

"I know. We saw a lot of accidents on our way here and the roads are very slick and icy. Looks like this snow storm is going to go on all night."

"You're safe and that's all that matters to me. My family will be over there soon. I just talked with my mother. She's excited about meeting you. So is everyone else."

"Derrick, how do the Montgomerys know so much about me?" she whispered. "I'm beginning to feel like the prodigal daughter."

"Oh, Chuck must have mentioned you to them. You think that's bad, wait until my family gets there. Brace yourself, baby. I'll be up to rescue you in the morning. I promise."

"Derrick, it's pretty bad out there. Your parents shouldn't risk it in this weather."

Derrick laughed. "Baby, the moment that Chuck called his parents to let them know that you were coming, stoves and ovens went on in every Jackson and Montgomery household. Four-wheel-drive vehicles, trucks and tractors were fired up, readied and the march was on!" he said, laughing.

"Why, Derrick, what's going on?"

"I've been talking about you a little bit myself. They know how special you are and how important our relationship is to me. We tend to get excited over these events."

"Events?"

"Sure, when a man brings a woman home to meet his family."

"But, Derrick, this was accidental. I mean, we came here because it was an emergency."

"Providence, baby. I would have wanted to prepare you a little better for this and I certainly wanted to be there with you, but I have confidence in you. You'll handle this with no sweat!"

"Derrick, what do I say to your parents?"

"Don't worry about it. You probably won't get a word in edgewise," he deadpanned. "I've got to run now, but I'll be there in the morning. Rest well."

They hung up, but Vivian was even more confused than before. She and Derrick had been dating for quite a while and sleeping together for nearly a year, but he had never said anything about taking her home to meet his family. Of course, they had talked about his family a lot. She knew all of the names and had seen scads of pictures. She knew some things about his sister, Sheila, and her husband, Bob, who was Chuck's brother, and their four children. Karyn and Ryan and their three children. Arlene and Dennis and their two children. His older brother, Grant, and his wife, Leigh, and his younger brother, Troy, who was still in college at Florida State. Of course, he had met her family after the Congressional hearing and again at Kenneth's and JeNelle's wedding. Everyone in her family thought that he was great, even though those were both brief occasions. She wondered what his family would think of her.

⊙━━◦

When Derrick Jackson hung up the telephone his thoughts of Vivian made him smile. He knew what she was in for when his family showed up. They would bathe her in the love that he was feeling for her. From the first minute that he saw her he knew that this would be no ordinary affair. No casual fling. The times that they had spent just laughing and talking were proof positive of that. She was very important to him. She electrified him with her ability to speak so eloquently about important social issues. Yet she could be so tender when they were just chatting and relaxing together. She had high moral character and a quick wit. There were times when they read each other's minds and other times when they would surprise each other. She trusted and respected him not because he had once played professional basketball and not because of his current profession. He knew that those things and the benefits that those things brought did not impress her. She dug below the facade to his very core. She got him. Period. She was a part of him, as natural as breathing in and out.

Though he was over ten years her senior, their times together had proven that they were compatible on every level despite the age difference. He knew that her career in law was very important to her. He wanted that for her, too. He had spent many nights with her, helping her study. Not that she needed his help, but he needed to be with her even if it meant propping themselves up in bed late into the night or getting up extra early in the morning to prep for an exam.

She didn't selfishly want him to alter his schedule the way some women demanded just so they could be together. Instead she'd be waiting for him no matter what time he finished for the day. She never complained when they couldn't be together, but he had sensed her occasional disappointment. This skiing weekend had been his idea as a way of showing his appreciation for her patience with him and his busy schedule. They hadn't been able to spend any quality time together since they were in Bimini. Now, he had disappointed her again, but again she had not complained. She had stopped by their favorite carryout and picked up a full-course dinner for him, wrapped it with a bow and a card telling him to take care of himself if he couldn't get away to join her. He wasn't going to let her down this time. Snow or no snow, he thought to himself, he would be there in the morning to be the first one to say good morning to her.

⚬══⊷

The door opened and a short, plump, Black woman with bright, expressive eyes came into the house followed by a very tall, burly Black man broadly smiling. Before they had even taken off their coats they walked directly to Vivian and hugged her.

"Esther, you were right! She is more beautiful than we had heard," the woman said, holding Vivian's shoulders and looking at her. "I'm Harriet Jackson and this is Grover. We're Derrick's parents."

"It's a pleasure to meet you both," Vivian said. "Derrick told me that you might be stopping by to say hello. I just got off the telephone with him."

"My dear, it's not just us. Everyone else is on the way, too."

"Everyone?"

"Sure, honey!" Harriet said, with a big smile and a firm grip on her. "We've been waiting a long time to meet you. We've been asking DJ to bring you to visit us, but he kept telling us that you had a full schedule and that you usually went home to South Carolina for holidays. Frankly, we were beginning to believe that you were a figment of DJ's imagination and entirely too good to be true, but Chucky Pie was singing your praises, too, so we knew that you were the real thing." She laughed. "Esther's been talking to your mama from time to time. We want to get to know your parents, too. They sound like good people from what we've heard."

"Thank you, Mrs. Jackson. I had no idea that Derrick had mentioned me to you."

"Mentioned you? The boy raves about you, honey," Grover said, laughing. "Can't shut him up most times. Everything is Vivian this and Vivian that."

Vivian blushed.

The door opened and in came more people than Vivian could count. They were everywhere. Derrick's three sisters, their spouses, and children and one of his two brothers with his wife and children. The Montgomerys' offspring and their wives and children descended as well. Aunts, uncles, and cousins were everywhere. A veritable feast was being brought in and prepared by the families who had been undaunted by the snowy, near-blizzard conditions. Vivian sensed that she was the center of attention for the two families and probably the topic of many discussions that they had been having. They hugged and squeezed her at every opportunity. Vivian was floored by it all. So were the other housemates who joined in easily with the two families. All except Gloria who seemed to be wearing a false smile, Vivian thought. The constant chatter and shrilled laughter were ear shattering, but Vivian was accustomed to it because it was reminiscent of her family's gatherings. In fact, it was just like being at home with her family. The easy laughter and fun of just being together. The jokes and camaraderie. The storytelling and the play making that added depth to each tale. As the afternoon and evening wore on, the families had told every story about Derrick since he was born and most about him and Chuck and their often misspent youth. Vivian had heard some of the tales, but the families added a different point of view; a lot more juicy detail.

Chuck stood apart, taking his families' uncensored accounts of his and Derrick's antics and exploits with chagrin or busying himself with stocking more firewood or playing with the children who crawled all over him at each opportunity. He feared that Vivian would discern how often he had talked about her to his family and what his true feelings were about her. Watching her interact so effortlessly with the families tore at him. She was magnificent, he thought. How she laughed or tilted her head or told a joke or told similar stories about her brothers and sister or even listened carefully to others. The light that danced in her eyes when she talked about Derrick was unmistakable. She was in love.

"DJ was real upset that he couldn't go with you for the whole week last year to your brother's wedding. He told us that he did get there in time to whisk you away to his place in Bimini right after the wedding," Sheila Jackson Montgomery said, smiling slyly.

"His place?" Vivian asked with surprise. "Derrick told me that the house in Bimini belonged to the medical practice."

Sheila clamped her hand over her mouth.

"You weren't supposed to tell that, honey," Bob Montgomery said, smiling and hugging his wife.

"Well," she sucked her teeth and grinned, "I forgot."

"DJ's not going to be happy about this, you know."

"Don't worry, Sheila, I won't say anything to your brother, but I don't understand why he didn't tell me about it himself."

"DJ did buy the place, but he leases it to the medical practice. He's embarrassed because he's doing so well. He doesn't like to show off. He's modest that way, but you already know that. We've all been to the house on vacations though," Bob said.

"Romantic vacations," Sheila added with a broad smile and a twinkle in her eyes.

Bob blushed red.

"Yes and each of your four children were conceived there, I might add," Grover Jackson hardily laughed at his daughter and son-in-law.

Vivian smiled. Bob and Sheila Montgomery, an interracial couple, seemed very happy to her. They had an easy manner with each other.

Special, it seemed. Vivian looked at Chuck and caught him staring at her with a faraway look in his eyes. She smiled and he seemed to catch himself.

"I can see why you think the Bimini house is so special. The place is fabulous," Vivian said.

"So, are you and DJ getting serious?" Grover asked.

Vivian was temporally speechless.

"By all accounts they are," Melissa chirped up. "They're always together—day and night," she added with a grin, overhearing the conversation.

Melissa sat on the edge of Vivian's chair and put her arm around her. Everyone ooed and laughed except Gloria.

"We're serious about *Star Wars*, and how to do the new Slides, and whether a tree falling in the woods actually makes a noise, if no one is there to hear it," Vivian retorted.

Esther laughed loudly. "I knew it. Chucky Pie told us that you had a good sense of humor. You're going to fit into these families just fine," she announced.

Chuck flushed. "Mom, I don't think that you should scare Vivian like that. After all, she hasn't said that she and Derrick are...you know..."

"Oh, DJ's serious, all right," Sheila chirped up. "I know my little brother," she said with a devilish smile. "One way or the other, one of you two boys was going to get Vivian into this family. Looks like DJ's the one..." Sheila choked, realizing what she had said.

The room was suddenly quiet as Sheila's words hung in the air.

"Yeah and lots of babies, too," Steven Montgomery said, breaking the uneasy silence. "We don't believe in planned parenthood in this family, as you can see," he said, laughing.

"And abortion is out of the question," Grant Jackson said, smiling at the baby in his arms. "There's nothing that Derrick hates more than abortion, so look out when you two finally get it together... Jacksons are going to be popping out like muffins."

Everyone laughed in agreement. Vivian smiled, but she felt like someone had plunged a knife into her heart. Then she felt a hand on her shoulder. She looked up to see Chuck's smiling face while he was holding his nephew, Randy.

"This little guy is the one who had us rushing up to take care of him," he said, handing Randy to her.

"Oh yes, I remember," she said, recovering with Chuck's help. "I should introduce you to my niece, Whitney Ivy. You two are about the same age." She smiled at the toddler.

"You're real good with babies, Vivian," Bob Montgomery said.

"Can't help it. They're so precious. Derrick and I visit these two orphanages where he has patients. There are so many babies in the world who need families. Families like yours." She smiled as she hugged Randy.

"Well, children, it's getting late and these grandbabies are dropping like flies," Harriet Jackson announced.

Vivian looked around, as she sat on the floor with the children surrounding her. She tried not to look at Chuck. She lifted Randy from her lap and hugged him. The children's parents began to gather up the sleeping offspring, dressing them for the weather, and loading them into their vehicles. They all hugged her and the other housemates as they began to leave.

"I'll take Vivian home with me," Harriet announced to Esther.

"Oh, no you won't, Harriet Jackson. DJ expects her to be right here in the morning and that's where she'll be," Esther said, with her hands on her hips in mocked fervor.

"Now you've had her all afternoon and evening, Esther Montgomery. It's my turn," Harriet retorted, mocking Esther.

"Now, Harriet, the girl has had a long day..." Steven interceded.

"Hold it, all of you," Grover said, holding up his hands. "Let's ask Vivian what she wants to do."

Everyone looked at Vivian.

"Uh, I'll sleep in the truck between the two houses," Vivian quipped.

Everyone laughed.

"All right, Esther, you win—this time, but I'll see you at our house for breakfast in the morning," Harriet announced, cupping her hands on Vivian's smiling face.

"That will be fine, Mrs. Jackson."

"Good, then come along, Grover. You've got to go get ready for breakfast."

"Yes, Harriet." Grover dramatically sighed.

They both kissed Vivian good night. Harriet and Esther embraced.

"She is wonderful just like DJ and Chucky Pie said, isn't she, Esther?"

"She's more than I expected. She's perfect, Harriet. It's just a shame that there aren't two of her so that both of our boys could be happy."

Vivian overheard the women chatting, as she was hugged by the other Montgomerys and Jacksons.

"Pretty intense, huh?" Chuck asked, standing next to Vivian as the families were leaving.

"Chucky Pie?"

"Oh, well, that's just what our families call me."

"DJ?"

Chuck hung his head.

"Well, Annie, you know how big families are. You come from one yourself."

"Yes, and I think that you and I have a few things to discuss, don't you?"

Chuck's heart raced. Vivian was looking directly into his eyes. He gave her a cryptic smile trying to avoid her stare.

"Uh, Ma, where do you want everyone to sleep?" Chuck asked, avoiding Vivian's obvious intention to discuss the evening's *faux pas* by Sheila.

"I'll show them," Steven said, as he and Esther left the room taking the housemates with them. "Come along, Vivian. I'll put you in Chucky Pie's room. It's all ready for you."

Derrick drove up to the Montgomery's house before dawn. He saw the remnants of the tire tracks in the snow and smiled. He knew that *'everyone'* must have been there. He went into the house and crept into each of the ten bedrooms searching for Vivian. Gloria woke up and saw him about to leave the bedroom where she and Melissa were sleeping.

"Derrick," she whispered so as not to wake Melissa.

Derrick went to Gloria and knelt down beside her bed. Gloria put her arm around him and pulled back her cover revealing her scantily clad body.

"You can sleep with me," she suggested.

"Uh, no thank you," Derrick said, removing her hand as he rose and left the room.

Gloria followed him into the hallway and grabbed his arm.

"Derrick, I don't think that you understand how I feel about you. I mean, I could really love a man who has your qualities, your body, your—" she said moving close and putting her arms around him.

Derrick didn't say anything. He removed her arms from around him and walked away. Finally he found Vivian in the first place that he thought he should have looked, Chuck's old bedroom. He and Chuck had spent many good times in that room as boys talking about the girls that they liked in school or the ones that liked them. Plotting their strategies about how to run basketball plays or just kicking back talking about the future and solving the world's troubles together. Back in the day the room held bunk beds. Now it held a single, king-sized bed to fit Chuck's adult size. The walls of that room carried the history of their friendship together in every picture and every poster. They had always been together it seemed to him. Even now with Vivian so important to both of them, they had found a way to keep their friendship together.

Derrick looked at her peaceful, sleeping face as he took off his cellphone and watch and placed them on a nightstand. He disrobed and slipped into bed with her. She did not wake. He folded her into his arms and held her close to him, listening to her breathing while kissing her forehead and caressed her gently. He fell asleep with Vivian in his arms.

"Coffee's ready, Mom," Chuck said, as his mother came into the kitchen still dressed in her sleeping attire.

"Chucky Pie, you're still the first one up in the morning," she said and sleepily smiled.

"It's that early childhood training. You and Pop had me up gathering eggs, milking cows, and shoveling cow pies before I went to school in the morning. DJ and I still can't sleep late in the morning because of that," he cryptically said.

Esther came up behind him, as he sat at the table and hugged him from behind. She rocked him in her arms. He leaned back into his mother's warm embrace and kissed the palm of both of her hands.

"I suspect that it's having that lovely Vivian Alexander in your old bedroom that got you up this early," she said, kissing the top of his head.

"DJ's here," Chuck spontaneously said, as he suddenly rose from the table and poured another cup of coffee for himself and one for his mother.

"I know. I heard him come in around 4:30. What's going on between DJ and Gloria Towson?"

"Oh you heard that too, did you?"

"Yes, but it's not like DJ to be carrying on an affair, especially not with a woman like Gloria when he's so serious about Vivian. I mean, Gloria's a very attractive woman, but Vivian, well she's in a class of her own."

"There's nothing going on between Gloria and DJ except in Gloria's mind."

"I didn't think so, but why is she acting like that? I mean, that nice David is gaga over her."

Chuck laughed. "Gloria knows that and she still treats him like shit...I mean, messes over him."

"Chucky Pie, you know I don't allow that kind of language to come out of my children's mouths no matter how grown you are!"

"Sorry, Mama, it just slipped out."

Esther put her hand on Chuck's. "Vivian is a wonderful girl, Chucky Pie. I just love her to bits. Your father does, too. You've always been a good judge of character. You've really found a gem in that young woman."

"So has DJ."

Esther shook her head. "I know, Son. Harriet and I have agonized over this dilemma. You and DJ have never had the same taste in women. We love you both so much and you're both like brothers to each other and you're both in love with the same woman. We don't know what to do."

"Don't worry your pretty head about it, Ma. I think that Vivian knows what to do."

"She doesn't know how you feel about her, does she? How can she be expected to make a decision between you two if she doesn't know all of the facts?"

"It's DJ, Ma. She's falling in love with him, but he hasn't told her yet about—"

"Oh no," Esther said, cupping her hand over her mouth. "Oh my Heaven! What is he thinking! He's got to tell her! If he doesn't, you must!"

"I've tried to talk with DJ, but you know how stubborn he can be. And, well, he's afraid of losing Vivian. He's scared to death that if she knew—"

"Vivian's not like that! I can tell!"

"He's not going to risk it. He's made that clear. He's forbidden me from telling her. We've had more than a few arguments over this. He's adamant. I love him and her, too, but I can't interfere."

"She's your friend, too. What's going to happen if she finds out that you knew and didn't tell her? That could ruin your friendship."

"Ruin it! It would end it! Vivian is an open, honest, and forthright woman. She won't tolerate deceit from anyone, including me. If I tell her, Derrick won't ever speak to me again. If I don't tell Vivian and she finds out, then she won't speak to me again. I'm damned if I do and I'm damned if I don't."

"Son, I didn't realize...I mean, you've been carrying this around all of this time."

"It's been hell, Ma, but I have to stay out of it. It's up to Derrick. It's his responsibility. It's his life."

"Good morning, Counselor," Derrick said, as Vivian awoke and found herself in his arms.

She lifted the covers and peeked at his nude body as he smiled at her.

"See something you like, Counselor?"

She smiled and snuggled close to him. "Oh yes. Good morning, Dr. Jackson. Weren't we scheduled for a therapy session this morning?"

"That can be arranged. I was feeling the need for a little TLC," he said, as Vivian stroked his body under the heavy quilt.

"You've come to the right place, Dr. Jackson, and at the right time. Now if we can just find that glove I believe that we'll be ready—"

Derrick reached down beside the bed and held up a condom. Vivian smiled.

"You do come prepared, don't you, Dr. Jackson?" she whispered, taking the condom from his hand.

"The point is, Counselor, I do cum a lot during your therapy sessions, so I have to come prepared," he said, holding up a box of forty-eight condoms and smiling broadly.

Vivian giggled. "Well, Doc, that box might get us through today, but what'll we do for the rest of the weekend?"

"Wing it," he said, as he passionately kissed her.

They made love. Derrick was panting hard after they both relaxed their sweat-laden bodies. He could barely catch his breath. He sat up, reached into his bag beside the bed, and swallowed two pills quickly with a bottle of mineral water that was sitting on the nightstand.

"What's that, Derrick?" Vivian asked. "Don't tell me that you have a headache. Not after how we've just made love."

"No, baby, those are vitamins. I need them when we make love. A man needs energy to go through your therapy sessions."

"You're my only patient, doctor or should I say DJ." She smiled.

"Oh, uh, you heard, huh?"

"Oh, yes, that and a lot more besides. You and Chucky Pie." She laughed. "Real unguided missiles!"

Derrick laughed and lay down beside Vivian.

"How bad was it?" he asked.

"Well, DJ, I can say clearly that I'm seeing you this morning from an entirely new point of view."

"That bad, huh?"

Vivian smiled. "So was her name Tina or Talia?"

"Oh God!" Derrick buried his face in his hand. "They told you *that* story?"

"Yes, now who was teaching who about how to have sex in the barn in the hayloft? I couldn't quite figure it out."

"Oops," he said. "It was a clinical exercise to determine unequivocally that there is no probative evidence that there is any difference between having sex between people with different colored complexions. It was all purely technical," he said, blushing.

"So who initiated this 'clinical exercise'?" Vivian mused.

"They did. I was merely assisting in the testing."

Vivian laughed.

"Well, I was," he defensively said. "Besides, that was more than twenty years ago."

"I believe you, baby." Vivian laughed. "I'm sure that at twelve years old you had a craving for scientific knowledge."

She buried her laughter in his chest.

"I was fourteen. Chuck was twelve, and I still do," Derrick said, as he rolled over on top of her. "So educate me, Counselor."

He kissed her and she responded passionately.

"There's so much more that I need to learn about making you happy," he said seriously.

"People can only be happy, baby. If it's not there, you can't force it. I am a happy person. Someone can make you laugh or make you cry, but no one can make you a happy person."

Derrick and Vivian sat in the family room of Harriet and Grover's home laughing and talking with his family after breakfast.

"More coffee, Vivian?" Harriet asked jovially.

"Yes, thank you, Mrs. Jackson, but I'll get it. Please don't bother yourself."

"No, I'll get it," Derrick intervened. "That's my mother's way of training us. I should have been the one to offer since you're my guest, right, Mom?"

"I'm glad to see that you haven't forgotten," Harriet said.

Derrick picked up the coffee mugs and went into the kitchen. Harriet followed while Vivian continued to have a lively conversation with Grover and the rest of Derrick's family.

"Derrick Jelon!" Harriet said sternly, as she closed the kitchen door behind her and marched up to her son. "Now that is a beautiful, intelligent, bright, sophisticated, and wonderful woman in there!"

"Uh oh, what did I do now? I know that tone, Mom," Derrick said, sitting down at the kitchen table.

"You haven't told her! That's unforgivable! You're in love with her and I think that she feels the same way about you. Why haven't you explained to her about—"

"Mom!" he forcefully interrupted. "I love you, but I'll handle this in my own way and in my own time! Did Chuck put this in your head?"

"No, he didn't! Esther did and she's worried! So am I! I'm not going to dance around this—"

"Mom!" Derrick said again, swelling up and rising to his feet. "I said that I'll handle it!"

Harriet's eyes flashed. She gritted her teeth, turned on her heels, and marched out of the kitchen. Derrick slumped against the kitchen counter. He knew that his mother was right. That he had not been completely forthcoming with Vivian, but he deeply loved her. Everything was going well with them. He wanted to ask her to marry him. To share his life… but, of course, what if he told her and she backed away from him? His thoughts raced. He needed just a little more time, and then he would tell her the truth and pop the question. He needed her permanently in his life.

"Well, family," Derrick said a while later as he rose from the sofa and grabbed Vivian's hand. "We've got some mountains to conquer."

Everyone moaned.

"Do you have to take Vivian away so soon, Uncle DJ?" Harrison Montgomery, Bob and Sheila's sixteen-year-old son, asked.

"If it's okay with you, Harrison, I promise that I'll come back, with or without your Uncle DJ to see you all again and, if your parents permit it, we'll talk about you spending some time with us in Washington this summer," Vivian said with a broad smile.

Harrison beamed and hugged her. "All right!" he yelled, giving her a high five. "Then maybe I can meet your sister, Aretha!"

"Oh, and how did you know about her?" Vivian asked with a sly smile.

"We've been writing to each other. She writes to everybody."

"Everybody?" Vivian asked in amazement.

"Yep," Harrison said, "everybody."

Vivian shook her head.

"You didn't know about this, Vivian?" Grover asked.

"No, but I shouldn't be surprised."

"See," Harrison said, pulling a neatly typed letter from his pocket. "This month's letter is all about your Fourth of July family reunion. Last month it was about Gregory's second year at UVA. Before that it was about your parents' anniversary party."

"No, Harrison, it was about JeNelle and Kenneth's announcement about their new set of twins, Jarrett and Justin" Grover corrected his grandson.

"Oh, that's right, Granddad. I forgot."

Vivian smiled. "That's my sister. I'm sure that we can arrange for you to meet her in person."

"She's taking flying lessons so she said that when she can solo she just might make this her first stop," Harrison said gleefully. "I've never known a girl flyer before."

"Why am I not surprised that she'd want to fly up here first?" Vivian mused.

Everyone laughed. They hugged each other and Vivian and Derrick went out into the bright, cold sunshine hand-in-hand. They all waved goodbye, as Derrick and Vivian drove away toward the Montgomery's farm. The snow plows had cleared the roads and Steve Montgomery was clearing the long driveway with his big plow, as Derrick and Vivian drove in. He waved and smiled as they passed him.

"Life goes on up here no matter what the weather," Vivian mused.

"Life goes on no matter what," Derrick said.

Vivian quizzically looked at Derrick, but they were already at the Montgomery's door so she didn't ask what his cryptic remark meant. They entered the Montgomery's home and heard the uproarious laughter and music coming from the family room.

"Well, you two, it's about time," Esther said, panting hard. "These young people were about to dance my feet off! That Bill Chandler is some smooth operator on a dance floor. If I was a few years younger… well," she said.

"And if I was straight and a few years older," Bill said, hugging Esther.

"Gay, bisexual or straight!" Esther insisted with a smile. "But I've got children older than you!"

"Let's get this crew out of here, Chuck, before we get into serious trouble," Derrick said.

Everybody moaned.

"They'll be back," Chuck said to his family."

"You promise, Uncle Chucky Pie," Thomas Montgomery, Bob's and Sheila's second son, pleaded.

"Tom, my boy, I guarantee it!" Chuck said, lifting the nine-year-old from the floor in a quick, smooth motion.

The boy giggled, as Chuck slung him over his shoulder. The other children clamored to be picked up.

"See what you started, Tom?" Chuck asked, as he tickled his nephew.

Tom laughed and wiggled, trying to get down.

"Do me next, Uncle Chucky Pie," Derrick teased.

"I got your Chucky Pie," Chuck retorted with a wink.

Derrick laughed and the two men started wrestling with each other. The children whooped and hollered and made loud clamorous noises.

"Enough, you two!" Esther scolded. "You two haven't changed a whit!"

The two men stopped their horsing around and grabbed Esther up between them kissing and hugging her.

"Just big kids, the both of you! Now you two stop playing with me or I'll have to get my strap after you," she said, giggling.

"Aww, come on and give me a big kiss, Ma," Chuck teased.

Esther complied and hugged and kissed Chuck.

"Me too," Derrick joked.

Esther cupped Derrick's face in her hands.

"Now you two take care of my Vivian," Esther scolded. "Don't you two let her hurt herself on those slopes, do you hear me?"

"Yes, ma'am," the two men said solemnly in unison.

Derrick kissed her and whispered in her ear. "It's going to be fine in the end. I promise you."

He released Esther and took Vivian's hand.

They all said their goodbyes more than a few times, lingering all the way to the cars with last minute hugs or kisses or messages. Derrick and Vivian rode in his Jeep Cherokee while Bill drove Vivian's 4X4.

"What was that about?" Vivian asked.

"What?"

"Between you and Esther Montgomery."

"I'm into older women. We're having this torrid little affair—"

"Now you tell me."

"I need my brown sugar, too, you know," he joked.

Vivian shook her head. "Derrick, was your mother upset about something this morning? She came out of the kitchen with tears in her eyes. I thought maybe you two had had an argument or something."

"My mother is a very emotional woman. That's what makes her so special. She's fine," he lied, but he had been caught off guard.

Finally they were away and headed to the ski slopes at Appalachian McCoy Resort and Country Club. When they arrived the lodge was packed with Ebon Ski, a national organization of Black skiers. The Georgetown crew parked their trucks and began unloading. Clearly this was going to be a party weekend, they had all said as they got out of their vehicles. Black men and women attired in their finest ski regalia were everywhere as more cars poured into the parking area to register. Derrick went inside to get them checked in, but was stopped each step of the way by people who recognized him and wanted to shake his hand or take a picture with him or women who wanted to offer him the key to their room.

The rest of the crew came into the lodge and milled around looking at all of the events that were scheduled for the four-day weekend or checked out the gift shops, ski shops, exercise room, sauna, lounges, indoor pool, and restaurants.

Vivian and Melissa found seats in the lobby lounge and gathered all of the luggage and ski equipment nearby. Three Black women sat talking as Vivian and Melissa sat down near them in front of a roaring fireplace with huge logs energetically burning. The Black women rolled their eyes at Melissa and turned up their noses at Vivian. Both Vivian and Melissa noticed their rude behavior.

"I don't know who Ms. Thang thinks she is bringing that ofay up here in this house," one Black woman said rather loudly to the other two women who both grunted in agreement.

"Maybe she be Ms. Daisy," another said, laughing.

"Nah, she probably de maid," another joked.

"What did I do, Vivian?" Melissa whispered, with concern.

"Nothing, Melissa, rudeness is an unfortunate human trait!" Vivian responded rather loudly. "Stupidity knows no boundaries!"

"Who you callin' stupid?" one of the women said, rolling her eyes at Vivian. "I know you not talkin' to me! Think you all of that with that ofay!"

"Kiss my—"

"Vivian!" Melissa interrupted.

"No, Melissa. I won't tolerate anyone disrespecting my friends like that!"

"It's fine, Vivian. I'm not offended. Please, let's not make a scene. We came here to have a good time and to ski," Melissa pleaded.

Vivian relaxed.

"Better had!" one woman said. "I think you should have known better than to bring that ofay up in here in the first place. She's probably just looking for some dark meat!"

Vivian's eyes flashed and she began to swell up with anger. "Tell it to someone who gives a damn about what you think!" Vivian railed.

Derrick rushed up as he noticed Vivian's demeanor. "*Whoa, whoa,* baby. What's the problem?" he asked, slipping between Vivian and the other women and holding Vivian in his arms.

The other women looked Derrick up and down and grinned.

"Nothing, Derrick," Vivian said, calming down.

Derrick saw Melissa's flushed complexion.

"Uh, come on, you two. We're all set," Derrick said, helping Melissa to her feet and hugging her and Vivian.

Derrick took the women toward their luggage and went to look for the rest of the Georgetown crew to distribute room keys.

"You didn't have to do that, Vivian," Melissa said, nearly in tears.

Vivian hugged her and Melissa returned her embrace.

"Yes, I did, my sister," Vivian whispered, as they held each other.

"I just don't understand what I did to them. I feel like I should apologize for something, but for what I don't know."

"You're not alone, Melissa. I shouldn't have come back at them like that either. I should have handled it better. Racism isn't practiced only by white people. It comes in all shades."

Later that night, the Georgetown crew sat in the lodge theater enjoying different comedy acts and comedians. They laughed at funny jokes and cheered along with the rest of the crowd from their position at a table center stage in front. A young, notable, Black male comedian was next and everyone stood to applaud when he entered the stage. He strutted around throwing his fist in the air and then pounding his chest. He grabbed the microphone.

"Niggas! Can I hear it for my niggas up in de house?"

The audience cheered loudly.

"We got some Super Bling Bling Niggas up in de house tonight!" the comedian said, as he began naming notable Black personalities in the audience who stood so that the audience could acknowledge them. "Right down here in front we got the big super nigga, my man, DJ Jackson, star basketball player extraordinary!" the comedian yelled. "And I see he brought a wetback, a red skin and some white folks with him tonight! He must want some cream for his coffee at bed time tonight!" the comedian joked. "Stand up, my nigga and take a bow!"

Derrick and Vivian looked at each other as the spotlight focused on them. They were reading each other's thoughts again. They stood up, motioned to their friends, and started leaving the theater.

The audience was stunned as they watched the group walk out. A hush fell over the theater. The comedian tried to recover, but couldn't as other people began to stand and leave. Outside the theater, a Black man approached Derrick and extended his hand.

"I'm Samuel Todd, President of Ebon Ski, Mr. Jackson. I apologize for what just happened in there. I want you and your friends to know that we're proud of what you did—walking out, I mean. You reminded us all that we haven't come as far as we think that we have."

Derrick shook Samuel's hand. "Thank you, Mr. Todd," Derrick said. "We do have to remember what our families and ancestors fought so hard to achieve. I won't tolerate being called names by anyone especially not from another Black man. I also won't have my friends insulted."

"Please call me Sam and you're right. We'll be more selective about who we book for our entertainment the next time. We'll also be sure to make it clear that everyone is invited to attend our skiing weekends, regardless of color."

"Good move, Sam. May I also suggest that you open your membership to all people?"

"You got it, Mr. Jackson! Please, I'd like for you and your friends to be our guests at the mixer tomorrow night in the ballroom."

Derrick turned and looked at his friends. They all nodded in agreement.

"Fine, Sam, we'll be there."

"Good. It's been a pleasure. You and your wife make a hell of a pair!" Sam said, as he shook Vivian's hand.

Derrick blushed as he looked at Vivian's face.

"We do, don't we?" he acknowledged.

Vivian shook her head and the other Georgetown crew members laughed as a crowd surrounded the crew shaking their hands and apologizing for the rudeness of the comedian.

Later the next day after a full day on the ski slopes, Derrick stood before a mirror dressing in his Ralph Lauren dark mustard-colored body shirt and brown pinstriped pleated trousers. He slipped into his unconstructed, dark rust-colored, suede jacket and was putting on his Rolex as Vivian stepped out of the bathroom. He turned and smiled broadly as he admired her bustier, tile-pattern, copper-tone, metallic, strapless, body dress. She slipped into some matching metallic sling-back pumps and noticed Derrick's stare.

"What?" she asked quizzically.

He shook his head slowly. "Umph! Umph! Umph! I wish that it wouldn't be better, but it always is!" he lamented, as a familiar gleam grew in his eyes.

"Look who's talking!" Vivian mused. "Talk about a heart stopper! Just don't wear that Adventurer cologne. It drives me crazy! I know what it's going to do to those five hundred or so other women at the mixer!"

"You mean this one," Derrick said, holding up the bottle. It was his signature scent and he owned the company that manufactured it and other unique fragrances.

"Yes," Vivian said.

"Drives you crazy, huh?" Derrick said, splashing it on liberally.

Vivian grinned as Derrick approached her. "Mmm, that's the one," she said, closing her eyes and inhaling deeply.

"Then maybe you'd better stay in my arms tonight just in case you need a little therapy for that insanity problem," he said, slipping his arms around her and kissing her on both breasts.

"We'd better get out of this suite or the only mixing I'm going to be doing will be in that Champagne-glass Jacuzzi and not in the ballroom."

Derrick laughed as he took Vivian's hand and they headed to the elevator. When the doors opened and they walked out into the lobby, they noticed the Georgetown crew standing and dressed to kill.

"*Whoa!*" they said simultaneously.

The Georgetown crew laughed at their expressions. Together they headed to the ballroom. As they approached the wide, but crowded, hallway outside the ballroom they could hear the band playing loudly and people dancing and clapping. It was going to be a great party from the sounds coming from inside. The crew waited their turn at the registration table and as they approached, Samuel Todd appeared in the doorway.

"Oh, Mr. and Mrs. Jackson's party," Sam said to the receptionists, as he ushered the Georgetown crew into the packed ballroom. Suddenly the music stopped and the spotlights flashed onto Derrick, Vivian, and the crew. There was dead silence as Samuel Todd led them in. Then applause started growing around the crowded room. Yells, whoops and hollers went up and people cheered loudly. The Georgetown crew was stunned as the applause grew louder and louder and reached a crescendo. Derrick put up his hand and smiled broadly. Vivian and the rest of the Georgetown crew cheered him, too. He reached for Vivian and kissed her in front of the cheering crowd.

"Speech! Speech! Speech!" the crowd chanted and applauded.

Derrick held on to Vivian's hand and went to the microphone as the crowd roared for him to speak. He motioned for his friends to follow. Derrick quieted the crowd and flashed his award-winning smile. The women openly swooned and Vivian laughed.

"Thank you, ladies and gentlemen. It's been a long time since I've heard that sound, but it's more important now than ever before. You can't determine where you're born or who your family is or the circumstances of your birth or the color of your skin. I was born in the slums of Philadelphia, but the slums were never born in me or in my family. My ancestors didn't raise me to judge people by the shades of their complexion.

"So I'm pleased to introduce to you my friends: Señora Anna Menendez-Gaza, Ms. Gloria Towson, Ms. Melissa Charles, Mr. William Chandler, Mr. Alan Lightfoot, Mr. David Carter, my best friend, Dr. Charles Montgomery, who you know as the famous ball player, Chucky P, and also the light in my life, Ms. Vivian Lynn Alexander. We, one and all, thank you. Now, let's party!"

The crowd erupted in applause and yells, as the Georgetown crew left the microphone and the music began to play. Vivian beamed with pride as Derrick gripped her hand and waded through the throngs of well-wishers. Derrick took Vivian into his arms to dance. He could see the tears in her beautiful eyes as she looked up at him. The pride in Vivian's face gripped him. She did not speak immediately, but continued to gaze at him.

"I keep hoping that it couldn't get better, but it always does," Vivian said, gazing into his eyes.

"I know that feeling well, Counselor." Derrick smiled back at her.

They kissed as the music played and they danced.

When the band began to play music suitable for a line dance, the Georgetown crew all got up on the dance floor and started doing a line dance that Chuck had taught them—The Down and Dirty. People gathered around them and started trying to emulate the complicated steps and movements. The crew led and the others began to follow along. The band kept the music going while more people began dancing to a new step and loving it. Even David knew how to step to the music and women were noticing how well he could move, too. Bill never had a problem attracting women. Gloria moved in beside him when other women seemed to be getting too close. Derrick and Vivian noticed her maneuver and smiled knowingly at each other.

Later, Derrick and Vivian approached their table and saw the three women who had been so rude, sitting and talking with Melissa. Melissa was flushed and laughing loudly when she looked up at Vivian.

"Oh, Vivian, let me introduce you to Delia Travis, Emory Davis, and Carla Thompson," Melissa said excitedly.

The three women rose from the table and looked at Vivian with blank expressions. Then Delia broke the uneasy calm.

"That phrase goes, 'Genius knows its limits, but stupidity knows no boundaries'."

The women looked at each other and broke out into laughter. They talked for some time, getting to know each other. Later, Vivian whispered to Derrick, "I was wrong. You make me very happy and it just keeps getting better and better!"

The ski slopes were packed as the crew spent the next few days enjoying their trip, drinking hot grog, swimming in the heated, indoor pool or playing tennis or racquetball in the indoor facilities. Each night they partied to near exhaustion with Ebon Ski and had breakfast with them before they hit the slopes.

"See you next time, Chuck," Emory said, as she hugged him. "Here are my address and telephone numbers in Denver. Let me know when you're in my neck of the woods."

She gave him a devilish smile and a wink, and he blushed as he returned the hug and glimpsed Vivian staring at his encounter.

"Vivian, it's been real," Emory Davis said with a smile and a hug. "Will we see you and Derrick next year?"

"We'll make a point of it, Emory. Don't forget though, we're going to be seeing each other at the Women's League Convention, too."

"Sure wish you'd bring Chuck along with you," she said as they parted.

Chuck blushed and continued loading luggage and ski equipment in his truck.

"I wonder why Emory wants me to bring you to Denver, Chuck," Vivian said, folding her arms across her chest, leaning against his truck, and grinning at him. "Could it be your bedside manner? Your charming country chic? Maybe it's the cowboy outfit or that curly brown hair of yours or your sultry brown eyes? What do you think, Chucky Pie?"

"Aw, Annie, what do I look like, the Ask Man or something?" he joked. "She's a nice lady. She likes country music, too. She loves Ray Charles' music."

Chuck was flushed, he knew. He and Emory had spent some intimate moments together in the heart-shaped Jacuzzi in her room, but it had been purely physical. He felt embarrassed that now Vivian, of all people, knew that something had happened. He was trying to read her expression, but was having great difficulty, so he looked away from her.

Derrick approached Vivian and Chuck and noticed something in how they were looking at each other. He couldn't figure it out, but there wasn't time to ask about it then as the rest of the group formed up to start the journey back to Washington, DC. It had been a great extended weekend and they had made new friends.

Chapter 34

"Ooowee, Cecil, you sure are looking good enough to eat! Don't she look good, Jessie?" Al Brown asked, licking his plump lips.

"You leave my girl alone, you old fool!" Cecil's mother, Jessie Jordon, said. "She's a professional now. Got too uppity to come 'round to see her mama anymore. Hangin' out with them other people."

"How are you feeling, Mama?" Cecil asked, as she put her purse on the table in her mother's living room, sat down on the sofa, and kicked off her shoes. She ignored her mother's comments.

"She feels real good to me," Al said, with a suggestive laugh playfully slapping Cecil's mother on the knee.

"Dry up, Al," Cecil deadpanned.

"Don't you be comin' in here playing Miss High and Mighty with me, Cecil Jordon. That's my man you talkin' to."

"Yeah, Mama, I know. You and Big Al are going to get married real soon."

"Yes we are, ain't we, Al?"

"Well, uh, uh, yeah, sure we is, Jessie. Soon as my ship come in, we gonna do it."

"Is that before or after you divorce Mrs. Brown, Al?" Cecil sarcastically asked.

"Never you mind 'bout that, Miss Missy," Jessie warned. "Where you been?"

"Working, Mama."

"You ain't had time to come see 'bout us?"

"I call you every week. I put money in your account every month. I can't run up here all the time."

"So why you here now?"

"Candice called me. She wanted me to meet her here. I had to be in town anyway."

"Yes, I know. I saw your picture in the society pages. Imagine that, Al. My daughter in high society with the white folks."

"I was raising money for a project."

"Didn't invite me along on this high society night."

"The next time I will, if you want me to."

"Humph! When's that gonna be?"

"I don't know, Mama. Look, where is Candice? I've got to pick up Janice."

"She'll be back soon. Probably still down at the hairdressers. You wanna beer?"

"No, it's a little early for me."

"Oh, so now you sayin' I'm a drunk!"

"Mama, I didn't say anything—"

"Shut the fuck up, Mama," Cybil Jordon railed, as she came into the living room. "Always riding Cecil's ass every time she comes here! Ray Ray, take these groceries in the kitchen and then you and Alfred come here and see your Aunt Cecil," Cybil ordered. "Hey, little sister, you looking real good. Saw that big ass ride of yours out front."

Cecil stood up and hugged her older, equally tall and statuesque sister.

"Ma, can I have some money to go to the arcade?"

Cybil slapped Alfred across the head. "Can't you speak to your aunt?" she growled.

"Ouch, Ma!" Alfred whined. "Always hittin' on somebody!"

"Watch yo mouth, boy, or I'll slap the black off you!"

"Alfred, baby, come here and give me some sugar," Cecil coaxed.

Alfred sauntered over to Cecil and flopped down beside her, pouting. Cecil hugged him and reached into her pocket. She slipped a twenty-dollar bill into his hand.

"You share that with Ray Ray," she whispered.

Alfred's face lit up. "Thanks, Aunt Cecil!" He beamed, as he gave her a big hug.

"I saw that, Cecil," Cybil said. "You gonna spoil these boys rotten."

"Can I go now, Ma?" Alfred whined.

"Don't I get no lovin'?"

"Aw, Ma," he whined.

"Oh, so maybe you wanna leave me and go live in that fancy condo with your Aunt Cecil now, huh?"

"Can I?" Alfred's face lit up again.

Cecil looked at Cybil in annoyance. "Alfred, soon as I get back from South Carolina you can come and spend a week with me."

"I got summer school. Mama won't let me."

"After summer school is over, we'll see what we can do before you go back to school in the fall."

"Yes!" Alfred yelled, jerking the air with his fist. "Ma, can I go?"

"Hell, what the fuck do I care! Go on now. Mind you be back here before them street lights come on. I don't wanna have to go lookin' for your black ass."

"Can I go, too, Mama?" Ray Ray asked. "I already put the food away."

"Yeah, get the hell out of here. But you two little Negros better not get yourself in no trouble or I'll beat your asses, you hear me?"

"Yes, Mama," the boys dryly chorused.

"Cybil, why do you have to treat those boys like that?"

"Don't you be tellin' me how to raise them boys of mine!"

"I'm not tellin' you anything. I'm just asking..."

"You don't know what you talkin' bout, bitch, so shut the fuck up!"

"You're right, Cybil. It's none of my business."

"Damn straight! Just 'cause you Miss Super Brain think you can come in here and tell me how to raise my boys. Why don't you go get your own babies and stop stickin' your nose in my business?"

"Cybil, I'm sorry that I said anything at all. You're right. I don't have any children so what do I know."

"A'ight den!" Cybil said, backing down. "Uh, you really gonna take those little children with you?"

"Yes, I can do that. I've got an expedition down in Mexico."

"Them boys can't swim. Don't you be drowin' my boys."

Cecil laughed. "I'll take care of them."

"Whatchu goin' to South Carolina for?" Al asked. "Don't nobody go to South Carolina on purpose," he said, laughing.

"Some friends invited me and Janice to their family reunion."

"These white folks?"

"No, Mama, they're mostly black."

"This somebody you screwin'?" Cybil asked.

"Just somebody I'm seeing."

"Them Southern boys hung like a damn horse, I hear. You gotta have a deep throat to suck on one'a dem cocksuckers," Cybil said, laughing. "Open your mouth, Cecil. Let me look down your throat," Cybil teased.

"Get out of my mouth, Cybil." Cecil laughed while playfully pushing her sister away.

"Ain't nobody's cock big as Big Al's here. Show um, baby," Jessie slurred.

"Naw, that's all right, Ma. I'll take your word for it," Cecil said, with a smirk.

"So when you goin'? To South Carolina, I mean," Cybil asked.

"Fourth of July weekend. Four or five days."

"Shit, you gonna miss the block party."

"I'm already committed."

"Must be a helluva man! What's his name?"

"Donald Dixon."

"Thought you was screwin' that big red Negro—uh—the one with the Benz."

"You mean Charles Easton?"

"Yeah, him—played football, didn't he?"

"Yeah, played in the pros. You get old fast in that game. He got cut from the 49ers and came back to San Diego to buy into some car dealerships."

"You still screwin' him, too, and this Negro Dixon?"

"Why you wanna know who I'm sleeping with? I don't ask you who's sleeping in your bed, do I?"

"I gots me a good Negro now. Good between the sheets, too."

"A'int nobody as good as Big Al between the sheet, right, baby?" Jessie said, swilling more beer and falling over on Al.

"Shut up, you old fool. Big Al ain't got no teef. He probably been gummin' your ass!" Cybil laughed.

"Damn! Where is Candice? I've got to go."

"Chill, Cecil! You come up here and can't sit a minute before you gotta be going somewhere. Make somebody think you shame of bein' from the 'hood."

Cecil took her cell phone from her purse, dialed Janice's number, and held the phone up to her ear. "It's just that I told Janice that I'd go to the cemetery with her and her grandparents... Janice?"

"Hi, Cecil."

"I'm sorry. I know I'm late. I'm still waiting for Candice."

"Don't worry about it. I figured that you got hung up. I'll go to the cemetery with my grandparents and my brother. Come by their house about five for dinner. Oh, how's your family?"

"Everybody's fine. Look, Janice, why don't I meet you at the cemetery?"

"Nah, you've wanted to see your family. Everybody will be back at the house by four or five. I'll see you then."

"Okay, girlfriend. You take it light."

"Will do."

Cecil closed the cell phone and sat back on the sofa.

"So what's up with Janice?"

"She's doing fine."

"Why she goin' to a cemetery? Somebody die or somethin'?"

"Yeah, you remember. I told you. Janice's mother and father were shot and killed in their little store during a robbery. Almost got her and her little brother, Adam, too."

"When that happen?"

"I don't know. It was before we met in undergrad. Janice was still in high school."

"So she goes to her people's grave?"

"Yes, every year to put flowers on their graves and the priest goes and says prayers."

"Damn, that's depressing."

"Hey! Hey! Hey!" Candice yelled Fat Albert style, coming in the front door.

"Where have you been, Candice?"

"Well hello to you, too," Candice Jordon said, facetiously rolling her eyes at Cecil and pursing her pouty lips.

"Candice, you asked me to meet you here nearly two hours ago."

"I had to get my 'do done—see," she said, turning around to show the intricately-woven, long, extension braids in her hair.

"Yeah, real nice, Candice. Now why did you ask me to come here on time if you were going to be late?"

"You got PMS or something, sistah woman? I told you I had to get shit sharp! My man's gonna pop the question tonight."

"Yeah right!"

"Well, he is!"

"Sure you're right!"

"You just wait and see."

"Candice, are you pregnant again?"

"Yeah, so?"

"Damn, when are you gonna learn! You been with this Negro for ten years! He's got a wife and four children at home! Two by that bitch over on Crenshaw and three with you!" Cybil railed. "The Negro ain't shit! He ain't nothin' but a cock hound and you keep givin' it up outta both panty legs! You stupid bitch! Don't you know nothin'?"

"Look who's talkin'! At least I know who the daddy is. You don't have a clue who gave you Ray Ray or Alfred, Cybil Jordon!"

"At least they was pretty Negros. Not like that old scab you been screwin'!"

"Pretty! Your Negros can't spell pretty!"

"Look, you two. I didn't come here to hear you fight. So what's the deal, Candice?"

"I need some money."

"I just gave you five hundred dollars last month, Candice."

"I'm a little short on the rent this month, that's all."

"Get it from that Negro of yours tonight when he, uh, pops the question," Cybil derisively interrupted. "See what that gets you."

Cecil reached for her purse.

"How much do you need?"

"A thousand."

"*What?*" Cecil railed. "Are you doing drugs or something?"

"My babies don't do no drugs!" Jessie interjected.

"Nah, Cecil, I just need a few things for the kids—you know—they need summer clothes and shit. They keep growin' outta everything."

"This is the last time, Candice. I'm not going to keep—"

"Shit, woman, you act like this is some big fuckin' deal or something! This is chump change to you. You got that big ass Jag sittin' right out front. Gettin' paid big, stupid money to go swimmin'. Doin' lectures and writing books that get you on book tours. Just cuz you got that PhD after your name you think everybody's got to bow down and kiss your hairy ass!"

"You want this money or not?" Cecil asked, holding out a check.

Candice snatched it out of her hand, turned on her heels, and walked out of the living room.

"Damn, Cecil, you take a lot of shit off that bitch. I'd kicked her ass if she treated me like that. The bitch didn't even say thank you! You forget where you come from or something?"

"No, I haven't forgotten. This is still East LA, but she's still my sister—she's no bitch!"

"Well *excuse* me!"

Cecil hugged her mother and then looked at Cybil.

"Tell Candice I'll be seeing her."

"Where you going?"

"Maybe I can still catch Janice."

"Ooowee, look at that big ass woman!" Al interjected. "Big ass, big tits and big legs! Fine lookin' woman there! She could be my daughter!"

Cecil ignored him and felt relieved as she left her mother's house. It was hard for her to come there now. She tried to stay a part of her family's life, but it wasn't her life anymore. They didn't seem to want to do anything with their lives anymore except drink beer, have babies and fight with each other. Well, if that's what they wanted they could have it, she thought, as she drove away.

Cecil walked quickly across the cemetery grounds toward Janice, her brother, her grandparents, and a few of their relatives and friends. The priest was giving a eulogy over the graves. Cecil slipped in beside Janice and laced her fingers with her friend's. Janice looked at Cecil and gave her a slight smile. They stood there hand-in-hand until the service ended.

"It don't make no sense. What did they ever do to deserve this?"

"Nothing, Janice. They didn't do anything. They were just in the wrong place at the wrong time."

"Wouldn't have happened if they lived in Goodwill."

"You don't know these things, Janice. It could have happened anywhere."

"You haven't been to Goodwill yet. You wait. You'll see what I mean. You get to die of old age there."

"Let's go, Janice. I'm hungry."

The two women started walking across the cemetery toward the cars.

"How did it go at your mother's place?"

"Same ol', same ol'. They still keep eating at each other."

"Candice wants money again?"

"How'd you guess?"

"She wanted to see you in person. Must have been big bucks this time."

"A thousand and she's pregnant."

"Same man?"

"Yeah, I guess."

"Big Al still around?"

"In the flesh," she said, grinning.

"What's up with Cybil and the boys?"

"Some people just shouldn't be mothers."

Janice laughed. "You've still got a family though, Cecil."

"I've got you," she said solemnly.

Janice nodded. "Let's go get something to eat and go home. I want to call James."

"Aw, Janice, that's all you do these days, is moon over James Dixon," Cecil teased.

"And why shouldn't I?"

"He's in South Carolina on a farm. Find somebody who can be around when you need to chill."

"It's not just about getting off, Cecil. I'm through with trying to make a man out of bits and pieces especially when the pieces don't fit and parts of the puzzle are missing. I can't do that anymore. James gives me a complete, uncomplicated picture with all the parts in the right place. No games just fact. Plain and simple. I like it like that. He can tell me how he feels not just what he thinks. He doesn't hide himself away and just give me little glimpses of himself. He's already complete."

"You sound like this thing with James is really getting serious."

"Well, hello, Ms. Jordon. It's about time you noticed."

"Well, Janice, whatever trips your trigger."

Chapter 35

"David, Mrs. Carter and I have been perplexed by your disregard of our instructions as it regards your behavior. It is our considered decision that you should return to the university to embark upon a career as a professor. Of course, this will require you to take additional courses leading to your doctorate, but Mrs. Carter and I are confident that you will be successful. If you prefer, you have our permission to choose between a doctorate in literature or music. Mrs. Carter, of course, would tutor you in that course and I will avail myself to you in the pursuit of literature. We have taken the liberty of speaking on your behalf to the University Chancellor who has assured us that such a course of action on your part would be welcomed. How say you?"

"Mr. Carter. Mrs. Carter. I have no comment."

"Then it is settled."

"On the contrary, Mr. Carter."

"David, this petulant behavior must cease!"

"Mr. Carter. Mrs. Carter. I trust that you will have a safe and enjoyable journey to England this season. I will take my leave of you now. Farewell," David said, as he left his parents standing at the international security departure gate at Dulles Airport. He felt a bit lightheaded, as he walked through the concourse toward the transport that would take him to the main terminal. Then out to the Washington Flyer taxicab stand and the twenty-mile journey to Georgetown and to Gloria.

He had never done that before. Disobeying his parents never ever crossed his mind. If it had, he certainly would have remembered. That would have been an act of cataclysmic proportions. His thoughts were not on the shocked expressions on his parents' faces. It was on the inestimable Gloria with her medium toast complexion, seductive brown eyes, flawless frame and thick, long black hair.

Standing with his parents, waiting to leave for Europe again seemed to have lost its luster. It certainly caused something rash to pop into his head. As eloquent as he could be, being with Gloria excited him in ways he had difficulty explaining. She was a raging storm that engulfed him and made him lose his footing. How to contain the whirlwind was his mission.

The taxicab pulled up in front of the Georgetown house and David paid the cab driver the exact amount. Then, as he got out he turned, took more bills from his wallet and did something else that he had never done before. He tipped the cabbie twenty percent. He smiled to himself as the cab driver expressed his appreciation in glowing terms and drove away. David stood and looked at the house, marveling more at what he had learned inside its inner sanctum than its imposing exterior. A revelation occurred to him. No matter what facade the exterior engenders, it's what's on the inside that makes the difference.

Derrick parked his car in the driveway and saw David standing, looking at the house.

"Hey, David, you with us?"

David's daze permitted Derrick to penetrate. "Greetings, Derrick. Yes, I am, as you say 'with you'."

"Glad to hear it. I thought you were scheduled to leave for England today with your parents for the summer."

"You are correct," David said, still looking at the house. "I have altered my itinerary. I will remain here for the summer. It's something that I've never done before."

"Yeah, I know. You've been doing quite a few things the past year that your housemates seem to think are out of character for you."

David looked toward Derrick. "I think that I've just discovered something."

"What's that?"

"Life."

"That's profound. What's led you to this discovery?"

"I'm not sure."

"You? Not sure of something? Now that's truly out of character for you."

"I know, but somehow it's invigorating," he said wistfully.

"Life does that to you. Searching for the answers to questions in your life create challenges that keep you vital and alive."

"I've looked at Vivian's license plate many times and seen the word EXPLORE, but until today it had no meaning for me. It is an invitation to a journey. To explore life. Life is a journey."

"You are waxing eloquent today, David."

"I'm beginning to explore my life today and every day."

The two men went into the house. Melissa was in the study searching for a book on the shelves that covered each wall and held volumes of books that would dwarf many law libraries.

"Mmmm, something smells good," Derrick said, entering the house and sniffing the air. "What's cooking, Melissa?"

"Derrick, hi, uh, I think it's your father. I mean, he and Anna are in the kitchen... Vivian's in the backyard playing with your nieces and nephews... uh, David, I thought that you were on your way to Europe. What happened? Did you miss your flight?"

"No, I decided not to go."

"You decided? What did your parents say about that?"

"I didn't ask them, but what are you searching for?"

"I can't find a volume of the United States Code," she said, still scouring the bookshelves.

"Which one?"

"Twenty-five. I'm looking for The Indian Mineral Development Act."

"Uh, 25 USC, pages 2101 to 2108. Public Law 97-382, I believe. Another tragedy of the American justice system," David said without difficulty.

Melissa looked at David in amazement. "You remember this stuff?"

"Certainly."

Melissa shook her head. "David, you're unreal."

"No, I am real, Melissa. See, I have mass and—"

"No, David, what I mean is that you have an incredible encyclopedic memory. I don't know how you do it. How you remember so much."

"To be exact, my memory is photographic. That is to say—"

"Never mind, David, I know what it means. Tell me about the Act."

"The Reagan administration blatantly and unabashedly maneuvered it through Congress and essentially undermined the basis for the environmental protection efforts only to the extent that it affected the Indian Nations. Of course, it was thinly veiled as a way of encouraging them toward economic self-sufficiency, but what it in fact did was to permit wholesale mining of their ancestral homelands. It was quite a transparent effort to steal yet another resource from the Indian Nations for Reagan's wealthy corporate cronies and, simultaneously, cutting sharply the United States' obligations to Native Americans.

"It was, of course, only the most recent in a long line of Acts geared to eject them from their homes and further disenfranchise them— essentially annihilate them. It's quite an embarrassment to civil justice to have the government of the United States openly and without conscience plot to destroy a once great and proud people in collusion with multilateral and multinational corporations and then to have the highest court in the land knowingly sanction such evil intent.

"The American Indian Religious Freedom Act in 1978 was another of such laws. There the Native American Nations, who had been forced into holding American citizenship against their will, could not exercise their right to religious freedom guaranteed to all Americans under the Free Exercise Clause of the First Amendment. Of course, the point here again was the Native American lands. Certain sacred spiritual practices could only be held in pristine surroundings. Meaning that the more land taken, usually unlawfully, meant that the Native American Nations had no place to practice their religion.

"In the same year, 1978, the Congress passed the Indian Child Welfare Act which essentially gave the government license to forcibly remove any Native American child from its parents and place the child in adoptive non-Indian homes furthering the government's genocidal intent. That's also in 15 USC.

"There are, I believe, eighteen Acts of Congress which attempt to further the unbridled genocide that has occurred since the late seventeen hundreds. However, as you have no doubt witnessed, the resiliency of the Native American people endures. They were invaded, conquered, decimated by disease, disenfranchised, separated from their native and spiritual customs and religious beliefs, and separated from their lands and their children—but still they survive."

"Our government has done all this?"

"The very same elected officials who depend on corporations for support repay that support by offering up laws which favor the wealthy. Justice is blind, Melissa, but the people should not be. We must be ever vigilant to protect the people not only from the corporations, but also from the government."

"It makes me wonder why I ever decided to become a lawyer. Maybe I should have become a congresswoman or senator. Then maybe I could do something to help."

"You still can. In addition, an attorney can become a judge. That's another way to help. You must, of course, strive to be impartial when rendering a decision—something that certain courts seem to have overlooked as it regards Native Americans."

"I know that you're right, David, but how can we right so many years of wrong from the bench?"

"Remember *Brown v. Board of Education* and *Plessey v. Ferguson*?"

"I see."

"Or better still, remember the Alexander family and their family creed or Benjamin Banneker, *'Presumption should never make us neglect that which appears easy to us, nor despair make us lose courage at the sight of difficulties'*."

"Thanks, David, but finding a way to help Alan when he's fighting both big corporations and big government is, in my mind, more than just 'difficulties'."

"If it is to be, it will be."

"Who said that?"

"I did."

Melissa smiled and continued discussing what she had learned and what she was hoping to find. David advised her that some of what she was looking for could probably be found at the Library of Congress, the National Archives, and the Bureau of Indian Affairs.

"What are you two conspirators up to?" Alan asked, as he entered the study.

"I've been picking David's brain for information concerning Acts of Congress. I was trying to find anything in the record that we could use to prove that the hearings leading up to the acts were influenced by big business and that the Congress erred in their decision-making and legislative processes, but all I can find are the final versions of the acts. Nothing on the House or Senate hearings or the legislative history."

"That's because they were closed-door sessions," Alan said. "I've spent all morning trying to get copies of the legislative history and hearing transcripts from some sixth-level bureaucrats and hit a stone wall," Alan said, frustrated. "All they needed to see was my red skin and suddenly they don't know what I'm asking for. I was speaking English—not Navajo!"

"Then let's see whether my skin and New England accent translate into something that they understand!" Melissa declared, visibly upset over the racism of which Alan had been subjected.

Alan and Melissa entered the Library of Congress separately and Melissa sauntered up to the Congressional desk. She batted her long lashes and deep blue eyes at the young, male, red-headed desk clerk, which immediately got his attention. She claimed to be a summer intern sent to copy a few records, as she leaned across the clerk's desk assuring that he would get a full view down her low-cut blouse while she whispered her request to see certain files. The desk clerk took the bait immediately and led her into a locked room filled with file drawers. He pointed out the files that she was looking for while Melissa wiggled and twisted, keeping his attention latched to her body as she retrieved just what she was looking for, the secret subcommittee records. The documents disclosed that certain politicians had stacked the witness list with pro-development industry forces and excluded any dissenters in the fact-finding process. Most of those politicians were still in Congress and had grown very powerful and wealthy in the process. The clerk was reluctant to let Melissa copy the files, so she turned up the flames by rubbing suggestively against the young man. Without further resistance, the man let Melissa have her way and she cooed her appreciation directly into the man's ear, rending him speechless.

After her success with the clerk, she and Alan poured over the papers and decided to find out how the politicians, most of whom had begun their political careers with little or no wealth, gained their financial windfalls. Melissa employed the same tactic with a clerk at the Library's Ethics Desk, where financial records were kept, but she was woefully unsuccessful. That clerk's steely demeanor did not melt under her womanly guile. Smarting over her defeat, she and Alan were leaving the Library when they bumped into Bill Chandler on his way to do a copyright search for one of his growing number of clients.

"What's up?" Bill asked.

"We've been trying to get copies of certain financial records and ethics filings for some politicians and some of the bureaucrats at a few federal agencies, but we can't get past the clerk," Alan said.

"Ethics and politicians, now that's a contradiction in terms," he quipped. "Is this more of your search for evidence about the Navajo lands?"

"A key element. We need to find out whether there is a common link between these politicians and where their money came from."

"Want some help?"

"Sure, but what can you do, Bill?"

"Point out the clerk and let's see."

Alan and Melissa hid behind the book stacks and pointed to the clerk who had refused Melissa access to the records. Bill approached the middle-aged man and a huge smile crossed his face. Within fifteen minutes, Bill walked out of the Library carrying a large folder filled with classified federal documents. Alan and Melissa were amazed as he handed the file to them.

"All right, you've got an hour—maybe two—to copy these files while I take Lancaster to a private lunch at the Ritz Hotel, Suite 414," Bill said, with a grin.

"Who's Lancaster?" Melissa asked.

"The desk clerk who wants to get laid by yours truly," he winked, as he walked back into the Library of Congress.

Melissa and Alan hurried to a quick copy center on Capitol Hill and copied the files. The information in the files clearly showed that extraordinary contributions were made to each politician's election campaign by several mining, forestry, and developer entities, but not much information was in the records concerning the politicians' personal assets.

Later that night, Melissa and Alan sat around the dinner table and told the other housemates what they had discovered and what else they needed to find. Their conversation went late into the evening, but when they finished talking, going over the mountains of files, and devouring two of Anna's freshly baked apples pies, a plan of action had been hatched. Alan would call the leaders of the other Native American Nations in the politicians' home districts and states and gather information from them. Vivian would search the computer networks for information on the mining, forestry, and developers who were heavy contributors to the politicians' campaigns. Bill would make a foray into the Internal Revenue Service offices. Gloria and David would take resumes to the politicians' offices and pose as young law school students searching for summer employment while they interviewed anyone on the politicians' staff about the congressperson or contacted acquaintances for quick coffee breaks and congressional gossip on the politicians. Melissa would contact her aristocratic, socialite, and private school cronies who were in Washington and/or on the social scene and pump them for information.

A week later, everyone's task was complete and Alan and Melissa sifted through everyone's notes and reports on what they had found. There was a link. In fact there were several glaring links. Corporations like ENRON, WorldCom, and Halliburton, and the people like the Koch brothers kept popping up. All of the politicians had received large campaign donations from the same corporate entities offshore. Their tax records indicated that they had all made the same investments in privately-held companies unrelated to the ones which made the domestic donations. Instead, these foreign corporations were spread around the globe. All of the politicians had, at one time or another, been key committee members on legislation that adversely affected the Native American Nations. The law students had a wealth of gossip, innuendo, and speculation about the politicians, the likes of which would have easily brought both houses of Congress to a screeching halt, but still more proof was necessary, they thought. On the surface, everything seemed to be above board. Melissa and Alan believed that if they released the information that they had, the politicians would be in a position to explain it all away as mere coincidence that they happened to appeal to the same industry leaders, made the same lucrative investments and, as for the gossip and innuendo, were concerned it could be viewed as libelous. They had a great deal more information though, with the help of their housemates, but they hadn't found the smoking gun.

Chapter 36

"So, when are you rolling out?" Kenneth asked Benny, as they sat on the deck of the Santa Barbara house watching JeNelle, her sons, and Whitney Ivy building castles in the sand and looking at the naval ships heading out into the Pacific Ocean.

"A few days. We don't really know," Benny answered, lacing his fingers behind his head and stretching his long frame out on the chaise lounge. "Pentagon's calling the shots on this one. My teams are ready."

"I'm glad that you decided to let Whitney stay with us while you're away."

"You know that I can't deny JeNelle anything, especially when you got her pregnant again," he laughed, "but how you are going to handle your pregnant wife, the twins, and Whitney at the same time is beyond me. My daughter is quite a little handful all by herself. I'm going to miss her though. She keeps me even and level."

"How long are you going to be away?" Kenneth poured another mimosa for them.

"I'm not going to be back in time for Vivian's graduation from law school, but I'll be home for the Fourth of July reunion. I'll come back through San Diego, drop my gear, and be on my way home all in the same day, I hope."

"Where are you headed?"

"Alaska and then Hawaii."

"Alaska?"

"Yeah, we're testing some new equipment to see how it performs in extreme temperatures. We tried it out in the tropics last month. Works real well."

"What equipment?"

"Something called a frequency surveillance system. Sounded like part of something that Cecil was working on. I hear that this system has been deployed worldwide. Must have been a real genius who put that little baby together. Nothing gets past us now, including bugs!"

"Bugs?"

"Yeah, this system is so sensitive that it picks up gnats!" Benny laughed. "Like I said, real genius."

"Oh, probably some kid in high school."

"Not this, KJ. This thing makes all of our other frequency surveillance equipment obsolete. No kid put that together."

"So now you're going to test it in extreme cold temperatures."

"Yeah, at least that's what they're telling us, but if you ask me, Papa One is going to be in the neighborhood."

"The president? In Alaska?"

"Sure. We're hauling out everything—F14s, F15s, stealth, carriers, frigates, cruisers. It's a hell of a big build up just for routine maneuvers to test equipment. Either that or we're preparing for an invasion," Benny sarcastically said.

"Let's hope not. Every time I hear about a country erupting in war, I think about G wanting to sign up."

"Yeah, I know. One military man is all this family needs. G's doing real well at UVA. Vivian's been dragging the housemates down to see him play. He's been scoring good numbers."

"He's been scoring even better numbers in his classes." Kenneth was pleased.

"Who wouldn't with Ms. Aretha Grace calling G all the time and writing to him, sending text and e-mail," Benny joked. "She even Skyes him daily."

"You'd think that she was the oldest Alexander sibling," Kenneth said, taking a sip of his drink.

"She's something for sure. Keeps telling me to stay 'pure' because Stacy's coming back." Benny laughed. "I'm not sure about our little sister. Sometimes I think that she's been through life a couple of times before. This couldn't be her first time through!"

"You know she's never been wrong before, though. She told me that JeNelle and I would finally get together and that we'd have a big happy family. Mom and Dad don't even question what she says. Maybe you'd better listen to her and stay 'pure'."

"Pure! I'm as pure as the arctic snow, at this point. I haven't even thought about sleeping with anyone. I'm damn close to being a virgin again," Benny deadpanned.

Kenneth nearly choked on his drink. He sat up and quizzically looked at his brother. "You mean that in all this time since Stacy's been gone you still haven't slept with anyone?" Kenneth asked in disbelief. "Not even Caroline Ann? Not even—"

"Nobody!" Benny assertively said.

"Man, this has got to go into somebody's record books! My brother, the original obey your thirst…Olympic-class lover…load and lock—"

"Has been taking matters into his own hands, if you know what I mean."

"Man, who would ever believe that you'd go on hiatus!" Kenneth emphatically said.

"Aw, as if you don't know what it's like. Your off switch didn't turn on for years at a time," Benny joked. "Not until Lisa Lambert switched you on. Now JeNelle must have you in the permanent on position!"

Benny saw something come over Kenneth's face.

"What is it, KJ?"

"Nothing."

"Your expression tells me that something's up."

Benny waited but Kenneth just looked toward the sea and JeNelle playing in the sand with Whitney and their twin boys. He knew Kenneth would never talk about his sex life even before he and JeNelle met. He was certain that if something was wrong, Kenneth wouldn't talk about it. He'd do something about it.

"Uh, you and Lisa aren't…"

Kenneth's head jerked around and he narrowed his eyes at Benny.

"Remember what we were taught, Benny. You keep your friends close and your enemies closer."

"Uh, that's what I said. I know that you and Lisa aren't playing Samson and Delilah," Benny said, shrinking under his older brother's glare. "Don seems to be spending a little of his time with Lisa though."

"Is he still seeing Cecil?"

"Yeah, our cousin seems to be the world-class lover, as usual."

"Is Cecil okay with that?"

"She seems to be. She says that there's nothing serious going on between them, but Janice and I aren't so sure. I mean, Don's been spending a lot of time following Cecil around on her expeditions and it's not because Cecil is pressing him."

"That's not Cecil's style. She's got a lot going for her. She's been writing some excellent articles for the *World Ecology Press* and she's been doing a lot of speaking engagements. She's even working with some at-risk young people in East LA, teaching them about the sea."

"Cecil's never been pressed to have a man around either. Neither she nor Janice even has to keep any telephone books. Their telephones come off the hooks, but they're cool with their action."

"Don will cool his extra curriculum when he wants to land Cecil."

"Cecil doesn't seem to care one way or the other, but Don! Now there's a real study in extremes for you. He tells me that he can't afford to get himself trapped into something long term and then proceeds to lay traps to capture Cecil," Benny said, confused.

"Yeah, but Cecil's on to that action. She's got the man trying to figure her out. He told me that she doesn't even call him. He has to call her."

"With Cecil, it's no game though. A man has to prove himself to her before she'll invest any time or energy in him. Many good men I know have tried and failed. She ain't no 'round-the-way-girl' as G would put it. She won't make any man a priority especially if he wants to treat her like an option."

The two brothers laughed.

"What kind of expeditions has Cecil been leading?"

"She's into everything. Global warming and the greenhouse effect, marine biotechnology, earthquakes, marine life and ecosystem research, ocean pollution, coastal-zone management, even ship and platform operations. You name it, she's into it."

"So when does Don get to see her if she's always on the move?"

"Don seems to be able to break free whenever she's diving to deploy and test some new deep-sea vehicle that she calls a Rover. Works with some type of buoy system. This Rover is a computer that processes and alters signals from the sea floor up to a depth of 6,000 meters. It's programmed to move from station to station along a set or random course. Bill helped her raise the capital she needed. Cecil's been deploying it to perform on-site chemical analysis and to gather data on the ecology of marine life and organic chemical cycling in the deepest parts of the ocean. She's very excited about this new technology, but Don seems to be just as interested in Cecil as she is in the technology. Janice and I are beginning to wonder about those two."

Kenneth laughed. "So what's Janice up to?"

"Oh, that's easy—James and the feeling is mutual," Benny said. "Janice has been paying as much attention to James as she has been paying to her work at the Salk Institute. She's deep into marine biotechnology and biomedicine. She's been developing pharmaceuticals from marine organisms. Antibiotics from marine microorganisms. She found some marine plant that produces beta carotene and another one that seems to inhibit the replication of the HIV virus."

"That's some pretty heavy stuff."

"Yeah, that's what's got James fence sitting."

"I heard Janice talking about this in Chicago. I still don't understand why James is hung up just because Janice is a scientist."

"Scientist extraordinaire. When she published her last article on the development of marine bacteria that can be used to remove toxic metals and other pollutants from ocean water and sediment, James was duly impressed. He's put Janice on some high pedestal that he thinks is outside of his reach."

"James is no country bumpkin. He's done very credible work in animal husbandry and new technology farming. He's got his double PhD and he's lecturing at SCU. He and Uncle Romelo run our family hydroponics farm business extremely well."

"You know that and I know that, but James doesn't think that his career compares to Janice's career. Janice seems to want to show him that she's a woman first and a scientist second."

"That's what she said and I say, good for her!"

Chapter 37

Deep in the cold, silent waters under the polar ice cap, a nuclear-propelled submarine stealthily moved through the icebergs on its way to perform another, top-secret, national-security mission.

"Captain, wake up, Sir! There's a message coming in on Security Channel Alpha!"

"What! What time is it, Ensign?" Captain Rourke asked, as he rolled out of his bunk on the nuclear submarine, *Sea Wolf*, planted his feet on the floor, and rubbed his eyes with the palms of his hands. The blue-green lights in his quarters laid a mystic haze over the small cubicle. "Did you say, Alpha Channel?" Captain Rourke excitedly asked.

"Yes, Sir!" the Ensign snapped.

"Go to Security Plan: EXPLORE, Ensign!"

"Yes, Sir, Captain!" the Ensign said, as he left the cubicle, pulled a revolver from his belt, and closed and locked the Captain's cubicle door. The Ensign stood guard, looking cautiously from side to side in the narrow passageway with his revolver cocked and ready.

Captain Rourke locked his door from the inside, pulled a failsafe lever in his cubicle, and a screen appeared. He peered into a retinal scanner, placed his hand over another scanner, and punched in a set of numbers in a certain sequence. He looked at his watch as the seconds ticked away. Numbers and symbols began to scramble across the bottom of the screen. The words: E N G A G E O R I O N crawled across the screen. He punched another set of numbers in sequence and looked at his watch again. O R I O N E N G A G E D came across the screen. He hurriedly scrambled the message, picked up a pair of headphones and put them on his head. He dialed a sequence of numbers and waited.

"Eagle," a voice came over the headphones.

"Orion," Rourke said.

"Copy that," the voice said.

Captain Rourke headed for the Command Center of the submarine.

"Attention!" the Deck Officer yelled, as the Captain entered the Command Center.

"All stop! Give me the Con! Clear the deck!" Captain Rourke bellowed.

The Navy men all set their equipment to central control and held up both hands when competed. They left their posts quickly and quietly, locking the doors to the Command Center behind them. Captain Rourke pulled the Failsafe lever, securing the Command Center. Then the Captain peered into another retinal scanner, placed his other hand over another scanner, and punched in more numbers in sequence. The numbers began to scramble and the words: E N G A G E P E G A S I S appeared. Another set of numbers appeared and the Captain keyed the numbers into the submarines guidance system. The words: P E G A S I S E N G A G E D flashed on the screen. The submarine moved into position.

"All hands, man your stations!" the Captain bellowed into the intercom.

"What's this about?" one Ensign asked another, as they resumed their posts.

"I haven't got a clue, but whatever it is, it's big!" he said with a sigh.

"You know, this top secret shit gives me the willies."

"Me, too. We've been out here for nearly four years and I still haven't seen the faces of those men in the forward section. All I know is that every time we go into auto drive we end up somewhere in the world and those men leave, we wait, and then they come back again. They don't even eat with us," another seasoned sailor added.

"We aren't at war with anybody, but Al-Qaeda or the Taliban extremists or at least we weren't when I signed on six months ago. That's something good, ain't it? Those men are probably Navy SEALs. They're one of those super-secret, elite organs that can get in and out of anyplace without being spotted. They've probably kept us out of more wars than we want to know about."

"Man, it still gives me the willies. Here we are sitting in a fuckin' nuclear tin can on more power than you need to light up a city the size of New York for a friggin' lifetime and it could all be over just like that," he said, as he snapped his finger.

"Ain't nobody crazy enough to mess with us! We got the best fighting force in the world!"

"Yeah, tell it to those fools who took down the World Trade Center. They must not have heard how good we are."

"Stow it, Ensign!" the Captain bellowed. "Rig for silent running!"

The men scrambled to their posts. The giant nuclear submarine cut through the depths of the ocean for twenty hours on a preset course with the destination unknown to anyone on board including Captain Rourke. When the submarine arrived at its destination, the propulsion systems shut down. Everyone was quiet and looked around at each other. Something was definitely different about this mission they knew.

A red telephone flashed in the captain's quarters and the Captain picked it up. He turned on a voice modulation and synchronization device.

"Do you know who I am?"

The captain looked at the two voice patterns on the monitor.

"Yes, Sir!" Captain Rourke said, as he nervously held the telephone in his hand.

"Go to Operation: Trojan," the voice said and disconnected.

Captain Rourke quickly, but nervously, entered the Command Center.

"Bring us up to periscope depth," he shouted.

He grabbed the arms of the periscope, as it rose and scanned the area.

"Hold steady on course 270 degrees north," he ordered, as he saw the aircraft carrier approaching on the port side. When it was alongside the carrier, Captain Rourke yelled, *"Blow all ballast! Surface! Surface!"* and sounded an alarm.

The Navy men scurried into position as the submarine rose to the surface.

"All stop! Clear the deck!" the Captain bellowed.

The men scurried out of the Command Center and locked the doors.

The captain pulled the security lever, automatically locking all doors, picked up a red telephone, and a voice acknowledged.

"Operation: Trojan engaged, Sir!" Captain Rourke said and hung up.

The hatch above the Command Center began to turn and then opened. Two male figures, with faces partially covered, climbed down into the submarine.

"Take me to Explorer One!" one of the figures ordered.

The captain led the two men, whose faces were still partially obscured, to a remote area of the submarine marked: **WARNING: NO ENTRY**.

"Stand guard here, Captain," one of the figures stated firmly.

The two men keyed in certain numbers on a door and the doors opened. A figure lay apparently sleeping in the tiny cubical. As the two men entered, laser beams pierced their cornea. The smaller framed person eased out of the bunk, holding two automatic weapons with laser beam sights on the intruders, and then snapped to attention, relaxing the weapons.

"At ease, Explorer One," the second figure said, uncovering his face and removing his hat. "It's a pleasure to finally meet you," the man said extending his hand.

"Thank you, Mr. President," Explorer One said, shaking hands with the President of the United States.

The President looked around the cubical, which allowed no room for movement with three people standing.

"May I sit down, Explorer One?" the President asked.

"Certainly, Sir!"

The President sat on the small bunk and motioned for everyone to relax.

"You've done an admiral job, Explorer One. I've come here to tell you that and that your missions have ended."

"It's over, sir?"

"Yes, your part in it is for the time being. You understand you may be called upon for covert duty at any time."

"Yes, Sir, I do understand. Thank you, Mr. President. May I ask whether the other eleven Explorers performed to your satisfaction, Sir?"

"Yes, they certainly did above and beyond, Explorer One. Each one that you picked for these missions and deployments has surpassed all expectations. You've lived under the most isolated and stressful situations over the recent past. You've done, what, over one hundred fifty-eight covert missions?"

"One fifty-nine, Sir. We completed one thirty days ago. We've found evidence that a multinational corporation is smuggling contraband into the US through various foreign ports and across the Mexican and Canadian boarders."

"I understand that you've become an expert marksman, martial arts expert, and survivalist. Your SEAL and Musaid training served you well. You've avoided having to use deadly force, but you've saved a couple of your team members' lives through sheer cunning, wit, and bravery far beyond what was expected. This last covert mission was a particularly dangerous one, they tell me. Frankly, we didn't believe that we were going to get all of you out alive."

"Sorry to worry you, Sir. The target had a unique security system. It took a few minutes longer to reconnoiter a new escape plan."

"I've been told. Alligators, poisonous snakes, and other deadly creatures."

"Yes, Sir."

"Tell me about this last mission, Explorer One, how your team escaped?

"We fried them, Sir. It's all in the report. The target was inland. Deep in a thick jungle. Tropical vegetation. On the way in, Mother One hosed the security with gasoline while we went in on wings inside the target drop zone perimeter. I got the transmitter set up and tapped into the communications network off the North Star satellite when it passed over. I uploaded the data from the target's computer system and then scrambled their operation. Perimeter security shut down without a signal. The Eagle and Wind Breeze covered the escape routes. Panther set the cover decoy and Jack the Ripper fried the second line security.

They never even knew we were there. Just looked like someone got careless with a match."

The President noticed the bandages on two fingers of Explorer One's left hand.

"What happened?" He pointed to the bandages.

"Oh, nothing much, Sir. We separated after the mission. Target security stepped on my fingers two clicks north of the beach extraction zone."

"You weren't captured?"

"Oh no, Sir. Target security probably thought that I was part of the vegetation. I was camouflaged. Target security walked over me twice, Sir. Caught my fingers the first time through. An inch right and it might have been my head, Sir. No damage, Sir. Just one broken, Sir."

The President shook his head. "And you swam back to the extraction point ten miles out at sea with a broken finger?"

"Only five clicks, Sir. The team dropped the props five clicks out. The propellers took us the rest of the way to the extraction zone. The *Sea Wolf* was right on schedule. It's all in the report, Sir."

"I've read Cobra Khan's reports to Delta. They were all well documented. So were all of the others. This last mission is the key to a very important plan. I can't tell you, but I'm sure that you know how critical it was and I hope that I'll never have to tell the American people either. I know that this tour of duty has been difficult, but it was a necessary test to determine whether the twelve of you could function under these circumstances and other nontraditional positions. Your multiple excursions into Iran netted a great deal of valuable Intel. As well as your work in Cuba, North Korea, Syria, Lebanon, and Pakistan. Destabilizing the drug cartels in Mexico and Afghanistan has put us ahead in the war on drugs. However, I'm curious. How did you come up with the code name Explorers?"

"It represented what we were doing, Mr. President. Exploring new career opportunities."

"Is that all, Explorer One?"

"No, Sir, but if you don't mind, Sir—"

"I understand."

"Thank you, Sir."

"You must remain silent about your missions as a member of a Navy Seal Team, and your work as a Musaid operative, until I'm prepared to announce it."

"Yes, Sir. I understand, Sir."

"How did the other SEALs on this team treat you?"

"They thought that I was a little weird, Sir, but as instructed, no one breached security. The SEALs are a top notched, totally dedicated operation, Sir."

The President laughed. "You've covered your identity well. If I didn't know better, I never would have suspected."

"Thank you, Sir."

"Well, Explorer One, let's get you top side. I'm sure that you've got someone waiting to see you."

"No, Sir. Not really, Sir. I'm ready for my next mission."

"Next mission? Don't you want to see that young man and daughter of yours or your family?"

"Young man, Sir?"

"Yes, this young man," the President said as he reached for a dossier on an iPad from his companion, opening it to a picture. "Major Benjamin Staton Alexander, Air Force. Code Name: EXPLORER. Over the years, he's tried everything to find you. Even got a few Congressmen and Senators skulking around. Had Washington leaking information like a sieve," the President said. "We didn't know what he was going to try next!"

"He did, Sir?"

"Yes. His brother, Kenneth Alexander, created a firestorm in Washington years ago. It's caused quite a change in the mood of the country. Dynamic young man. I arranged to meet him socially through a California State judge who's an old friend of mine. I wanted to see if I could persuade the young man to work for the party. Told me that he was willing to make a small donation to my campaign if I would tell him where you were. When I told him that it was a matter of national security, he turned me down flat. Said that he was just a 'Country Boy' with ancestors who taught him about integrity, honor, respect, and commitment. That was the most cleverly ambiguous rejection I've ever had. The whole family seems to be fiercely independent. Do you have any influence with Kenneth Alexander?"

"No, Sir. I've never met him, but I've met the rest of the family. They have a tradition of dedication to excellence. Nothing in this universe can influence them or dissuade them from that goal."

The President laughed. "I know. Kenneth Alexander almost put the military out of business. I respect him and his family though. You're in good company, Commander."

"Commander?"

"Yes, you've earned it and the gratitude of a grateful President and nation for your selfless sacrifices. The computer data that you transmitted links a major offshore conglomerate to a number of illegal and potentially dangerous operations in the States."

"Just doing my job, Sir, but I can't tell you how much this means to me."

"I can see it on your face, Explorer One. Now let's get you out of here. Admiral Gordon, here, is beginning to turn green around the gills from claustrophobia."

"Yes, Sir!"

Explorer One stood on the deck of the huge aircraft carrier and watched as the President's helicopter lifted off. Tears formed.

"All right, Commander Greene, I've been instructed by POTUS himself to give you anything and everything that you want," Admiral Gordon said, with a broad smile.

"Admiral, I'd kill for a real bath in hot water with lots of bubbles."

Admiral Gordon laughed. "You've got it, Commander, and anything else that you want."

The Admiral led the Commander to some nicely appointed quarters on the aircraft carrier, which included a whirlpool tub already churning and bubbling. The Commander's eyes lit up.

"I've been saving something for you, Commander," the Admiral said, as he led her into the room and closed the door. "I know that you'll understand my inability to give this to you before now, but your mission required the highest security measures."

The Admiral placed a large hand-carved safe box on a table and keyed numbers in sequence. He opened the box and pulled out letters addressed to Lieutenant Stacy Greene, c/o Admiral Clarence Gordon. The post mark read, Goodwill, Summer County, South Carolina. Stacy sat down nearly dazed by the sheer number of envelopes. They had all been opened and apparently read.

"For security reasons, I've read these letters and seen the pictures that the Alexander family sent to you. It's none of my business, Stacy, but that family cares a helluva lot for you. Your daughter is a beautiful little girl, too. I've been watching her grow each year through these pictures."

Stacy opened each picture in sequence according to the postmark date. There were pictures of Whitney Ivy and Benny together, smiling. Stacy began to feel her emotions uncontrollably rising after viewing only a few pictures. She put everything back into the box and closed it.

"Thank you, Admiral," she said, regaining her composure.

"Aren't you going to look at those, Stacy? There are letters there from Major Alexander, too."

"No, Admiral. That was another life. I've got to move on. What's my next mission?"

Admiral Gordon critically looked at Stacy. He reached across the table and took her hand.

"Stacy, your eyes tell me that you have some unresolved business to take care of before we talk about your next mission. Don't you think that you should resolve that first?"

Stacy pulled her hand back and sat back in her chair.

"I did resolve it, Clarence, when I left San Diego. Captain, I mean, Major Alexander only wanted his daughter and to marry JeNelle Towson. By now that should have happened and they should be very happy together as a family. I respect Major Alexander. He was my best friend."

"Still is, apparently. By the way that he's torn up Washington looking for you, it seems to me to be a lot more than friendship."

"No, Clarence, we were just friends and sometimes lovers. That's how his daughter was conceived. We had an unguarded moment. An accidental liaison which I feared could have wrecked his chances with the woman he loved. I didn't want JeNelle Towson to misunderstand my relationship with Major Alexander. He truly loves her."

"Well, you never know with relationships, Stacy, but I think that you ought to find out and stop sacrificing your feelings for what might be the case. I think that I can arrange for you two to see each other very soon if you like."

"No, there's nothing left between us. I do want to know how Major Alexander and his daughter are doing though. I have some friends in San Diego who should know. Maybe I'll contact them from wherever I'm assigned for my next tour of duty."

"You're a credit to the Navy and I'm proud to have you under my command, but the Navy needs whole people. People who are happy and fulfilled professionally, emotionally, and mentally. You've proven yourself to be a top officer in this Navy, fully capable of handling yourself in any situation come hell or high water. Now, I can't order you to deal with your relationship with Major Alexander, but I strongly suggest that you do and that's all that I'm going to say on that topic. In the meantime, I have some disturbing news for you."

Stacy's concern was evident when she sat up in her chair.

"What is it, Clarence?"

"The FBI and the Secret Service tell me that your brother, Russell, is running with a bunch of gang bangers. Nothing too serious yet, they don't think, but according to reports, he's getting in over his head. Your father has been working long hours and the FBI doesn't think that he's fully aware of what Russell has been up to."

"How serious is this, Clarence? I mean, has Russell done anything illegal?"

"No, but according to the FBI this gang 'makes their bones' so to speak by killing someone at random. That's their initiation into the gang. The gangs aren't just some thugs on the street. They're a well-organized drug ring that has connections with organized crime, money laundering, and contraband. You may not know this, but Russell could get himself killed if he keeps going in the wrong direction."

"Oh no!" Stacy said quietly in horror. "I know all too well what can happen. I lost my twin sister to drugs when we were only thirteen. Russell was only a little boy at the time. Have you been sending my paycheck to my father?"

"Yes, every month. The Secret Service relocated them, just like they do to protect all SEAL Team members' families when necessary. We established the blind savings account just as you requested. Your father and brother are in Asheville, North Carolina. That's where the Secret Service thought that they would be safe."

"What about my mother? Has the FBI or Secret Service been able to find her?"

"She's moved around a lot. They've kept up with her though. The last report said that she was somewhere in Michigan."

Stacy suddenly felt emotionally drained. She had been fighting to keep her country safe while her family was in eminent danger.

"I need to find my father and brother and see what I can do to help before I take on another mission."

"I think that would be wise. The post as Naval Attaché to the Japanese Government assigned to our Embassy in Tokyo, Japan, can wait another month or two, Commander Greene."

Stacy's eyes suddenly brightened.

"Do you mean it? Me, heading up our naval delegation in Japan?"

She nearly leaped from her seat. Admiral Gordon smiled at her enthusiasm.

"Who else could we pick for such an important post, Stacy? Anyone who could perform as you have as a Navy SEAL and as a Musaid Officer could handle these diplomatic duties with no problem. The fact that you fluently speak Japanese, Mandarin, Chinese, and Korean and understand their customs did have a little to do with it," Clarence slyly smiled. "Also, we want you strategically placed if we need to rapidly deploy you for covert missions in the Far or Middle East. You're still on covert mission status assigned to The Nursery. The rest of Team: Explorers will also be assigned to The Nursery, but strategically deployed."

"That's good to know, but I'm a Black woman. That's already two strikes against me when it comes to much of the oriental culture."

"The Japanese delegation in Washington was very impressed by you at their embassy party years ago. They're swift. They knew that you were guiding me carefully through my limited diplomatic ability with them. You kept me from making a compete fool of myself. I know what you're capable of and so does the Japanese delegation. The others will learn. This posting will give you career advancement possibilities to a strategic post for the Joint Chiefs of Staff. Even if they didn't respect you, and they do, I'd send you anyway. They'd just have to undergo a cultural revolution! I'm sending them my best officer regardless of color or gender. If they don't like it, then tough!"

"I could kiss you, but I'm not sure that Isabel would appreciate that."

"The General is not here, now is she, Commander?"

Stacy hugged Clarence and kissed him on the cheek. Clarence blushed.

"Now you get some rest. We'll be in Hawaii in a week. Then I want you to go take care of the other parts of your life. I'll make arrangement for your transport."

"Thanks, Clarence—I mean Admiral Gordon," Stacy said, with a smile and a salute.

Clarence patted her hand. "I mean *all* of your issues, Commander." He left her stateroom.

When he entered his own quarters, he opened his safe and retried a secure phone. "Delta, expect the fish to swim in your direction soon. I've completed my mission. Now it's up to you."

"Copy that." The voice said and was gone.

Stacy knew that the Admiral was referring to Benny and Whitney Ivy. When the Admiral left her quarters, she sat back in her chair and looked at the steel box. She was tempted to open it, but brushed off the temptation and started pulling off her clothes. Moments later she slid into the whirlpool bath and moaned in ecstasy as the water bubbled and swirled around her. She tightly closed her eyes and let her head slip below the warm, churning water. When she surfaced, she felt renewed.

She lay there in the water and the dream that she had for over four years reappeared to her. There was no fighting it as she had done before. She could see the vision of her and Benny in the Chalet in Vail having sex over and over again in the large whirlpool tub.

She recalled his handsome face and strong, muscular body. The hair that covered his chest, his rock-hard abdomen, and six-pack abs, down between his thick sculptured thighs. She also recalled each instance of their sexual encounters and the levels of ecstasy that they had reached together. Unbelievable levels so filled with brightness and excitement that were beyond the ability to describe. Lying with him in the afterglow of each union was a treasure. How he touched and caressed her and made her tingle. How excited he was every day of her pregnancy. How they found new ways to have sex when she was too large to be much of a challenge for him, but her thirst for him was insatiable. She couldn't understand it. From the very moment that she realized that she was pregnant, she craved him.

She smiled to herself. Some women craved pickles or ice cream or watermelon or pizza, but having sex with Benny was her aphrodisiac. He never let her down and always made her feel like it was the very first time that they had sex.

They had done so much together as friends and lovers. Quiet times when he would hold her or reach for her hand. He knew and understood what having a baby for him meant to her career. He let her know each day how much he appreciated her sacrifice by the things that he did for and with her. She knew that on many occasions he had hard, tedious, and mentally draining missions of his own to contend with, but he never let her feel his fatigue. He would spend every possible moment with her that he could and he never complained once.

It wasn't just the exciting and blissful sexual encounters that occurred to her now. It was the peace and tranquility of Goodwill, Summer County, South Carolina, and the multitude of loving family members and friends who constituted the Alexander family clan. She recalled each happy face from the fun-filled weekend that they spent there, enjoying the simple pleasures of life. Sitting around the big table in the country kitchen, with Sylvia, Bernard, Vivian, Gregory and Aretha. Going to Gregory's basketball game. The extraordinary family picnic that followed the game. Aretha's piano recital and the special gesture that Aretha made by playing a tune just for her on the piano. That tune, "Do You Know," had haunted her every day since Aretha first played it and sustained her on some of the most harrowing intrigues as a member of the Navy SEAL Team or a Musaid Officer into hostile territories.

The memories of Goodwill, South Carolina, were in stark contrast to her youth in the slums of Chicago's Cabrini Green's tenement buildings. The filth and obscene graffiti. The rats and roaches. The pimps and the prostitutes. The alcoholics and the bums. The drug pushers and thugs stalking the community. Young and old dying on the streets, in alleys, and in the hallways of her building. Finding her twin sister, Casey, against the door of their two-room flat with a needle still stuck in her arm. Her mother, Helen, deserting them unable to bear the pain of their hopeless existence. Her father, Willis Greene, and his determination to hold on to her and her brother, Russell, with little or no job and few prospects because of his limited education. He was not an educated man, but he never feared hard work. Willis would do what he had to do to make an honest dollar. Sometimes drowning his agonies in beer, but never failing to support her and Russell. They didn't have much, but they never went to bed with an empty belly. They had a roof over their heads and clothes on their backs. Her father would take any and every menial job that he could find. All too often being forced to leave her and Russell alone to fend for themselves because he could not afford a babysitter when he found work. She had learned to survive and take care of herself and her little brother long before she became a Navy SEAL. She had to, no one else was there to protect them while her father worked. It was only her presence of mind and a seven-inch switch blade that had kept her from being gang raped on more than a few occasions like other young girls who had been caught off guard. Basketball had been her ticket out of Cabrini Green and she played it as if her life depended on it because it did. Now she feared that her brother had not learned how to survive the devastation of living in an underprivileged neighborhood.

That it had followed him to Asheville, North Carolina. She knew that many years had passed since she had seen her father and brother, but she needed to be with what was left of her family. The Alexanders taught her something about how to love family. It was a lesson that she had vowed never to forget.

Chapter 38

Benny and his teams of jet fighter pilots circled widely around the area of the ocean as the President's helicopter landed on the deck of the USS Gettysburg.

"Papa One is secured, Explorer. Tag Team two is flying relief. Over."

"That's a roger, Baby Bird. I copy that. The Eagle has landed."

Benny landed his F14 on the deck of the USS Gettysburg aircraft carrier and taxied to the off-load area. The icy wind cut through his body as his bubble top opened and he slid out of his helmet and harness.

"Welcome aboard, Major," a ground crew Ensign said with a sharp salute, as he shimmied up the ladder of the aircraft and reached for Benny's helmet, case, and gear.

Benny returned the salute and immediately disembarked the aircraft, following the Ensign down the ladder. He grabbed the earphones that he was handed while another Ensign handed him a heavy jacket with a hood. Benny's jet disappeared below deck as he talked to his teams while they circled and began to land in precise patterns and roll to the off-load ramp. No sooner than one plane was off loaded to the lower deck another one landed.

"Keep that nose up, Beckmann... All right, Troy, bring her home to papa... Nice line up, Steward... Come on, Gettis, let's do this today..." Benny was saying to his teams.

"Begging your pardon, Sir," an Ensign yelled over the roar of the aircraft engines, "Admiral Gordon sends his regards and requests the pleasure of your teams' and your company in the officers' mess, Sir."

"Okay, Ensign." Benny quickly yelled back, with an answering salute, but kept his attention on his team's landing precision and process.

The President stood with Admiral Gordon as the officer's passed through the receiving line, shaking the President's hand. Admiral Gordon introduced each officer as they approached. Benny led his teams through the line.

"And this is our Air Force leader," Admiral Gordon started to say, but the President interrupted him.

"Alexander, isn't it?" the President asked, as Benny approached.

"Yes, Sir, Major Benjamin S. Alexander, Sir, 99th Tactical Jet Fighter Squadron out of March Air Force Base, Sir." Benny snapped a salute, which the President returned.

"Enjoyed watching you and your men landing today, Major Alexander. Fine job you've been doing I hear," he said, extending his hand.

"Thank you, Sir," Benny said, accepting his hand for a shake.

"Met your brother, Kenneth, a while back out in Santa Barbara. Johnny Worthington introduced me to him and his lovely wife, JeNelle, while I was on vacation. Fine man. Hell of a hardball player, too!"

"Yes, Sir. I'm also acquainted with Judge Worthington. He officiated at Kenneth and JeNelle's wedding. It's interesting that my brother never mentioned meeting you before to me, but I agree with you, Sir, my brother is the best. It's a pleasure to meet you, Sir," Benny said, as he started to move away and shake Admiral Gordon's hand.

"Major," the President called and motioned for Benny to stand beside him. "Introduce me to your officers, please."

Benny fell in line beside the President and introduced each of his captains and their lieutenants as they passed through the receiving line. Admiral Gordon had a faint smile on his face, which seemed to signal something that Benny didn't understand.

"Well, Major, I've been seeing your family everywhere these days," the President said.

"Sir?"

"Your sister, Vivian, made Law Review again at Georgetown and I hear that she turned down several very lucrative offers to go into the private sector and decided to go into public service working on Senator

Mitchell's Committee. Your brother, Gregory, seems to be making a name for himself in the college sports community, and I hear that your father is making a successful run at the South Carolina State Senate as an independent of all things!"

Benny smiled. "Yes, Sir. My family has been a bit active."

"A bit? Your sister has had my wife working hard on a number of issues. There has been no peace in the White House since those two met," the President emphatically said.

"Yes, Sir, but the best is yet to come. My sister, Aretha Grace, isn't out of high school yet."

"Another Alexander getting ready to take on the world?"

"The universe, Sir."

The President shook his head, as he walked around the room talking with the other officers, but he kept Benny at his side. Benny was confused over all of the attention that he was receiving and especially over the strange smile that Admiral Gordon was wearing.

After the officers dined with the President, Benny took his teams into a debriefing room to talk.

"What was that all about, Major?" Captain Troy asked, as Benny's team members gathered around.

"I heard that Papa One asked for your team specifically, Major," Captain Bredin excitedly said.

"Yeah, I heard that, too, Major. What gives?" another officer asked.

"Men, I haven't got a clue, but if I had to guess, I'd say that Papa One knows that the best jet fighter teams in the military are in the Air Force's 99th Tactical Jet Fighter Squadron!" Benny broadly smiled.

His men cheered loudly. He settled them down and they began their debriefing session which lasted for a couple of hours. Then the session was over.

"All right, the 99th Tact is on the flight line at 0430," Benny said, "so sleep fast."

The men all groaned.

"Then it's off to Hawaii," he added.

The men all cheered and headed out of the briefing room portal.

Benny was asleep in his small cubical when he felt the engines of the huge aircraft carrier come to a stop. He looked at his watch. It was 0200. He rolled over and went back to sleep. At 0400 he heard the Navy jets and then helicopters taking off. He rolled over and tried to go back to sleep, but his eyes glimpsed his small pictures on the side table. A small double frame with a picture of Whitney Ivy and one of Stacy that he always carried when he traveled. He rolled onto his back and laced his fingers behind his head. He closed his eyes and visualized Stacy's face in his mind. How she touched him. How the scent of her hair and her body electrified him. How she felt on top of him, beside him, beneath him. How she had that quick, gleaming, but sometimes devilish, smile that thrilled him to his core. How her face glowed when she was talking about something she learned or another mission that she was to be a part of. How she walked with a quick pace and how she jogged or swam when she was pushing herself and her endurance level. How she curled up in bed surrounded by manuals when she was studying or researching. How she smugly beat him at poker or chess or backgammon. How her belly rose with Whitney Ivy inside. He felt his nature rising and saw the scant cover over his body twitching with the anticipation of another release.

As Benny approached the ready room at 0420 he noticed Admiral Gordon going into one of the larger officer's quarters with another person. He started to call out to the Admiral to ask him about Stacy again, but changed his mind. He had talked with the Admiral before many times and each time the Admiral refused to divulge Stacy's whereabouts. Benny hurried to meet his team leaders and to prepare to leave for Hawaii.

"What was that sub parked next to us this morning for?" Captain Bredin was asking another officer as Benny entered the Ready Room.

"Beats me! Some strange goings on around here before the President lifted off," Captain Troy said. "I couldn't see it. Was it one of ours?"

"Yeah, one of those big suckers! Nuclear. Never seen one up close before, but when I heard these seadogs scrambling I took a quick look.

Saw Papa One and Admiral Gordon... oh and somebody else climbing out of that mother before the Secret Service and MP's moved me out. Maybe it was some kind of drill."

"Shit no! You don't get Papa One and the Admiral up at 0330 for some damn drill, Troy! It was probably some of that top secret shit!"

"Attention!" Captain Troy yelled when he noticed Benny entering the Ready Room.

"At ease, Gentlemen. Good Morning. Orders of the Day," Benny began.

The aviators silenced and slid into their seats as Benny outlined their mission and flight schedules.

"All right, men. Keep your feet dry. No fly-bys, no hand stands, and no grand stands," Benny ordered. "Dismissed!"

The aviators scrambled to their aircraft. Benny took the lead as his engines fired up with a deafening roar. He signaled his ready status, and in seconds he was catapulted into the air. He flew north, circled and watched as his teams on the tiny aircraft carrier below joined up in formation. They flew west and then south to Hawaii as the sun began to illuminate the sky from the east.

On the fourth day of the drill, Markham Air Force Base was a welcome sight after hours of flight time. As they maneuvered into various attack patterns, Benny looked down from his F-14 and noticed the USS Gettysburg surrounded by frigates, cruisers and destroyers on a dead run to the naval port at Pearl Harbor. The ships were still a couple hundred miles out at sea, but he knew that they would make landfall by the next day.

"Major Alexander?" the young corporal said, with a salute as Benny finished debriefing his teams after that day's combat exercise.

"Yes, at ease, Corporal." Benny saluted.

"You're wanted in HQ, Sir."

"Thanks, Corporal. Do you know what this is about?"

"No, Sir. They just sent me down here to find you, Sir."

"Thank you, Corporal." Benny saluted.

Benny slung his flight gear over his shoulder.

"What gives, Major?" Captain Troy asked.

"Beats me."

"Something must be up, Major. Scuttlebutt has it that you're in line for a promotion."

Benny laughed.

"Why are you laughing, Major? You certainly deserve it. You've worked harder than anyone else to keep us in A-1 condition."

"That's what they pay me for, Captain."

"Maybe they're going to pay you what you're worth now," Captain Troy said.

Benny gave him a cryptic smile, but did not answer him. He proceeded into the headquarters building at Markham Air Force Base and straight to Major General Polimo's office. "Go right in, Major Alexander," Polimo's Master Sergeant said, with a big smile on his dark complexioned face. "They're waiting for you."

"What's this about?" Benny asked.

"Progress, Major," the Black man said, smiling.

Benny went into the office and was greeted by four generals.

"Major Alexander reporting as ordered, Sir!" he said, with a crisp salute.

"At ease, Major," Major General Caldwell, Benny's Commanding Officer, said with a smile and extending his hand. "I think you know these other officers."

"Yes, Sir," Benny said, glancing at the other generals with whom he had worked with before.

"Take a load off, Major."

"Thank you, Sir." Benny sat and patiently waited.

"Major, we've been reviewing your file. You've had quite an illustrious career. Major Benjamin Staten Alexander, Code Name EXPLORER, Jet Squadron leader, 99th Jet Fighter Tactical, code name : BENNY AND THE JETS. You received your Bachelor of Science degree and graduated in the top five percent in your academy class at Colorado Springs, Colorado. Broke all records on proficiency at the flight training facility at Vance AFB in Enid, Oklahoma. From there right into active combat duty in Iraq and Afghanistan. You flew more missions than anyone else. You've been credited with saving a lot of lives because of the number of sorties you've flown. Then Squadron Officer School and Air Command at Andrews AFB in Maryland, and your master's degree in personnel management at UC-San Diego while at March AFB for what, five years now?"

"Yes, Sir, but is there some problem, Sir?"

The generals all laughed.

"No, Major, there's no problem. Let me continue."

"Yes, Sir."

"Now you've been on exchange duty with the Navy at Miramar Naval Air or at North Island Naval Air in San Diego. Instructor pilot and check-point pilot on the T-37, F-4, F-14 and F-15, Aircraft commander, standardizations and evaluation flight examiner, candidate counselor and recruiter specialist, operations officer, and deputy chief of staff for operations. You're rated as a Command Pilot with more than 4,200 flight hours. You're qualified on the T-33, T-37, F-4, F-14, F-15, F-16, F-111 and C-135. You've received the Distinguished Service Medal, Legion of Merit, Distinguished Flying Cross with oak leaf cluster, Defense Meritorious Service Medal, Meritorious Service Medal with fifteen oak leaf clusters, Air Force Commendation Medal, Air Force Outstanding Unit Award, Joint Service Achievement Medal, Combat Readiness Medal, Outstanding Airman of the Year, etc., etc., etc. You've created a realistic combat training course unmatched by any other courses that we've been using at the academies to train our young pilots. You've got the best record of any of our other jet pilot commands and you've just completed another mission receiving top honors with this all-out drill. You've put together a crack team of officers who all seem to think that you can walk on water and not get your feet wet!"

The generals all laughed. Benny gave them a slight smile.

"You seem to know what you're doing, Major."

"Thank you, Sir, but it's the teams that I serve with that make it all work. They're the best in the military."

"They seem to think that you're the best in the military and we agree. We've received a flood of requests from young pilots who want to transfer into your command. The training courses that you've been conducting around the country seem to have inspired a lot of our young officers to want to work under you."

"There're a lot of bright and energetic young men and women serving in the military today, Sir. It's been a distinct pleasure to work with all of them."

"Well, it seems that the feeling is mutual, Major, so how are we going to solve this dilemma?"

"Dilemma, Sir?"

"Yes, Major, how are we going to get these bright, young men and women under your command?"

"Well, Sir, I have ten captains now, who I believe should be promoted. I've written the performance appraisals and recommendations and I believe that they're well qualified to handle training new officers."

"So that's your suggested solution? Promote your captains and have them do the training?"

"Yes, Sir. They deserve it. They have all worked hard and distinguished themselves as officers. I'd trust any one of them with my life, Sir."

"You've had quite a life for your young years, Major. How have you accomplished so much in a relatively short period of time, and we understand that you're raising a beautiful little girl alone?"

"I have a responsibility to fulfill my obligations to my family, Sir."

"How so?"

"My parents and my ancestors, Sir. They've made an investment in me. Whatever I've done or achieved is because of them and their struggles."

"From your background, Major, we see that you could have had a stellar career and a very lucrative life as a civilian playing professional basketball, but you chose the Air Force instead. Not a very lucrative career choice. Although you seem to have made some very wise investments according to your financial statements. Why did you do that, Major?"

"Jets, Sir. I've always wanted to fly jets. My parents taught me and my sisters and brothers what their ancestors taught them: to decide what it is that we want and then to make it happen, but to always work for the common good. That's what I'm teaching my daughter. My parents taught me that I had options in my life. I chose the path less traveled so that I could explore something different and work for the common good."

"Very noble and awesome undertaking, Major."

"You don't know my parents, Sir. They expect the best from us. Nothing more and nothing less. I may have had options, but I certainly didn't have any choice on that score. Bernard and Sylvia Alexander, my grandparents, aunts and uncles, cousins, and the rest of my family made that crystal clear to each and every generation of our family."

The generals all laughed.

"That's what I've taught my teams, Sir. That's why I think that they are ready for a greater leadership role."

"We agree, Major. We've reviewed and approved your recommendations. Your captains and lieutenants will be promoted, but we have an even better solution."

"What's that, Sir?"

"We've decided to promote you, Colonel Alexander. We believe that you've got the right stuff to continue the fine work that you've been doing."

"'Colonel'? Did you say 'Colonel' Alexander?"

"Yes," Major General Caldwell said with a broad smile.

"You meant to say Lieutenant Colonel, didn't you, Sir?"

"No, Colonel Alexander. Are you questioning my memory? Don't you think that we generals know what the order of promotion is in this command?"

"Yes Sir... I mean, no, Sir . . . I mean, thank you, Sir."

The generals all laughed and Major General Caldwell presented Benny with a small purple box that held the American eagle insignia.

"I guess we have your ancestors and family to thank for your success, Colonel Alexander."

"I'll tell them that you said that, Sir." Benny broadly smiled. "We're having our annual family reunion on the Fourth of July in Goodwill, South Carolina."

"Well, Colonel Alexander, let's go see your men. They're all waiting for you in the Officers' Mess."

"They knew about this, Sir?"

"Knew about it?" he laughed. "They're the ones who wrote letters to us recommending you."

Benny smiled, as he and the generals left the Major General's office. The Master Sergeant snapped a crisp salute, as Benny came through the door.

"Congratulations, Colonel Alexander," the aide beamed.

Benny saw the pride welling up in the aide's demeanor.

"Thank you, Soldier!" Benny said, returning the salute and shaking the aide's hand.

They gave each other a warm, knowing handshake.

The party that Benny's teams threw for him was loud and raucous. They told outrageous tales about him and jokingly mocked him but affectionately. Tales about his exploits with women and his professional demeanor also got a wide airing. It was a roast of the highest order with each of his captains and lieutenants telling their funniest tales with little regard for the truth, but in good-natured fun and humor. The group of one hundred or so was enthralled in side-splitting laughter for hours. Then it was Benny's turn to address his crew and the others who were assembled.

Benny's extemporaneous comments were well received by his audience. People pumped his hand and enthusiastically clapped him on his back. Later as the din of well-wishers subsided, he walked alone on the dock and watched as the USS Gettysburg glided into port. Military families, waiting for their loved ones to return, waved at the Navy men and women lined up on the deck of the aircraft carrier. Thoughts of Stacy were strong as he involuntarily found himself waving along with the rest of the crowd. One of his teams streaked by overhead in perfect formation headed for Hickham Air Force Base and the successful completion of another tour of duty.

"Very interesting comments, sir," a voice said behind him.

Benny turned to see JC Baker, now demoted to Lieutenant Colonel.

"JC," he dryly acknowledged him.

Baker snapped a salute and Benny returned it.

"Permission to speak freely, Sir."

"At ease, Lieutenant Colonel. Permission granted," Benny said.

Baker relaxed, took out a cigarette and lit it. He motioned to Benny's new insignia.

"Congratulations on your promotion. You deserve it." He looked away from Benny. "Long time between hellos, Benny," Baker said, dragging on the cigarette.

"Thanks, I didn't know that you were stationed here."

"I've been here for a couple of months. I thought your brother might have mentioned it to you."

"Kenneth? Why? What has he got to do with where you're stationed?"

"Saw him up in Alaska years ago when he was on his honeymoon. Married that lady friend of yours, I hear."

"That doesn't tell me what I asked you."

"I know. Ask your brother what he did. All I know is that I asked for his help and he gave it. I appreciate it. After what I got him into, I'm surprised that he even spoke to me."

"Perhaps it's because he has integrity."

Baker looked away and took another drag. "Guess you're still pissed off, too."

"If Kenneth can get past this, so can I."

Baker didn't look at Benny. He nodded toward the aircraft carrier.

"You waiting for someone special off the Gettysburg?"

"No, just killing time before I head back to March tomorrow."

"That was Lieutenant Greene you were talking about in your remarks, wasn't it?"

"Yes, it was."

"I guess you don't know where she is yet either."

"No, I don't. Do you know something about where she is?"

"All I was able to find out was that she picked eleven women for some special training. She wasn't in the states. If she was, I would have been able to find her."

"Any idea what country she's in?"

"Still got a thing for her, I see, but no. Whatever she's into has national security written all over it." He turned and looked directly at Benny. "You should have asked your commander-in-chief. I hear he has a lot of respect for you and your family. He probably would have told you where she is and even arranged for you two to get together."

"The President? He doesn't get involved in troop deployments."

"You should spend some time in Washington at the Pentagon, Colonel. You'd learn a lot more than you can sixty thousand feet in the air," Baker said, flicking away his cigarette. "A lot more. I don't think you understand how powerful your family is, and I'm not just talking about your brother."

Baker saluted and walked away.

As the aircraft carrier slowly glided into port at Pearl Harbor, Hawaii, Stacy saw Air Force jets flying overhead. A crack team just like Benny's, she thought, as she watched them fly in precise formation. She was so proud of what he had accomplished. He was a top notch Air Force pilot and officer destined to do great things in his career. She hoped that JeNelle would not only love him and Whitney, but respect him and his professionalism and talent. He was made of the right stuff, she thought. A caring, dedicated officer who was confident and sure of his abilities and direction; he flew intuitively and effortlessly in his universe. He stood head and shoulders above his contemporaries with an ever-deepening interest in and dedication to his craft. He created different and higher expectations for himself meeting each challenge, triumph and discovery with great enthusiasm. Never yielding to any uncertainties about his skills or abilities. He had clarity of his direction and was exhilarated by it. She, too, knew what feeling that rush was about. It generated great body heat between them and sent them into hours of euphoric orbit in their universe together.

Stacy shook off her strong thoughts of Benny. Perhaps it was seeing the F-14 Eagle jet fighters that ignited her thoughts of and desires for him. Or perhaps it was the Air Force officers who were standing on the distant dock waving as the aircraft carrier slowed to a stop and dropped anchor.

"Commander?" the young Ensign was saying, "Commander Greene?"

"Oh, yes, I'm Commander Greene, Ensign," Stacy said, still unaccustomed to her new rank.

The young Ensign saluted sharply. Stacy returned the salute.

"At ease, Ensign."

"Thank you, Commander. Begging your pardon for disturbing you, Commander, but I tried getting your attention. You seemed lost in your thought, Sir,—I mean, Ma'am," the young Ensign stumbled.

Stacy realized that her short Navy haircut and white Navy dress uniform with slacks made her look more masculine than feminine. She would have to try to remember that she was still a woman, but she had no tools to work with. Living for many years as a Navy SEAL had erased the feminine style of dress from her mind.

"That's all right, Ensign. What did you want?"

"I'm your driver and assistant, Commander. Ensign D. Tulaine."

"Driver? Who gave you those orders, Tulaine?"

"The Admiral, himself, Sir—I mean, Ma'am. All Commanders are entitled to a driver, Sir,—I mean—"

"Don't worry about it, Tulaine. It'll grow on you," Stacy said, as she mused to herself. "I'm countermanding the Admiral's orders, Ensign. I don't need a driver."

"Begging your pardon, Sir, but the Admiral said that would be your position and that I wasn't to take no shit off you. Those were his exact words, Commander, not mine. He said that if you didn't let me carry your duffle and be your driver he'd have me skinny dipping off an iceberg in Alaska, Sir. Please, Commander Greene, I'm from Southern Louisiana. Me and icebergs don't mix, Sir."

Stacy laughed. "Okay, Ensign. Lead the way."

As Stacy saluted the mast, the flag, and disembarked the USS Gettysburg, the Ensign led her to a waiting car complete with Commander Flags flying on each side of the hood. *Clarence is going to pay for this*, she mused as Ensign Tulaine opened the car door for her. She looked up at the Command Center of the aircraft carrier where she knew that Admiral Gordon was probably sitting, smiling to himself over the discomfort that she was feeling about being pampered and treated with such courtesies.

She was taken directly to a waiting Navy transport aircraft and flown to San Diego, the headquarters for the Navy's Pacific Fleet operations and the largest Naval Air Station on the West Coast. She could see the condo where Benny had lived as the aircraft began its final approach for landing. It was strange being back in the United States after so many years abroad, particularly in San Diego, she thought. There were so many memories of Benny there. She wondered whether Cecil and Janice still lived in the same building as Benny. She would call at the first opportunity, but first she felt that she needed a makeover, if only to help Ensign Tulaine discern her gender more easily. He waited patiently while she went into the beauty salon and spa and got the works. She knew that her makeover had been successful when she emerged from the salon and Ensign Tulaine's eyes bugged out of his head, a huge smile crossed his face, and he skipped around the car to get into the driver's seat. She noticed that he kept peeking at her in his rear view mirror.

"Keep your eyes on the road, Ensign Tulaine," Stacy had to caution more than once.

"Yes, Ma'am!" he snapped each time with a broad grin, but eventually he'd again nearly wreck the car taking quick glimpses at her.

It was worth the grip that she spent for the makeover and for the packages of makeup, moisturizers, skin creams, and cleansers. She stopped at a mall so that she could buy some civilian clothes, undergarments and shoes. Now she felt more like a woman. They pulled into the jetport in front of the Navy Mess Hall.

"Commander, your flight to North Carolina will be leaving at 1400 hours. You might want to wait inside, Ma'am. It's more comfortable in there and I'll come for you when the flight is ready to depart."

"Thank you, Ensign Tulaine."

Stacy went into the Navy Mess Hall and several officers saluted her as Ensign Tulaine led the way. She was about to be seated when a familiar voice called to her.

"Lieutenant Greene," the voice said, grabbing her from behind and kissing her on the back of the neck.

She turned around.

"Oh, Bruce, how are you?" she said, trying to hide her disappointment that it wasn't Benny.

"*Whoa!*" he said quickly, "Look at you—*Commander* Greene? I don't know where you've been hiding, but you look fantastic!"

"Thanks, Bruce, you look great, too. How have you been keeping yourself?"

Bruce was awestruck. He could barely keep his mind on what he was saying. "Fine, fine, Stacy. I've missed you, you know," Bruce said, moving in close to her. "Any chance that I can get to see you tonight for dinner and some dancing?"

"You're sweet, Bruce, but I'm shipping out in a few minutes. Have you seen any of the old crew?"

"Yes, as a matter of fact I've been seeing quite a lot of Cecil Jordon—Dr. Jordon."

"Cecil got her doctorate?" Stacy asked, excited.

"Yeah, so did Janice Atterly."

"That's wonderful. Please tell them both how proud I am for them. So you and Cecil are an item, huh?"

"Sort of. She's seeing some other guy, too, but she's making me walk slower. Still, she knows that I still have this passion for you," he said, placing his hand on hers.

"Down, Bruce. You know that it was just friendship between us, not passion," Stacy said, with a smile pulling her hand back.

"It could have been a lot more if Alexander wasn't around."

The mere mention of Benny's name made her heart flutter.

"How is he, Bruce? Have you seen him lately?"

"No, not lately. Ran in to him one night at Jason's with Cecil, Janice, and another beauty. I don't remember her name, but I think that the man has been sucking in too much pure oxygen in those clouds. He was wearing a wedding band and talking about—"

"Commander Greene, your transport is ready. We'll have to hurry."

"Thank you, Ensign. I'll be there."

"Do you have to go so soon, Stacy? We have a lot to catch up on."

"Sorry, Bruce. It was good seeing you again," Stacy said, as she rose from the table, kissed Bruce on the cheek, and was out the door.

Bruce went to the telephone and dialed Benny's telephone number. The answering machine picked up.

"Benny, this is Bruce Payton. I just saw Stacy Greene. Give me a call when you get in."

Stacy climbed into the transport. As she sat down and buckled up, Bruce's comment about Benny being with a beautiful woman and wearing a wedding band stabbed deeply into her heart. Benny and JeNelle were married, she thought to herself. She wanted to be happy for him and for Whitney. She didn't realize that tears had formed in her eyes.

"Are you all right, Commander?" Ensign Tulaine asked, with some concern in his voice.

He had startled her.

"Yes, of course, Ensign. I just heard some good news about some friends of mine."

"Oh, okay, Commander. I just wanted to tell you that we're in a holding pattern. We'll be lifting off shortly."

"Thank you, Ensign." Then she had a thought. "Ensign, do we have a land line aboard?"

"Yes, Commander, I'll get it."

Ensign Tulaine returned with a cell phone and Stacy dialed Cecil at work.

"Hey there, girlfriend," Stacy said when Cecil answered. "Or should I say Dr. Girlfriend."

"Stacy? Stacy Greene is that you?!" Cecil screamed. "My God it is you! Where are you? I'm coming right over! Stacy where the hell have you been! I need to talk... and ..."

"Slow down, Cecil, I'm just calling to congratulate you on receiving your doctorate. I'm so proud of you. I hear that Janice got hers, too!"

"Yeah, yeah! Where are you? Tell me and I'll be right over. I'm on my way!"

"I'm just leaving, Cecil, but tell me how are Benny, JeNelle, and Whitney?"

"Well, JeNelle is just great. She's Mrs. Alexander now. She just had a second set of twin boys and she and—"

The engines revved up and Stacy could no longer hear what Cecil was saying, but she had heard enough already. She closed the cell phone and laid her head back against the headrest. The loud roaring engines drowned out her sobs. Benny and JeNelle were not only married, but they now had four boys. Whitney had four little brothers. She kept thinking of this to herself as the aircraft journeyed eastward.

No one was at home whenStacy entered the small house on College Street in Asheville, North Carolina. She flipped on the light and looked around at the unkempt condition of the house. Dropping her duffle bag on the floor, she flopped in to a big chair with a dingy slip cover that was next to a window. She noticed that the walls were drab and were badly in need of a few coats of paint. The globe on the ceiling light was dirty and dusty and full of dead moths. Newspapers were scattered around. Dust was thick on the old, worn out furniture. Air did not seem to be circulating in the stifling room. Oil spots were on the floor and the doorway that led into the kitchen. Dishes were piled high in the rusty-looking, porcelain sink. The trashcan overflowed and smelled to high heaven. The kitchen table was full of papers and barely allowed space for eating. The kitchen floor looked muddy and a trail of ants marched to and from a morsel of food beside the refrigerator door. The only bathroom was no better. Dirty clothes piled up in one corner, blocking her way to the commode.

Stacy sighed at the depressing conditions. She removed her Navy uniform and put on her Navy shorts and top. She started in the living room, cleaning in places that appeared never to have been cleaned before. She washed the kitchen walls. Then scrubbed the stubborn grease that refused to disappear. She washed the dishes, cleaned the floor, and refrigerator throwing out molded food and sour milk. She cleaned the oven, then the bathroom, separating the laundry and washing one load after the other, and hanging the clothes outside for drying. For more than three hours Stacy worked steadily. Then she found a market and bought enough food to feed an army. When she returned to the house she cooked dinner and set the table, putting fresh flowers in a jelly jar and burning scented candles. She looked at her watch. It was 9:30 P.M. and no one was at home yet. She sat on the sofa and waited. Finally, at 10:45 P.M. a car pulled into the yard. She heard heavy footsteps approaching. When the door opened, Willis Greene came in. His eyes lit up as he saw his daughter and the condition of the house.

"Stacy! Stacy girl!" he said as he hugged her. "When you git chere? Why didn't yous tell me yous were comin?"

There was joy in his voice and his face, Stacy thought.

"Hi, Dad," Stacy said with tears in her eyes, as she hugged him.

He was covered with garage smells and oils. Black greasy soot on his hands, but she didn't care. She was in her father's arms. She was home with her family.

"Dad? Yous nair call me dat 'fore, but I be likin' how it be soundin'."

"I know. I've always called you Willis, but you're my father. You raised me and you deserve the respect."

Willis beamed with pride. "Let me be lookin' at ya, Stacy girl! Gosh, you be lookin' great!" His eyes began to water. He wiped them on his dirty sleeve. "It be so good to see ya again affer all dese years!"

"It's good to be home with you again, Dad. Where's Russell? Is he with you?"

"Russell? You means dat boy ain't in here yet?"

"No, Dad. I've been here for hours and Russell never came home."

"I'll kill him!" Willis said between gritted teeth. "I done told dat boy to be coming home right affer summer school. He be hangin' 'round getting' into no good! Wait 'til I gets my hands on dat boy!" Willis bellowed.

"Dad, calm down. Why don't you go get cleaned up and get comfortable? I've cooked dinner. Russell will probably be home soon and we can all sit down and have a good meal together."

Willis looked at Stacy's calm and lovely face.

"Looka me. I be so happy to see ya and I already be tryin' to spoil your surprise. Just give me a minute and I be right witcha, Stacy girl." Willis lumbered toward the bathroom and suddenly turned. He went back to Stacy and hugged her again. "Thank ya for comin' home. The house never be lookin' better," he said, as he released her and went into the bathroom.

Willis' appreciation of her efforts made Stacy beam with pride.

Just as Willis came out of his bedroom freshly showered and dressed in clean clothes, the front door opened and Russell lumbered in. Stacy was putting the food on the table in the kitchen and looked up. She smiled broadly, as she wiped her hands and went toward her brother.

"Russell," she called out with joy at seeing her nearly grown brother. "Come here and give me a big hug!"

Russell dodged her and looked at her menacingly. "Who you, bitch?" he growled.

Stacy's heart sank. "It's me, Russell. Your sister, Stacy."

"Yeah, whatever," he scowled walking away from her.

His father stopped him and grabbed his arm. "Why you be actin' like dat? Dat be your sistah! Your kin come to visit chew! Show some respect! And where you been anyways, boy? Didn't I tells you to come to de house affer school?" Willis bellowed.

"Git the fuck off me, old man!" Russell angrily said. "I oughtta just put a cap in yo Black ass!"

"Russell, that's your father you're speaking to. What's gotten into you?" Stacy asked concerned.

Russell pulled away from his father and pulled a silver nine-millimeter Glock from his pocket.

Willis' eyes opened wide, but with one smooth motion Stacy kicked the gun from Russell's hand, grabbed him by the throat, and threw him to the floor with her knee in his chest. Russell's eyes blinked wildly. In a split second, Stacy had reacted with deadly force. The defensive maneuver was so instinctive that she had not even thought of what she was doing until Russell was on the floor gasping for air.

He saw her hand cocked in a deadly position and felt her other hand grasping his throat. Stacy got up and pulled Russell to his feet before he realized that he was being lifted. Tension hung like a wet blanket in the air.

"Oh, my God," she said, hugging him, "I could have killed you. I'm sorry, baby."

Tears were forming in her eyes. Russell pushed away from her, rubbing his chest and neck. He didn't speak but walked away, went into his room, and slammed the door. Stacy buried her face in her hands. Willis, who was dazed by his daughter's unbelievable swift action, went to her and held her.

"Child, I ain't even gonna ask you where you leant ta do dat," he whispered, stroking her hair and rocking her.

Stacy composed herself and reached for the gun. She popped the chamber and checked it for ammunition. The gun wasn't loaded. She sighed in relief, as she dismantled it like the professional that she had become. Her father was looking on in amazement.

"Come on, Dad, let's eat before this dinner gets cold," she said, now in full possession of herself. Like any successful mission, she knew that she had to have a plan to get the results she needed.

Willis complied, went into the kitchen and saw that it was clean, with the flowers on the table and candles burning. His chipped, mismatched plates were shining and the flatware sat proudly on the folded paper towel napkins. He smiled at his daughter and sniffed the air.

"Look real nice in cheer, Stacy girl. You done good! Whatcha cookin?"

Stacy pulled the macaroni and cheese from the oven, along with a pot roast. The string beans were piping hot, as well as the candied yams and dinner rolls. She served Willis' plate and then her own. The lemonade was poured into jelly jar glasses that were filled with ice. Sitting down, she bowed her head. When she looked up, Willis was watching at her. He snapped his attention back to his plate.

"Mmm," he said, as he tasted the food. "Dis be real good, Stacy girl. You knows whatcha be doin' round a kitchen!"

"Thanks, Dad."

"'Dad'," he repeated, letting the word roll off his tongue slowly. "I like dat. I like de way you be sayin' dat!"

Stacy laughed. "I guess it does sound a little strange."

"Never you mind, Stacy girl. I be likin' Dad better," he said, with a smile. "Shows respect! I like dat!"

They laughed, but Stacy still felt badly about Russell. She hated that the first impression that she had left with her brother after so many years of being apart and out of touch was one of deadly force.

After dinner, Willis washed the dishes and Stacy knocked on Russell's door. He didn't answer after the second knock so she peeked in. He was laying on his bed in the dimly lit room with an artist pad and pencil in his hand. He put them down and turned his back to her when she entered.

"Russell, I'm sorry for what I did to you," Stacy said, as she stroked his bare back.

He pulled away from her touch. Her eyes became accustomed to the dimness and she looked around the room. Drawings of peaceful scenes hung on the walls. She picked up the pad that he had been drawing in and flipped through the pages. She stopped on an unfinished sketch of a house by a waterfall in the woods. She marveled at how good it was and how good all of the pictures were. It reminded her of her mother, whose delicate hands had drawn many beautiful pictures when she and her twin sister were very young.

"You're quite an artist, Russell," she said softly, admiring the pictures.

Russell turned swiftly, snatched the pad from her hand, and threw it down on the floor.

"That doesn't make it any worse, Russell. It's still very good," she said calmly and quietly.

"What chew want in here?" he asked gruffly.

"How about some dinner? I set a plate aside to keep your dinner warm for you."

"Ain't hungry!" he growled.

"I'll just leave it there on the stove for you. Maybe you'll be hungry later," she said, as she kissed his shoulder. She got up from the bed and left the room.

Willis had finished washing the dishes and was sitting in the kitchen. Stacy sat across from him and noticed his sad expression.

"Just don't know what ta do wit' dat boy no more. Bringin' a gun in dis here house. It ain't much, but it be home. Don't need no gun in dis here house," Willis lamented.

"I'll be here for a while, Dad. Maybe I can help."

Willis looked into his daughter's eyes and reached across the table. She reached for his hand.

"It be good to have you home, Stacy girl. Real good."

They talked for a while and then Stacy curled up on the sofa to sleep. Late into the night her eyes opened as she heard Russell creep across the room to the kitchen. She did not move or let on that she was awake. She heard him gobbling down the food in the kitchen and then felt his presence standing over her before he headed for the front door.

"You didn't wash the plate," she said quietly.

He stood motionless. She flipped on the lamp at her head and looked at her watch. It was 2:30 A.M.

"I ain't no bitch! You want dat plate washed, din you wash it! I'm goin' out!"

"I'm going with you then. I like nighttime strolls," she said, as she sat up on the sofa.

"Who axed you? Didn't nobody ax you to go nowhere!" he growled. "Didn't nobody ax you to come here messin' up everything, bitch!"

Stacy got up and walked up to Russell. He backed up from her advance, but she got dead in his face and put her hands on the door above his shoulders, pinning him against the door.

"What was that you called me?" she asked in a low, menacing tone, looking into his eyes.

Russell didn't answer.

"I'm your sister, Russell, and I love you whether you believe me or not. I came home because I need you and our father. Now, it's too bad if you're not happy with this arrangement, but I'm here. Live with it. You can give me attitude twenty-four seven, but I'm still going to be your sister and I'm still going to love you," she said in the same low, menacing tone.

She released him, walked back to the sofa, and lay down. Russell stood by the door not looking at her. He started toward his room.

"Wash that plate, Russell," Stacy said quietly.

Russell stood motionless for a moment and then went into the kitchen.

"And use soap," she added.

She heard Russell washing the plate and placing it in the drying rack. He headed for his room.

"Good night, little brother," she said quietly, as she turned out the light. "I love you."

The next morning, Stacy was up making breakfast when Willis came out of his bedroom. He entered the kitchen and sniffed the air.

"Good morning, Dad," Stacy said, with a smile. She hugged him and kissed him on the cheek.

"You still here? I thought you was a dream. Smells good in here. Like real family."

Stacy smiled, as she served his plate with eggs, bacon, hominy grits, stewed apples and hot biscuits. Willis' eyes lit up, as she placed the plate on the table. He dug right in. Stacy stopped him and sat across from him. She bowed her head and said a silent prayer.

"Now let's eat," she said, as she poured the orange juice and the coffee.

She buttered the biscuits and put the grape jelly in front of him. Then she went to Russell's door and knocked.

"Breakfast is ready," she said, as she peeked in.

Russell rolled over and looked at her. "Ain't hungry," he growled.

"Russell Greene, I've been standing over that stove and you're going to sit down at the table and have breakfast with us. Now you can do this my way or you can do it your way, but little brother, believe me when I tell you that it's going to be done. Oh, by the way, good morning."

Russell didn't answer. He rolled off the bed, brushed by her, and headed for the kitchen. She stopped him.

"Wash your face and brush your teeth before you come to the table."

Russell mumbled something under his breath, but he complied. Stacy placed a plate before him, as he sat down.

"What time do you have to be in summer school, Russell?" Stacy asked.

"Why you wanna know?" he growled.

"I thought that I'd go with you and meet your teachers."

"You trippin'! I ain't takin' no bit... nobody to school wit' me! I ain't no baby!"

"Fine, then I'll meet you after school and you can introduce me to them then."

"Huh! You don't need to be doing dat!"

"I know that I don't have to do it, but I want to do it."

Russell rolled his eyes and ate his breakfast. After breakfast, Stacy was cleaning the kitchen as Russell headed out of the door. She called after him, and grabbed her keys and purse. She caught him and beckoned him to get into the car. He complied, reluctantly, and directed her to the school. When they arrived he was out of the car in a flash. Stacy parked the car around the corner and waited. When Russell came running around the corner and saw her sitting on the trunk of the car, he stopped in his tracks. Stacy got off the car, locked her arm in his, and walked him back to school. She entered his classroom and took a seat at the rear.

"Well, Mr. Greene, it's been a while since we've seen you," the tall, muscular, Black male teacher said. "And to what do we owe the honor of your presence today?"

Russell rolled his sullen eyes and stared in the opposite direction.

"Well, let's try another question, Mr. Greene. Who's the lovely young woman who has accompanied you here this morning?"

"Sistah," he growled lowly.

"Pleased to meet you, Ms. Greene. You're welcome here. I'm Mr. Dixon. I teach English and math," he said, extending his hand.

Stacy shook it. "I'm Stacy Greene, Mr. Dixon. Russell's sister. It's a pleasure to meet you."

"May I ask what you do professionally, Ms. Greene?"

"I'm a naval officer," Stacy said, trying to discern why he had asked.

The class of twenty students either laughed in disbelief or ooed, but the teacher leaned against the blackboard confidently in a way that for some reason reminded Stacy of Benny's sexy stance.

"What rank are you, Ms. Greene?" he asked with a smirk on his face.

"Commander."

Now the class really broke up into uproarious laughter. Stacy rose from her seat and walked through the seats to the front of the room.

"Oh, so you don't believe that I'm an officer in the United States Navy, huh?" she asked, smiling at the class.

"Nah," some of them said in unison. "No way! A sistah! Huh!"

"Okay," she said, with a quirky smile. "Give me five minutes."

Stacy hurried to the car, pulled a new uniform from her luggage in the trunk of the car, and returned to the classroom fully dressed.

"*Attention!*" she bellowed from the classroom door.

The students all jumped and turned around as she came in. Russell buried his face in his hands and slouched down in his seat. Stacy marched to his seat and took his hands from his face.

"I'm nothing to be ashamed of, Russell," she whispered, as she continued to the front of the classroom.

The students were awestruck. One young girl raised her hand and Stacy acknowledged her.

"Do the men soldiers have to salute you?" the girl asked timidly.

Stacy smiled. "Only when I'm in uniform and only if I'm a higher rank than they are."

Another girl raised her hand.

"Would you please tell me your name, when you ask your questions?" Stacy asked with a smile.

"My name be Rochel. How you learnt to talk white?"

Stacy laughed. "You mean I don't sound like I'm a Black woman?"

"Naw," the group answered.

"Well, seeing is believing, isn't it? Am I Black?" Stacy asked while meandering through the seats.

"Yeah," they all said.

"Am I a woman?" she asked.

"Yeah," they all answered.

"Well then, this must be what a Black woman sounds like, wouldn't you agree, Mr. Dixon?"

The teacher was sitting in his chair admiring the view of Stacy in uniform. He smiled at her. Hands began to fly up all over the classroom.

Stacy answered each person. The fifty-minute session flew by. Even Russell was sitting up in his seat listening to the questions and his sister's answers. When the class ended, young people came up to her, admired the medals on her uniform, the gold braids around her sleeves and on her hat. They all shook her hand as they left the room.

"That's what I'm gonna be when I grows up!" one girl said to another.

"Me too!" the other girl answered.

Stacy laughed as she overheard the girls' conversation.

"Thank you, Commander Greene. I hope that you know what an inspiration you were to the class today and to me," he said, holding Stacy's hand.

"Thank you. I enjoyed it."

"Commander, may I call you later? Say Friday or Saturday?"

"We don't have a telephone. Thanks anyway," Stacy said, as she walked toward her brother who was standing by the door.

Young people were asking him questions, as she walked up.

"Yeah, that's right! She's my sister," he was saying.

His hands were stuck down in his pockets and he looked down at the floor. Stacy slipped her arm in his and guided him down the hallway.

"Well, little brother, how did I do?" she asked, with a smile, peeking under her brother's face.

"A'ight, I guess," he said quietly.

She smiled to herself. "All right, what's next?"

Russell stopped in his tracks. "You gonna go to all my classes?"

"Yep. All day, every day. I'm going to spend time with you because I love you."

Russell didn't look up. He sauntered to this next class with his sister holding his arm. Students gawked at them as they passed, but Russell didn't seem to mind.

After school that first day Stacy drove them to a paint store and purchased both indoor and outdoor paint. She and Russell began painting the house every day after she helped him study. He still wasn't fully accepting her return, but he was not openly hostile. He even washed the dishes after she cooked. Willis was thoroughly pleased at what they were doing. On the weekend the three of them went to a matinee movie in a shopping mall and had pizza afterward. They sat in the pizza parlor and Russell finally asked her a direct question.

"So where you been?"

"After I left the Naval Academy in Annapolis, Maryland, I was assigned to the Pentagon in Washington, DC. Then, I was stationed in San Diego for a while and later on an aircraft carrier in the North Pacific.

"Where dat? Dat North Pacific place?"

"The Pacific Ocean, Russell."

"Oh," he said.

Stacy realized that he didn't have a clue about what or where the Pacific Ocean was. After the pizza, they walked around the shopping mall. Stacy went into a bookstore and made a few purchases. Later that night as Willis dished up sherbet in the new bowls that Stacy bought, Stacy sat on the sofa next to Russell.

"Here, these are for you," she said, handing the packages to him.

"What's dis?" he asked.

"Open it and see, Russell."

He opened one bag and found a beautiful map of the planet.

"This is where I've been Russell," she said, pointing to the Pacific Ocean. "And this is where we are now."

Russell looked intrigued by the vastness of it all, as Stacy pointed to other countries and oceans on the map.

"And this is where I'll be stationed next."

"What's dat word?"

"Tokyo, Japan."

"Day Chinks like at dat store?"

"No, Russell. They're Chinese. Not Chinks. I'll be in Japan. The people there are called Japanese."

"Well day all look alike to me."

"They aren't, Russell, just as we as Black people are different, so are they. Maybe you'll come and visit me in Japan."

"How I gotta git dare?"

"Fly, Russell."

"Nah, dats too far on dat lil' plane."

"What little plane, Russell? You'd be on a big 747 jumbo jet."

"Dat lil' plane like what dat pilot Alexander be flyin'."

Stacy was so shocked that she could barely catch her breath. "Benjamin Alexander?" she asked.

"Yeah, him."

"When did you meet Benjamin?"

"He and dat weird sistah of his and dat brother, Gregory, dey came here last year with his lil' girl. Den he came back last Easter with his weird sister and took me flyin' to an Air Force base. He even let his weird sister fly de plane!"

Stacy couldn't believe what she was hearing.

"Dad, is this true? Benny Alexander was here in Asheville?"

"Yeah, he been lookin' for ya. Call me at de garage e'ry now and again. Been sending pictures of Whitney to me, too. Said he'd be back on the Fourth of July. Even 'vited me and de boy to come to his family reunion."

"What did he want?"

"Just said he wanted to talk ta ya. Didn't give no reason. Pretty lil' baby girl though. Cute as a button. Looked just like you and..." Willis cut off his thought. "Yeah, real cute baby."

Stacy didn't know what to make of it. She sat back on the sofa. *Why would Benny be tracking down her family*, she wondered, *and how did he find them? Was something wrong with Whitney? Was she ill?* She dismissed the thought. Admiral Gordon would have told her if that were the case. Nevertheless, she was confused.

"You gonna eat dat?" Russell asked, pointing to the sherbet.

"No, Russell, you may have it," she said, still trying to gather her thoughts.

She looked at her watch. "Come on, Russell, let's find a telephone booth."

Russell got up and followed her, still eating her sherbet. They drove to a corner store. Russell sat in the car while Stacy called Benny's telephone number in San Diego. The answering machine picked up. She was surprised that he had the same telephone number. She left a message and hung up. She dialed the Alexander's number, but just as a female voice answered, Stacy sensed danger and hung up. She turned to see five, grizzly-looking men with matching blue rags tied around their heads crowding in around her.

"May I help you, gentlemen?" she asked calmly.

"Yeah, bitch! You can give me some of that phine pussy you got 'tween yo legs!" one man said, advancing toward her.

"Yeah and you can give me some head," another one said.

"I don't think so, my brothers, so if you'll excuse me—"

"Where the fuck you think you be goin', bitch?"

"You gonna be my bitch tonight! Maybe tomorrow night, too!"

"Home, my brother!" Stacy said, sizing up her options. Five wasn't too many to handle. She checked each one and was ready to go into attack mode.

Unexpectedly, Russell broke through the group and stood in front of Stacy.

"Ain't gonna be like dat, Crip. Dis here be my sistah! Ain't gonna be dissin' my family!"

"Where you been, Streetwise, you little red punk? We been lookin' for your lil' scrawny redbone ass!"

"Like I say, Crip, dis here be family, man! Ain't nobody takin' nothin' here!"

Suddenly red and blue strobe lights flashing in sequence were around them. The men backed off.

"What's the problem here?" a big, burly police officer asked, then got out of the police cruiser brandishing a night stick.

Another officer stood by the cruiser with a gun pointed in their direction.

"No problem, officer," Stacy said, stepping in front of Russell. "These gentlemen were just waiting to use the telephone. Uh, may I show you some ID?"

The officer nodded and Stacy held up one hand and reached in her pocket for her ID card. She took it out carefully and handed it to the officer.

"Navy, huh?"

"Yes, officer. Just home on leave visiting my family. This is my brother. If it's all the same to you, we'll be leaving now."

The police officer handed the ID card back to Stacy and motioned for her and Russell to leave.

"All right, gentlemen," the officer said to the other men, "You know the drill. Assume the position."

Russell didn't say anything as they drove home. They pulled into the front yard and got out of the car.

"Russell," Stacy said, as they crossed the yard. "Thank you for what you did for me back there."

"Yeah, right," he said softly, looking down at the ground, kicking at the dirt with his hands in his pockets.

"Could I get a hug?" she asked smiling at him.

He didn't look up, but moved toward her. She wrapped her arms around him and squeezed. He slowly took his hands out of his pockets and embraced her gently at first then he squeezed her.

"That was very brave of you, Russell, protecting me like that," she said, looking into his face.

He smiled slightly. "Protecting you!" he said, still holding her, "I was just trying to keep you from kickin' dey asses with dat kung fu shit!" He smiled broadly and hugged her again.

Stacy laughed as they went inside.

Later that night as Stacy lay on the sofa, she could not sleep. Her mind raced. She wondered why Benny was going to all the trouble to find her. Then she remembered what Clarence Gordon said about Benny tearing up Washington looking for her. Maybe something was in those letters that she left on the aircraft carrier. Now she wished that she had read them, but it was too late. The carrier was far out at sea now.

Her vision of her and Benny together returned. She had tried to put him out of her mind after she learned that he was married to JeNelle and that they had two sets of twin baby boys. Whitney now had little brothers who she knew Benny would teach to be explorers just like him.

Her thoughts were interrupted when she heard Russell come out of his bedroom. He stood beside the sofa a second or two, spread a blanket on the floor beside the sofa, placed the pillow on the floor, and lay down. Tears formed in her eyes. They had slept on pallets on the floor together when he was just a baby. The floor and the bath tub were the safest places to be when gangs were shooting up their old neighborhood. She rolled off the sofa and wrapped her arms around him. He snuggled close to her and kissed her on the cheek. They slept there together the rest of the night, wrapped in each other's embrace.

In the morning, Stacy heard Willis come out of his bedroom. He paused and looked at the sight of his two children sleeping together on the floor. Stacy looked up and smiled at her father, as she eased out of Russell's embrace. He was snoring quietly. She followed her father into the kitchen and made coffee. She sat across the red Formica table from him.

"Dad, tell me about my family."

"There ain't much to tell, Stacy. Don't know my peoples. Grew up in an orphanage in Kentucky. Ran away when I was younger den Russell. I done odd jobs and farm work and knocked round.

"One day I been workin' dis here big farm in Ballard County and I sees dis pretty lil' thing sittin' on de back steps of dis big house. She be cryin' somethin' awful. So I goes up to hur and ax hur what de trouble be. She say dat de man inside on top of hur mama agin. So I peek through de screen and dis white man, he be doin' his business on top of dis Negro woman on the floor in de kitchen. De Negro woman, she be cryin', but she don't be hollowin' or nothin', so I takes de girl's hand an walk down the lane. She look white, but I done seen lots of dem chillin' made from a white man and a Negro woman, so I knows she be black. I talk nice to hur and affer while we start spendin' time together. She tell me dat white man be her daddy. Dey been dare on dat farm since she were born into dis here world and err time dat white man wife go to town—dat white man go to town on hur mama.

"One day de girl, she come flyin' down the lane. Dress half tore off, cryin' and screamin', I goes to hur and she say dis other man, he affer hur now. He try to kiss hur and tare hur clothes off. Hur mama, she tell her to come git me and to run away far and not let dat other white man catch up to hur.

"Well sah, I had 'bout twenty dollar in my pocket, but we starts ta walkin—going north out of Kentucky. We end up in Chicago. Den you and your sistah be born. We both had to meet dat dare mule, but peoples they be thinkin' your mama were white. She be waitressin' at some place and I go by to pick hur up. Soon as deys sees me, she'd git fired. Den, mens be botherin' her when she come home thinkin' she be a white woman livin' with a Negro man in Cabrini Green. She git raped in de hall, but wouldn't nobody tell me who done it. Good thing too 'cause I'd kill't 'em iffin I would have got my hands on 'em. Yo mama, she say she don't wanna live iffin I hurt somebody and den gotta go ta jail, so we try to keep goin' on. Nobody in de Negro places would be hirin' her 'cause dey think she white. She don't wanna work in no white folk's kitchen 'cause of what happen to hur mama. She 'fraid dat some white man gonna want to put his hands on hur and she 'fraid I'd find out 'bout it. She got down on hur self. She got de misery real bad. Den one day you come home and finds yo sistah, well yo mama, she couldn't take no mo. She left me dis note sayin' she sorry and all, but she couldn't help it. I look ery'where for hur. I know'd she be scared out dere alone. I never see her again.

"She sho' did have a nice way wit' hur. Quiet. Kinda shy, pretty girl. Made nice pictures. Just like dat boy dere. Yeah, she be a good girl. She try to be nice to ery'body. Didn't never smoke or drink or nuthin'. Always trying to make things better for you chilluns. De life. It just took my Helen's heart away."

Stacy recognized the anguish in her father's eyes, as he talked about her mother. She had not thought about it before, but it was clear to her now that her father still deeply loved her mother.

Stacy's eyes watered, as he talked. She wiped her tears. "Russell's listening," she whispered to her father.

He peeked over her shoulder into the living room.

"How you know dat?" he asked.

"I know. He's been awake for a while now."

Willis shook his head amazed at his daughter and sipped his coffee.

Russell got up off the floor and came into the kitchen.

"Good morning, little brother," Stacy said cheerfully. "You sleep well?"

"Not wit'chall in here yakin'," he growled. "What'chall takin' 'bout?"

"You heard us, Russell. It's no secret," Stacy said.

"Yeah, well I don't wanna hear nothin' 'bout dat ho."

Willis' eyes narrowed and he balled up his fist. He leaped up from the table, but Stacy was between them quicker than a flash.

"Dad, you said that you wanted to put in some extra work at the garage. I'm sorry about breakfast. Do you mind picking up something on your way? I'll make a big Sunday dinner tonight."

Willis looked at Stacy a long moment before he relaxed nodding his head. "Naw, naw, baby girl, I don't mind," he said, still starring his son down. "I'll be home round one o'clock." He poured out the rest of his coffee, then marched out of the house.

Stacy turned to face Russell. "That's our mother that you're talking about, Russell. No matter what she's done, she still brought us into this world. We have no right to judge her. She's still our family."

"Ain't no muva of mine!" he growled.

Stacy did not argue. She was a realist. It was going to take time and patience to reach through her brother's defense mechanisms. She put her arm around Russell and smiled.

"How about you make breakfast while I shower?"

Russell cut his eyes at her. "What chew wanna eat?"

"Whatever you want to make. Surprise me," Stacy said with a smile.

She left Russell in the kitchen and went into the bathroom to shower. Her father's sadness haunted her. Willis had lost so much in his life. He was only sixteen years older than her. Still young enough to be her older brother. No family to help him go through life. No history of warm childhood memories. Just loss and despair. A dead child, a lost wife, a daughter who had all but deserted him and an only son, hell bent on self-destruction. So different from Benny's rich family history and traditions. Loving and caring for children, relatives, and friends. Living comfortably in the bosom of the South—living with and in Goodwill. As she was getting out of the shower, Stacy heard voices. She wrapped a towel around her body and was drying her hair with another towel as she came out of the bathroom.

"Was someone at the door, Russell?" she asked, as she walked into the living room.

"Morning, Commander Greene," Russell's teacher said, standing before her.

He quickly turned his back.

Stacy smiled. "Good morning. This is certainly a surprise."

"A pleasant one, I hope, Commander," he said, still with his back to her.

Stacy was caught off guard. "What can we do for you this morning?"

"I was wondering whether we could go somewhere and maybe have breakfast."

Stacy slipped her arm into Russell's. "I'm sorry, but my brother has made breakfast for me and, as you can see, I'm not ready to receive visitors this early in the morning."

"Well, I can wait. Maybe we can have lunch or dinner?"

"I thank you for your offer, but I'm booked solid for the day. Maybe another time."

"How about Monday brunch? Say about 11:30 A.M.?"

"You certainly are persistent," Stacy said.

"Is that a yes, Commander?"

"That's a maybe. Give me a phone number where I can reach you later today and we'll discuss it."

The teacher wrote a number on a business card and handed it to Stacy.

"I'll be looking forward to hearing from you, Commander," he said, as he walked out the front door and got into his car.

Stacy didn't answer. After he left, she slipped into her shorts and a top and went into the kitchen. Russell had two bowls of cereal on the table with orange juice and toast. He was pouring coffee into her cup when she came in. She noticed the bunch of freshly-picked wild flowers in the jelly jar vase.

"This looks great, Russell," she cheerfully said, with a smile.

She kissed her brother on the cheek. He was strangely quiet, she thought.

He sat down across from her. "You didn't have to do dat," Russell said, looking down at his cereal. "Mr. Dixon ain't a bad man. He new in town. He don't know a whole lot of peoples. He even axed me to kinda show him round. Said he wanted to be my friend an all."

"I'm sure that he's probably a very nice man, Russell, but I'm here to spend my time with you and our father."

He was quite again. "But didn't you ever want to love somebody, Stacy?"

The question grabbed her in the pit of her stomach. She had to recover from her thoughts of Benny and their daughter. "I did love someone once, Russell," she said, not knowing why she had said it.

"Din why you leave him?"

"It's complicated," she said, eating her cereal and trying to act naturally.

Russell was quiet. "It was dat Alexander, wasn't it?"

"Yes, but like I said, it was complicated."

"What, he didn't want chew?"

"No, I mean, we were just friends."

"Din why you have dat baby?"

The questions were getting to be too painful for Stacy, but she didn't want to cut off her communication with her brother. He was beginning to feel more comfortable with her. She gathered herself. Russell was looking her in her eyes. He was waiting for an answer. Stacy took a deep breath.

"Benny Alexander and I didn't use protection once and I got pregnant. It wasn't planned or anything like that. We were just friends. You're old enough to understand that you don't necessarily have to be in love to have sex. We were both involved in our careers and I didn't want to have a baby, but he did. He wouldn't go along with my plan to have an abortion. He was my best friend so I agree to have the baby because the baby meant so much to him and to his family. When Whitney was born I left for a new assignment."

"Jus' like dat? You mean you jus' up and left?" Russell incredulously, disdainfully asked.

Stacy recognized the anger growing in Russell's face.

"No, Russell, I mean, I had to go. I had a job to do, a mission to fulfill," she said almost pleading for his understanding.

"Naw! Naw! You copped out! You jus' up and drop dat baby and walk away jus' like dat ho did! You a ho jus' like her! You went away when I was little and never came back! Now you come back here talkin' 'bout you love me! You don't love me! You don't love nobody 'ceptin' yourself! What 'bout dat baby? Who she spose to love? Her ho of a mama done left her!"

Russell was seething with anger. He was pouring out all of the hurt and frustration inside him. Tears were streaming down Stacy's face. She reached for Russell, but he pulled away from her and stormed out of the kitchen into the back yard. He kicked over the paint cans that were sitting in the yard. Stacy watched him from the kitchen as he walked away. She saw him bury his face in his hands then wipe his face on his arm. He wasn't facing her, but she knew that he was crying. The vision of his handsome face contorted into pain and agony tore at her very core. She had not realized how deeply her leaving home affected her brother.

She felt the pain when her sister died in her arms and when her mother left, but Stacy dealt with that pain. She knew that she had to go on. She had to survive. She had not let herself think about it. She had buried that agony deep in her soul, but she could see that Russell could not bury his pain the way that she had been able to do. His pain was intensified because she left him too, just like their sister and their mother.

What would Whitney think? Would she understand why she left? Why she never came back? What would Benny and JeNelle tell her about her family? About her? Nothing in her years of training taught her how to love family. She only knew about duty; how to serve and protect. Benny and his family had done that. Now she felt empty. Lost without something to give to her brother to help him learn to love family. To trust family. She couldn't give up though. She and Russell had come too far to let it slip away.

She went into the yard and approached him from behind. She wrapped her arms around him, pinning his arms against his body. He struggled to free himself from her, but she held on tightly not letting him get away from her. Eventually his efforts to free himself subsided and his body shook with emotion as he cried aloud not hiding his pain. She cried too. They let themselves feel the pain of the losses that they shared. It was the first time that she had cried about her sister or her mother. She had never mourned them. She had kept it all pinned up and locked away inside of her for all of those years.

"You may not believe it now, Russell, but I do love you. You and Willis are all that I have. We are all that we have," Stacy said, as she released him and moved around to face him.

He looked at the ground, avoiding her eyes. She lifted his chin to face her. She wanted him to know and believe that he meant everything to her and that she needed his love as much as he needed hers.

To be continued . . .

AUTHOR BIO

Ann Jeffries is a native of Washington, D. C. She is an only child who enjoyed the benefits of a private school education at Allen in Asheville, NC, and a public education at the University of Maryland. She began writing fiction for her own amusement.

Ann is the recipient of many awards for leadership and public service. A speaker at colleges and universities and conferences and conventions, she has extensively traveled the North American continent, Asia and Europe. Among other things, she is an entrepreneur, an avid viewer of public television and a voracious reader of fiction.

Ms. Jeffries' pride and joy are her family, particularly her Fabulous Four grands. She lives in Maryland and South Carolina.